The Collected
Supernatural and Weird
Fiction of
Vernon Lee
Volume 2

The Collected Supernatural and Weird Fiction of Vernon Lee Volume 2

Including One Novel "Louis Norbert",
One Novelette and Nine Short Stories
of the Strange and Unusual

Vernon Lee

LEONAUR

The Collected
Supernatural and Weird
Fiction of
Vernon Lee
Volume 2
Including One Novel "Louis Norbert", One Novelette and Nine Short Stories
of the Strange and Unusual
by *Vernon Lee*

FIRST EDITION

Leonaur is an imprint
of Oakpast Ltd

ISBN: 978-0-85706-685-5 (hardcover)
ISBN: 978-0-85706-686-2 (softcover)

http://www.leonaur.com

Contents

A Wicked Voice

A story from *Hauntings*

To M.W., in remembrance of the last song at Palazzo Barbaro,

Chi ha inteso, intenda.

They have been congratulating me again today upon being the only composer of our days—of these days of deafening orchestral effects and poetical quackery—who has despised the new-fangled nonsense of Wagner, and returned boldly to the traditions of Handel and Gluck and the divine Mozart, to the supremacy of melody and the respect of the human voice.

O cursed human voice, violin of flesh and blood, fashioned with the subtle tools, the cunning hands, of Satan! O execrable art of singing, have you not wrought mischief enough in the past, degrading so much noble genius, corrupting the purity of Mozart, reducing Handel to a writer of high-class singing-exercises, and defrauding the world of the only inspiration worthy of Sophocles and Euripides, the poetry of the great poet Gluck? Is it not enough to have dishonoured a whole century in idolatry of that wicked and contemptible wretch the singer, without persecuting an obscure young composer of our days, whose only wealth is his love of nobility in art, and perhaps some few grains of genius?

And then they compliment me upon the perfection with which I imitate the style of the great dead masters; or ask me very seriously whether, even if I could gain over the modern public to this bygone style of music, I could hope to find singers to perform it. Sometimes, when people talk as they have been talking today, and laugh when I declare myself a follower of Wagner, I burst into a paroxysm of unintelligible, childish rage, and exclaim, "We shall see that some day!"

Yes; some day we shall see! For, after all, may I not recover from this strangest of maladies? It is still possible that the day may come when all these things shall seem but an incredible nightmare; the day when *Ogier the Dane* shall be completed, and men shall know whether I am a follower of the great master of the Future or the miserable singing-masters of the Past. I am but half-bewitched, since I am conscious of the spell that binds me. My old nurse, far off in Norway, used to tell me that were-wolves are ordinary men and women half their days, and that if, during that period, they become aware of their horrid transformation they may find the means to forestall it. May this not be the case with me? My reason, after all, is free, although my artistic inspiration be enslaved; and I can despise and loathe the music I am forced to compose, and the execrable power that forces me.

Nay, is it not because I have studied with the doggedness of hatred this corrupt and corrupting music of the Past, seeking for every little peculiarity of style and every biographical trifle merely to display its vileness, is it not for this presumptuous courage that I have been overtaken by such mysterious, incredible vengeance?

And meanwhile, my only relief consists in going over and over again in my mind the tale of my miseries. This time I will write it, writing only to tear up, to throw the manuscript unread into the fire. And yet, who knows? As the last charred pages shall crackle and slowly sink into the red embers, perhaps the spell may be broken, and I may possess once more my long-lost liberty, my vanished genius.

It was a breathless evening under the full moon, that implacable full moon beneath which, even more than beneath the dreamy splendour of noon-tide, Venice seemed to swelter in the midst of the waters, exhaling, like some great lily, mysterious influences, which make the brain swim and the heart faint—a moral malaria, distilled, as I thought, from those languishing melodies, those cooing vocalizations which I had found in the musty music-books of a century ago. I see that moonlight evening as if it were present. I see my fellow-lodgers of that little artists' boarding-house. The table on which they lean after supper is strewn with bits of bread, with napkins rolled in tapestry rollers, spots of wine here and there, and at regular intervals chipped pepper-pots, stands of toothpicks, and heaps of those huge hard peaches which nature imitates from the marble-shops of Pisa. The whole *pension*-full is assembled, and examining stupidly the engraving which the American etcher has just brought for me, knowing me to be mad about eighteenth century music and musicians, and having noticed, as he turned over the heaps of penny prints in the square of San Polo, that the portrait is that of a singer of those days.

Singer, thing of evil, stupid and wicked slave of the voice, of that instrument which was not invented by the human intellect, but begotten of the body, and which, instead of moving the soul, merely stirs up the dregs of our nature! For what is the voice but the Beast calling, awakening that other Beast sleeping in the depths of mankind, the Beast which all great art has ever sought to chain up, as the archangel chains up, in old pictures, the demon with his woman's face? How could the creature attached to this voice, its owner and its victim, the singer, the great, the real singer who once ruled over every heart, be otherwise than wicked and contemptible? But let me try and get on with my story.

I can see all my fellow-boarders, leaning on the table, contemplating the print, this effeminate *beau*, his hair curled into *ailes de pigeon*, his sword passed through his embroidered pocket, seated under a triumphal arch somewhere among the clouds, surrounded by puffy Cupids and crowned with laurels by a bouncing goddess of fame. I hear again all the insipid exclamations, the insipid questions about this singer:—"When did he live? Was he very famous? Are you sure, Magnus, that this is really a portrait,"

&c. &c. And I hear my own voice, as if in the far distance, giving them all sorts of information, biographical and critical, out of a battered little volume called *The Theatre of Musical Glory; or, Opinions upon the most Famous Chapel-masters and Virtuosi of this Century*, by Father Prosdocimo Sabatelli, Barnalite, Professor of Eloquence at the College of Modena, and Member of the Arcadian Academy, under the pastoral name of Evander Lilybaean, Venice, 1785, with the approbation of the Superiors.

I tell them all how this singer, this Balthasar Cesari, was nicknamed Zaffirino because of a sapphire engraved with cabalistic signs presented to him one evening by a masked stranger, in whom wise folk recognized that great cultivator of the human voice, the devil; how much more wonderful had been this Zaffirino's vocal gifts than those of any singer of ancient or modern times; how his brief life had been but a series of triumphs, petted by the greatest kings, sung by the most famous poets, and finally, adds Father Prosdocimo, "courted (if the grave Muse of history may incline her ear to the gossip of gallantry) by the most charming nymphs, even of the very highest quality."

My friends glance once more at the engraving; more insipid remarks are made; I am requested—especially by the American young ladies—to play or sing one of this Zaffirino's favourite songs—"For of course you know them, dear Maestro Magnus, you who have such a passion for all old music. Do be good, and sit down to the piano." I refuse, rudely enough, rolling the print in my fingers. How fearfully this cursed heat, these cursed moonlight nights, must have unstrung me! This Venice would certainly kill me in the long-run! Why, the sight of this idiotic engraving, the mere name of that coxcomb of a singer, have made my heart beat and my limbs turn to water like a love-sick hobbledehoy.

After my gruff refusal, the company begins to disperse; they prepare to go out, some to have a row on the lagoon, others to saunter before the *cafés* at St. Mark's; family discussions arise, gruntings of fathers, murmurs of mothers, peals of laughing from young girls and young men. And the moon, pouring in by the wide-open windows, turns this old palace ballroom, nowadays an inn dining-room, into a lagoon, scintillating, undulating like the other lagoon, the real one, which stretches out yonder furrowed by invisible *gondolas* betrayed by the red prow-lights. At last the whole lot of them are on the move. I shall be able to get some quiet in my room, and to work a little at my opera of *Ogier the Dane*. But no! Conversation revives, and, of all things, about that singer, that Zaffirino, whose absurd portrait I am crunching in my fingers.

The principal speaker is Count Alvise, an old Venetian with dyed whiskers, a great check tie fastened with two pins and a chain; a threadbare patrician who is dying to secure for his lanky son that pretty American girl, whose mother is intoxicated by all his mooning anecdotes about the past glories of Venice in general, and of his illustrious family in particular. Why, in Heaven's name, must he pitch upon Zaffirino for his mooning, this old duffer of a patrician?

"Zaffirino,—ah yes, to be sure! Balthasar Cesari, called Zaffirino," snuffles the voice of Count Alvise, who always repeats the last word of every sentence at least three times. "Yes, Zaffirino, to be sure! A famous singer of the days of my forefathers; yes, of my forefathers, dear lady!" Then a lot of rubbish about the former greatness of Venice, the glories of old music, the former Conservatoires, all mixed up with anecdotes of Rossini and Donizetti, whom he pretends to have known intimately. Finally, a story, of course containing plenty about his illustrious family:—"My great grand-aunt, the Procuratessa Vendramin, from whom we have inherited our estate of Mistrà, on the Brenta"—a hopelessly muddled story, apparently, fully of digressions, but of which that singer Zaffirino is the hero. The narrative, little by little, becomes more intelligible, or perhaps it is I who am giving it more attention.

"It seems," says the Count, "that there was one of his songs in particular which was called the 'Husbands' Air'—*L'Aria dei Marit*—because they didn't enjoy it quite as much as their better-halves. . . . My grand-aunt, Pisana Renier, married to the

11

Procuratore Vendramin, was a patrician of the old school, of the style that was getting rare a hundred years ago. Her virtue and her pride rendered her unapproachable. Zaffirino, on his part, was in the habit of boasting that no woman had ever been able to resist his singing, which, it appears, had its foundation in fact—the ideal changes, my dear lady, the ideal changes a good deal from one century to another!—and that his first song could make any woman turn pale and lower her eyes, the second make her madly in love, while the third song could kill her off on the spot, kill her for love, there under his very eyes, if he only felt inclined.

"My grandaunt Vendramin laughed when this story was told her, refused to go to hear this insolent dog, and added that it might be quite possible by the aid of spells and infernal pacts to kill a *gentildonna*, but as to making her fall in love with a lackey—never! This answer was naturally reported to Zaffirino, who piqued himself upon always getting the better of anyone who was wanting in deference to his voice. Like the ancient Romans, *parcere subjectis et debellare superbos*. You American ladies, who are so learned, will appreciate this little quotation from the divine Virgil. While seeming to avoid the Procuratessa Vendramin, Zaffirino took the opportunity, one evening at a large assembly, to sing in her presence. He sang and sang and sang until the poor grand-aunt Pisana fell ill for love. The most skilful physicians were kept unable to explain the mysterious malady which was visibly killing the poor young lady; and the Procuratore Vendramin applied in vain to the most venerated Madonnas, and vainly promised an altar of silver, with massive gold candlesticks, to Saints Cosmas and Damian, patrons of the art of healing.

"At last the brother-in-law of the Procuratessa, Monsignor Almorò Vendramin, Patriarch of Aquileia, a prelate famous for the sanctity of his life, obtained in a vision of Saint Justina, for whom he entertained a particular devotion, the information that the only thing which could benefit the strange illness of his sister-in-law was the voice of Zaffirino. Take notice that my poor grand-aunt had never condescended to such a revelation.

"The *Procuratore* was enchanted at this happy solution; and his lordship the Patriarch went to seek Zaffirino in person, and carried him in his own coach to the Villa of Mistrà, where the *Procuratessa* was residing.

"On being told what was about to happen, my poor grand-aunt went into fits of rage, which were succeeded immediately by equally violent fits of joy. However, she never forgot what was due to her great position. Although sick almost unto death, she had herself arrayed with the greatest pomp, caused her face to be painted, and put on all her diamonds: it would seem as if she were anxious to affirm her full dignity before this singer.

"Accordingly she received Zaffirino reclining on a sofa which had been placed in the great ballroom of the Villa of Mistrà, and beneath the princely canopy; for the Vendramins, who had intermarried with the house of Mantua, possessed imperial fiefs and were princes of the Holy Roman Empire. Zaffirino saluted her with the most profound respect, but not a word passed between them. Only, the singer inquired from the *Procuratore* whether the illustrious lady had received the Sacraments of the Church. Being told that the Procuratessa had herself asked to be given extreme unction from the hands of her brother-in-law, he declared his readiness to obey the orders of His Excellency, and sat down at once to the harpsichord.

"Never had he sung so divinely. At the end of the first song the Procuratessa Vendramin had already revived most extraordinarily; by the end of the second she appeared entirely cured and beaming with beauty and happiness; but at the third air— the *Aria dei Mariti*, no doubt—she began to change frightfully; she gave a dreadful cry, and fell into the convulsions of death. In a quarter of an hour she was dead! Zaffirino did not wait to see her die. Having finished his song, he withdrew instantly, took post-horses, and travelled day and night as far as Munich. People remarked that he had presented himself at Mistrà dressed in mourning, although he had mentioned no death among his relatives; also that he had prepared everything for his departure, as if fearing the wrath of so powerful a family.

"Then there was also the extraordinary question he had asked before beginning to sing, about the Procuratessa having confessed and received extreme unction.... No, thanks, my dear lady, no cigarettes for me. But if it does not distress you or your charming daughter, may I humbly beg permission to smoke a cigar?"

And Count Alvise, enchanted with his talent for narrative, and sure of having secured for his son the heart and the dollars of his fair audience, proceeds to light a candle, and at the candle one of those long black Italian cigars which require preliminary disinfection before smoking.

... If this state of things goes on I shall just have to ask the doctor for a bottle; this ridiculous beating of my heart and disgusting cold perspiration have increased steadily during Count Alvise's narrative. To keep myself in countenance among the various idiotic commentaries on this cock-and-bull story of a vocal coxcomb and a vaporing great lady, I begin to unroll the engraving, and to examine stupidly the portrait of Zaffirino, once so renowned, now so forgotten. A ridiculous ass, this singer, under his triumphal arch, with his stuffed Cupids and the great fat winged kitchen-maid crowning him with laurels. How flat and vapid and vulgar it is, to be sure, all this odious eighteenth century!

But he, personally, is not so utterly vapid as I had thought. That effeminate, fat face of his is almost beautiful, with an odd smile, brazen and cruel. I have seen faces like this, if not in real life, at least in my boyish romantic dreams, when I read Swinburne and Baudelaire, the faces of wicked, vindictive women. Oh yes! he is decidedly a beautiful creature, this Zaffirino, and his voice must have had the same sort of beauty and the same expression of wickedness....

"Come on, Magnus," sound the voices of my fellow-boarders, "be a good fellow and sing us one of the old chap's songs; or at least something or other of that day, and we'll make believe it was the air with which he killed that poor lady."

"Oh yes! the *Aria dei Mariti*, the 'Husbands' Air,'" mumbles old Alvise, between the puffs at his impossible black cigar. "My poor grand-aunt, Pisana Vendramin; he went and killed her with those songs of his, with that *Aria dei Mariti.*"

I feel senseless rage overcoming me. Is it that horrible palpitation (by the way, there is a Norwegian doctor, my fellow-countryman, at Venice just now) which is sending the blood to my brain and making me mad? The people round the piano, the furniture, everything together seems to get mixed and to turn into moving blobs of colour. I set to singing; the only thing which remains distinct before my eyes being the portrait of Zaffirino, on the edge of that boarding-house piano; the sensual, effeminate face, with its wicked, cynical smile, keeps appearing and disappearing as the print wavers about in the draught that makes the candles smoke and gutter. And I set to singing madly, singing I don't know what.

Yes; I begin to identify it: 'tis the *Biondina in Gondoleta*, the only song of the eighteenth century which is still remembered by the Venetian people. I sing it, mimicking every old-school grace; shakes, cadences, languishingly swelled and diminished notes, and adding all manner of buffooneries, until the audience, recovering from its surprise, begins to shake with laughing; until I begin to laugh myself, madly, frantically, between the phrases of the melody, my voice finally smothered in this dull, brutal laughter.... And then, to crown it all, I shake my fist at this long-dead singer, looking at me with his wicked woman's face, with his mocking, fatuous smile.

"Ah! you would like to be revenged on me also!" I exclaim. "You would like me to write you nice *roulades* and flourishes, another nice *Aria dei Mariti*, my fine Zaffirino!"

★★★★★★

That night I dreamed a very strange dream. Even in the big half-furnished room the heat and closeness were stifling. The air seemed laden with the scent of all manner of white flowers, faint and heavy in their intolerable sweetness: tuberoses, gardenias, and jasmines drooping I know not where in neglected vases. The moonlight had transformed the marble floor around me into a shallow, shining, pool. On account of the heat I had exchanged my bed for a big old-fashioned sofa of light wood, painted with little nosegays and sprigs, like an old silk; and I lay there, not attempting to sleep, and letting my thoughts go vaguely to my opera of *Ogier the Dane*, of which I had long finished writing the words, and for whose music I had hoped to find some inspiration in this strange Venice, floating, as it were, in the stagnant lagoon of the past. But Venice had merely put all my ideas into hopeless confusion; it was as if there arose out of its shallow waters a miasma of long-dead melodies, which sickened but intoxicated my soul. I lay on my sofa watching that pool of whitish light, which rose higher and higher, little trickles of light meeting it here and there, wherever the moon's rays struck upon some polished surface; while huge shadows waved to and fro in the draught of the open balcony.

I went over and over that old Norse story: how the Paladin, Ogier, one of the knights of Charlemagne, was decoyed during his homeward wanderings from the Holy Land by the arts of an enchantress, the same who had once held in bondage the great Emperor Caesar and given him King Oberon for a son; how Ogier had tarried in that island only one day and one night, and yet, when he came home to his kingdom, he found all changed, his friends dead, his family dethroned, and not a man who knew his face; until at last, driven hither and thither like a beggar, a poor minstrel had taken compassion of his sufferings and given him all he could give—a song, the song of the prowess of a hero dead for hundreds of years, the Paladin Ogier the Dane.

The story of Ogier ran into a dream, as vivid as my waking thoughts had been vague. I was looking no longer at the pool of moonlight spreading round my couch, with its trickles of light and looming, waving shadows, but the *frescoed* walls of a great saloon. It was not, as I recognized in a second, the dining-room of that Venetian palace now turned into a boarding-house. It was a far larger room, a real ballroom, almost circular in its octagon shape, with eight huge white doors surrounded by *stucco* mouldings, and, high on the vault of the ceiling, eight little galleries or recesses like boxes at a theatre, intended no doubt for musicians and spectators. The place was imperfectly lighted by only one of the eight chandeliers, which revolved slowly, like huge spiders, each on its long cord. But the light struck upon the gilt *stuccoes* opposite me, and on a large expanse of *fresco*, the sacrifice of Iphigenia, with Agamemnon and Achilles in Roman helmets, lappets, and knee-breeches.

It discovered also one of the oil panels let into the mouldings of the roof, a goddess in lemon and lilac draperies, foreshortened over a great green peacock. Round the room, where the light reached, I could make out big yellow satin sofas and heavy gilded consoles; in the shadow of a corner was what looked like a piano, and farther in the shade one of those big canopies which decorate the anterooms of Roman palaces. I looked about me, wondering where I was: a heavy, sweet smell, reminding me of the flavour of a peach, filled the place.

Little by little I began to perceive sounds; little, sharp, metallic, detached notes, like those of a mandolin; and there was united to them a voice, very low and sweet, almost a whisper, which grew and grew and grew, until the whole place was filled with that exquisite vibrating note, of a strange, exotic, unique quality. The note went on, swelling and swelling. Suddenly there was a horrible piercing shriek, and the thud of a body on the floor, and all manner of smothered exclamations. There, close by the canopy, a light suddenly appeared; and I could see, among the dark figures moving to and fro in the room, a woman lying on the ground, surrounded by other women.

Her blond hair, tangled, full of diamond-sparkles which cut through the half-darkness, was hanging dishevelled; the laces of her bodice had been cut, and her white breast shone among the sheen of jewelled brocade; her face was bent forwards, and a thin white arm trailed, like a broken limb, across the knees of one of the women who were endeavouring to lift her. There was a sudden splash of water against the floor, more confused exclamations, a hoarse, broken moan, and a gurgling, dreadful sound. . . .
I awoke with a start and rushed to the window.

17

Outside, in the blue haze of the moon, the church and belfry of St. George loomed blue and hazy, with the black hull and rigging, the red lights, of a large steamer moored before them. From the lagoon rose a damp sea-breeze. What was it all? Ah! I began to understand: that story of old Count Alvise's, the death of his grand-aunt, Pisana Vendramin. Yes, it was about that I had been dreaming.

I returned to my room; I struck a light, and sat down to my writing-table. Sleep had become impossible. I tried to work at my opera. Once or twice I thought I had got hold of what I had looked for so long. . . . But as soon as I tried to lay hold of my theme, there arose in my mind the distant echo of that voice, of that long note swelled slowly by insensible degrees, that long note whose tone was so strong and so subtle.

★★★★★★

There are in the life of an artist moments when, still unable to seize his own inspiration, or even clearly to discern it, he becomes aware of the approach of that long-invoked idea. A mingled joy and terror warn him that before another day, another hour have passed, the inspiration shall have crossed the threshold of his soul and flooded it with its rapture. All day I had felt the need of isolation and quiet, and at nightfall I went for a row on the most solitary part of the lagoon. All things seemed to tell that I was going to meet my inspiration, and I awaited its coming as a lover awaits his beloved.

I had stopped my *gondola* for a moment, and as I gently swayed to and fro on the water, all paved with moonbeams, it seemed to me that I was on the confines of an imaginary world. It lay close at hand, enveloped in luminous, pale blue mist, through which the moon had cut a wide and glistening path; out to sea, the little islands, like moored black boats, only accentuated the solitude of this region of moonbeams and wavelets; while the hum of the insects in orchards hard by merely added to the impression of untroubled silence. On some such seas, I thought, must the Paladin Ogier, have sailed when about to discover that during that sleep at the enchantress's knees centuries had elapsed and the heroic world had set, and the kingdom of prose had come.

While my *gondola* rocked stationary on that sea of moon-beams, I pondered over that twilight of the heroic world. In the soft rattle of the water on the hull I seemed to hear the rattle of all that armour, of all those swords swinging rusty on the walls, neglected by the degenerate sons of the great champions of old. I had long been in search of a theme which I called the theme of the "Prowess of Ogier;" it was to appear from time to time in the course of my opera, to develop at last into that song of the Minstrel, which reveals to the hero that he is one of a long-dead world. And at this moment I seemed to feel the presence of that theme. Yet an instant, and my mind would be overwhelmed by that savage music, heroic, funereal.

Suddenly there came across the lagoon, cleaving, checkering, and fretting the silence with a lacework of sound even as the moon was fretting and cleaving the water, a ripple of music, a voice breaking itself in a shower of little scales and cadences and trills.

I sank back upon my cushions. The vision of heroic days had vanished, and before my closed eyes there seemed to dance mul-titudes of little stars of light, chasing and interlacing like those sudden vocalizations.

"To shore! Quick!" I cried to the *gondolier.*

But the sounds had ceased; and there came from the orchards, with their mulberry-trees glistening in the moonlight, and their black swaying cypress-plumes, nothing save the confused hum, the monotonous chirp, of the crickets.

I looked around me: on one side empty dunes, orchards, and meadows, without house or steeple; on the other, the blue and misty sea, empty to where distant islets were profiled black on the horizon.

A faintness overcame me, and I felt myself dissolve. For all of a sudden a second ripple of voice swept over the lagoon, a shower of little notes, which seemed to form a little mocking laugh.

Then again all was still. This silence lasted so long that I fell once more to meditating on my opera. I lay in wait once more for the half-caught theme. But no. It was not that theme for which I was waiting and watching with baited breath. I realized my delusion when, on rounding the point of the Giudecca, the murmur of a voice arose from the midst of the waters, a thread of sound slender as a moonbeam, scarce audible, but exquisite, which expanded slowly, insensibly, taking volume and body, taking flesh almost and fire, an ineffable quality, full, passionate, but veiled, as it were, in a subtle, downy wrapper. The note grew stronger and stronger, and warmer and more passionate, until it burst through that strange and charming veil, and emerged beaming, to break itself in the luminous facets of a wonderful shake, long, superb, triumphant.

There was a dead silence.

"Row to St. Mark's!" I exclaimed. "Quick!"

The *gondola* glided through the long, glittering track of moonbeams, and rent the great band of yellow, reflected light, mirroring the cupolas of St. Mark's, the lace-like pinnacles of the palace, and the slender pink belfry, which rose from the lit-up water to the pale and bluish evening sky.

In the larger of the two squares the military band was blaring through the last spirals of a *crescendo* of Rossini. The crowd was dispersing in this great open-air ballroom, and the sounds arose which invariably follow upon out-of-door music. A clatter of spoons and glasses, a rustle and grating of frocks and of chairs, and the click of scabbards on the pavement. I pushed my way among the fashionable youths contemplating the ladies while sucking the knob of their sticks; through the serried ranks of respectable families, marching arm in arm with their white frocked young ladies close in front. I took a seat before Florian's, among the customers stretching themselves before departing, and the waiters hurrying to and fro, clattering their empty cups and trays. Two imitation Neapolitans were slipping their guitar and violin under their arm, ready to leave the place.

"Stop!" I cried to them; "don't go yet. Sing me something— sing *La Camesella* or *Funiculì, funiculà*—no matter what, provided you make a row;" and as they screamed and scraped their utmost,

I added, "But can't you sing louder, d—n you!—sing louder, do you understand?"

I felt the need of noise, of yells and false notes, of something vulgar and hideous to drive away that ghost-voice which was haunting me.

******

Again and again I told myself that it had been some silly prank of a romantic amateur, hidden in the gardens of the shore or gliding unperceived on the lagoon; and that the sorcery of moonlight and sea-mist had transfigured for my excited brain mere humdrum roulades out of exercises of Bordogni or Crescentini.

But all the same I continued to be haunted by that voice. My work was interrupted ever and *anon* by the attempt to catch its imaginary echo; and the heroic harmonies of my Scandinavian legend were strangely interwoven with voluptuous phrases and florid cadences in which I seemed to hear again that same accursed voice.

To be haunted by singing-exercises! It seemed too ridiculous for a man who professedly despised the art of singing. And still, I preferred to believe in that childish amateur, amusing himself with warbling to the moon.

One day, while making these reflections the hundredth time over, my eyes chanced to light upon the portrait of Zaffirino, which my friend had pinned against the wall. I pulled it down and tore it into half a dozen shreds. Then, already ashamed of my folly, I watched the torn pieces float down from the window, wafted hither and thither by the sea-breeze. One scrap got caught in a yellow blind below me; the others fell into the canal, and were speedily lost to sight in the dark water. I was overcome with shame. My heart beat like bursting. What a miserable, unnerved worm I had become in this cursed Venice, with its languishing moonlights, its atmosphere as of some stuffy *boudoir*, long unused, full of old stuffs and *potpourri*!

That night, however, things seemed to be going better. I was able to settle down to my opera, and even to work at it. In the intervals my thoughts returned, not without a certain pleasure, to those scattered fragments of the torn engraving fluttering down to the water. I was disturbed at my piano by the hoarse voices and the scraping of violins which rose from one of those music-boats that station at night under the hotels of the Grand Canal. The moon had set. Under my balcony the water stretched black into the distance, its darkness cut by the still darker outlines of the flotilla of *gondolas* in attendance on the music-boat, where the faces of the singers, and the guitars and violins, gleamed reddish under the unsteady light of the Chinese-lanterns.

"*Jammo, jammo; jammo, jammo jà*," sang the loud, hoarse voices; then a tremendous scrape and twang, and the yelled-out burden, "*Funiculì, funiculà; funiculì, funiculà; jammo, jammo, jammo, jammo, jammo jà.*"

Then came a few cries of "*Bis, Bis!*" from a neighbouring hotel, a brief clapping of hands, the sound of a handful of coppers rattling into the boat, and the oar-stroke of some *gondolier* making ready to turn away.

"Sing the *Camesella*," ordered some voice with a foreign accent.

"No, no! *Santa Lucia.*"

"I want the *Camesella.*"

"No! *Santa Lucia.* Hi! sing *Santa Lucia*—d'you hear?"

The musicians, under their green and yellow and red lamps, held a whispered consultation on the manner of conciliating these contradictory demands. Then, after a minute's hesitation, the violins began the prelude of that once famous air, which has remained popular in Venice—the words written, some hundred years ago, by the patrician Gritti, the music by an unknown composer—*La Biondina in Gondoleta.*

That cursed eighteenth century! It seemed a malignant fatality that made these brutes choose just this piece to interrupt me.

At last the long prelude came to an end; and above the cracked guitars and squeaking fiddles there arose, not the expected nasal chorus, but a single voice singing below its breath.

My arteries throbbed. How well I knew that voice! It was singing, as I have said, below its breath, yet none the less it sufficed to fill all that reach of the canal with its strange quality of tone, exquisite, far-fetched.

They were long-drawn-out notes, of intense but peculiar sweetness, a man's voice which had much of a woman's, but more even of a chorister's, but a chorister's voice without its limpidity and innocence; its youthfulness was veiled, muffled, as it were, in a sort of downy vagueness, as if a passion of tears withheld.

There was a burst of applause, and the old palaces re-echoed with the clapping. "Bravo, bravo! Thank you, thank you! Sing again—please, sing again. Who can it be?"

And then a bumping of hulls, a splashing of oars, and the oaths of *gondoliers* trying to push each other away, as the red prow-lamps of the *gondolas* pressed round the gaily lit singing-boat.

But no one stirred on board. It was to none of them that this applause was due. And while everyone pressed on, and clapped and vociferated, one little red prow-lamp dropped away from the fleet; for a moment a single *gondola* stood forth black upon the black water, and then was lost in the night.

For several days the mysterious singer was the universal topic. The people of the music-boat swore that no one besides themselves had been on board, and that they knew as little as ourselves about the owner of that voice. The *gondoliers*, despite their descent from the spies of the old Republic, were equally unable to furnish any clue. No musical celebrity was known or suspected to be at Venice; and everyone agreed that such a singer must be a European celebrity. The strangest thing in this strange business was, that even among those learned in music there was no agreement on the subject of this voice: it was called by all sorts of names and described by all manner of incongruous adjectives; people went so far as to dispute whether the voice belonged to a man or to a woman: everyone had some new definition.

In all these musical discussions I, alone, brought forward no opinion. I felt a repugnance, an impossibility almost, of speaking about that voice; and the more or less commonplace conjectures of my friend had the invariable effect of sending me out of the room.

Meanwhile my work was becoming daily more difficult, and I soon passed from utter impotence to a state of inexplicable agitation. Every morning I arose with fine resolutions and grand projects of work; only to go to bed that night without having accomplished anything. I spent hours leaning on my balcony, or wandering through the network of lanes with their ribbon of blue sky, endeavouring vainly to expel the thought of that voice, or endeavouring in reality to reproduce it in my memory; for the more I tried to banish it from my thoughts, the more I grew to thirst for that extraordinary tone, for those mysteriously downy, veiled notes; and no sooner did I make an effort to work at my opera than my head was full of scraps of forgotten eighteenth century airs, of frivolous or languishing little phrases; and I fell to wondering with a bitter-sweet longing how those songs would have sounded if sung by that voice.

At length it became necessary to see a doctor, from whom, however, I carefully hid away all the stranger symptoms of my malady. The air of the lagoons, the great heat, he answered cheerfully, had pulled me down a little; a tonic and a month in the country, with plenty of riding and no work, would make me myself again. That old idler, Count Alvise, who had insisted on accompanying me to the physician's, immediately suggested that I should go and stay with his son, who was boring himself to death superintending the maize harvest on the mainland: he could promise me excellent air, plenty of horses, and all the peaceful surroundings and the delightful occupations of a rural life—"Be sensible, my dear Magnus, and just go quietly to Mistrà."

Mistrà—the name sent a shiver all down me. I was about to decline the invitation, when a thought suddenly loomed vaguely in my mind.

"Yes, dear Count," I answered; "I accept your invitation with gratitude and pleasure. I will start tomorrow for Mistrà."

★★★★★★

The next day found me at Padua, on my way to the Villa of Mistrà. It seemed as if I had left an intolerable burden behind me. I was, for the first time since how long, quite light of heart. The tortuous, rough-paved streets, with their empty, gloomy *porticoes*; the ill-plastered palaces, with closed, discoloured shutters; the little rambling square, with meagre trees and stubborn grass; the Venetian garden-houses reflecting their crumbling graces in the muddy canal; the gardens without gates and the gates without gardens, the avenues leading nowhere; and the population of blind and legless beggars, of whining sacristans, which issued as by magic from between the flag-stones and dust-heaps and weeds under the fierce August sun, all this dreariness merely amused and pleased me. My good spirits were heightened by a musical mass which I had the good fortune to hear at St. Anthony's.

Never in all my days had I heard anything comparable, although Italy affords many strange things in the way of sacred music. Into the deep nasal chanting of the priests there had suddenly burst a chorus of children, singing absolutely independent of all time and tune; grunting of priests answered by squealing of boys, slow Gregorian modulation interrupted by jaunty barrel-organ pipings, an insane, insanely merry jumble of bellowing and barking, mewing and cackling and braying, such as would have enlivened a witches' meeting, or rather some mediaeval Feast of Fools. And, to make the grotesqueness of such music still more fantastic and Hoffmannlike, there was, besides, the magnificence of the piles of sculptured marbles and gilded bronzes, the tradition of the musical splendour for which St. Anthony's had been famous in days gone by.

I had read in old travellers, Lalande and Burney, that the Republic of St. Mark had squandered immense sums not merely on the monuments and decoration, but on the musical establishment of its great cathedral of *Terra Firma*. In the midst of this ineffable concert of impossible voices and instruments, I tried

25

to imagine the voice of Guadagni, the *soprano* for whom Gluck had written *Che farò senza Euridice*, and the fiddle of Tartini, that Tartini with whom the devil had once come and made music. And the delight in anything so absolutely, barbarously, grotesquely, fantastically incongruous as such a performance in such a place was heightened by a sense of profanation: such were the successors of those wonderful musicians of that hated eighteenth century!

The whole thing had delighted me so much, so very much more than the most faultless performance could have done, that I determined to enjoy it once more; and towards vesper-time, after a cheerful dinner with two bagmen at the inn of the Golden Star, and a pipe over the rough sketch of a possible *cantata* upon the music which the devil made for Tartini, I turned my steps once more towards St. Anthony's.

The bells were ringing for sunset, and a muffled sound of organs seemed to issue from the huge, solitary church; I pushed my way under the heavy leathern curtain, expecting to be greeted by the grotesque performance of that morning.

I proved mistaken. Vespers must long have been over. A smell of stale incense, a crypt-like damp filled my mouth; it was already night in that vast cathedral. Out of the darkness glimmered the votive-lamps of the chapels, throwing wavering lights upon the red polished marble, the gilded railing, and chandeliers, and plaqueing with yellow the muscles of some sculptured figure. In a corner a burning taper put a halo about the head of a priest, burnishing his shining bald skull, his white surplice, and the open book before him. "Amen" he chanted; the book was closed with a snap, the light moved up the apse, some dark figures of women rose from their knees and passed quickly towards the door; a man saying his prayers before a chapel also got up, making a great clatter in dropping his stick.

The church was empty, and I expected every minute to be turned out by the sacristan making his evening round to close the doors. I was leaning against a pillar, looking into the greyness of the great arches, when the organ suddenly burst out into a series of chords, rolling through the echoes of the church: it seemed to be the conclusion of some service. And above the organ rose the notes of a voice; high, soft, enveloped in a kind of downiness, like a cloud of incense, and which ran through the mazes of a long cadence. The voice dropped into silence; with two thundering chords the organ closed in. All was silent. For a moment I stood leaning against one of the pillars of the nave: my hair was clammy, my knees sank beneath me, an enervating heat spread through my body; I tried to breathe more largely, to suck in the sounds with the incense-laden air. I was supremely happy, and yet as if I were dying; then suddenly a chill ran through me, and with it a vague panic. I turned away and hurried out into the open.

The evening sky lay pure and blue along the jagged line of roofs; the bats and swallows were wheeling about; and from the belfries all around, half-drowned by the deep bell of St. Anthony's, jangled the peel of the *Ave Maria*.

★★★★★★

"You really don't seem well," young Count Alvise had said the previous evening, as he welcomed me, in the light of a lantern held up by a peasant, in the weedy back-garden of the Villa of Mistrà. Everything had seemed to me like a dream: the jingle of the horse's bells driving in the dark from Padua, as the lantern swept the acacia-hedges with their wide yellow light; the grating of the wheels on the gravel; the supper-table, illumined by a single petroleum lamp for fear of attracting mosquitoes, where a broken old lackey, in an old stable jacket, handed round the dishes among the fumes of onion; Alvise's fat mother gabbling dialect in a shrill, benevolent voice behind the bullfights on her fan; the unshaven village priest, perpetually fidgeting with his glass and foot, and sticking one shoulder up above the other.

And now, in the afternoon, I felt as if I had been in this long, rambling, tumble-down Villa of Mistrà—a villa three-quarters of which was given up to the storage of grain and garden tools, or to the exercise of rats, mice, scorpions, and centipedes—all my life; as if I had always sat there, in Count Alvise's study, among

27

the pile of undusted books on agriculture, the sheaves of accounts, the samples of grain and silkworm seed, the ink-stains and the cigar-ends; as if I had never heard of anything save the cereal basis of Italian agriculture, the diseases of maize, the *peronospora* of the vine, the breeds of bullocks, and the iniquities of farm labourers; with the blue cones of the Euganean hills closing in the green shimmer of plain outside the window.

After an early dinner, again with the screaming gabble of the fat old Countess, the fidgeting and shoulder-raising of the unshaven priest, the smell of fried oil and stewed onions, Count Alvise made me get into the cart beside him, and whirled me along among clouds of dust, between the endless glister of poplars, acacias, and maples, to one of his farms.

In the burning sun some twenty or thirty girls, in coloured skirts, laced bodices, and big straw-hats, were threshing the maize on the big red brick threshing-floor, while others were winnowing the grain in great sieves. Young Alvise III. (the old one was Alvise II.: everyone is Alvise, that is to say, Lewis, in that family; the name is on the house, the carts, the barrows, the very pails) picked up the maize, touched it, tasted it, said something to the girls that made them laugh, and something to the head farmer that made him look very glum; and then led me into a huge stable, where some twenty or thirty white bullocks were stamping, switching their tails, hitting their horns against the mangers in the dark. Alvise III. patted each, called him by his name, gave him some salt or a turnip, and explained which was the Mantuan breed, which the Apulian, which the Romagnolo, and so on.

Then he bade me jump into the trap, and off we went again through the dust, among the hedges and ditches, till we came to some more brick farm buildings with pinkish roofs smoking against the blue sky. Here there were more young women threshing and winnowing the maize, which made a great golden Danaë cloud; more bullocks stamping and lowing in the cool darkness; more joking, fault-finding, explaining; and thus through five farms, until I seemed to see the rhythmical rising and falling of the flails against the hot sky, the shower of golden grains, the yellow dust from the winnowing-sieves on to the bricks, the switching of innumerable tails and plunging of innumerable horns, the glistening of huge white flanks and foreheads, whenever I closed my eyes.

"A good day's work!" cried Count Alvise, stretching out his long legs with the tight trousers riding up over the Wellington boots. "Mamma, give us some aniseed-syrup after dinner; it is an excellent restorative and precaution against the fevers of this country."

"Oh! you've got fever in this part of the world, have you? Why, your father said the air was so good!"

"Nothing, nothing," soothed the old Countess. "The only thing to be dreaded are mosquitoes; take care to fasten your shutters before lighting the candle."

"Well," rejoined young Alvise, with an effort of conscience, "of course there *are* fevers. But they needn't hurt you. Only, don't go out into the garden at night, if you don't want to catch them. Papa told me that you have fancies for moonlight rambles. It won't do in this climate, my dear fellow; it won't do. If you must stalk about at night, being a genius, take a turn inside the house; you can get quite exercise enough."

After dinner the aniseed-syrup was produced, together with brandy and cigars, and they all sat in the long, narrow, half-furnished room on the first floor; the old Countess knitting a garment of uncertain shape and destination, the priest reading out the newspaper; Count Alvise puffing at his long, crooked cigar, and pulling the ears of a long, lean dog with a suspicion of mange and a stiff eye. From the dark garden outside rose the hum and whirr of countless insects, and the smell of the grapes which hung black against the starlit, blue sky, on the trellis. I went to the balcony. The garden lay dark beneath; against the twinkling horizon stood out the tall poplars. There was the sharp cry of an owl; the barking of a dog; a sudden whiff of warm, enervating perfume, a perfume that made me think of the taste of certain peaches, and suggested white, thick, wax-like petals. I seemed to have smelt that flower once before: it made me feel languid, almost faint.

"I am very tired," I said to Count Alvise. "See how feeble we city folk become!"

★★★★★★

But, despite my fatigue, I found it quite impossible to sleep. The night seemed perfectly stifling. I had felt nothing like it at Venice. Despite the injunctions of the Countess I opened the solid wooden shutters, hermetically closed against mosquitoes, and looked out.

The moon had risen; and beneath it lay the big lawns, the rounded tree-tops, bathed in a blue, luminous mist, every leaf glistening and trembling in what seemed a heaving sea of light. Beneath the window was the long trellis, with the white shining piece of pavement under it. It was so bright that I could distinguish the green of the vine-leaves, the dull red of the catalpa-flowers. There was in the air a vague scent of cut grass, of ripe American grapes, of that white flower (it must be white) which made me think of the taste of peaches all melting into the delicious freshness of falling dew. From the village church came the stroke of one: Heaven knows how long I had been vainly attempting to sleep.

A shiver ran through me, and my head suddenly filled as with the fumes of some subtle wine; I remembered all those weedy embankments, those canals full of stagnant water, the yellow faces of the peasants; the word malaria returned to my mind. No matter! I remained leaning on the window, with a thirsty longing to plunge myself into this blue moon-mist, this dew and perfume and silence, which seemed to vibrate and quiver like the stars that strewed the depths of heaven. . . . . . What music, even Wagner's, or of that great singer of starry nights, the divine Schumann, what music could ever compare with this great silence, with this great concert of voiceless things that sing within one's soul?

As I made this reflection, a note, high, vibrating, and sweet, rent the silence, which immediately closed around it. I leaned out of the window, my heart beating as though it must burst. After a brief space the silence was cloven once more by that note, as the darkness is cloven by a falling star or a firefly rising slowly like a rocket. But this time it was plain that the voice did not come, as I had imagined, from the garden, but from the house itself, from some corner of this rambling old villa of Mistrà.

Mistrà—Mistrà! The name rang in my ears, and I began at length to grasp its significance, which seems to have escaped me till then. "Yes," I said to myself, "it is quite natural." And with this odd impression of naturalness was mixed a feverish, impatient pleasure. It was as if I had come to Mistrà on purpose, and that I was about to meet the object of my long and weary hopes.

Grasping the lamp with its singed green shade, I gently opened the door and made my way through a series of long passages and of big, empty rooms, in which my steps re-echoed as in a church, and my light disturbed whole swarms of bats. I wandered at random, farther and farther from the inhabited part of the buildings.

This silence made me feel sick; I gasped as under a sudden disappointment.

All of a sudden there came a sound—chords, metallic, sharp, rather like the tone of a mandolin—close to my ear. Yes, quite close: I was separated from the sounds only by a partition. I fumbled for a door; the unsteady light of my lamp was insufficient for my eyes, which were swimming like those of a drunkard. At last I found a latch, and, after a moment's hesitation, I lifted it and gently pushed open the door. At first I could not understand what manner of place I was in. It was dark all round me, but a brilliant light blinded me, a light coming from below and striking the opposite wall. It was as if I had entered a dark box in a half-lighted theatre. I was, in fact, in something of the kind, a sort of dark hole with a high balustrade, half-hidden by an up-drawn curtain. I remembered those little galleries or recesses for the use of musicians or lookers-on—which exist under the ceiling of the ballrooms in certain old Italian palaces.

Yes; it must have been one like that. Opposite me was a vaulted ceiling covered with gilt mouldings, which framed great time-blackened canvases; and lower down, in the light thrown up from below, stretched a wall covered with faded *frescoes*. Where had I seen that goddess in lilac and lemon draperies foreshortened over a big, green peacock? For she was familiar to me, and the *stucco* Tritons also who twisted their tails round her gilded frame. And that *fresco*, with warriors in Roman *cuirasses* and green and blue *lappets*, and knee-breeches—where could I have seen them before? I asked myself these questions without experiencing any surprise. Moreover, I was very calm, as one is calm sometimes in extraordinary dreams—could I be dreaming?

I advanced gently and leaned over the balustrade. My eyes were met at first by the darkness above me, where, like gigantic spiders, the big chandeliers rotated slowly, hanging from the ceiling. Only one of them was lit, and its Murano-glass pendants, its carnations and roses, shone opalescent in the light of the guttering wax. This chandelier lighted up the opposite wall and that piece of ceiling with the goddess and the green peacock; it illumined, but far less well, a corner of the huge room, where, in the shadow of a kind of canopy, a little group of people were crowding round a yellow satin sofa, of the same kind as those that lined the walls. On the sofa, half-screened from me by the surrounding persons, a woman was stretched out: the silver of her embroidered dress and the rays of her diamonds gleamed and shot forth as she moved uneasily. And immediately under the chandelier, in the full light, a man stooped over a harpsichord, his head bent slightly, as if collecting his thoughts before singing.

He struck a few chords and sang. Yes, sure enough, it was the voice, the voice that had so long been persecuting me! I recognized at once that delicate, voluptuous quality, strange, exquisite, sweet beyond words, but lacking all youth and clearness. That passion veiled in tears which had troubled my brain that night on the lagoon, and again on the Grand Canal singing the *Biondina*, and yet again, only two days since, in the deserted cathedral of Padua. But I recognized now what seemed to have been hidden from me till then, that this voice was what I cared most for in all the wide world.

The voice wound and unwound itself in long, languishing phrases, in rich, voluptuous *rifioriruras*, all fretted with tiny scales and exquisite, crisp shakes; it stopped ever and *anon*, swaying as if panting in languid delight. And I felt my body melt even as wax in the sunshine, and it seemed to me that I too was turning fluid and vaporous, in order to mingle with these sounds as the moonbeams mingle with the dew.

Suddenly, from the dimly lighted corner by the canopy, came a little piteous wail; then another followed, and was lost in the singer's voice. During a long phrase on the harpsichord, sharp and tinkling, the singer turned his head towards the dais, and there came a plaintive little sob. But he, instead of stopping, struck a sharp chord; and with a thread of voice so hushed as to be scarcely audible, slid softly into a long *cadenza*. At the same moment he threw his head backwards, and the light fell full upon the handsome, effeminate face, with its ashy pallor and big, black brows, of the singer Zaffirino. At the sight of that face, sensual and sullen, of that smile which was cruel and mocking like a bad woman's, I understood—I knew not why, by what process—that his singing *must* be cut short, that the accursed phrase *must* never be finished. I understood that I was before an assassin, that he was killing this woman, and killing me also, with his wicked voice.

I rushed down the narrow stair which led down from the box, pursued, as it were, by that exquisite voice, swelling, swelling by insensible degrees. I flung myself on the door which must be that of the big saloon. I could see its light between the panels. I bruised my hands in trying to wrench the latch. The door was fastened tight, and while I was struggling with that locked door I heard the voice swelling, swelling, rending asunder that downy veil which wrapped it, leaping forth clear, resplendent, like the sharp and glittering blade of a knife that seemed to enter deep into my breast. Then, once more, a wail, a death-groan, and that dreadful noise, that hideous gurgle of breath strangled by a rush of blood. And then a long shake, acute, brilliant, triumphant.

The door gave way beneath my weight, one half crashed in. I entered. I was blinded by a flood of blue moonlight. It poured in through four great windows, peaceful and diaphanous, a pale blue mist of moonlight, and turned the huge room into a kind of submarine cave, paved with moonbeams, full of shimmers, of pools of moonlight. It was as bright as at midday, but the brightness was cold, blue, vaporous, supernatural. The room was completely empty, like a great hayloft. Only, there hung from the ceiling the ropes which had once supported a chandelier; and in a corner, among stacks of wood and heaps of Indian-corn, whence spread a sickly smell of damp and mildew, there stood a long, thin harpsichord, with spindle-legs, and its cover cracked from end to end.

I felt, all of a sudden, very calm. The one thing that mattered was the phrase that kept moving in my head, the phrase of that unfinished cadence which I had heard but an instant before. I opened the harpsichord, and my fingers came down boldly upon its keys. A jingle-jangle of broken strings, laughable and dreadful, was the only answer.

Then an extraordinary fear overtook me. I clambered out of one of the windows; I rushed up the garden and wandered through the fields, among the canals and the embankments, until the moon had set and the dawn began to shiver, followed, pursued forever by that jangle of broken strings.

People expressed much satisfaction at my recovery. It seems that one dies of those fevers.

Recovery? But have I recovered? I walk, and eat and drink and talk; I can even sleep. I live the life of other living creatures. But I am wasted by a strange and deadly disease. I can never lay hold of my own inspiration. My head is filled with music which is certainly by me, since I have never heard it before, but which still is not my own, which I despise and abhor: little, tripping flourishes and languishing phrases, and long-drawn, echoing cadences.

O wicked, wicked voice, violin of flesh and blood made by

the Evil One's hand, may I not even execrate thee in peace; but is it necessary that, at the moment when I curse, the longing to hear thee again should parch my soul like hell-thirst? And since I have satiated thy lust for revenge, since thou hast withered my life and withered my genius, is it not time for pity? May I not hear one note, only one note of thine, O singer, O wicked and contemptible wretch?

Prince Alberic and the Snake Lady

A Story from *Pope Jacynth and Other Fantastic Tales*

In the year 1701, the Duchy of Luna became united to the Italian dominions of the Holy Roman Empire, in consequence of the extinction of its famous ducal house in the persons of Duke Balthasar Maria and of his grandson Alberic, who should have been third of the name. Under this dry historical fact lies hidden the strange story of Prince Alberic and the Snake Lady.

1

The first act of hostility of old Duke Balthasar towards the Snake Lady, in whose existence he did not, of course, believe, was connected with the arrival at Luna of certain tapestries after the designs of the famous Monsieur le Brun, a present from his Most Christian Majesty King Lewis the XIV. These Gobelins, which represented the marriage of Alexander and Roxana, were placed in the throne-room, and in the most gallant suite of chambers overlooking the great rockery garden, all of which had been completed by Duke Balthasar Maria in 1680; and, as a consequence, the already existing tapestries, silk hangings, and mirrors painted by Marius of the Flowers, were transferred into other apartments, thus occasioning a general re-hanging of the Red Palace at Luna.

These magnificent operations, in which, as the court poets sang, Apollo and the Graces lent their services to their beloved patron, aroused in Duke Balthasar's mind a sudden curiosity to see what might be made of the rooms occupied by his grandson and heir, and which he had not entered since Prince Alberic's christening. He found the apartments in a shocking state of neglect, and the youthful prince unspeakably shy and rustic; and he determined to give him at once an establishment befitting his age, to look out presently for a princess worthy to be his wife, and, somewhat earlier, for a less illustrious but more agreeable lady to fashion his manners.

Meanwhile, Duke Balthasar Maria gave orders to change, the tapestry in Prince Alberic's chamber. This tapestry was of old and Gothic taste, extremely worn, and represented Alberic the Blond and the Snake Lady Oriana, as described in the Chronicles of Archbishop Turpin and the poems of Boiardo. Duke Balthasar Maria was a prince of enlightened mind and delicate taste; the literature as well as the art of the dark ages found no grace in his sight; he reproved the folly of feeding the thoughts of youth on improbable events; besides, he disliked snakes and was afraid of the devil. So he ordered the tapestry to be removed and another, representing Susanna and the Elders, to be put in its stead. But when Prince Alberic discovered the change, he cut Susanna and the Elders into strips with a knife he had stolen out of the ducal kitchens (no dangerous instruments being allowed to young princes before they were of an age to learn to fence) and refused to touch his food for three days.

The tapestry over which little Prince Alberic mourned so deeply had indeed been both tattered and Gothic. But for the boy it possessed an inexhaustible charm. It was quite full of things, and they were all delightful. The sorely-frayed borders consisted of wonderful garlands of leaves and fruits and flowers, tied at intervals with ribbons, although they seemed all to grow like tall narrow bushes, each from a big vase in the bottom corner, and made of all manner of different plants. There were bunches of spiky bays, and of acorned oak leaves; sheaves of lilies and heads of poppies, gourds, and apples and pears, and hazelnuts and mulberries, wheat ears, and beans, and pine tufts. And in each of these plants, of which those above named are only a very few, there were curious live creatures of some sort—various birds, big and little, butterflies on the lilies, snails, squirrels, mice, and rabbits, and even a hare, with such pointed ears, darting among the spruce fir.

Alberic learned the names of most of these plants and creatures from his nurse, who had been a peasant, and he spent much ingenuity seeking for them in the palace gardens and terraces; but there were no live creatures there, except snails and toads, which the gardeners killed, and carp swimming about in the big tank, whom Alberic did not like, and who were not in the tapestry; and he had to supplement his nurse's information by that of the grooms and scullions, when he could visit them secretly. He was even promised a sight, one day, of a dead rabbit—the rabbit was the most fascinating of the inhabitants of the tapestry border—but he came to the kitchen too late, and saw it with its pretty fur pulled off, and looking so sad and naked that it made him cry. But Alberic had grown so accustomed to never quitting the Red Palace and its gardens, that he was usually satisfied with seeing the plants and animals in the tapestry, and looked forward to seeing the real things only when he should be grown up. 'When I am a man,' he would say to himself—for his nurse scolded him for saying it to her—'I will have a live rabbit of my own.'

The border of the tapestry interested Prince Alberic most when he was very little—indeed, his remembrance of it was older than that of the Red Palace, its terraces and gardens—but gradually he began to care more and more for the picture in the middle.

There were mountains, and the sea with ships; and these first made him care to go on to the topmost palace terrace and look at the real mountains and the sea beyond the roofs and gardens; and there were woods of all manner of tall trees, with clover and wild strawberries growing beneath them; and roads, and paths, and rivers, in and out; these were rather confused with the places where the tapestry was worn out, and with the patches and mendings thereof, but Alberic, in the course of time, contrived to make them all out, and knew exactly whence the river came which turned the big mill-wheel, and how many bends it made

38

before coming to the fishing-nets; and how the horsemen must cross over the bridge, then wind behind the cliff with the chapel, and pass through the wood of pines in order to get from the castle in the left-hand corner nearest the bottom to the town, over which the sun was shining with all its beams, and a wind blowing with inflated cheeks on the right hand close to the top.

The centre of the tapestry was the most worn and discoloured; and it was for this reason perhaps that little Alberic scarcely noticed it for some years, his eye and mind led away by the bright red and yellow of the border of fruit and flowers, and the still vivid green and orange of the background landscape. Red, yellow, and orange, even green, had faded in the centre into pale blue and lilac; even the green had grown an odd dusty tint; and the figures seemed like ghosts, sometimes emerging and then receding again into vagueness.

Indeed, it was only as he grew bigger that Alberic began to see any figures at all; and then, for a long time he would lose sight of them. But little by little, when the light was strong, he could see them always; and even in the dark make them out with a little attention. Among the spruce firs and pines, and against a hedge of roses, on which there still lingered a remnant of redness, a knight had reined in his big white horse, and was putting one arm round the shoulder of a lady, who was leaning against the horse's flank. The knight was all dressed in armour—not at all like that of the equestrian statue of Duke Balthasar Maria in the square, but all made of plates, with plates also on the legs, instead of having them bare like Duke Balthasar's statue; and on his head he had no wig, but a helmet with big plumes.

It seemed a more reasonable dress than the other, but probably Duke Balthasar was right to go to battle with bare legs and a kilt and a wig, since he did so. The lady who was looking up into his face was dressed with a high collar and long sleeves, and on her head she wore a thick circular garland, from under which the hair fell about her shoulders. She was very lovely, Alberic got to think, particularly when, having climbed upon a chest of drawers, he saw that her hair was still full of threads of gold, some of them quite loose because the tapestry was so rubbed. The knight and his horse were of course very beautiful, and he liked the way in which the knight reined in the horse with one hand, and embraced the lady with the other arm.

But Alberic got to love the lady most, although she was so very pale and faded, and almost the colour of the moonbeams through the palace windows in summer. Her dress also was so beautiful and unlike those of the ladies who got out of the coaches in the Court of Honour, and who had on hoops and no clothes at all on their upper part. This lady, on the contrary, had that collar like a lily, and a beautiful gold chain, and patterns in gold (Alberic made them out little by little) all over her bodice. He got to want so much to see her skirt; it was probably very beautiful too, but it so happened that the inlaid chest of drawers before mentioned stood against the wall in that place, and on it a large ebony and ivory crucifix, which covered the lower part of the lady's body.

Alberic often tried to lift off the crucifix, but it was a great deal too heavy, and there was not room on the chest of drawers to push it aside, so the lady's skirt and feet were invisible. But one day, when Alberic was eleven, his nurse suddenly took a fancy to having all the furniture shifted. It was time that the child should cease to sleep in her room, and plague her with his loud talking in his dreams. And she might as well have the handsome inlaid chest of drawers, and that nice pious crucifix for herself next door, in place of Alberic's little bed. So one morning there was a great shifting and dusting, and when Alberic came in from his walk on the terrace, there hung the tapestry entirely uncovered. He stood for a few minutes before it, riveted to the ground. Then he ran to his nurse, exclaiming: 'O, nurse, dear nurse, look—the lady—!'

For where the big crucifix had stood, the lower part of the beautiful pale lady with the gold-thread hair was now exposed. But instead of a skirt, she ended off in a big snake's tail, with scales of still most vivid (the tapestry not having faded there) green and gold.

The nurse turned round.

'Holy Virgin,' she cried, 'why, she's a serpent!' Then, noticing the boy's violent excitement, she added, 'You little ninny, it's only Duke Alberic the Blond, who was your ancestor, and the Snake Lady.'

Little Prince Alberic asked no questions, feeling that he must not. Very strange it was, but he loved the beautiful lady with the thread of gold hair only the more because she ended off in the long twisting body of a snake. And that, no doubt, was why the knight was so very good to her.

2

For want of that tapestry, poor Alberic, having cut its successor to pieces, began to pine away. It had been his whole world; and now it was gone he discovered that he had no other. No one had ever cared for him except his nurse, who was very cross. Nothing had ever been taught him except the Latin catechism; he had had nothing to make a pet of except the (sit carp, supposed to be four hundred years old, in the tank; he had nothing to play with except a gala coral with bells by Benvenuto Cellini, which Duke Balthasar Maria had sent him on his eighth birthday. He had never had anything except a Grandfather, and had never been outside the Red Palace.

Now, after the loss of the tapestry, the disappearance of the plants and flowers and birds and beasts on its borders, and the departure of the kind knight on the horse and the dear golden-haired Snake Lady, Alberic became aware that he had always hated both his grandfather and the Red Palace.

The whole world, indeed, were agreed that Duke Balthasar was the most magnanimous and fascinating of monarchs, and that the Red Palace of Luna was the most magnificent and delectable of residences. But the knowledge of this universal opinion, and the consequent sense of his own extreme unworthiness, merely exasperated Alberic's detestation, which, as it grew, came to identify the Duke and the Palace as the personification and visible manifestation of each other. He knew now—oh, how well!—every time that he walked on the terrace or in the garden (at the hours when no one else ever entered them) that he had always abominated the brilliant tomato-coloured plaster which gave the palace its name: such a pleasant, gay colour, people would remark, particularly against the blue of the sky.

Then there were the twelve Caesars—they were the twelve Caesars, but multiplied over and over again—busts with flying draperies and spiky garlands, one over every first-floor window, hundreds of them, all fluttering and grimacing round the place. Alberic had always thought them uncanny; but now he positively avoided looking out of the window, lest his eye should catch the *stucco* eyeball of one of those Caesars in the opposite wing of the building. But there was one thing more especially in the Red Palace, of which a bare glimpse had always filled the youthful Prince with terror, and which now kept recurring to his mind like a nightmare.

This was no other than the famous grotto of the Court of Honour. Its roof was ingeniously inlaid with oyster-shells, forming elegant patterns, among which you could plainly distinguish some colossal satyrs; the sides were built of rockery, and in its depths, disposed in a most natural and tasteful manner, was a herd of life-size animals all carved out of various precious marbles. On holidays the water was turned on, and spurted about in a gallant fashion. On such occasions persons of taste would flock to Luna from all parts of the world to enjoy the spectacle. But ever since his earliest infancy Prince Alberic had held this grotto in abhorrence.

The oyster-shell satyrs on the roof frightened him into fits, particularly when the fountains were playing; and his terror of the marble animals was such that a bare allusion to the porphyry rhinoceros, the giraffe of Cipollino, and the *verde* antique monkeys, set him screaming for an hour. The grotto, moreover, had become associated in his mind with the other great glory of the Red Palace, to wit, the domed chapel in which Duke Balthasar Maria intended erecting monuments to his immediate ancestors, and in which he had already prepared a monument for himself. And the whole magnificent palace, grotto, chapel and all, had become mysteriously connected with Alberic's grandfather, owing to a particularly terrible dream. When the boy was eight years old, he was taken one day to see his grandfather.

It was the feast of St Balthasar, one of the Three Wise Kings from the East, as is well known. There had been firing of mortars and ringing of bells ever since daybreak. Alberic had his hair curled, was put into new clothes (his usual raiment being somewhat tattered), a large nosegay was placed in his hand, and he and his nurse were conveyed by complicated relays of lackeys and of pages up to the ducal apartments. Here, in a crowded outer room, he was separated from his nurse and received by a gaunt person in a long black robe like a sheath, and a long shovel hat, whom Alberic identified many years later as his grandfather's Jesuit confessor. He smiled a long smile, discovering a prodigious number of teeth, in a manner which froze the child's blood; and lifting an embroidered curtain, pushed Alberic into his grandfather's presence.

Duke Balthasar Maria, called in all Italy the ever young prince, was at his toilet He was wrapped in a green Chinese wrapper, embroidered with gold *pagodas*, and round his head was tied an orange scarf of delicate fabric. He was listening to the performance of some fiddlers; and of a lady dressed as a nymph, who was singing the birthday ode with many shrill trills and quavers; and meanwhile his face, in the hands of a valet, was being plastered with a variety of brilliant colours. In his green and gold wrapper and orange head-dress, with the strange patches of vermilion and white on his cheeks, Duke Balthasar looked to the diseased fancy of his nephew as if he had been made of various precious metals, like the celebrated effigy he had erected of himself in the great burial-chapel.

But, just as Alberic was mustering up courage and approaching his magnificent grandparent, his eye fell upon a sight so mysterious and terrible that he fled wildly out of the ducal presence. For through an open door he could see in an adjacent closet a man dressed in white, combing the long flowing locks of what he recognised as his grandfather's head, stuck on a short pole in the light of a window.

That night Alberic had seen in his dreams the ever young Duke Balthasar Maria descend from his niche in the burial-chapel; and, with his Roman lappets and corselet visible beneath the green bronze cloak embroidered with gold *pagodas*, march down the great staircase into the Court of Honour, and ascend to the empty place at the end of the rockery grotto (where, as a matter of fact, a statue of Neptune, by a pupil of Bernini, was placed some months later), and there, raising his sceptre, receive the obeisance of all the marble animals—the giraffe, the rhinoceros, the stag, the peacock, and the monkeys. And behold I suddenly his well-known features waxed dim, and beneath the great curly peruke there was a round blank thing—a barber's block!

Alberic, who was an intelligent child, had gradually learned to disentangle this dream from reality; but its grotesque terror never vanished from his mind, and became the core of all his feelings towards Duke Balthasar Maria and the Red Palace.

3

The news—which was kept back as long as possible—of the destruction of Susanna and the Elders threw Duke Balthasar Maria into a most violent rage with his grandson. The boy should be punished by exile, and exile to a terrible place; above all, to a place where there was no furniture to destroy. Taking due counsel with his Jesuit, his jester, and his dwarf, Duke Balthasar decided that in the whole Duchy of Luna there was no place more fitted for the purpose than the Castle of Sparkling Waters.

For the Castle of Sparkling Waters was little better than a ruin, and its sole inhabitants were a family of peasants. The original cradle of the House of Luna, and its principal bulwark against invasion, the castle had been ignominiously discarded and forsaken a couple of centuries before, when the dukes had built the rectangular town in the plain; after which it had been used as a quarry for ready-cut stone, and the greater part carted off to rebuild the town of Luna, and even the central portion of the Red

Palace. The castle was therefore reduced to its outer circuit of walls, enclosing vineyards and orange-gardens, instead of moats and yards and towers, and to the large gate tower, which had been kept, with one or two smaller buildings, for the housing of the farmer, his cattle, and his stores.

Thither the misguided young prince was conveyed in a carefully shuttered coach and at a late hour of the evening, as was proper in the case of an offender at once so illustrious and so criminal. Nature, moreover, had clearly shared Duke Balthasar Maria's legitimate anger, and had done her best to increase the horror of this just though terrible sentence. For that particular night the long summer broke up in a storm of fearful violence; and Alberic entered the ruined castle amid the howling of wind, the rumble of thunder, and the rush of torrents of rain.

But the young prince showed no fear or reluctance; he saluted with dignity and sweetness the farmer and his wife and family, and took possession of his attic, where the curtains of an antique and crazy four-poster shook in the draught of the unglazed windows, as if he were taking possession of the gala chambers of a great palace.

'And so,' he merely remarked, looking round him with reserved satisfaction, 'I am now in the castle which was built by my ancestor and namesake, the Marquis Alberic the Blond.'

He looked not unworthy of such illustrious lineage, as he stood there in the flickering light of the pine-torch: tall for his age, slender and strong, with abundant golden hair falling about his very white face.

That first night at the Castle of Sparkling Waters, Alberic dreamed without end about his dear, lost tapestry. And when, in the radiant autumn morning, he descended to explore the place of his banishment and captivity, it seemed as if those dreams were still going on. Or had the tapestry been removed to this spot, and become a reality in which he himself was running about?

The gate tower in which he had slept was still intact and chivalrous. It had battlements, a drawbridge, a great escutcheon

45

with the arms of Luna, just like the castle in the tapestry. Some vines, quite loaded with grapes, rose on the strong cords of their fibrous wood from the ground to the very roof of the town, exactly like those borders of leaves and fruit which Alberic had loved so much. And, between the vines, all along the masonry, were strung long narrow ropes of maize, like garlands of gold.

A plantation of orange-trees filled what had once been the moat; lemons were *spalliered* against the delicate pink brickwork. There were no lilies, indeed, but big carnations hung down from the tower windows, and a tall oleander, which Alberic mistook for a special sort of rose-tree, shed its blossoms on to the draw-bridge. After the storm of the night, birds were singing all round; not indeed as they sang in spring, which Alberic, of course, did not know, but in a manner quite different from the canaries in the ducal aviaries at Luna. Moreover, other birds, wonderful white and gold creatures, some of them with brilliant tails and scarlet crests, were pecking and strutting and making curious noises in the yard. And—could it be true?—a little way further up the hill, for the castle walls climbed steeply from the seaboard, in the grass beneath the olive-trees, white creatures were running in and out—white creatures with pinkish lining to their ears, undoubtedly—as Alberic's nurse had taught him on the tapestry—undoubtedly *rabbits*.

Thus Alberic rambled on, from discovery to discovery, with the growing sense that he was in the tapestry, but that the tapestry had become the whole world. He climbed from terrace to terrace of the steep olive-yard, among the sage and the fennel tufts, the long red walls of the castle winding ever higher on the hill. And on the very top of the hill was a high terrace surrounded by towers, and a white shining house with columns and windows, which seemed to drag him upwards.

It was, indeed, the citadel of the place, the very centre of the castle.

Alberic's heart beat strangely as he passed beneath the wide arch of delicate ivy-grown brick, and clambered up the rough-paved path to the topmost terrace. And there he actually forgot the tapestry. The terrace was laid out as a vineyard, the vines trellised on the top of stone columns; at one end stood a clump of trees, pines, and a big ilex and a walnut, whose shrivelled leaves already strewed the grass. To the back stood a tiny little house all built of shining marble, with two large rounded windows divided by delicate pillars, of the sort (as Alberic later learned) which people built in the barbarous days of the Goths. Among the vines, which formed a vast arbour, were growing, in open spaces, large orange and lemon trees, and flowering bushes of rosemary, and pale pink roses. And in front of the house, under a great umbrella pine, was a well, with an arch over it and a bucket hanging to a chain.

Alberic wandered about in the vineyard, and then slowly mounted the marble staircase which flanked the white house. There was no one in it The two or three small upper chambers stood open, and on their blackened floor were heaped sacks, and faggots, and fodder, and all manner of coloured seeds. The unglazed windows stood open, framing in between their white pillars a piece of deep blue sea. For there, below, but seen over the tops of the olive-trees and the green leaves of the oranges and lemons, stretched the sea, deep blue, speckled with white sails, bounded by pale blue capes, and arched over by a dazzling pale blue sky. From the lower storey there rose faint sounds of cattle, and a fresh, sweet smell as of grass and herbs and coolness, which Alberic had never known before.

How long did Alberic stand at that window? He was startled by what he took to be steps close behind him, and a rustle as of silk. But the rooms were empty, and he could see nothing moving among the stacked up fodder and seeds. Still, the sounds seemed to recur, but now outside, and he thought he heard someone in a very low voice call his name. He descended into the vineyard; he walked round every tree and every shrub, and climbed upon the broken masses of rose-coloured masonry, crushing the scented ragwort and peppermint with which they were overgrown. But all was still and empty. Only, from far, far below, there rose a stave of peasant's song.

47

The great gold balls of oranges, and the delicate yellow lemons, stood out among their glossy green against the deep blue of the sea; the long bunches of grapes hung, filled with sunshine, like clusters of rubies and jacinths and topazes, from the trellis which patterned the pale blue sky. But Alberic felt not hunger, but sudden thirst, and mounted the three broken marble steps of the well. By its side was a long narrow trough of marble, such as stood in the court at Luna, and which, Alberic had been told, people had used as coffins in pagan times. This one was evidently intended to receive water from the well, for it had a mark in the middle, with a spout; but it was quite dry and full of wild herbs, and even of pale, prickly roses. There were garlands carved upon it, and people with twisted snakes about them; and the carving was picked out with golden brown minute mosses.

Alberic looked at it, for it pleased him greatly; and then he lowered the bucket into the deep well, and drank. The well was very, very deep. Its inner sides were covered, as far as you could see, with long delicate weeds like pale green hair, but this faded away in the darkness. At the bottom was a bright space, reflecting the sky, but looking like some subterranean country. Alberic, as he bent over, was startled by suddenly seeing what seemed a face filling up part of that shining circle; but he remembered it must be his own reflection, and felt ashamed. So, to give himself courage, he bent over again, and sang his own name to the image. But instead of his own boyish voice he was answered by wonderful tones, high and deep alternately, running through the notes of a long, long cadence, as he had heard them on holidays at the Ducal Chapel at Luna.

When he had slaked his thirst, Alberic was about to unchain the bucket, when there was a rustle hard by, and a sort of little hiss, and there rose from the carved trough, from among the weeds and roses, and glided on to the brick of the well, a long, green, glittering thing. Alberic recognised it to be a snake; only, he had no idea it had such a flat, strange little head, and such a long forked tongue, for the lady on the tapestry was a woman from the waist upwards. It sat on the opposite side of the well, moving its long neck in his direction, and fixing him with its small golden eyes.

Then, slowly, it began to glide round the well circle towards him. Perhaps it wants to drink, thought Alberic, and tipped the bronze pitcher in its direction. But the creature glided past, and came around and rubbed itself against Alberic's hand. The boy was not afraid, for he knew nothing about snakes; but he started, for, on this hot day, the creature was icy cold. But then he felt sorry. 'It must be dreadful to be always so cold,' he said; 'come, try and get warm in my pocket.'

But the snake merely rubbed itself against his coat, and then disappeared back into the carved sarcophagus.

4

Duke Balthasar Maria, as we have seen, was famous for his unfading youth, and much of his happiness and pride was due to this delightful peculiarity. Any comparison, therefore, which might diminish it, was distasteful to the ever young sovereign of Luna; and when his son had died with mysterious suddenness, Duke Balthasar Maria's grief had been tempered by the consolatory fact that he was now the youngest man at his own court. This very natural feeling explains why the Duke of Luna had put behind him for several years the fact of having a grandson, painful because implying that he was of an age to be a grandfather. He had done his best, and succeeded not badly, to forget Alberic while the latter abode under his own roof; and now that the boy had been sent away to a distance, he forgot him entirely for the space of several years.

But Balthasar Maria's three chief counsellors had no such reason for forgetfulness; and so, in turn, each unknown to the other, the Jesuit, the dwarf, and the jester sent spies to the Castle of Sparkling Waters, and even secretly visited that place in person. For by the coincidence of genius, the mind of each of these profound politicians, had been illuminated by the same remarkable thought, to wit: that Duke Balthasar Maria, unnatural as it seemed, would some day have to die, and Prince Alberic, if still alive, become duke in his stead. Those were the times of subtle statecraft; and the Jesuit, the dwarf, and the jester were notable statesmen even in their day. So each of them had provided himself with a scheme, which, in order to be thoroughly artistic, was twofold and, so to speak, double-barrelled. Alberic might live or he might die, and therefore Alberic must be turned to profit in either case. If, to invert the chances, Alberic should die before coming to the throne, the Jesuit, the dwarf, and the jester had each privately determined to represent this death as purposely brought about by himself for the benefit of one of the three powers which would claim the duchy in case of extinction of the male line.

The Jesuit had chosen to attribute the murder to devotion to the Holy See; the dwarf had preferred to appear active in favour of the King of Spain; and the jester had decided that he would lay claim to the gratitude of the Emperor. The very means which each would pretend to have used had been thought out: poison in each case, only while the dwarf had selected henbane, taken through a pair of perfumed gloves, and the jester pounded diamonds mixed in champagne, the Jesuit had modestly adhered to the humble cup of chocolate, which, whether real or fictitious, had always stood his order in such good stead. Thus did each of these wily courtiers dispose of Alberic in case he should die.

There remained the alternative of Alberic continuing to live; and for this the three rival statesmen were also prepared. If Alberic lived, it was obvious that he must be made to select one of the three as his sole minister, and banish, imprison, or put to death the other two. For this purpose it was necessary to secure his affection by gifts, until he should be old enough to understand that be had actually owed his life to the passionate loyalty of the Jesuit, or the dwarf, or the jester, each of whom had saved him from the atrocious enterprises of the other two counsellors of Balthasar Maria—nay, who knows? perhaps from the malignity of Balthasar Maria himself.

In accordance with these subtle machinations, each of the three statesmen determined to outwit his rivals by sending young Alberic such things as would appeal most strongly to a poor young prince living in banishment among peasants, and wholly unsupplied with pocket-money. The Jesuit expended a considerable sum on books, magnificently bound with the arms of Luna; the dwarf prepared several suits of tasteful clothes; and the jester selected, with infinite care, a horse of equal and perfect gentleness and mettle.

And, unknown to one another, but much about the same period, each of the statesmen sent his present most secretly to Alberic. Imagine the astonishment and wrath of the Jesuit, the dwarf, and the jester, when each saw his messenger come back from Sparkling Waters with his gift returned, and the news that Prince Alberic was already supplied with a complete library, a handsome wardrobe, and not one, but two horses of the finest breed and training; nay, more unexpected stilly that while returning the gifts to their respective donors, he had rewarded the messengers with splendid liberality.

The result of this amazing discovery was much the same in the mind of the Jesuit, the dwarf, and the jester. Each instantly suspected one or both of his rivals; then, on second thoughts, determined to change the present to one of the other items (horse, clothes, or books, as the case might be), little suspecting that each of them had been supplied already; and, on further reflection, began to doubt the reality of the whole business, to suspect connivance of the messengers, intended insult on the part of the prince; and, therefore, decided to trust only to the evidence of his own eyes in the matter.

Accordingly, within the same few months, the Jesuit, the dwarf, and the jester, feigned grievous illness to their ducal master, and while everybody thought them safe in bed in the Red Palace at Luna, hurried, on horseback, or in a litter, or in a coach, to the Castle of Sparkling Waters.

The scene with the peasant and his family, young Alberic's host, was identical on the three occasions; and, as the farmer saw that each of these personages was willing to pay liberally for absolute secrecy, he very consistently swore to supply that *desideratum* to each of the three great functionaries. And similarly, in all three cases, it was deemed preferable to see the young prince first from a hiding-place, before asking leave to pay their respects.

The dwarf, who was the first in the field, was able to hide very conveniently in one of the cut velvet plumes which surmounted Alberic's four-post bedstead, and to observe the young prince as he changed his apparel. But he scarcely recognised the Duke's grandson. Alberic was sixteen, but far taller and stronger than his age would warrant His figure was at once manly and delicate, and full of grace and vigour of movement. His long hair, the colour of floss silk, fell in wavy curls, which seemed to imply almost a woman's care and coquetry. His hands also, though powerful, were, as the dwarf took note, of princely form and whiteness.

As to his garments, the open doors of his wardrobe displayed every variety that a young prince could need; and, while the dwarf was watching, he was exchanging a russet and purple hunting-dress, cut after the Hungarian fashion with cape and hood, and accompanied by a cap crowned with peacock's feathers, for a habit of white and silver, trimmed with Venetian lace, in which he intended to honour the wedding of one of the farmer's daughters. Never, in his most genuine youth, had Balthasar Maria, the ever young and handsome, been one-quarter as beautiful in person or as delicate in apparel as his grandson in exile among poor country folk.

The Jesuit, in his turn, came to verify his messenger's extraordinary statements. Through the gap between two rafters he was enabled to look down on to Prince Alberic in his study. Magnificently bound books lined the walls of the closet, and in their gaps hung valuable prints and maps. On the table were heaped several open volumes, among globes both terrestrial and celestial; and Alberic himself was leaning on the arm of a great chair, reciting the verses of Virgil in a most graceful chant. Never had the Jesuit seen a better-appointed study nor a more precocious young scholar.

As regards the jester, he came at the very moment that Alberic was returning from a ride; and, having begun life as an acrobat, he was able to climb into a large ilex which commanded an excellent view of the castle yard.

Alberic was mounted on a splendid jet-black barb, magnificently caparisoned in crimson and gold Spanish trappings. His groom—for he had even a groom—was riding a horse only a shade less perfect: it was white and he was black—a splendid negro such as only great princes own. When Alberic came in sight of the farmer's wife, who stood shelling peas on the doorstep, he waved his hat with infinite grace, caused his horse to *caracole* and rear three times in salutation, picked an apple up while cantering round the castle yard, threw it in the air with his sword and cut it in two as it descended, and did a number of similar feats such as are taught only to the most brilliant cavaliers. Now, as he was going to dismount, a branch of the ilex cracked, the black barb reared, and Alberic, looking up, perceived the Jester moving in the tree.

'A wonderful parti-coloured bird!' he exclaimed, and seized the fowling-piece that hung to his saddle. But before he had time to fire the jester had thrown himself down and alighted, making three somersaults, on the ground.

'My Lord,' said the jester, 'you see before you a faithful subject who, braving the threats and traps of your enemies, and, I am bound to add, risking also your Highnesses sovereign displeasure, has been determined to see his prince once more, to have the supreme happiness of seeing him at last clad and equipped and mounted—'

'Enough!' interrupted Alberic sternly. 'You need say no more. You would have me believe that it is to you I owe my horses and books and clothes, even as the dwarf and the Jesuit tried to make me believe about themselves last month. Know, then, that Alberic of Luna requires gifts from none of you. And now, most miserable councillor of my unhappy grandfather, begone!'

The jester checked his rage, and tried, all the way back to Luna, to get at some solution of this intolerable riddle. The Jesuit and the dwarf— the scoundrels—had been trying *their* hand then! Perhaps, indeed, it was their blundering which had ruined his own perfectly-concocted scheme. But for their having come and claimed gratitude for gifts they had not made, Alberic would perhaps have believed that the jester had not merely offered the horse which was refused, but had actually given the two which had been accepted, and the books and clothes (since there had been books and clothes given) into the bargain.

But then, had not Alberic spoken as if he were perfectly sure from what quarter all his possessions had come? This reminded the jester of the allusion to the Duke Balthasar Maria; Alberic had spoken of him as unhappy. Was it, could it be, possible that the treacherous old wretch had been keeping up relations with his grandson in secret, afraid—for he was a miserable old coward at bottom—both of the wrath of his three counsellors, and of the hatred of his grandson? Was it possible, thought the jester, that not only the Jesuit and the dwarf, but the Duke of Luna also, had been intriguing against him round young Prince Alberic?

Balthasar Maria was quite capable of it; he might be enjoying the trick he was playing his three masters—for they were his masters; he might be preparing to turn suddenly upon them with his long neglected grandson like a sword to smite them. On the other hand, might this not be a mere mistaken supposition on the part of Prince Alberic, who, in his silly dignity, preferred to believe in the liberality of his ducal grandfather than in that of his grandfather's servants? Might the horses, and all the rest, not really be the gift of either the dwarf or the Jesuit, although neither had got the credit for it? 'No, no,' exclaimed the jester, for he hated his fellow-servants worse than his master, 'anything better than that! Rather a thousand times that it were the Duke himself who had outwitted them.'

Then, in his bitterness, having gone over the old arguments again and again, some additional circumstances returned to his memory. The black groom was deaf and dumb, and the peasants, it appeared, had been quite unable to extract any information from him. But he had arrived with those particular horses only a few months ago; a gift, the peasants had thought, from the old Duke of Luna. But Alberic, they had said, had possessed other horses before, which they had also taken for granted had come from the Red Palace. And the clothes and books had been accumulating, it appeared, ever since the prince's arrival in his place of banishment.

Since this was the case, the plot, whether on the part of the Jesuit or the dwarf, or on that of the duke himself, had been going on for years before the jester had bestirred himself! Moreover, the prince not only possessed horses, but he learned to ride, he not only had books, but he had learned to read, and even to read various tongues; and finally, the prince was not only clad in princely garments, but he was every inch of him a prince. He had then been consorting with other people than the peasants at Sparkling Waters. He must have been away—or—someone must have come. He had not been living in solitude.

But when—how—and above all, who?

And again the baffled jester revolved the probabilities concerning the dwarf, the Jesuit, and the duke. It must be—it could be no other—it evidently could only be—.

'Ah!' exclaimed the unhappy diplomatist;' if only one could believe in magic!'

And it suddenly struck him, with terror and mingled relief, 'Was it magic?'

But the jester, like the dwarf and the Jesuit, and the Duke of Luna himself, was altogether superior to such foolish beliefs.

5

The young Prince of Luna had never attempted to learn the story of Alberic the Blond and the Snake Lady. Children sometimes conceive an inexplicable shyness, almost a dread, of knowing more on some subject which is uppermost in their thoughts; and such had been the case of Duke Balthasar Maria's grandson. Ever since the memorable morning when the ebony crucifix had been removed from in front of the faded tapestry, and the whole figure of the Snake Lady had been for the first time revealed, scarcely a day had passed without their coming to the boy's mind: his nurse's words about his ancestors Alberic and the Snake Lady Oriana.

But, even as he had asked no questions then, so he had asked no questions since; shrinking more and more from all further knowledge of the matter. He had never questioned his nurse; he had never questioned the peasants of Sparkling Waters, although the story, he felt quite sure, must be well known among the ruins of Alberic the Blond's own castle. Nay, stranger still, he had never mentioned the subject to his dear godmother, to whom he had learned to open his heart about all things, and who had taught him all that he knew.

For the duke's jester had guessed rightly that, during these years at Sparkling Waters, the young prince had not consorted solely with peasants. The very evening after his arrival, as he was sitting by the marble well in the vineyard, looking towards the sea, he had felt a hand placed lightly on his shoulder, and looked up into the face of a beautiful lady dressed in green.

'Do not be afraid,' she had said, smiling at his terror. 'I am not a ghost, but alive like you; and I am, though you do not know it, your godmother. My dwelling is close to this castle, and I shall come every evening to play and talk with you, here by the little white palace with the pillars, where the fodder is stacked. Only, you must remember that I do so against the wishes of your grandfather and all his friends, and that if ever you mention me to any one, or allude in any way to our meetings, I shall be obliged to leave the neighbourhood, and you will never see me again. Some day when you are big you will learn why; till then you must take me on trust And now what shall we play at?'

And thus his godmother had come every evening at sunset, just for an hour and no more, and had taught the poor solitary little prince to play (for he had never played) and to read, and to manage a horse, and, above all, to love: for, except the old tapestry in the Red Palace, he had never loved anything in the world.

Alberic told his dear godmother everything, beginning with

the story of the two pieces of tapestry, the one they had taken away and the one he had cut to pieces; and he asked her about all the things he ever wanted to know, and she was always able to answer. Only about two things they were silent: she never told him her name nor where she lived, nor whether Duke Balthasar Maria knew her (the boy guessed that she had been a friend of his father's); and Alberic never revealed the fact that the tapestry had represented his ancestor and the beautiful Oriana; for, even to his dear godmother, and most perhaps to her, he found it impossible even to mention Alberic the Blond and the Snake Lady.

But the story, or rather the name of the story he did not know, never loosened its hold on Alberic's mind. Little by little, as he grew up, it came to add to his life two friends, of whom he never told his godmother. They were, to be sure, of such sort, however different, that a boy might find it difficult to speak about without feeling foolish. The first of the two friends was his own ancestor, Alberic the Blond; and the second that large tame grass snake whose acquaintance he had made the day after his arrival at the castle. About Alberic the Blond he knew indeed but little, save that he had reigned in Luna many hundreds of years ago, and that he had been a very brave and glorious prince indeed, who had helped to conquer the Holy Sepulchre with Godfrey and Tancred and the other heroes of Tasso.

But, perhaps in proportion to this vagueness, Alberic the Blond served to personify all the notions of chivalry which the boy had learned from his godmother, and those which bubbled up in his own breast. Nay, little by little the young prince began to take his unknown ancestor as a model, and in a confused way, to identify himself with him. For was he not fair-haired too, and Prince of Luna, *Alberic*, third of the name, as the other had been first? Perhaps for this reason he could never speak of this ancestor with his godmother. She might think it presumptuous and foolish; besides, she might perhaps tell him things about Alberic the Blond which would hurt him; the poor young prince, who had compared the splendid reputation of his own grandfather with the miserable reality, had grown up precociously sceptical.

As to the snake, with whom he played every day in the grass, and who was his only companion during the many hours of his godmother's absence, he would willingly have spoken of her, and had once been on the point of doing so, but he had noticed that the mere name of such creatures seemed to be odious to his godmother. Whenever, in their readings, they came across any mention of serpents, his godmother would exclaim, 'Let us skip that,' with a look of intense pain in her usually cheerful countenance. It was a pity, Alberic thought, that so lovely and dear a lady should feel such hatred towards any living creature, particularly towards a kind which, like his own tame grass snake, was perfectly harmless. But he loved her too much to dream of thwarting her; and he was very grateful to his tame snake for having the tact never to show herself at the hour of his god-mother's visits.

But to return to the story represented on the dear, faded tap-estry in the Red Palace.

When Prince Alberic, unconscious to himself, was beginning to turn into a full-grown and gallant-looking youth, a change began to take place in him, and it was about the story of his ancestor and the Lady Oriana. He thought of it more than ever, and it began to haunt his dreams; only it was now a vague-ly painful thought; and, while dreading still to know more, he began to experience a restless, miserable craving to know all. His curiosity was like a thorn in his flesh, working its way in and in; and it seemed something almost more than curiosity. And yet, he was still shy and frightened of the subject; nay, the greater his craving to know, the greater grew a strange certainty that the knowing would be accompanied by evil. So, although many people could have answered—the very peasants, the fish-ermen of the coast, and first and foremost, his godmother—he let months pass before he asked the question. It, and the answer, came of a sudden.

There came occasionally to Sparkling Waters an old man, who united in his tattered person the trades of mending crockery and reciting fairy tales. He would seat himself in summer, under the spreading fig-tree in the castle yard, and in winter by the peasants' deep, black chimney, alternately boring holes in pipkins, or gluing plate edges, and singing, in a cracked, nasal voice, but not without dignity and charm of manner, the stories of the King of Portugal's cowherd, of the feathers of the griffin, or some of the many *stanzas* of *Orlando* or *Jerusalem Delivered* which he knew by heart. Our young prince had always avoided him, partly from a vague fear of a mention of his ancestor and the Snake Lady, and partly because of something vaguely sinister in the old man's eye. But now he awaited with impatience the vagrant's periodical return, and on one occasion, summoned him to his own chamber.

'Sing me,' he commanded, 'the story of Alberic the Blond and the Snake Lady.'

The old man hesitated, and answered with a strange look— 'My Lord, I do not know it.'

A sudden feeling, such as the youth had never experienced before, seized hold of Alberic. He did not recognise himself. He saw and heard himself, as if it were someone else, nod first at some pieces of gold, of those his godmother had given him, and then at his fowling-piece hung on the wall; and as he did so he had a strange thought: 'I must be mad.' But he merely said, sternly—

'Old man, that is not true. Sing that story at once, if you value my money and your safety.'

The vagrant took his white-bearded chin in his hand, mused, and then, fumbling among the files and drills and pieces of wire in his tool-basket, which made a faint metallic accompaniment, he slowly began to chant the following *stanzas*:—

6

Now listen, courteous prince, to what befell your ancestor, the valorous Alberic, returning from the Holy Land.

Already a year had passed since the strongholds of Jerusa- lem had fallen beneath the blows of the faithful, and since the

Sepulchre of Christ had been delivered from the worshippers of Macomet. The great Godfrey was enthroned as its guardian, and the mighty barons, his companions, were wending their way homewards—Tancred, and Bohemund, and Reynold, and the rest

The valorous Alberic, the honour of Luna, after many perilous adventures, brought by the anger of the wizard Macomet, whom he had offended, was shipwrecked on his homeward way, and cast, alone of all his great army, upon the rocky shore of an unknown island. He wandered long about, among woods and pleasant pastures, but without ever seeing any signs of habitation; nourishing himself solely on berries and clear water, and taking his rest in the green grass beneath the trees. At length, after some days of wandering, he came to a dense forest, the like of which he had never seen before, so deep was its shade and so tangled were its boughs. He broke the branches with his iron-gloved hand, and the air became filled with the croaking and screeching of dreadful night-birds.

He pushed his way with shoulder and knee, trampling the broken leafage under foot, and the air was filled with the roaring of monstrous lions and tigers. He grasped his sharp double-edged sword and hewed through the interlaced branches, and the air was filled with the shrieks and sobs of a vanquished city. But the knight of Luna went on, undaunted, cutting his way through the enchanted wood. And behold! as he issued thence, there was before him a lordly castle, as of some great prince, situate in a pleasant meadow among running streams.

And as Alberic approached, the portcullis was raised, and the drawbridge lowered; and there arose sounds of fifes and bugles, but nowhere could he descry any living wight around. And Alberic entered the castle, and found therein guardrooms full of shining arms, and chambers spread with rich stuffs, and a banqueting-hall, with a great table laid and a chair of state at the end. And as he entered a concert of invisible voices and instruments greeted him sweetly, and called him by name, and bid him be welcome; but not a living soul did he see. So he sat him down at the table, and as he did so, invisible hands filled his cup and his plate, and ministered to him with delicacies of all sorts.

Now, when the good knight had eaten and drunken his fill, he drank to the health of his unknown host, declaring himself the servant thereof with his sword and heart. After which, weary with wandering, he prepared to take rest on the carpets which strewed the ground; but invisible hands unbuckled his armour, and clad him in silken robes, and led him to a couch all covered with rose-leaves. And when he had lain himself down, the concert of invisible singers and players put him to sleep with their melodies.

It was the hour of sunset when the valorous baron awoke, and buckled on his armour, and hung on his thigh the great sword Brillamorte; and invisible hands helped him once more.

The knight of Luna went all over the enchanted castle, and found all manner of rarities, treasures of precious stones, such as great kings possess, and stores of gold and silver vessels, and rich stuffs, and stables full of fiery coursers ready caparisoned; but never a human creature anywhere. And, wondering more and more, he went forth into the orchard, which lay within the castle walls. And such another orchard, sure, was never seen, since that in which the hero Hercules found the three golden apples and slew the great dragon. For you might see in this place fruit-trees of all kinds, apples and pears, and peaches and plums, and the goodly orange, which bore at the same time fruit and delicate and scented blossom.

And all around were set hedges of roses, whose scent was even like heaven; and there were other flowers of all kinds, those into which the vain Narcissus turned through love of himself, and those which grew, they tell us, from the blood-drops of fair Venus's minion; and lilies of which that messenger carried a sheaf who saluted the meek damsel, glorious above all womankind. And in the trees sang innumerable birds; and others, of unknown breed, joined melody in hanging cages and aviaries. And in the orchard's midst was set a fountain, the most wonderful e'er made, its waters running in green channels among the flowered grass.

For that fountain was made in the likeness of twin naked maidens, dancing together, and pouring water out of pitchers as they did so; and the maidens were of fine silver, and the pitchers of wrought gold, and the whole so cunningly contrived by magic art that the maidens really moved and danced with the waters they were pouring out—a wonderful work, most truly. And when the kKnight of Luna had feasted his eyes upon this marvel, he saw among the grass, beneath a flowering almond-tree, a sepulchre of marble, cunningly carved and gilded, on which was written, 'Here is imprisoned the Fairy Oriana, most miserable of all fairies, condemned for no fault, but by envious powers, to a dreadful fate,'—and as he read, the inscription changed, and the sepulchre showed these words:

'O knight of Luna, valorous Alberic, if thou wouldst show thy gratitude to the hapless mistress of this castle, summon up thy redoubtable courage, and, whatsoever creature issue from my marble heart, swear thou to kiss it three times on the mouth, that Oriana may be released.'

And Alberic drew his great sword, and on its hilt, shaped like a cross, he swore.

Then wouldst thou have heard a terrible sound of thunder, and seen the castle walls rock. But Alberic,' nothing daunted, repeats in a loud voice, 'I swear,' and instantly that sepulchre's lid upheaves, and there issues thence and rises up a great green snake, wearing a golden crown, and raises itself and fawns towards the valorous knight of Luna. And Alberic starts and recoils in terror. For rather, a thousand times, confront alone the armed hosts of all the heathen, than put his lips to that cold, creeping beast I And the serpent looks at Alberic with great gold eyes, and big tears issue thence, and it drops prostrate on the grass; and Alberic summons courage and approaches; but when the serpent glides along his arm, a horror takes him, and he falls back, unable. And the tears stream from the snake's golden eyes, and moans come from its mouth.

And Alberic runs forward, and seizes the serpent in both

arms, and lifts it up, and three times presses his warm lips against its cold and slippery skin, shutting his eyes in horror. And when the knight of Luna opens them again, behold! O wonder! in his arms no longer a dreadful snake, but a damsel, richly dressed and beautiful beyond compare.

7

Young Alberic sickened that very night, and lay for many days raging with fever. The peasant's wife and a good neighbouring priest nursed him unhelped, for when the messenger they sent arrived at Luna, Duke Balthasar was busy rehearsing a grand ballet in which he himself danced the part of Phoebus Apollo; and the ducal physician was therefore despatched to Sparkling Waters only when the young prince was already recovering.

Prince Alberic undoubtedly passed through a very bad illness, and went fairly out of his mind for fever and ague.

He raved so dreadfully in his delirium about enchanted tapestries and terrible grottoes. Twelve Caesars with rolling eyeballs, barbers' blocks with perukes on them, monkeys of *verde* antique, and porphyry rhinoceroses, and all manner of hellish creatures, that the good priest began to suspect a case of demoniac possession, and caused candles to be kept lighted all day and all night, and holy water to be sprinkled, and a printed form of exorcism, absolutely sovereign in such trouble, to be nailed against the bed-post. On the fourth day the young prince fell into a profound sleep, from which he awaked in apparent possession of his faculties.

'Then you are not the porphyry rhinoceros?' he said, very slowly, as his eye fell upon the priest; 'and this is my own dear little room at Sparkling Waters, though I do not understand all those candles. I thought it was the great hall in the Red Palace, and that all those animals of precious marbles, and my grandfather, the duke, in his bronze and gold robes, were beating me and my tame snake to death with harlequins' laths. It was terrible. But now I see it was all fancy and delirium.'

The poor youth gave a sigh of relief, and feebly caressed the rugged old hand of the priest, which lay upon his counterpane. The prince stayed for a long while motionless, but gradually a strange light came into his eyes, and a smile on to his lips. Presently he made a sign that the peasants should leave the room, and taking once more the good priest's hand, he looked solemnly in his eyes, and spoke in an earnest voice. 'My father,' he said, 'I have seen and heard strange things in my sickness, and I cannot tell for certain now what belongs to the reality of my previous life, and what is merely the remembrance of delirium. On this I would fain be enlightened. Promise me, my father, to answer my questions truly, for this is a matter of the welfare of my soul, and therefore of your own.'

The priest nearly jumped on his chair. So he had been right. The demons had been trying to tamper with the poor young prince, and now he was going to have a fine account of it all.

'My son,' he murmured, 'as I hope for the spiritual welfare of both of us, I promise to answer all your interrogations to the best of my powers. Speak without reticence.'

Alberic hesitated for a moment, and his eyes glanced from one long lit taper to the other.

'In that case,' he said slowly. 'let me conjure you, my father, to tell me whether or not there exists a certain tradition in my family, of the loves of my ancestor, Alberic the Blond, with a certain Snake Lady, and how he was unfaithful to her, and failed to disenchant her, and how a second Alberic, also my ancestor, loved this same Snake Lady, but failed before the ten years of fidelity were over, and became a monk. . . . Does such a story exist, or have I imagined it all during my sickness?'

'My son,' replied the good priest testily, for he was most horribly disappointed by this speech, 'it is scarce fitting that a young prince but just escaped from the jaws of death—and, perhaps, even from the insidious onslaught of the Evil One—should give his mind to idle tales like these.'

'Call them what you choose,' answered the prince gravely, 'but remember your promise, father. Answer me truly, and presume not to question my reasons.'

The priest started. What a hasty ass he had been! Why, these were probably the demons talking out of Alberic's mouth, causing him to ask silly irrelevant questions in order to prevent a good confession. Such were notoriously among their stock tricks! But he would outwit them. If only it were possible to summon up St Paschal Baylon, that new fashionable saint who had been doing such wonders with devils lately! But St Paschal Baylon required not only that you should say several rosaries, but that you should light four candles on a table and lay a supper for two; after that there was nothing he would not do.

So the priest hastily seized two candlesticks from the foot of the bed, and called to the peasant's wife to bring a clean napkin and plates and glasses; and meanwhile endeavoured to detain the demons by answering the poor prince's foolish chatter, 'Your ancestors, the two Alberics—a tradition in your serene family—yes, my Lord—there is such—let me see, how does the story go?—ah yes—this demon, I mean this Snake Lady was a—what they call a fairy—or witch, *malefica* or *stryx* is, I believe, the proper Latin expression—who had been turned into a snake for her sins—good woman, woman, is it possible you cannot be a little quicker in bringing those plates for His Highness's supper? The Snake Lady—let me see—was to cease altogether being a snake if a cavalier remained faithful to her for ten years, and at any rate turned into a woman every time a cavalier was found who had the courage to give her a kiss as if she were not a snake—a disagreeable thing, besides being mortal sin.

'As I said just now, this enabled her to resume temporarily her human shape, which is said to have been fair enough; but how can one tell? I believe she was allowed to change into a woman for an hour at sunset, in any case and without anybody kissing her, but only for an hour. A very unlikely story, my Lord, and not a very moral one, to my thinking!'

And the good priest spread the tablecloth over the table, wondering secretly when the plates and glasses for St. Paschal Baylon would make their appearance. If only the demon could be prevented from beating a retreat before all was ready! 'To return to the story about which Your Highness is pleased to inquire,' he continued, trying to gain time by pretending to humour the demon who was asking questions through the poor prince's mouth, 'I can remember hearing a poem before I took orders—a foolish poem too, in a very poor style, if my memory is correct—that related the manner in which Alberic the Blond met this Snake Lady, and disenchanted her by performing the ceremony I have alluded to.

'The poem was frequently sung at fairs and similar resorts of the uneducated, and, as remarked, was a very inferior composition indeed. Alberic the Blond afterwards came to his senses, it appears, and after abandoning the Snake Lady fulfilled his duty as a prince, and married the princess. . . . I cannot exactly remember what princess, but it was a very suitable marriage, no doubt, from which Your Highness is of course descended.

'As regards the Marquis Alberic, second of the name, of whom it is accounted that he died in odour of sanctity (and indeed it is said that the facts concerning his beatification are being studied in the proper quarters), there is a mention in a life of Saint Fredevaldus, bishop and patron of Luna, printed at the beginning of the present century at Venice, with approbation and licence of the authorities and inquisition, a mention of the fact that this Marquis Alberic the second had contracted, having abandoned his lawful wife, a left-handed marriage with this same Snake Lady (such evil creatures not being subject to natural death), she having induced him thereunto in hope of his proving faithful ten years, and by this means restoring her altogether to human shape.

'But a certain holy hermit, having got wind of this scandal, prayed to St. Fredevaldus as patron of Luna, whereupon St. Fredevaldus took pity on the Marquis Alberic's sins, and appeared to him in a vision at the end of the ninth year of his irregular connection with the Snake Lady, and touched his heart so thoroughly that he instantly forswore her company, and handing the Marquisate over to his mother, abandoned the world and entered the order of St. Romwald, in which he died, as remarked, in odour of sanctity, in consequence of which the present dDuke, Your Highness's magnificent grandfather, is at this moment, as befits so pious a prince, employing his influence with the Holy Father for the beatification of so glorious an ancestor.

'And now, my son,' added the good priest, suddenly changing his tone, for he had got the table ready, and lighted the candles, and only required to go through the preliminary invocation of St. Paschal Baylon—'and now, my son, let your curiosity trouble you no more, but endeavour to obtain some rest, and if possible—'

But the prince interrupted him.

'One word more, good Father,' he begged, fixing him with earnest eyes; 'is it known what has been the fate of the Snake Lady?'

The impudence of the demons made the priest quite angry, but he must not scare them before the arrival of St Paschal, so he controlled himself, and answered slowly by gulps, between the lines of the invocation he was mumbling under his breath:

'My Lord—it results from the same life of St. Fredevaldus, that . . . (in case of property lost, fire, flood, earthquake, plague) . . . that the Snake Lady (thee we invoke, most holy Paschal Baylon!). The Snake Lady being of the nature of fairies, cannot die unless her head be severed from her trunk, and is still haunting the world, together with other evil spirits, in hopes that another member of the house of Luna (Thee we invoke, most holy Paschal Baylon!)—may succumb to her arts and be faithful to her for the ten years needful to her disenchantments— (most holy Paschal Baylon!—and most of all—on thee we call—for aid against the . . .)—'

But before the priest could finish his invocation, a terrible shout came from the bed where the sick prince was lying—

'O Oriana, Oriana!' cried Prince Alberic, sitting up in his bed with a look which terrified the priest as much as his voice. 'O Oriana, Oriana!' he repeated, and then fell back exhausted and broken.

'Bless my soul!' cried the priest, almost upsetting the table;

'why, the demon has already issued out of him! Who would have guessed that St Paschal Baylon performed his miracles as quick as that?'

8

Prince Alberic was awakened by the loud trill of a nightingale. The room was bathed in moonlight, in which the tapers, left burning round the bed to ward off evil spirits, flickered yellow and ineffectual. Through the open casement came, with the scent of freshly-cut grass, a faint concert of nocturnal sounds: the silvery vibration of the cricket, the reed-like quavering notes of the leaf frogs, and, every now and then, the soft note of an owlet, seeming to stroke the silence as the downy wings growing out of the temples of the Sleep God might stroke the air. The nightingale had paused; and Alberic listened breathless for its next burst of song.

At last, and when he expected it least, it came, liquid, loud, and triumphant; so near that it filled the room and thrilled through his marrow like an unison of Cremona viols. It was singing on the pomegranate close outside, whose first buds must be opening into flame-coloured petals. For it was May. Alberic listened; and collected his thoughts, and understood. He arose and dressed, and his limbs seemed suddenly strong, and his mind strangely clear, as if his sickness had been but a dream. Again the nightingale trilled out, and again stopped. Alberic crept noiselessly out of his chamber, down the stairs and into the open.

Opposite, the moon had just risen, immense and golden, and the pines and the cypresses of the hill, the furthest battlements of the castle walls, were printed upon it like delicate lace. It was so light that the roses were pink, and the pomegranate flower scarlet, and the lemons pale yellow, and the vines bright green, only differently coloured from how they looked by day, and as if washed over with silver. The orchard spread uphill, its twigs and separate leaves all glittering as if made of diamonds, and its tree-trunks and *spalliers* weaving strange black patterns of shadow. A little breeze shuddered up from the sea, bringing the scent of the irises grown for their root among the cornfields below.

The nightingale was silent. But Prince Alberic did not stand waiting for its song. A spiral dance of fire-flies, rising and falling like a thin gold fountain, beckoned him upwards through the dewy grass. The circuit of castle walls, jagged and battlemented, and with tufts of trees profiled here and there against the resplendent blue pallor of the moonlight, seemed twined and knotted like huge snakes around the world.

Suddenly, again, the nightingale sang—a throbbing, silver song. It was the same bird, Alberic felt sure; but it was in front of him now, and was calling him onwards. The fireflies wove their golden dance a few steps in front, always a few steps in front, and drew him uphill through the orchard.

As the ground became steeper, the long trellises, black and crooked, seemed to twist and glide through the blue moonlit grass like black gliding snakes, and, at the top, its marble *pillarets* clear in the light, slumbered the little Gothic palace of white marble. From the solitary sentinel pine broke the song of the nightingale. This was the place. A breeze had risen, and from the shining moonlit sea, broken into causeways and flotillas of smooth and fretted silver, came a faint briny smell, mingling with that of the irises and blossoming lemons, with the scent of vague ripeness and freshness. The moon hung like a silver lantern over the orchard; the wood of the trellises patterned the blue luminous heaven; the vine-leaves seemed to swim, transparent, in the shining air. Over the circular well, in the high grass, the fireflies rose and fell like a thin fountain of gold. And, from the sentinel pine, the nightingale sang.

Prince Alberic leant against the brink of the well, by the trough carved with antique designs of serpent-bearing *maenads*. He was wonderfully calm, and his heart sang within him. It was, he knew, the hour and place of his fate.

The nightingale ceased: and the shrill song of the crickets was suspended. The silvery luminous world was silent.

A quiver came through the grass by the well, a rustle through the roses. And, on the well's brink, encircling its central blackness, glided the snake.

'Oriana!' whispered Alberic. 'Oriana!' She paused, and stood almost erect. The prince put out his hand, and she twisted round his arm, extending slowly her chilly coil to his wrist and fingers.

'Oriana!' whispered Prince Alberic again. And raising his hand to his face, he leaned down and pressed his lips on the little flat head of the serpent. And the nightingale sang. But a coldness seized his heart, the moon seemed suddenly extinguished, and he slipped away in unconsciousness.

When he awoke the moon was still high. The nightingale was singing its loudest. He lay in the grass by the well, and his head rested on the knees of the most beautiful of ladies. She was dressed in cloth of silver which seemed woven of moon mists, and shimmering moonlit green grass. It was his own dear godmother.

9

When Duke Balthasar Maria had got through the rehearsals of the ballet called *Daphne Transformed*, and finally danced his part of Phoebus Apollo to the infinite delight and glory of his subjects, he was greatly concerned, being benignly humoured, on learning that he had very nearly lost his grandson and heir. The dwarf, the Jesuit, and the jester, whom he delighted in pitting against one another, had severally accused each other of disrespectful remarks about the dancing of that ballet; so Duke Balthasar determined to disgrace all three together and inflict upon them the hated presence of Prince Alberic. It was, after all, very pleasant to possess a young grandson, whom one could take to one's bosom and employ in being insolent to one's own favourites. It was time, said Duke Balthasar, that Alberic should learn the habits of a court and take unto himself a suitable princess.

The young prince accordingly was sent for from Sparkling Waters, and installed at Luna in a wing of the Red Palace, overlooking the Court of Honour, and commanding an excellent view of the great rockery, with the *verde* antique apes and the porphyry rhinoceros. He found awaiting him on the great staircase a magnificent staff of servants, a master of the horse, a grand cook, a barber, a hairdresser and assistant, a fencing-master, and four fiddlers. Several lovely ladies of the court, the principal ministers of the crown, and the Jesuit, the dwarf, and the jester, were also ready to pay their respects.

Prince Alberic threw himself out of the glass coach before they had time to open the door, and bowing coldly, ascended the staircase, carrying under his cloak what appeared to be a small wicker cage. The Jesuit, who was the soul of politeness, sprang forward and signed to an officer of the household to relieve His Highness of this burden. But Alberic waved the man off; and the rumour went abroad that a hissing noise had issued from under the prince's cloak, and, like lightning, the head and forked tongue of a serpent.

Half an hour later the official spies had informed Duke Balthasar that his grandson and heir had brought from Sparkling Waters no apparent luggage save two swords, a fowling-piece, a volume of Virgil, a branch of pomegranate blossom, and a tame grass snake.

Duke Balthasar did not like the idea of the grass snake; but wishing to annoy the jester, the dwarf, and the Jesuit, he merely smiled when they told him of it, and said: 'The dear boy! What a child he is! He probably, also, has a pet lamb, white as snow, and gentle as spring, mourning for him in his old home! How touching is the innocence of childhood! Heigho! I was just like that myself not so very long ago.' Whereupon the three favourites and the whole Court of Luna smiled and bowed and sighed: 'How lovely is the innocence of youth!' while the duke fell to humming the well-known air, *Thyrsis was a shepherd-boy,* of which the ducal fiddlers instantly struck up the *ritornel.*

'But,' added Balthasar Maria, with that subtle blending of majesty and archness in which he excelled all living princes, 'but it is now time that the prince, my grandson, should learn'—here he put his hand on his sword and threw back slightly one curl of his jet-black peruke—'the stern exercises of Mars; and also, let us hope, the freaks and frolics of Venus.'

Saying which, the old sinner pinched the cheek of a lady of the very highest quality, whose husband and father were instantly congratulated by the whole court.

Prince Alberic was displayed next day to the people of Luna, standing on the balcony among a tremendous banging of mortars; while Duke Balthasar explained that he felt towards this youth all the fondness and responsibility of an elder brother. There was a grand ball, a gala opera, a review, a very high mass in the cathedral; the dwarf, the Jesuit, and the jester each separately offered his services to Alberic in case he wanted a loan of money, a love-letter carried, or in case even (expressed in more delicate terms) he might wish to poison his grandfather. Duke Balthasar Maria, on his side, summoned his ministers, and sent couriers, booted and liveried, to three great dukes of Italy, carrying each of them, in a morocco wallet emblazoned with the arms of Luna, an account of Prince Alberic's lineage and person, and a request for particulars of any marriageable princesses and dowries to be disposed of.

10

Prince Alberic did not give his grandfather that warm satisfaction which the old duke had expected. Balthasar Maria, entirely bent upon annoying the three favourites, had said, and had finally believed, that he intended to introduce his grandson to the delights and duties of life, and in the company of this beloved stripling, to dream that he, too, was a youth once more: a statement which the court took with due deprecatory reverence, as the duke was well known never to have ceased to be young.

But Alberic did not lend himself to so touching an idyll. He behaved, indeed, with the greatest decorum, and manifested the utmost respect for his grandfather. He was marvellously assiduous in the council chamber, and still more so in following the military exercises and learning the trade of a soldier. He surprised everyone by his interest and intelligence in all affairs of state; he more than surprised the court by his readiness to seek knowledge about the administration of the country and the condition of the people. He was a youth of excellent morals, courage, and diligence; but, there was no denying it, he had positively no conception of *sacrificing to the Graces*. He sat out, as if he had been watching a review, the delicious operas and superb ballets which absorbed half the revenue of the duchy. He listened, without a smile of comprehension, to the witty innuendoes of the ducal table. But worst of all, he had absolutely no eyes, let alone a heart, for the fair sex.

Now Balthasar Maria had assembled at Luna a perfect bevy of lovely nymphs, both ladies of the greatest birth, whose husbands received most honourable posts, military and civil, and young females of humbler extraction, though not less expensive habits, ranging from singers and dancers to slave-girls of various colours, all dressed in their appropriate costume: a galaxy of beauty which was duly represented by the skill of celebrated painters on all the walls of the Red Palace, where you may still see their faded charms, habited as Diana, or Pallas, or in the spangles of Columbine, or the turban of Sibyls.

These ladies were the object of Duke Balthasar's most munificently divided attentions; and in the delight of his new-born family affection, he had promised himself much tender interest in guiding the taste of his heir among such of these nymphs as had already received his own exquisite appreciation. Great, therefore, was the disappointment of the affectionate grandfather when his dream of companionship was dispelled, and it became hopeless to interest young Alberic in anything at Luna save despatches and cannons.

The court, indeed, found the means of consoling Duke Balthasar for this bitterness by extracting therefrom a brilliant comparison between the unfading grace, the vivacious, though majestic, character of the grandfather, and the gloomy and pedantic personality of the grandson. But, although Balthasar Maria would only smile at every new proof of Alberic's bearish obtuseness, and ejaculate in French, 'Poor child! he was born old, and I shall die young!' the reigning prince of Luna grew vaguely to resent the peculiarities of his heir.

In this fashion things proceeded in the Red Palace at Luna, until Prince Alberic had attained his twenty-first year.

He was sent, in the interval, to visit the principal courts of Italy, and to inspect its chief curiosities, natural and historical, as befitted the heir to an illustrious state. He received the golden rose from the Pope in Rome; he witnessed the festivities of Ascension Day from the *Doge's* barge at Venice; he accompanied the Marquis of Montferrat to the camp under Turin; he witnessed the launching of a galley against the Barbary corsairs by the Knights of St Stephen in the port of Leghorn, and a grand bullfight and burning of heretics given by the Spanish Viceroy at Palermo; and he was allowed to be present when the celebrated Dr. Borri turned two brass buckles into pure gold before the Archduke at Milan.

On all of which occasions the heir-apparent of Luna bore himself with a dignity and discretion most singular in one so young. In the course of these journeys he was presented to several of the most promising heiresses in Italy, some of whom were of so tender age as to be displayed in jewelled swaddling clothes on brocade cushions; and a great many possible marriages were discussed behind his back. But Prince Alberic declared for his part that he had decided to lead a single life until the age of twent- eight or thirty, and that he would then require the assistance of no ambassadors or chancellors, but find for himself the future Duchess of Luna.

All this did not please Balthasar Maria, as indeed nothing else about his grandson did please him much. But, as the old duke did not really relish the idea of a daughter-in-law at Luna, and as young Alberic's whimsicalities entailed no expense, and left him entirely free in his business and pleasure, he turned a deaf ear to the criticisms of his counsellors, and letting his grandson inspect fortifications, drill soldiers, pore over parchments, and mope in his wing of the palace, with no amusement save his repulsive tame snake, Balthasar Maria composed and practised various ballets, and began to turn his attention very seriously to the completion of the rockery grotto and of the sepulchral chapel, which, besides the Red Palace itself, were the chief monuments of his glorious reign.

It was the growing desire to witness the fulfilment of these magnanimous projects which led the duke of Luna into unexpected conflict with his grandson. The wonderful enterprises above-mentioned involved immense expenses, and had periodically been suspended for lack of funds. The collection of animals in the rockery was very far from complete. A camelopard of spotted alabaster, an elephant of Sardinian jasper, and the entire families of a cow and sheep, all of correspondingly rich marbles, were urgently required to fill up the corners. Moreover, the supply of water was at present so small that the fountains were dry save for a couple of hours on the very greatest holidays; and it was necessary for the perfect naturalness of this ingenious work that an aqueduct twenty miles long should pour perennial streams from a high mountain lake into the grotto of the Red Palace.

The question of the sepulchral chapel was, if possible, even more urgent, for, after every new ballet, Duke Balthasar went through a fit of contrition, during which he fixed his thoughts on death; and the possibilities of untimely release, and of burial in an unfinished mausoleum, filled him with terrors. It is true that Duke Balthasar had, immediately after building the vast domed chapel, secured an effigy of his own person before taking thought for the monuments of his already buried ancestors, and the statue, twelve feet high, representing himself in coronation robes of green bronze brocaded with gold, holding a sceptre, and bearing on his head, of purest silver, a spiky coronet set with diamonds, was one of the curiosities which travellers admired most in Italy.

But this statue was unsymmetrical, and moreover, had a dismal suggestiveness, so long as surrounded by empty niches; and the fact that only one-half of the pavement was inlaid with discs of sardonyx, jasper, and camelian, and that the larger part of the walls were rough brick without a vestige of the mosaic pattern of *lapis-lazuli*, malachite, pearl, and coral, which had been begun round the one finished tomb, rendered the chapel as poverty-stricken in one aspect as it was magnificent in another. The finishing of the chapel was therefore urgent, and two more bronze statues were actually cast, those, to wit, of the duke's father and grandfather, and mosaic workmen called from the Medicean works in Florence. But, all of a sudden, the ducal treasury was discovered to be empty, and the ducal credit to be exploded.

State lotteries, taxes on salt, even a sham crusade against the *Dey* of Algiers, all failed to produce any money. The alliance, the right to pass troops through the duchy, the letting out of the ducal army to the highest bidder, had long since ceased to be a source of revenue either from the Emperor, the King of Spain, or the Most Christian One.

The Serene Republics of Venice and Genoa publicly warned their subjects against lending a single sequin to the Duke of Luna; the Dukes of Mantua and Modena began to worry about bad debts; the Pope himself had the atrocious taste to make complaints about suppression of church dues and interception of Peter's pence. There remained to the bankrupt Duke Balthasar Maria only one hope in the world—the marriage of his grandson.

There happened to exist at that moment a sovereign of incalculable wealth, with an only daughter of marriageable age. But this potentate, although the nephew of a recent Pope, by whose confiscations his fortunes were founded, had originally been a dealer in such goods as are comprehensively known as drysalting; and, rapacious as were the Princes of the Empire, each was too much ashamed of his neighbours to venture upon alliance with a family of so obtrusive an origin.

Here was Balthasar Maria's opportunity: the drysalter prince's *ducats* should complete the rockery, the aqueduct, and the chapel; the drysalter's daughter should be wedded to Alberic of Luna, that was to be third of the name.

11

Prince Alberic sternly declined. He expressed his dutiful wish that the grotto and the chapel, like all other enterprises undertaken by his grandparent, might be brought to an end worthy of him. He declared that the aversion to drysalters was a prejudice unshared by himself. He even went so far as to suggest that the eligible princess should marry, not the heir-apparent, but the reigning duke of Luna. But, as regarded himself, he intended, as stated, to remain for many years single. Duke Balthasar had never in his life before seen a man who was determined to oppose him. He felt terrified and became speechless in the presence of young Alberic.

Direct influence having proved useless, the duke and his counsellors, among whom the Jesuit, the dwarf, and the jester had been duly reinstated, looked round for means of indirect persuasion or coercion. A celebrated Venetian beauty was sent for to Luna—a lady frequently employed in diplomatic missions, which she carried through by her unparalleled grace in dancing. But Prince Alberic, having watched her for half an hour, merely remarked to his equerry that his own tame grass snake made the same movements as the lady infinitely better and more modestly. Whereupon this means was abandoned. The dwarf then suggested a new method of acting on the young prince's feelings.

This, which he remembered to have been employed very successfully in the case of a certain duchess of Malfi, who had given her family much trouble some generations back, consisted in dressing a number of domestics up as ghosts and devils, hiring some genuine lunatics from a neighbouring establishment, and introducing them at dead of night into Prince Alberic's chamber. But the prince, who was busy at his orisons, merely threw a heavy stool and two candlesticks at the apparitions; and, as he did so, the tame snake suddenly rose up from the floor, growing colossal in the act, and hissed so terrifically that the whole party fled down the corridor. The most likely advice was given by the Jesuit. This truly subtle diplomatist averred that it was useless trying to act upon the prince by means which did not already affect him; instead of clumsily constructing a lever for which there was no fulcrum in the youth's soul, it was necessary to find out whatever leverage there might already exist.

Now, on careful inquiry, there was discovered a fact which the official spies, who always acted by precedent and pursued their inquiries according to the rules of the human heart as taught by the Secret Inquisition of the Republic of Venice, had naturally failed to perceive. This fact consisted in a rumour, very vague but very persistent, that Prince Alberic did not inhabit his wing of the palace in absolute solitude. Some of the pages attending on his person affirmed to have heard whispered conversations in the prince's study, on entering which they had invariably found him alone; others maintained that, during the absence of the prince from the palace, they had heard the sound of his private harpsichord, the one with the story of Orpheus and the view of Soracte on the cover, although he always kept its key on his person.

A footman declared that he had found in the prince's study, and among his books and maps, a piece of embroidery certainly not belonging to the prince's furniture and apparel, moreover, half finished, and with a needle sticking in the canvas; which piece of embroidery the prince had thrust into his pocket But, as none of the attendants had ever seen any visitor entering or issuing from the prince's apartments, and the professional spies had ransacked all possible hiding-places and modes of exit in vain, these curious indications had been neglected, and the opinion had been formed that Alberic being, as everyone could judge, somewhat insane, had a gift of ventriloquism, a taste for musical boxes, and a proficiency in unmanly handicrafts which he carefully secreted.

These rumours had at one time caused great delight to Duke Balthasar; but he had got tired of sitting in a dark cupboard in his grandson's chamber, and had caught a bad chill looking through his keyhole; so he had stopped all further inquiries as officious fooling on the part of impudent lacqueys.

But the Jesuit foolishly adhered to the rumour. 'Discover *her,*' he said, 'and work through her on Prince Alberic' But Duke Balthasar, after listing twenty times to this remark with the most delighted interest, turned round on the twenty-first time and gave the Jesuit a look of Jove-like thunder.

'My father,' he said, 'I am surprised—I may say more than surprised—at a person of your cloth descending so low as to make aspersions upon the virtue of a young prince reared in my palace and born of my blood. Never let me hear another word about ladies of light manners being secreted within these walls.'

Whereupon the Jesuit retired, and was in disgrace for a fortnight, till Duke Balthasar woke up one morning with a strong apprehension of dying.

But no more was said of the mysterious female friend of Prince Alberic, still less was any attempt made to gain her intervention in the matter of the drysalter princess's marriage.

12

More desperate measures were soon resorted to. It was given out that Prince Alberic was engrossed in study; and he was forbidden to leave his wing of the Red Palace, with no other view than the famous grotto with the *verde* antique apes and the porphyry rhinoceros. It was published that Prince Alberic was sick; and he was confined very rigorously to a less agreeable apartment in the rear of the palace, where he could catch sight of the plaster laurels and draperies, and the rolling plaster eyeball of one of the twelve Caesars under the cornice. It was judiciously hinted that the prince had entered into religious retreat; and he was locked and bolted into the state prison, alongside of the unfinished sepulchral chapel, whence a lugubrious hammering came as the only sound of life. In each of these places the recalcitrant youth was duly argued with by some of his grandfather's familiars, and even received a visit from the old duke in person. But threats and blandishments were all in vain, and Alberic persisted in his refusal to marry.

It was now six months since he had seen the outer world, and six weeks since he had inhabited the state prison, every stage in

79

his confinement, almost every day thereof, having systematically deprived him of some luxury, some comfort, or some mode of passing his time. His harpsichord and foils had remained in the gala wing overlooking the grotto. His maps and books had not followed him beyond the higher story with the view of the twelfth Caesar. And now they had taken away from him his Virgil, his inkstand and paper, and left him only a book of hours.

Balthasar Maria and his counsellors felt intolerably baffled. There remained nothing further to do; for if Prince Alberic were publicly beheaded, or privately poisoned, or merely left to die of want and sadness, it was obvious that Prince Alberic could no longer conclude the marriage with the drysalter princess, and that no money to finish the grotto and the chapel, or to carry on court expenses, would be forthcoming.

It was a burning day of August, a Friday, thirteenth of that month, and after a long prevalence of enervating *sirocco*, when the old duke determined to make one last appeal to the obedience of his grandson. The sun, setting among ominous clouds, sent a lurid orange gleam into Prince Alberic's prison chamber, at the moment that his ducal grandfather, accompanied by the jester, the dwarf, and the Jesuit, appeared on its threshold after prodigious clanking of keys and clattering of bolts. The unhappy youth rose as they entered, and making a profound bow, motioned his grandparent to the only chair in the place.

Balthasar Maria had never visited him before in this his worst place of confinement; and the bareness of the room, the dust and cobwebs, the excessive hardness of the chair, affected his sensitive heart; and, joined with irritation at his grandson's obstinacy and utter depression about the marriage, the grotto, and the chapel, actually caused this magnanimous sovereign to burst into tears and bitter lamentations.

'It would indeed melt the heart of a stone,' remarked the jester sternly, while his two companions attempted to soothe the weeping duke—'to see one of the greatest, wisest, and most valorous princes in Europe reduced to tears by the undutifulness of his child.'

'Princes, nay kings and emperors' sons,' exclaimed the dwarf, who was administering Melissa water to the duke, 'have perished miserably for much less.'

'Some of the most remarkable personages of sacred history are stated to have incurred eternal perdition for far slighter offences,' added the Jesuit.

Alberic had sat down on the bed. The tawny sunshine fell upon his figure. He had grown very thin, and his garments were inexpressibly threadbare. But he was spotlessly neat, his lace band was perfectly folded, his beautiful blond hair flowed in exquisite curls about his pale face, and his whole aspect was serene and even cheerful. He might be twenty-two years old, and was of consummate beauty and stature.

'My Lord,' he answered slowly, 'I entreat Your Serene Highness to believe that no one could regret more deeply than I do such a spectacle as is offered me by the tears of a duke of Luna. At the same time, I can only reiterate that I accept no responsibility . . . . '

A distant growling of thunder caused the old duke to start, and interrupted Alberic's speech.

'Your obstinacy, my Lord,' exclaimed the dwarf, who was an excessively choleric person, 'betrays the existence of a hidden conspiracy most dangerous to the state.'

'It is an indication,' added the jester, 'of a highly deranged mind.'

'It seems to me,' whispered the Jesuit, 'to savour most undoubtedly of devilry.'

Alberic shrugged his shoulders. He had risen from the bed to close the grated window, into which a shower of hail was suddenly blowing with unparalleled violence, when the old duke jumped on his seat, and, with eyeballs starting with terror, exclaimed, as he tottered convulsively, 'The serpent! the serpent!'

For there, in a corner, the tame grass snake was placidly coiled up, sleeping.

'The snake! the devil! Prince Alberic's pet companion!' exclaimed the three favourites, and rushed towards that corner.

Alberic threw himself forward. But he was too late. The jester, with a blow of his harlequin's lath, had crushed the head of the startled creature; and, even while he was struggling with him and the Jesuit, the dwarf had given it two cuts with his Turkish scimitar.

'The snake! the snake!' shrieked Duke Balthasar, heedless of the desperate struggle.

The warders and equerries waiting outside thought that Prince Alberic must be murdering his grandfather, and burst into prison and separated the combatants.

'Chain the rebel! the wizard! the madman!' cried the three favourites.

Alberic had thrown himself on the dead snake, which lay crushed and bleeding on the floor; and he moaned piteously.

But the prince was unarmed and overpowered in a moment. Three times he broke loose, but three times he was recaptured, and finally bound and gagged, and dragged away. The old duke recovered from his fright, and was helped up from the bed on to which he had sunk. As he prepared to leave, he approached the dead snake, and looked at it for some time. He kicked its mangled head with his ribboned shoe, and turned away laughing.

'Who knows,' he said, 'whether you were not the Snake Lady? That foolish boy made a great fuss, I remember, when he was scarcely out of long clothes, about a tattered old tapestry representing that repulsive story.'

And he departed to supper.

13

Prince Alberic of Luna, who should have been third of his name, died a fortnight later, it was stated, insane. But those who approached him maintained that he had been in perfect possession of his faculties; and that if he refused all nourishment during his second imprisonment, it was from set purpose. He was removed at night from his apartments facing the grotto with the *verde* antique monkeys and the porphyry rhinoceros, and hastily buried under a slab, which remained without any name or date, in the famous mosaic sepulchral chapel.

Duke Balthasar Maria survived him only a few months. The old duke had plunged into excesses of debauchery with a view, apparently, to dismissing certain terrible thoughts and images which seemed to haunt him day and night, and against which no religious practices or medical prescription were of any avail. The origin of these painful delusions was probably connected with a very strange rumour, which grew to a tradition at Luna, to the effect that when the prison room occupied by Prince Alberic was cleaned, after that terrible storm of the 13th August of the year 1700, the persons employed found in a corner, not the dead grass snake, which they had been ordered to cast into the palace drains, but the body of a woman, naked, and miserably disfigured with blows and sabre cuts.

Be this as it may, history records as certain that the house of Luna became extinct in 1701, the duchy lapsing to the Empire. Moreover, that the mosaic chapel remained for ever unfinished, with no statue save the green bronze and gold one of Balthasar Maria above the nameless slab covering Prince Alberic. The rockery also was never completed; only a few marble animals adorning it besides the porphyry rhinoceros and the *verde* antique apes, and the water-supply being sufficient only for the greatest holidays. These things the traveller can report. Also that certain chairs and curtains in the porter's lodge of the now long-deserted Red Palace are made of the various pieces of an extremely damaged arras, having represented the story of Alberic the Blond and the Snake Lady.

The Doll
A.k.a. *The Image*

I believe that's the last bit of *bric-à-brac* I shall ever buy in my life (she said, closing the Renaissance casket)—that and the Chinese dessert set we have just been using. The passion seems to have left me utterly. And I think I can guess why. At the same time as the plates and the little coffer I bought a thing—I scarcely know whether I ought to call it a thing—which put me out of conceit with ferreting about among dead people's properties. I have often wanted to tell you all about it, and stopped for fear of seeming an idiot. But it weighs upon me sometimes like a secret; so, silly or not silly, I think I should like to tell you the story. There, ring for some more logs, and put that screen before the lamp.

It was two years ago, in the autumn, at Foligno, in Umbria. I was alone at the inn, for you know my husband is too busy for my *bric-à-brac* journeys, and the friend who was to have met me fell ill and came on only later. Foligno isn't what people call an interesting place, but I liked it. There are a lot of picturesque little towns all round; and great savage mountains of pink stone, covered with ilex, where they roll faggots down into the torrent beds, within a drive. There's a full, rushing little river round one side of the walls, which are covered with ivy; and there are fifteenth-century *frescoes*, which I dare say you know all about. But, what of course I care for most, there are a number of fine old palaces, with gateways carved in that pink stone, and courts with pillars, and beautiful window gratings, mostly in good enough repair, for Foligno is a market town and a junction, and altogether a kind of metropolis down in the valley.

Also, and principally, I liked Foligno because I discovered a delightful curiosity-dealer. I don't mean a delightful curiosity shop, for he had I nothing worth twenty *francs* to sell; but a delightful, enchanting old man. His Christian name was Orestes, and that was enough for me. He had a long white beard and such kind brown eyes, and beautiful hands; and he always carried an earthenware brazier under his cloak. He had taken to the curiosity business from a passion for beautiful things, and for the past of his native place, after having been a master mason. He knew all the old chronicles, lent me that of Matarazzo, and knew exactly where everything had happened for the last six hundred years.

He spoke of the Trincis, who had been local despots, and of St. Angela, who is the local saint, and of the Baglionis and Cæsar Borgia and Julius II, as if he had known them; he showed me the place where St. Francis preached to the birds, and the place where Propertius—was it Propertius or Tibullus?—had had his farm; and when he accompanied me on my rambles in search of *bric-à-brac* he would stop at corners and under arches and say, "This, you see, is where they carried off those Nuns I told you about; that's where the Cardinal was stabbed. That's the place where they razed the palace after the massacre, and passed the plough-share through the ground and sowed salt." And all with a vague, far-off, melancholy look, as if he lived in those days and not these.

Also he helped me to get that little velvet coffer with the iron clasps, which is really one of the best things we have in the house. So I was very happy at Foligno, driving and prowling about all day, reading the chronicles Orestes lent me in the evening; and I didn't mind waiting so long for my friend who never turned up. That is to say, I was perfectly happy until within three days of my departure. And now comes the story of my strange purchase.

Orestes, with considerable shrugging of shoulders, came one

morning with the information that a certain noble person of Foligno wanted to sell me a set of Chinese plates. "Some of them are cracked," he said; "but at all events you will see the inside of one of our finest palaces, with all its rooms as they used to be—nothing valuable; but I know that the *signora* appreciates the past wherever it has been let alone."

The palace, by way of exception, was of the late seventeenth century, and looked like a barracks among the neat little carved Renaissance houses. It had immense lions' heads over all the windows, a gateway in which two coaches could have met, a yard where a hundred might have waited, and a colossal staircase with *stucco* virtues on the vaultings. There was a cobbler in the lodge and a soap factory on the ground floor, and at the end of the colonnaded court a garden with ragged yellow vines and dead sunflowers.

"*Grandiose*, but very coarse—almost eighteenth century," said Orestes as we went up the sounding, low-stepped stairs. Some of the dessert set had been placed, ready for my inspection, on a great gold console in the immense escutcheoned anteroom. I looked at it, and told them to prepare the rest for me to see the next day. The owner, a very noble person, but half ruined—I should have thought entirely ruined, judging by the state of the house—was residing in the country, and the only occupant of the palace was an old woman, just like those who raised the curtains for you at church doors.

The palace was very grand. There was a ballroom as big as a church, and a number of reception rooms, with dirty floors and eighteenth-century furniture, all tarnished and tattered, and a gala room, all yellow satin and gold, where some emperor had slept; and there were horrible racks of faded photographs on the walls, and two-penny screens, and Berlin wool cushions, attesting the existence of more modern occupants.

I let the old woman unbar one painted and gilded shutter after another, and open window after window, each filled with little greenish panes of glass, and followed her about passively, quite happy, because I was wandering among the ghosts of dead people. "There is the library at the end here," said the old woman, "if the *signora* does not mind passing through my room and the ironing-room; it's quicker than going back by the big hall." I nodded, and prepared to pass as quickly as possible through an untidy-looking servants' room, when I suddenly stepped back. There was a woman in 1820 costume seated opposite, quite motionless. It was a huge doll. She had a sort of Canova classic face, like the pictures of Mme. Pasta and Lady Blessington. She sat with her hands folded on her lap and stared fixedly.

"It is the first wife of the count's grandfather," said the old woman. "We took her out of her closet this morning to give her a little dusting."

The doll was dressed to the utmost detail. She had on open-work silk stockings, with sandal shoes, and long silk embroidered mittens. The hair was merely painted, in flat bands narrowing the forehead to a triangle. There was a big hole in the back of her head, showing it was cardboard.

"Ah," said Orestes, musingly, "the image of the beautiful countess! I had forgotten all about it. I haven't seen it since I was a lad," and he wiped some cobweb off the folded hands with his red handkerchief, infinitely gently. "She used still to be kept in her own *boudoir*."

"That was before my time," answered the housekeeper. "I've always seen her in the wardrobe, and I've been here thirty years. Will the care to see the old count's collection of medals?" Orestes was very pensive as he accompanied me home

"That was a very beautiful lady," he said shyly, as we came within sight of my inn; "I mean the first wife of the grandfather of the present count. She died after they had been married a couple of years. The old count, they say, went half crazy. He had the doll made from a picture, and kept it in the poor lady's room, and spent several hours in it every day with her. But he ended by marrying a woman he had in the house, a laundress, by whom he had had a daughter."

"What a curious story!" I said, and thought no more about it.

But the doll returned to my thoughts, she and her folded hands, and wide open eyes, and the fact of her husband's having ended by marrying the laundress. And next day, when we returned to the palace to see the complete set of old Chinese plates, I suddenly experienced an odd wish to see the doll once more. I took advantage of Orestes, and the old woman, and the count's lawyer being busy deciding whether a certain dish cover which my maid had dropped, had or had not been previously chipped, to slip off and make my way to the ironing-room.

The doll was still there, sure enough, and they hadn't found time to dust her yet. Her white satin frock, with little *ruches* at the hem, and her short bodice, had turned grey with engrained dirt; and her black fringed kerchief was almost red. The poor white silk mittens and white silk stockings were, on the other hand, almost black. A newspaper had fallen from an adjacent table on to her knees, or been thrown there by someone, and she looked as if she were holding it. It came home to me then that the clothes which she wore were the real clothes of her poor dead original.

And when I found on the table a dusty, unkempt wig, with straight bands in front and an elaborate jug handle of curls behind, I knew at once that it was made of the poor lady's real hair. "It is very well made," I said shyly, when the old woman, of course, came creaking after me. She had no thought except that of humouring whatever caprice might bring her a tip. So she smirked horribly, and, to show me that the image was really worthy of my attention, she proceeded in a ghastly way to bend the articulated arms, and to cross one leg over the other beneath the white satin skirt.

"Please, please, don't do that!" I cried to the old witch. But one of the poor feet, in its sandaled shoe, continued dangling and wagging dreadfully.

I was afraid lest my maid should find me staring at the doll. I felt I couldn't stand my maid's remarks about her. So, though fascinated by the fixed dark stare in her Canova goddess or Ingres Madonna face, I tore myself away and returned to the inspection

88

of the dessert set.

I don't know what that doll had done to me; but I found that I was thinking of her all day long. It was as if I had just made a new acquaintance of a painfully interesting kind, rushed into a sudden friendship with a woman whose secret I had surprised, as sometimes happens, by some mere accident. For I somehow knew everything about her, and the first items of information which I gained from Orestes—I ought to say that I was irresistibly impelled to talk about her with him—did not enlighten me in the least, but merely confirmed what I was aware of. The doll—for I made no distinction between the portrait and the original—had been married straight out of the convent, and, during her brief wedded life, been kept secluded from the world by her husband's mad love for her, so that she had remained a mere shy, proud, inexperienced child.

Had she loved him? She did not tell me that at once. But gradually I became aware that in a deep, inarticulate way she had really cared for him more than he cared for her. She did not know what answer to make to his easy, overflowing, garrulous, demonstrative affection; he could not be silent about his love for two minutes, and she could never find a word to express hers, painfully though she longed to do so. Not that he wanted it; he was a brilliant, will-less, lyrical sort of person, who knew nothing of the feelings of others and cared only to welter and dissolve in his own.

In those two years of ecstatic, talkative, all-absorbing love for her he not only forswore all society and utterly neglected his affairs, but he never made an attempt to train this raw young creature into a companion, or showed any curiosity as to whether his idol might have a mind or a character of her own. This indifference she explained by her own stupid, inconceivable incapacity for expressing her feelings; how should he guess at her longing to know, to understand, when she could not even tell him how much she loved him? At last the spell seemed broken: the words and the power of saying them came; but it was on her death-bed. The poor young creature died in child-birth, scarcely more than a child herself.

There now! I know even you would think it all silliness. I know what people are—what we all are—how impossible it is ever *really* to make others feel in the same way as ourselves about anything. Do you suppose I could have ever told all this about the doll to my husband? Yet I tell him everything about myself and I know he would have been quite kind and respectful. It was silly of me ever to embark on the story of the doll with any one; it ought to have remained a secret between me and Orestes. *He,* I really think, would have understood all about the poor lady's feelings, or known it already as well as I.

Well, having begun, I must go on, I suppose. I knew all about the doll when she was alive—I mean about the lady—and I got to know, in the same way, all about her after she was dead. Only I don't think I'll tell you. *Basta:* the husband had the doll made, and dressed it in her clothes, and placed it in her *boudoir,* where not a thing was moved from how it had been at the moment of her death. He allowed no one to go in. and cleaned and dusted it all himself, and spent hours every day weeping and moaning before the doll. Then, gradually, he began to look at his collection of medals, and to resume his rides; but he never went into society, and never neglected spending an hour in the *boudoir* with the doll.

Then came the business with the laundress. And then he sent the doll into a wardrobe? Oh no; he wasn't that sort of man. He was an idealizing, sentimental, feeble sort of person, and the amour with the laundress grew up quite gradually in the shadow of the inconsolable passion for the wife. He would never have married another woman of his own rank, given *her* son a stepmother (the son was sent to a distant school and went to the bad); and when he *did* marry the laundress it was almost in his dotage, and because she and the priests bullied him so fearfully about legitimating that other child. He went on paying visits to the doll for a long time, while the laundress idyll went on quite peaceably.

Then, as he grew old and lazy, he went less often; other people were sent to dust the doll, and finally she was not dusted at all. Then he died, having quarrelled with his son and got to live like a feeble old boor, mostly in the kitchen. The son— the doll's son—having gone to the bad, married a rich widow. It was she who refurnished the *boudoir* and sent the doll away. But the daughter of the laundress, the illegitimate child, who had become a kind of housekeeper in her half-brother's palace, nourished a lingering regard for the doll, partly because the old count had made such a fuss about it, partly because it must have cost a lot of money, and partly because the lady had been a *real* lady. So when the *boudoir* was refurnished she emptied out a closet and put the doll to live there; and she occasionally had it brought out to be dusted.

Well, while all these things were being borne in upon me there came a telegram saying my friend was not coming on to Foligno, and asking me to meet her at Perugia. The little Renaissance coffer had been sent to London; Orestes and my maid and myself had carefully packed every one of the Chinese plates and fruit dishes in baskets of hay. I had ordered a set of the "*Archivio Storico*" as a parting gift for dear old Orestes—I could never have dreamed of offering him money, or cravat pins, or things like that—and there was no excuse for staying one hour more at Foligno.

Also I had got into low spirits of late—I suppose we poor women cannot stay alone six days in an inn, even with *bric-à-brac* and chronicles and devoted maids—and I knew I should not get better till I was out of the place. Still I found it difficult, nay, impossible, to go. I will confess it outright: I couldn't abandon the doll. I couldn't leave her, with the hole in her poor cardboard head, with the Ingres Madonna features gathering dust in that filthy old woman's ironing-room. It was just impossible. Still go I must. So I sent for Orestes. I knew exactly what I wanted; but it seemed impossible, and I was afraid, somehow, of asking him. I gathered up my courage, and, as if it were the most natural thing in the world, I said—

"Dear Signor Oreste, I want you to help me to make one last

purchase. I want the count to sell me the—the portrait of his grandmother; I mean the doll."

I had prepared a speech to the effect that Orestes would easily understand that a life-size figure so completely dressed in the original costume of a past epoch would soon possess the highest historical interest, etc. But I felt that I neither needed nor ventured to say any of it. Orestes, who was seated opposite me at table—he would only accept a glass of wine and a morsel of bread, although I had asked him to share my hotel dinner—Orestes nodded slowly, then opened his eyes out wide, and seemed to frame the whole of me in them. It wasn't surprise. He was weighing me and my offer.

"Would it be very difficult?" I asked. "I should have thought that the count—"

"The count," answered Orestes drily, "would sell his soul, if he had one, let alone his grandmother, for the price of a new trotting pony."

Then I understood.

"Signor Oreste," I replied, feeling like a child under the dear old man's glance, "We have not known one another long, so I cannot expect you to trust me yet in many things. Perhaps also buying furniture out of dead people's houses to stick it in one's own is not a great recommendation of one's character. But I want to tell you that I am an honest woman according to my lights, and I want you to trust me in this matter."

Orestes bowed. "I will try and induce the count to sell you the doll," he said.

I had her sent in a closed carriage to the house of Orestes. He had, behind his shop, a garden which extended into a little vineyard, whence you could see the circle of great Umbrian mountains; and on this I had had my eye.

Signor Oreste," I said, "will you be very kind, and have some faggots—I have seen some beautiful faggots of myrtle and bay in your kitchen—brought out into the vineyard; and may I pluck some of your chrysanthemums?" I added.

We stacked the faggots at the end of the vineyard, and placed the doll in the midst of them, and the chrysanthemums on her knees. She sat there in her white satin Empire frock, which, in the bright November sunshine, seemed white once more, and sparkling. Her black fixed eyes stared as in wonder on the yellow vines and reddening peach trees, the sparkling dewy grass of the vineyard, upon the blue morning sunshine, the misty blue amphitheatre of mountains all round.

Orestes struck a match and slowly lit a pine cone with it; when the cone was blazing he handed it silently to me. The dry bay and myrtle blazed up crackling, with a fresh resinous odour; the doll was veiled in flame and smoke. In a few seconds the flame sank, the smouldering faggots crumbled. The doll was gone. Only, where she had been, there remained in the embers something small and shiny. Orestes raked it out and handed it to me. It was a wedding ring of old-fashioned shape, which had been hidden under the silk mitten. "Keep it, *signora*," said Orestes; "you have put an end to her sorrows."

Faustus and Helena

Notes on the Supernatural in Art

There is a story, well-known throughout the sixteenth century, which tells how Doctor Faustus of Wittemberg, having made over his soul to the fiend, employed him to raise the ghost of Helen of Sparta, in order that she might become his paramour. The story has no historic value, no scientific meaning; it lacks the hoary dignity of the tales of heroes and demi-gods, wrought, vague, and colossal forms, out of cloud and sunbeam, of those tales narrated and heard by generations of men deep hidden in the stratified ruins of lost civilisation, carried in the races from India to Hellas, and to Scandinavia. Compared with them, this tale of Faustus and Helena is paltry and brand-new; it is not a myth, nay, scarcely a legend; it is a mere trifling incident added by humanistic pedantry to the ever-changing medieval story of the man who barters his soul for knowledge, the wizard, alchemist, philosopher, printer, Albertus, Bacon, or Faustus.

It is a part, an unessential, subordinate fragment, valued in its day neither more nor less than any other part of the history of Doctor Faustus, narrated cursorily by the biographer of the wizard, overlooked by some of the ballad rhymers, alternately used and rejected by the playwrights of puppet-shows; given by Marlowe himself no greater importance than the other marvellous deeds, the juggling tricks and magic journeys of his hero.

But for us, the incident of Faustus and Helena has a meaning, a fascination wholly different from any other portion of the story; the other incidents owe everything to artistic treatment:

this one owes nothing. The wizard Faustus, awaiting the hour which will give him over to Hell, is the creation of Marlowe; Gretchen is even more completely the creation of Goethe; the fiend of the Englishman is occasionally grand, the fiend of the German is throughout masterly; in all these cases we are in the presence of true artistic work, of stuff rendered valuable solely by the hand of the artist, of figures well defined and finite, and limited also in their power over the imagination. But the group of Faustus and Helena is different; it belongs neither to Marlowe nor to Goethe, it belongs to the legend. It does not give the complete and limited satisfaction of a work of art; it has the charm of the fantastic and fitful shapes formed by the flickering firelight or the wreathing mists; it haunts like some vague strain of music, drowsily heard in half-sleep.

It fills the fancy, it oscillates and transforms itself; the artist may see it, attempt to seize and embody it for evermore in a definite and enduring shape, but it vanishes out of his grasp, and the forms which should have inclosed it are mere empty sepulchres, haunted and charmed merely by the evoking power of our own imagination. If we are fascinated by the Lady Helen of Marlowe, walking, like some Florentine goddess, with embroidered kirtle and Madonna face, across the study of the old wizard of Wittemberg; if we are pleased by the stately pseudo-antique Helena of Goethe, draped in the drapery of Thorwaldsen's statues, and speaking the language of Goethe's own Iphigenia, as she meets the very modern Faust, gracefully masqued in medieval costume; if we find in these attempts, the one unthinking and imperfect, the other laboured and abortive, something which delights our fancy, it is because our thoughts wander off from them and evoke a Faustus and Helena of our own, different from the creations of Marlowe and of Goethe; it is because in these definite and imperfect artistic forms, there yet remains the suggestion of the subject with all its power over the imagination.

We forget Marlowe, and we forget Goethe, to follow up the infinite suggestion of the legend. We cease to see the Elizabethan and the pseudo-antique Helen; we lift our imagination from

the book and see the medieval street at Wittemberg, the ga-
bled house of Faustus, all sculptured with quaint devices and
grotesque forms of apes and cherubs and flowers; we penetrate
through the low brown rooms, filled with musty books and
mysterious ovens and retorts, redolent with strange scents of
alchemy, to that innermost secret chamber, where the old wizard
hides, in the depths of his medieval house, the immortal woman,
the god-born, the fatal, the beloved of Theseus and Paris and
Achilles; we are blinded by this sunshine of antiquity pent up in
the oaken-panelled chamber, such as Dürer might have etched;
and all around we hear circulating the mysterious rumours of
the neighbours, of the *burghers* and students, whispering shyly of
Dr. Faustus and his strange guest, in the beer-cellars and in the
cloisters of the old university town.

And gazing thus into the fantastic intellectual mist which has
risen up between us and the book we were reading, be it Marlowe or Goethe, we cease, after a while, to see Faustus or Helena,
we perceive only a chaotic fluctuation of incongruous shapes;
scholars in furred robes and caps pulled over their ears, *burghers*
wives with high sugar-loaf coif and slashed bodices, with hands
demurely folded over their prayer-books, and knights in armour
and immense plumes, and haggling Jews, and tonsured monks,
descended out of panels of Wohlgemuth and the engravings of
Dürer, mingling with, changing into processions of naked ath-
letes on foaming short-maned horses, of draped Athenian maidens carrying baskets and sickles, and priests bearing oil-jars and
torches, all melting into each other, indistinct, confused, like the
images in a dream; vague crowds, phantoms following in the
wake of the spectre woman of antiquity, beautiful, unimpas-
sioned, ever young, luring to Hell the wizard of the Middle
Ages.

Why does all this vanish as soon as we once more fix our
eyes upon the book? Why can our fancy show us more than can
the artistic genius of Marlowe and of Goethe? Why does Marlowe, believing in Helen as a satanic reality, and Goethe, striv-
ing after her as an artistic vision, equally fail to satisfy us? The

question is intricate: it requires a threefold answer, dependent on the fact that this tale of Faustus and Helena is in fact a tale of the supernatural—a weird and colossal ghost-story, in which the actors are the spectre of antiquity, ever young, beautiful, radiant, though risen from the putrescence of two thousand years; and the Middle Ages, alive, but toothless, palsied, and tottering. Why neither Marlowe nor Goethe have succeeded in giving a satisfactory artistic shape to this tale is explained by the necessary relations between art and the supernatural, between our creative power and our imaginative faculty; why Marlowe has failed in one manner and Goethe in another is explained by the fact that, as we said, for the first the tale was a supernatural reality, for the second a supernatural fiction.

What are the relations between art and the supernatural? At first sight the two appear closely allied: like the supernatural, art is born of imagination; the supernatural, like art, conjures up unreal visions. The two have been intimately connected during the great ages of the supernatural, when instead of existing merely in a few disputed traditional dogmas, and in a little discredited traditional folklore, it constituted the whole of religion and a great part of philosophy. Gods and demons, saints and spectres, have afforded at least one-half of the subjects for art. The supernatural, in the shape of religious mythology, had art bound in its service in antiquity and the Middle Ages; the supernatural, in the shape of spectral fancies, regained its dominion over art with the advent of romanticism. From the gods of the *Iliad* down to the Commander in *Don Giovanni*, from the sylvan divinities of Praxiteles to the fairies of Shakespeare, from the Furies of Æschylus to the Archangels of Perugino, the supernatural and the artistic have constantly appeared linked together.

Yet, in reality, the hostility between the supernatural and the artistic is well-nigh as great as the hostility between the supernatural and the logical. Critical reason is a solvent, it reduces the phantoms of the imagination to their most prosaic elements; artistic power, on the other hand, moulds and solidifies them into distinct and palpable forms: the synthetical definiteness of art is as sceptical as the analytical definiteness of logic. For the supernatural is necessarily essentially vague, and art is necessarily essentially distinct: give shape to the vague and it ceases to exist. The task set to the artist by the dreamer, the prophet, the priest, the ghost-seer of all times, is as difficult, though in the opposite sense, as that by which the little girl in the Venetian fairy tale sought to test the omnipotence of the emperor. She asked him for a very humble dish, quite simple and not costly, a pat of butter broiled on a gridiron.

The emperor desired his cook to place the butter on the gridiron and light the fire; all was going well, when, behold! the butter began to melt, trickled off, and vanished. The artists were asked to paint, or model, or narrate the supernatural; they set about the work in good conscience, but see, the supernatural became the natural, the gods turned into men, the Madonnas into mere mothers, the angels into armed striplings, the phantoms into mere creatures of flesh and blood.

There are in reality two sorts of supernatural, although only one really deserves the name. A great number of beliefs in all mythologies are in reality mere scientific errors—abortive attempts to explain phenomena by causes with which they have no connection—the imagination plays not more part in them than in any other sort of theorising, and the notions that unlucky accidents are due to a certain man's glance, that certain formulæ will bring rain or sunshine, that miraculous images will dispel pestilence, and kings of England cure epilepsy, must be classed under the head of mistaken generalizations, not very different in point of fact from exploded scientific theories, such as Descartes' vortices, or the innate ideas of scholasticism. That there was a time when animals spoke with human voice may seem to us a piece of fairy-lore, but it was in its day a scientific hypothesis as brilliant and satisfying as Darwin's theory of evolution.

We must, therefore, in examining the relations between art and the supernatural, eliminate as far as possible this species of scientific speculation, and consider only that supernatural which really deserves the name, which is beyond and outside the limits of the possible, the rational, the explicable—that supernatural which is due not to the logical faculties, arguing from wrong premises, but to the imagination wrought upon by certain kinds of physical surroundings.

The divinity of the earlier races is in some measure a mistaken scientific hypothesis of the sort we have described, an attempt to explain phenomena otherwise inexplicable. But it is much more: it is the effect on the imagination of certain external impressions, it is those impressions brought to a focus, personified, but personified vaguely, in a fluctuating ever-changing manner; the personification being continually altered, reinforced, blurred out, enlarged, restricted by new series of impressions from without, even as the shape which we puzzle out of congregated cloud-masses fluctuates with their every movement—a shifting vapour now obliterates the form, now compresses it into greater distinctness: the wings of the fantastic monster seem now flapping leisurely, now extending bristling like a griffon's; at one moment it has a beak and talons, at others a mane and hoofs; the breeze, the sunlight, the moonbeam, form, alter, and obliterate it.

Thus is it with the supernatural: the gods, moulded out of cloud and sunlight and darkness, are for ever changing, fluctuating between a human or animal shape, god or goddess, cow, ape, or horse, and the mere natural phenomenon which impresses the fancy. Pan is the weird, shaggy, cloven-footed shape which the goat-herd or the huntsman has seen gliding among the bushes in the grey twilight; his is the piping heard in the tangle of reeds, marsh lily, and knotted nightshade by the riverside: but Pan is also the wood, with all its sights and noises, the solitude, the gloom, the infinity of rustling leaves, and cracking branches; he is the greenish-yellow light stealing in amid the boughs; he is the breeze in the foliage, the murmur of unseen waters, the mist hanging over the damp sward, the ferns and grasses which entangle the feet, and the briars which catch in the hair and garments are his grasp; and the wanderer dashes through the thickets with a sickening fear in his heart, and sinks down on the outskirts of the forest, gasping, with sweat-clotted hair, overcome by this glimpse of the great god.

In this constant renewal of the impressions on the fancy, in this unceasing shaping and reshaping of its creations, consisted the vitality of the myths of paganism, from the scorching and pestilence-bearing gods of India to the divinities shaped out of tempest and snowdrift of Scandinavia; they were constantly issuing out of the elements, renewed, changed, ever young, under the exorcism not only of the priest and of the poet, but of the village boor; and on this unceasing renovation depended the sway which they maintained, without ethical importance to help them, despite philosophy and Christianity. Christianity, born in an age of speculation and eclecticism, removed its divinities, its mystic figures, out of the cosmic surroundings of paganism; it forbade the imagination to touch or alter them, it regularised, defined, explained, placed the Saviour, the Virgin, the saints and angels, into a kind of supersensuous world of logic, logic adapted to Heaven, and different therefore from the logic of earth, but logic none the less.

Christianity endowed them with certain definite attributes, not to be found among mortals, but analogous in a manner to mortal attributes; the Christian supernatural system belongs mainly to the category of mistaken scientific systems; its peculiarities are due, not to overwrought fancy, but to overtaxed reason. Thus the genuine supernatural was well-nigh banished by official Christianity, regulated as it was by a sort of congress of men of science, who eliminated, to the best of their powers, any vagaries of the imagination which might show themselves in their mystico-logic system. But the imagination did work nevertheless, and the supernatural did reappear, both within and without the Christian system of mythology. The Heaven of theology was too ethical, too logical, too positive, too scientific, in accordance with the science of the Middle Ages, for the minds of humanity at large; the scholars and learned clergy might study and expound it, but it was insufficient for the ignorant. The imagination reappeared once more.

To the monk arose out of the silence and gloom of the damp,

lichen-grown crypt, out of the fœtid emanations of the charnal-house, strange forms of horror which lurked in his steps and haunted his sleep after fasting and scourging and vigils; devils and imps horrible and obscene, which the chisel of the stone-cutter vainly attempted to reproduce, in their fluctuating abomination, on the capitals and gargoyles of cloister and cathedral. To the artisan, the weaver pent up in some dark cellar into which the daylight stole grey and faint from the narrow strip of blue sky between the overhanging eaves, for him, the hungry and toil-worn and weary of soul, there arose out of the hum of the street above, out of the half-lit dust, the winter damp and summer suffocation of the underground workshop, visions and sounds of sweetness and glory, misty clusters of white-robed angels shedding radiance around them, swaying in mystic linked dances, mingling with the sordid noises of toil seraphic harmonies, now near, now dying away into distance, voices singing of the sunshine and flowers of Paradise.

And for others, for the lean and tattered peasant, with the dull, apathetic resignation of the starved and goaded ox or horse, sleeping on the damp clay of his hut and eating strange flourless bread, and stranger carrion flesh, there came a world of the supernatural, different from that of the monk or the artisan, at once terrifying and consoling; the divinities cast out by Christianity, the divinities for ever newly begotten by nature, but begotten of a nature miserably changed, born in exile and obloquy and persecution, fostered by the wretched and the brutified; differing from the gods of antiquity as the desolate heath, barren of all save stones and prickly furze and thistle, differs from the fertile pasture-land; as the forests planted over the cornfield, whence issue wolves, and the Baron's harvest-trampling horses, differ from the forests which gave their oaks and pines to Tyrian ships; divinities warped, and crippled, grown hideous and malignant and unhappy in the likeness of their miserable votaries.

This is the real supernatural, born of the imagination and its surroundings, the vital, the fluctuating, the potent; and it is this which the artist of every age, from Phidias to Giotto, from

Giotto to Blake, has been called upon to make known to the multitude. And there had been artistic work going on unnoticed long before the time of any painter or sculptor or poet of whom we have any record; mankind longed from the first to embody, to fix its visions of wonder, it set to work with rough unskilful fingers moulding into shape its divinities.

Rude work, ugly, barbarous, blundering scratchings on walls, kneaded clay vessels, notched sticks, nonsense rhymes; but work nevertheless which already showed that art and the supernatural were at variance, the beaked and clawed figures outlined on the wall were compromises between the man and the beast, but definite compromises, so much and no more of the man, so much and no more of the beast; the goddess on the clay vessels became a mere little owl; the divinities even in the nonsense verses were presented now as very distinct cows, now as very distinct clouds, or very distinct men and women; the vague, fluctuating impressions oscillating before the imagination like the colours of a dove's wing, or the pattern of a shot silk, interwoven, unsteady, never completely united into one, never completely separated into several, were rudely seized, disentangled by art; part was taken, part thrown aside; what remained was homogeneous, definite, unchanging; it was what it was and could never be aught else.

Goethe has remarked, with a subjective simplicity of irreverence which is almost comical, that as God created man in his image, it was only fair that man, in his turn, should create God in *his* image. But the decay of pagan belief was not, as Hegel imagines, due to the fact that Hellenic art was anthropomorphic. The gods ceased to be gods not merely because they became too like men, but because they became too like anything definite. If the ibis on the amulet, or the owl on the terra-cotta, represents a more vital belief in the gods than does the Venus of Milo or the Giustiniani Minerva, it is not because the idea of divinity is more compatible with an ugly bird than with a beautiful woman, but because whereas the beautiful woman, exquisitely wrought by a consummate sculptor, occupied the mind of the artist and of the beholder with the idea of her beauty, to the exclusion of all else, the rudely-engraven ibis, or the badly-modelled owlet, on the other hand, served merely as a symbol, as the recaller of an idea; the mind did not pause in contemplation of the bird, but wandered off in search of the god: the goggle eyes of the owl and the beak of the ibis were soon forgotten in the contemplation of the vague, ever transmuted visions of phenomena of sky and light, of semi-human and semi-bestial shapes, of confused half-embodied forces; in short, of the supernatural.

But the human shape did most mischief to the supernatural, merely because the human shape was the most absolute, the most distinct of all shapes: a god might be symbolised as a beast, but he could only be pourtrayed as a man; and if the portrait was correct, then the god was a man, and nothing more. Even the most fantastic among pagan supernatural creatures, those strange monsters who longest kept their original dual nature—the centaurs, satyrs, and tritons—became, beneath the chisel of the artist, mere aberrations from the normal, rare, and curious types like certain fair-booth phenomena, but perfectly intelligible and rational; the very chimæra, she who was to give her name to every sort of unintelligible fancy, became, in the *bas-reliefs* of the story of Bellerophon a mere singular mixture between a lion, a dog, and a bird—a cross-breed which happens not to be possible, but which an ancient might well have conceived as adorning some distant zoological collection.

How much more rationalised were not the divinities in whom only a peculiar shape of the eye, a certain structure of the leg, or a definite fashion of wearing the hair remained of their former nature. Learned men, indeed, tell us that we need only glance at Hera to see that she is at bottom a cow; at Apollo, to recognise that he is but a stag in human shape: or at Zeus, to recognise that he is, in point of fact, a lion.

Yet it remains true that we need only walk down the nearest street to meet ten ordinary men and women who look more like various animals than do any antique divinities, and who can yet never be said to be in reality cows, stags, or lions. The same applies to the violent efforts which are constantly being made to show in the Greek and Latin poets a distinct recollection of the cosmic nature of the gods, construing the very human movements, looks, and dress of divinities into meteorological phenomena, as has been done even by Mr. Ruskin, in his *Queen of the Air*, despite his artist's sense, which should have warned him that no artistic figure, like Homer's divinities, can possibly be at the same time a woman and a whirlwind.

The gods did originally partake of the character of cosmic phenomena, as they partook of the characters of beasts and birds, and of every other species of transformation, such as we may watch in dreams; but as soon as they were artistically embodied, this transformation ceased, the nature had to be specified in proportion as the form became distinct; and the drapery of Pallas, although it had inherited its purple tint from the storm-cloud, was none the less, when it clad the shoulders of the goddess, not a storm-cloud, but a piece of purple linen.

"What do you want of me?" asks the artist.

"A god," answers the believer.

"What is your god to be like?" asks the artist.

"My god is to be a very handsome warrior, a serene heaven, which is occasionally overcast with clouds, which clouds are sometimes very beneficial, and become (and so does the god at those moments) heavy-uddered cows; at others, they are dark, and cause annoyance, and then they capture the god, who is the light (but he is also the clouds, remember), and lock him up in a tower, and then he frees himself, and he is a neighing horse, and he is sitting on the prancing horse (which is himself, you know, and is the sky too), in the shape of two warriors, and also———"

"May Cerberus devour you!" cries the artist. "How can I represent all this? Do you want a warrior, or a cow, or the heavens, or a horse, or do you want a warrior with the hoofs of a horse and the horns of a cow? Explain, for, by Juno, I can give you only one of these at a time."

Thus, in proportion as the gods were subjected to artistic manipulation, whether by sculptor or poet, they lost their supernatural powers. A period there doubtless was when the gods stood out quite distinct from nature, and yet remained connected with it, as the figures of a high relief stand out from the background; but gradually they were freed from the chaos of impressions which had given them birth, and then, little by little, they ceased to be gods; they were isolated from the world of the wonderful, they were respectfully shelved off into the region of the ideal, where they were contemplated, admired, discussed, but not worshipped even like their statues by Praxiteles and their pictures by Parrhasius.

The divinities who continued to be reverenced were the rustic divinities and the foreign gods and goddesses; the divinities which had been safe from the artistic desecration of the cities, and the divinities which were imported from hieratic, unartistic countries like Egypt and Syria; on the one hand, the gods shaped with the pruning-knife out of figwood, and stained with ochre or wine-lees, grotesque mannikins, standing like scarecrows, in orchard or corn-field, to which the peasants crowded in devout procession, leading their cleanly-dressed little ones, and carrying gifts of fruit and milk, while the listless Tibullus, fresh from sceptical Rome, looked on from his doorstep, a vague, childish veneration stealing over his mind; on the other hand, the monstrous goddesses, hundred-breasted or ibis-headed, half hidden in the Syrian and Egyptian temples, surrounded by mysterious priests, swarthy or effeminate, in mitres and tawny robes, jangling their *sistra* and clashing their cymbals, moving in mystic or frenzied dances, weird, obscene, and unearthly, to the melancholy drone of Phrygian or Egyptian music, sending a shudder through the atheist Catullus, and filling his mind with ghastly visions of victims of the great goddess, bleeding, fainting, lashed on to madness by the wrath of the terrible divinity.

These were the last survivors of paganism, and to their protection clung the old gods of Greece and Rome, reduced to human level by art, stripped naked by sculptor and poet and muffling themselves in the homely or barbaric garments of lowborn or outlandish usurpers; art had been a worse enemy than scepticism: Apelles and Scopas had done more mischief than Epicurus.

Christian art was, perhaps, more reverent in intention, but not less desecrating in practice; even the Giottesques turned Christ, the Virgin, and the Saints, into mere Florentine men and women; even Angelico himself, although a saint, was unable to show Paradise except as a flowery meadow, under a highly gilded sky, through which moved ladies and youths in most artistic but most earthly embroidered garments; and Hell except as a very hot place where men and women were being boiled and broiled and baked and fried and roasted by very comic little weasel-snouted fiends, which on a carnival car would have made Florentines roar with laughter. The real supernatural was in the cells of fever-stricken, starved visionaries; it was in the contagious awe of the crowd sinking down at the sight of the stained napkin of Bolsena; in that soiled piece of linen was Christ, and God, and Paradise; in that and not in the panels of Angelico and Perugino, or in the *frescoes* of Signorelli and Filippino.

Why? Because the supernatural is nothing but ever-renewed impressions, ever-shifting fancies; and that art is the definer, the embodier, the analytic and synthetic force of form. Every artistic embodiment of impressions or fancies implies isolation of those impressions or fancies, selection, combination and balancing of them; that is to say, diminution—nay, destruction of their inherent power.

As, in order to be moulded, the clay must be separated from the mound; as, in order to be carved, the wood must be cut off from the tree; as, in order to be re-shaped by art, the mass of atoms must be rudely severed; so also the mental elements of art, the mood, the fancy must be severed from the preceding and succeeding moods or fancies; artistic manipulation requires that its intellectual, like its tangible materials, cease to be vital, but the materials, mental or physical, are not only deprived of vitality and power of self-alteration; they are combined in given proportions, the action of the one on the other destroys in great part the special power of each; art is proportion, and proportion is restriction. Last of all, but most important, these isolated, no longer vital materials, neutralised by each other, are further reduced to insignificance by becoming parts of a whole conception; their separate meaning is effaced by the general meaning of the work of art; art bottles lightning to use it as white colour, and measures out thunder by the beat of the chapel-master's roll of notes.

But art does not merely restrict impressions and fancies within the limits of form; in its days of maturity and independence it restricts yet closer within the limits of beauty. Partially developed art, still unconscious of its powers and aims, still in childish submission to religion, sets to work conscientiously, with no other object than to embody the supernatural; if the supernatural suffers in the act of embodiment, if the fluctuating fancies which are Zeus or Pallas are limited and curtailed, rendered logical and prosaic even in the wooden pre-historic idol or the roughly kneaded clay owlet, it is by no choice of the artist—his attempt is abortive, because it is thwarted by the very nature of his art.

But when art is mature, things are different; the artist, conscious of his powers, instinctively recognising the futility of aiming at the embodiment of the supernatural, dragged by an irresistible longing to the display of his skill, to the imitation of the existing and to the creation of beauty, ceases to strain after the impossible and refuses to attempt anything beyond the possible. The art, which was before a mere insufficient means, is now an all-engrossing aim; unconsciously, perhaps, to himself, the artist regards the subject merely as a pretext for the treatment; and where the subject is opposed to such treatment as he desires, he sacrifices it. He may be quite as conscientious as his earliest predecessor, but his conscience has become an artistic conscience, he sees only as much as is within art's limits; the gods, or the saints, which were cloudy and supernatural to the artist of immature art, are definite and artistic to the artist of mature art; he can think, imagine, feel only in a given manner; his religious conceptions have taken the shape of his artistic creations; art has destroyed the supernatural, and the artist has swallowed up the believer.

The attempts at supernatural effects are almost always limited to a sort of symbolical abbreviation, which satisfies the artist and his public respecting the subject of the work, and lends it a traditional association of the supernatural; a few spikes round the head of a young man are all that remains of the solar nature of Apollo; the little budding horns and pointed ears of the satyr must suffice to recall that he was once a mystic fusion of man and beast and forest; a gilded disc behind the head is all that shows that Giotto's figures are immortals in glory; and a pair of wings is all that explains that Perugino's St. Michael is not a mere dainty mortal warrior; the highest mysteries of Christianity are despatched with a triangle and an open book, to draw which Raphael might employ his colour-grinder, while he himself drew the finely-draped baker's daughter from Trastevere.

In all these cases the artist refused to grapple with the supernatural, and dismissed it with a mere stereotyped symbol, not more artistic than the names which he might have engraved beneath each figure. Religious associations were thus awakened without the artist, whether of the time of Pericles or of the time of Leo X., giving himself further trouble; the diffusion of religious ideas and feeling spared art from being religious. Let us, therefore, in order to judge fairly of what art can or cannot do for the supernatural, seek for one of the very rare instances in which the artist has had no symbolical abbreviations at his disposal, and has been obliged, if he would awaken any idea in the mind of the spectator, to do so by means of his artistic creations. The number of such exceptional instances is extremely limited in the great art of antiquity and the Renaissance, when artistic subjects were almost always traditionally religious or plainly realistic, and consequently intelligible at first sight.

There is, however, an example, and that example is a masterpiece. It is the engraving by Agostino Veneziano, after a lost drawing by Raphael, generally called "Lo Stregozzo," and representing a witch going to the Sabbath. Through a swampy country, amidst rank and barren vegetation, sweeps the triumphal procession—strange, beautiful, and ghastly; a naked boy dashes headlong in front, bestriding a long-haired he-goat, and blowing a horn, little stolen children packed behind on his saddle; on he dashes, across the tufts of marsh-lily and bulrush, across the stagnant-pools of water, clearing the way and announcing his mistress the witch. She thrones, old, parched, lank, high on the top of an unearthly car, made of the spine and ribs of some antediluvian creature, with springs and traces of ghastly jaw and collar and thigh bones, supported on either side by galloping skeletons, skeletons made up of skeletons, of all that is strangest in the bones and beaks of beasts and birds, on which ride young fauns and satyrs. To her chariot, by a yoke of human bones, are harnessed two stalwart naked youths, and two others sustain its plough-like end; grand, magnificently moving figures, bounding forward like wild horses, the unearthly carriage swinging and creaking as they go.

And, as they go, brushing through the high, dry, maremma-grass, the witch cowers on her chariot, clutching in one hand a heap of babies, in the other a vessel filled with fire, whose smoke, mingling with her long, dishevelled hair, floats behind, sweeping through the rank vegetation, curling and eddying into vague, strange semblances of lions, apes, chimæras. Forward dashes the outrunner on his goat, onward bound the naked litter-bearers; up gallop the fauns and satyrs on the fleshless, monstrous carcases; up and down sways the creaking, cracking chariot of bones; one moment more, and the wild, splendid, hideous triumph will have swept out of sight, leaving behind only trampled marsh-plants and a trail of fantastic, lurid smoke among the ruffled, moaning reeds and grasses.

Such is Raphael's *Stregozzo*. It is a master-piece of drawing and of pictorial fancy, it is perhaps the highest achievement of great art in the direction of the supernatural: for Dürer is often hideous, Rembrandt always obscure, and the moderns, like Blake and Doré, distinctly run counter to the essential nature of art in their attempts after vagueness. When once told the subject of the print, by Agostino Veneziano, our imagination easily flies off on to the track of the supernatural; but, in so doing, it leaves the work behind, and on return to it we experience a return to the natural. If, on the other hand, we are not told the subject of the print, we very possibly see nothing supernatural in it: there are splendid figures worthy of Michael Angelo, and grotesque fancies, in the shape of the skeletons and coach of bones, worthy of Leonardo; as a whole, the print is striking, beautiful, and problematic, but it falls short of the effect which would be produced by the mere words "a witch riding through a marsh on a chariot of bones," if left to insinuate themselves into the imagination.

Of the really supernatural, there is in it but one touch: and that in the only part of the drawing which is left vague; it is the confused shapes assumed by the eddying smoke among the rushes. All the rest is outside the region of the supernatural: it is problematic in subject, but clear, harmonious, and beautiful in treatment; the imagination may wander off from it, but in its presence it must remain passive. With this masterpiece we would fain compare a picture which seems to deal with a cognate subject; a picture as suggestive as it is absolutely artistically worthless.

We saw it once, many years ago, among a heap of rubbishy smudges at a picture-dealer's in Rome, and we have never forgotten it—a picture painted by some German smearer of the early sixteenth century; very ugly, stupid, and unattractive; ill drawn, ill composed, of a uniform hard, vulgar brown. It represented, with no attempt at perspective, a level country spread out like a map, dotted here and there with little spired and turretted towns, also a castle or two, a few trees and some rivers, disposed with a child's satisfaction with their mere indication, as much as to say—"here is a town, there is a castle." Some peasants were represented working in the fields, a little train of horsemen coming out of a castle, and near one of the chess-board castles a grass plot with half-a-dozen lit stakes, to which tiny figures were carrying faggots, while men-at-arms and *burghers*, no bigger than flies, looked on.

In the foreground of the great flat expanse lay a boor, a fellow dressed like a field-labourer, in heavy sleep on the ground. Round him on the grass were marked curious circles, and in them was moving a strange figure, in cloak and helmet, with clawed wings and horns, leering horridly, moving round on tiptoe, his arms outstretched, as if gradually encircling the sleeper in order to pounce upon him; despite the complete absence of artistic skill, the gradual inevitable approach of the demon, the irresistible network of circles with which he was surrounding his prey, was perfectly indicated.

Above, in the sky, two figures, half demon, half dragon, floated leisurely, like a moored boat, as if a guard of the devil below. What is the exact subject of this picture? No one can tell; but its meaning is intense for the imagination, it has the frightful suggestiveness of some old book on witchcraft, prosaic and curt; of a page opened at random of Sprenger's *Malleus Malificarum*. Yes; over the plain, the towns, and castles, monotonous and dull, the fiends are hovering; even over the stakes where their votaries are being burnt; and see, the peasant asleep in the field, with his spade and hoe beside him, is being surrounded by magic circles, by the invisible nets of the demon, who prowls round him like a kite ready to pounce on to its quarry.

Why is there no need to write the word *witchcraft* beneath this picture? Why can this nameless smearer succeed where Raphael has failed? Because he is content to suggest to the imagination, and lets it create for itself its world of the supernatural; because he is not an artist, and because Raphael is; because he suggests everything and shows nothing, while Raphael creates, defines, perfects, gives form to that which is by its nature formless.

If we would bring home to ourselves this action of art on the supernatural, we must examine the only species of supernatural which still retains vitality, and can still be deprived of it by art. That which remains to us of the imaginative workings of the past is traditional and well-nigh effete: we have poems and pictures, Vedic hymns, Hebrew psalms, and Egyptian symbols; we have folklore and dogma; remnants of the supernatural, some labelled in our historic museums, where they are scrutinised, catalogue and eye-glass in hand; others dusty on altars and in chapels, before which we uncover our heads and cast down our eyes: relics of dead and dying faiths, of which some are daily being transferred from the church to the museum; art cannot deprive any of these of that imaginative life and power which they have long ceased to possess.

We have forms of the supernatural in which we believe from acquiescence of habit, but they are not vital; we have a form of the supernatural in which, from logic and habit, we disbelieve, but which is vital; and this form of the supernatural is the ghostly. We none of us believe in ghosts as logical possibilities, but we most of us conceive them as imaginative probabilities; we can still feel the ghostly, and thence it is that a ghost is the only thing which can in any respect replace for us the divinities of old, and enable us to understand, if only for a minute, the imaginative power which they possessed, and of which they were despoiled not only by logic, but by art. By *ghost* we do not mean the vulgar apparition which is seen or heard in told or written tales; we mean the ghost which slowly rises up in our mind, the haunter not of corridors and staircases, but of our fancies.

Just as the gods of primitive religions were the undulating, bright heat which made mid-day solitary and solemn as midnight; the warm damp, the sap-riser and expander of life; the sad dying away of the summer, and the leaden, suicidal sterility of winter; so the ghost, their only modern equivalent, is the damp, the darkness, the silence, the solitude; a ghost is the sound of our steps through a ruined cloister, where the ivy-berries and convolvulus growing in the fissures sway up and down among the sculptured foliage of the windows, it is the scent of mouldering plaster and mouldering bones from beneath the broken pavement; a ghost is the bright moonlight against which the cypresses stand out like black hearse-plumes, in which the blasted grey olives and the gnarled fig-trees stretch their branches over the broken walls like fantastic, knotted, beckoning fingers, and the abandoned villas on the outskirts of Italian towns, with the birds flying in and out of the unglazed windows, loom forth white and ghastly; a ghost is the long-closed room of one long dead, the faint smell of withered flowers, the rustle of long-unmoved curtains, the yellow paper and faded ribbons of long-unread letters ... each and all of these things, and a hundred others besides, according to our nature, is a ghost, a vague feeling we can scarcely describe, a something pleasing and terrible which invades our whole consciousness, and which, confusedly embodied, we half dread to see behind us, we know not in what shape, if we look round.

Call we in our artist, or let us be our own artist; embody, let us see or hear this ghost, let it become visible or audible to others besides ourselves; paint us that vagueness, mould into shape that darkness, modulate into chords that silence—tell us the character and history of those vague beings. . . . set to work boldly or cunningly. What do we obtain? A picture, a piece of music, a story; but the ghost is gone. In its stead we get oftenest the mere image of a human being; call it a ghost if you will, it is none. And the more complete the artistic work, the less remains of the ghost. Why do those stories affect us most in which the ghost is heard but not seen? Why do those places affect us most of which we merely vaguely know that they are haunted? Why most of all those which look as if they might be haunted? Why, as soon as a figure is seen, is the charm half-lost?

And why, even when there is a figure, is it kept so vague and mist-like? Would you know Hamlet's father for a ghost unless he told you he was one? and can you remember it long while he speaks in mortal words? and what would be Hamlet's father without the terrace of Elsinore, the hour, and the moonlight? Do not these embodied ghosts owe what little effect they still possess to their surroundings, and are not the surroundings the real ghost?

Throw sunshine on to them, and what remains? Thus we have wandered through the realm of the supernatural in a manner neither logical nor business-like, for logic and business-likeness are rude qualities, and scare away the ghostly; very far away do we seem to have rambled from Dr. Faustus and Helen of Sparta;

but in this labyrinth of the fantastic there are sudden unexpected turns—and see, one of these has suddenly brought us back into their presence. For we have seen why the supernatural is always injured by artistic treatment, why therefore the confused images evoked in our mind by the mere threadbare tale of Faustus and Helena are superior in imaginative power to the picture carefully elaborated and shown us by Goethe. We can now understand why under his hand the infinite charm of the weird meeting of antiquity and the Middle Ages has evaporated. We can explain why the strange fancy of the classic Walpurgis-night, in the second part of *Faust*, at once stimulates the imagination and gives it nothing.

If we let our mind dwell on that mysterious Pharsalian plain, with its glimmering fires and flamelets alone breaking the darkness, where Faust and Mephistopheles wandering about meet the spectres of antiquity, shadowy in the gloom—the sphinxes crouching, the sirens, the dryads and oreads, the griffons and cranes flapping their unseen wings overhead; where Faust springs on the back of Chiron, and as he is borne along sickens for sudden joy when the centaur tells him that Helen has been carried on that back, has clasped that neck; when we let our mind work on all this, we are charmed by the weird meetings, the mysterious shapes which elbow us; but let us take up the volume and we return to barren prose, without colour or perfume.

Yet Goethe felt the supernatural as we feel it, as it can be felt only in days of disbelief, when the more logical we become in our ideas, the more we view nature as a prosaic machine constructed by no one in particular, the more poignantly, on the other hand, do we feel the delight of the transient belief in the vague and the impossible; the greater the distinctness with which we see and understand all around us, the greater the longing for a momentary half-light in which forms may appear stranger, grander, vaguer than they are. We moderns seek in the world of the supernatural a renewal of the delightful semi-obscurity of vision and keenness of fancy of our childhood; when a glimpse into fairyland was still possible, when things appeared in false lights, brighter, more important, more magnificent than now.

Art indeed can afford us calm and clear enjoyment of the beautiful—enjoyment serious, self-possessed, wide-awake, such as befits mature intellects; but no picture, no symphony, no poem, can give us that delight, that delusory, imaginative pleasure which we received as children from a tawdry engraving or a hideous doll; for around that doll there was an atmosphere of glory. In certain words, in certain sights, in certain snatches of melody, words, sights, and sounds which we now recognise as trivial, commonplace, and vulgar, there was an ineffable meaning; they were spells which opened doors into realms of wonder; they were precious in proportion as they were misappreciated.

We now appreciate and despise; we see, we no longer imagine. And it is to replace this uncertainty of vision, this liberty of seeing in things much more than there is, which belongs to man and to mankind in this childhood, which compensated the Middle Ages for starvation and pestilence, and compensates the child for blows and lessons, it is to replace this that we crave after the supernatural, the ghostly—no longer believed, but still felt.

It was from this sickness of the prosaic, this turning away from logical certainty, that the men of the end of the eighteenth and the beginning of this century, the men who had finally destroyed belief in the religious supernatural, who were bringing light with new sciences of economy, philology, and history— Schiller, Goethe, Herder, Coleridge—left the lecture-room and the laboratory, and set gravely to work on ghostly tales and ballads. It was from this rebellion against the tyranny of the possible that Goethe was charmed with that culmination of all impossibilities, that most daring of ghost stories, the story of Faustus and Helena. He felt the seduction of the supernatural, he tried to embody it—and he failed.

The case was different with Marlowe. The bringing together of Faustus and Helena had no special meaning for the man of the sixteenth century, too far from antiquity and too near the Middle Ages to perceive as we do the strange difference between them; and the supernatural had no fascination in a time when it was all permeating and everywhere mixed with prose. The whole play of Dr. *Faustus* is conceived in a thoroughly realistic fashion; it is tragic, but not ghostly. To Marlowe's audience, and probably to Marlowe himself, despite his atheistic reputation, the story of Faustus's wonders and final damnation was quite within the realm of the possible; the intensity of the belief in the tale is shown by the total absence of any attempt to give it dignity or weirdness.

Faustus evokes Lucifer with a pedantic semi-biblical Latin speech; he goes about playing the most trumpery conjuror's tricks—snatching with invisible hands the food from people's lips, clapping horns and tails on to courtiers for the Emperor's amusement, letting his legs be pulled off like boots, selling wisps of straw as horses, doing and saying things which could appear tragic and important, nay, even serious, only to people who took every second cat for a witch, who burned their neighbours for vomiting pins, who suspected devils at every turn, as the great witch-expert Sprenger shows them in his horribly matter-of-fact manual.

We moderns, disbelieving in devilries, would require the most elaborately romantic and poetic accessories—a splendid lurid back-ground, a magnificent Byronian invocation of the fiend. The Mephistophilis of Marlowe, in those days when devils still dwelt in people, required none of Goethe's wit or poetry; the mere fact of his being a devil, with the very real association of flame and brimstone in this world and the next, was sufficient to inspire interest in him; whereas in 1800, with Voltaire's novels and Hume's treatises on the table, a dull devil was no more endurable than any other sort of bore. The very superiority of Marlowe is due to this absence of weirdness, to this complete realism; the last scene of the English play is infinitely above the end of the second part of *Faust* in tragic grandeur, just because Goethe made abortive attempts, after a conscious and artificial supernatural, while Marlowe was satisfied with perfect reality of situation.

The position of Faustus, when the years of his pact have expired, and he awaits midnight, which will give him over to Lucifer, is as thoroughly natural in the eyes of Marlowe as is in the eyes of Shelley the position of Beatrice Cenci awaiting the moment of execution. The conversation between Faustus and the scholars, after he has made his will, is terribly life-like: they disbelieve at first, pooh-pooh his danger; then, half-convinced, beg that a priest may be fetched; but Faustus cannot deal with priests. He bids them, in agony, go pray in the next room. "Aye, pray for me, pray for me, and what noise soever you hear, come not unto me, for nothing can save me . . . . Gentlemen, farewell; if I live till morning, I'll visit you; if not, Faustus is gone to hell." Faustus remains alone for the one hour which separates him from his doom; he clutches at the passing time, he cries to the hours to stop with no rhetorical figure of speech, but with a terrible reality of agony:

Let this hour be but
A year, a month, a week, a natural day,
That Faustus may repent and save his soul.

Time to repent, time to recoil from the horrible gulf into which he is being sucked; Christ, will Christ's blood not save him? He would leap up to heaven and cling fast, but Lucifer drags him down. He would seek annihilation in nature, be sucked into its senseless, feelingless mass . . . .and, meanwhile, the time is passing, the interval of respite is shrinking and dwindling. Would that he were a soulless brute and might perish, or that at least eternal hell were finite—a thousand, a hundred thousand years let him suffer, but not for ever and without end! Midnight begins striking. With convulsive agony he exclaims as the rain patters against the window:

O soul, be changed into small water-drops,
And fall into the ocean, ne'er be found.

But the twelfth stroke sounds; Lucifer and his crew enter; and when next morning the students, frightened by the horrible tempest and ghastly noises of the night, enter his study, they find

Faustus lying dead, torn and mangled by the demon. All this is not supernatural in our sense; such scenes as this were real for Marlowe and his audience. Such cases were surely not unfrequent; more than one man certainly watched through such a night in hopeless agony, conscious, like Faustus, of pact with the fiend—awaiting, with earth and heaven shut and bolted against him, eternal hell.

In this story of Doctor Faustus, which, to Marlowe and his contemporaries, was not a romance but a reality, the episode of the evoking of Helen is extremely secondary in interest. To raise a dead woman was not more wonderful than to turn wisps of straw into horses, and it was perhaps considered the easier of the two miracles; the sense of the ordinary ghostly is absent, and the sense that Helen is the ghost of a whole long-dead civilisation, that sense which is for us the whole charm of the tale, could not exist in the sixteenth century. Goethe's Faust feels for Helen as Goethe himself might have felt, as Winckelmann felt for a lost antique statue, as Schiller felt for the dead Olympus: a passion intensely imaginative and poetic, born of deep appreciation of antiquity, the essentially modern, passionate, nostalgic craving for the past.

In Marlowe's play, on the contrary, Faustus and the students evoke Helen from a confused pedantic impression that an ancient lady must be as much superior to a modern lady as an ancient poem, be it even by Statius or Claudian, must be superior to a modern poem—it is a humanistic fancy of the days of the revival of letters. But, by a strange phenomenon, Marlowe, once realising what Helen means, that she is the fairest of women, forgets the scholarly interest in her. Faustus, once in presence of the wonderful woman, forgets that he had summoned her up to gratify his and his friends' pedantry; he sees her, loves her, and bursts out into the splendid tirade full of passionate fancy:

Was this the face that launched a thousand ships,
And burnt the topless towers of Ilium?
Sweet Helen, make me immortal with a kiss!
Her lips suck forth my soul! See, where it flies!

Come, Helen, come, give me my soul again
Here will I dwell, for Heaven is in these lips
And all is dross that is not Helena.
I will be Paris, and for love of thee,
Instead of Troy shall Wittenberg be sacked;
And I will combat with weak Menelaus,
And wear thy colours on my plumed crest;
Yea, I will wound Achilles in the heel
And then return to Helen for a kiss.
Oh! thou art fairer than the evening air
Clad in the beauty of a thousand stars;
Brighter art thou than flaming Jupiter
When he appeared to hapless Semele;
More lovely than the monarch of the sky
In wanton Arethusa's azure arms;
And none but thou shalt be my paramour.

This is real passion for a real woman, a woman very different from the splendid semi-vivified statue of Goethe, the Helen with only the cold, bloodless, intellectual life which could be infused by enthusiastic studies of ancient literature and art, gleaming bright like marble or a spectre. This Helena of Marlowe is no antique; the Elizabethan dramatist, like the painter of the fifteenth century, could not conceive the purely antique, despite all the translating of ancient writers, and all the drawing from ancient marbles. One of the prose versions of the story of Faustus, contains a quaint account of Helen, which sheds much light on Marlowe's conception:

This lady appeared before them in a most rich gowne of purple velvet, costly imbrodered; her haire hanged downe loose, as faire as the beaten gold, and of such length that it reached downe to her hammes; having most amorous cole-black eyes, a sweet and pleasant round face, with lips as red as a cherry; her cheeks of a rose colour, her mouth small, her neck white like a swan; tall and slender of personage; in summe, there was no imperfect place in her; she looked around about with a rolling hawk's eye, a smiling and wanton countenance, which neerehand inflamed the hearts of all the students, but that they persuaded themselves she was a spirit, which make them lightly passe away such fancies.

This fair dame in the velvet embroidered gown, with the long, hanging hair, this Helen of the original Faustus legend, is antique only in name; she belongs to the race of medieval and modern women—the Lauras, Fiammettas, and Simonettas of Petrarch, Boccaccio, and Lorenzo dei Medici; she is the sister of that slily sentimental *coquette*, the Monna Lisa of Leonardo. The strong and simple women of Homer, and even of Euripides, majestic and matronly even in shame, would repudiate this slender, smiling, ogling beauty; Briseis, though the captive of Achilles' spear, would turn with scorn from her. The antique woman has a dignity due to her very inferiority and restrictedness of position; she has the simplicity, the completeness, the absence of everything suggestive of degradation, like that of some stately animal, pure in its animal nature.

The modern woman, with more freedom and more ideal, rarely approaches to this character; she is too complex to be perfect, she is frail because she has an ideal, she is dubious because she is free, she may fall because she may rise. Helen deserted Menelaus and brought ruin upon Troy, therefore, in the eyes of antiquity, she was the victim of fate, she might be unruffled, spotless, majestic; but to the man of the sixteenth century she was merely frail and false. The rolling hawk's eye and the wanton smile of the old legend-monger would have perplexed Homer, but they were necessary for Marlowe; his Helen was essentially modern, he had probably no inkling that an antique Helen as distinguished from a modern could exist. In the paramour of Faustus he saw merely the most beautiful woman, some fair and wanton creature, dressed not in chaste and majestic antique drapery, but in fantastic garments of lawn, like those of Hero in his own poem:

The lining purple silk, with gilt stars drawn;
Her wide sleeves green, and bordered with a grove
Where Venus, in her naked glory strove
To please the careless and disdainful eyes
Of proud Adonis, that before her lies;
Her kirtle blue. . . .
Upon her head she wore a myrtle wreath
From whence her veil reached to the ground beneath;
Her veil was artificial flowers and leaves
Whose workmanship both man and beast deceives.

Some slim and dainty goddess of Botticelli, very mortal withal, long and sinuous, tightly clad in brocaded garments and clinging cobweb veils, beautiful with the delicate, diaphanous beauty, rather emaciated and hectic, of high rank, and the conscious, elaborate fascination of a woman of fashion—a creature whom, like the Gioconda, Leonardo might have spent years in decking and painting, ever changing the ornaments and ever altering the portrait; to whom courtly poets like Bembo and Castiglione might have written scores of sonnets and *canzoni* to her hands, her eyes, her hair, her lips, a fanciful inventory to which she listened languidly under the cypresses of Florentine gardens.

Some such being, even rarer and more dubious for being an exotic in the England of Elizabeth, was Marlowe's Helen; such, and not a ghostly figure, descended from a pedestal, white and marble-like in her unruffled drapery, walking with solid step and unswerving, placid glance through the study, crammed with books, and vials, and strange instruments, of the medieval wizard of Wittenberg. Marlowe deluded himself as well as Faustus, and palmed off on to him a mere modern lady. To raise a real spectre of the antique is a craving of our own century; Goethe attempted to do it and failed, for what reasons we have seen; but we have all of us the charm wherewith to evoke for ourselves a real Helena, on condition that, unlike Faustus and unlike Goethe, we seek not to show her to others, and remain satisfied if the weird and glorious figure haunt only our own imagination.

Pope Jacynth

A Story from *Pope Jacynth and Other Fantastic Tales*
Forming a portion of the *Codex Eburneus* of the suppressed
Abbey of Nonantola

1

It was Pope Jacynth who built anew the basilica over the bodies of the holy martyrs, Paul and John, brothers; and who wainscoted the choir, and laid down the flooring, and set up the columns of the nave, a row on either side, all of precious marble. And it was of his death and the marvellous thing which was seen afterward, showing indeed the justice of God and His infinite mercy, that the following tale is told.

This Jacynth, whose name in the world and in the cloister was Odo, was known all through Italy, and through the Marquisate of Tuscany and the County of Benevento, and the Kingdom of Sicily and such dominions as belonged to the Grecian Emperors, for his great and unparalleled humility and his exceeding ardent and exclusive love of God. And in these lay his ruin. For, even as is written in the book of the Prophet Job, which it were sin for any layman to read, and damnation for any clerk to translate, that the Lord allowed Satan to try his faithful servant with many plagues and doubts and evil incitements, so it pleased Him who is the Mirror of all Truth, to make a wager with Satan concerning the soul of this man Odo or otherwise Jacynth. And this when he was still in his mother's womb.

For the Lord said to Satan: 'I grant leave that thou tempt any man whatsoever at My choice among such as shall be born into the world before the sun, which turns for ever round earth, shall have gone back to the spot where it now is.'

And Satan caused the man Odo, afterwards Jacynth, to be born to the greatest dignity in his land, even to be firstborn of Averard, Marquis of Tusculum. But Odo cared not for the greatness of his birth, and the wealth of his father's house. And, being only fourteen years of age, he fled from his parents and went on the ship of a certain mariner, who brought wine and tanned hides and fair white stone for building from Greece, Istria, and Salernum, to the port of Rome, which is below Mount Aventine, and took back the fleece of sheep and thin cheese, and slabs of porphyry and serpentine from the temples of the heathen.

But Satan caused Odo to grow most marvellously in beauty and shapeliness of body and loveliness of countenance and sweetness of voice, so that pirates captured him and sold him, being eighteen years of age, to Alecto, Queen of the Amazons, which inhabit the isles beyond the pillars of Hercules, and are most wondrously fair women. And Queen Alecto became enamoured of the beauty of Odo, otherwise Jacynth, and offered him her love and every delight. But Jacynth scourged himself with ropes of thistles, and ate only of the fruit of the prickly pear and drank only of water from the marshes; and he shaved his head and stained his face with certain herbs, and consorted with lepers, and spurned the queen and her delicates.

Then Satan caused Odo, otherwise Jacynth, to increase most mightily in strength and courage, so that he could wrestle with the lions in the desert and cleave a strong man in twain with one blow. So that the people, seeing his might and wondering greatly thereat) made him their captain, captain even over hundreds, that he might avenge them on certain wicked kings, their neighbours, and clear the country of robbers and wild beasts. But when he had put the kings in chains and thrown the robbers into dungeons, and exterminated the wild beasts, Jacynth, who was then called Odo, put up his sword and allowed not that any man should be killed or sold into captivity, and bade them desist from slaying the hares and deer and wild asses, saying that these also were creatures of God and worthy of kindness. And he was at this time thirty-two years of age.

Then Satan caused Odo, later to be called Jacynth, to exceed all other men in subtlety of mind. And he learned all languages, both living and dead, as those of the Grecians, Romans, Ethiopians, and even of Armorica and Taprobane; and studied all books on philosophy, divine and natural astrology, medicine, music, alchemy, the properties of herbs and numbers, magic and poetry and rhetoric, whatsoever books have been written since the building of Babel, when all languages were dispersed. And he went from place to place teaching and disputing; and whithersoever he went, and mostly in Paris and at Salernum, did he challenge all doctors, rabbis, and men of learning to discuss with him on any subject of their choosing, and always did he demonstrate before all men that their arguments were wrong and their science vain. But when Odo, otherwise Jacynth, had done this, he burned his books, save the gospels, and retired to a monastery of his founding. And he was at this time forty and five years of age.

Then Satan caused Odo, later called Jacynth, to become wondrously knowing of the heart of man and his wickedness, and wondrous full of unction and fervour, and all men came to his monastery, which was called Clear Streams, and listened to his preaching and reformed their ways, and many put themselves under his rule, and of these there were such multitudes that the monastery would not hold them, and others had to be built in all parts of the world. And kings and emperors confessed to him their sins, and stood at his bidding clothed in sackcloth at the church door, singing the penitential psalms and holding lighted tapers.

But Odo, later called Jacynth, instituted abbots and heads of the order, and for himself retired into the wild places of the mountains and built himself there a hermitage of stone quarried with his own hands, and planted fruit-trees and pot-herbs, and lived there alone, praying and meditating, high up near the wellhead of the river which runs down through the woods to the

Tyrrhene Sea. And he was sixty years of age.

And Satan went up before the Lord and said, 'Verily I can tempt him yet grant me, I pray Thee, but the use of Thine own tools, and I will bring Thee the soul of this man bound in mortal sin.'

And the Lord answered, 'I grant it'

And at the prayer of Satan, God caused him to be acclaimed as pope. And the cardinals and prelates and princes of the earth journeyed to the hermitage, and sought for the man Odo, who henceforth was to be called Jacynth. And they found him in his orchard pruning a fig-tree, and by his side were the herbs for his supper in a clean platter, and the gospel lay on his lectern, and there stood by it a tame goat, ready to be milked; and on a hook hung his red hat, and a crucifix was by the lectern. And in the wall of his garden, which was small, with a well in the midst and set round with wooden pillars, was a window, with a pillar carved of stone in the middle, and through the window one could see the oak woods below, and the olive-yards, and the river winding through the valley, and the Tyrrhene Sea, with ships sailing, in the distance.

Now when he saw the cardinals and prelates and princes of the earth, Odo, who was thenceforth called Jacynth, put down his pruning-hook; and when he had heard their message he wept, and knelt before the crucifix, and wept again, and cried, 'Woe's me! Terrible are the trials of Thy servants, O Lord, and great must be Thy mercy.' But he went with them to be crowned Pope, because his heart was full of humbleness and the love of God. And Pope Jacynth, formerly Odo, was seventy-five years of age when they set him on his throne.

And the Lord called to him Satan, and was angered, and said, 'What wilt thou do next. Accursed One?'

And Satan replied, 'I will do no more, O Lord. Suffer this man but to live the space of five years, and then watch we for our wager.'

And they took Pope Jacynth, once called Odo, and carried him to the palace, which is over against the Church of St Peter, and before which stands the pine cone of brass, made as a talisman by the Emperor Adrian. And they arrayed him in fine linen from Egypt, and silk from Byzantium, as befits a Pope; and his cope was of beaten gold, even gold beaten to the thinness of a leaf, wrought all over with the history of our Lord and His Apostles, with a border of lambs and lilies, a lamb and a lily all the way turn about And his stole was likewise of gold, gold plates cunningly riveted, and it was set all round with precious stones, emeralds, and opals, and beryls and sardonyxes, and the stone called *Melitta*, all perfectly round and the size of a pigeon's egg; and two goodly graven stones of the ancients, one showing a chariot-race and the other the effigy of the Emperor Galba, most cunningly cut in relief.

And his mitre also was of riveted gold, and inside it was fastened the lance-head of Longinus, which touched the flesh of our Lord; and on the outside it was bordered with pearls, and in its midst was a sapphire the size of a swan's egg, worked marvellously into a cup, which was the cup that the Angel brought to our Lord. And when they had arrayed Pope Jacynth in this apparel, they placed him in his chair, which was of cedar-wood covered with plates of gold, and they bore him, eight bearers, namely, three counts, three marquises, a duke and the Exarch of the Pentapolis, on their shoulders; and the cushions of his chair were of silk. And over him they bore a canopy embroidered most marvellously with the signs of the Zodiac by the Matrons of Amalfi. And before him went two carrying fans of the feathers of the white peacock, and two bearing censers filled with burning ambergris, and six blowing on clarions of silver.

And in this manner was he enthroned above the place where rests the body of the Apostle, behind the ambones of onion stone, and the railing of alabaster openwork showing peacocks and vine leaves, and under the dome where our Lord sits in judgment on a ground of purple and sea-green and gold, and the holy lambs pasture on green enamel, each with a palm tree by his side, and the great gold vine rises on a ground of turquoise blue. And on either side of the throne was a column of precious marble taken from a temple of the heathen, even a column of red porphyry from the temple of Mars, and a column of alabaster, cunningly fluted, from the temple of Apollo. And the bells in the belfry, which is set with discs of serpentine and platters from Majorca, began to ring, and the trumpets to sound, and all the people sang the psalm *Magnificat* And the heart of Pope Jacynth, formerly called Odo, was filled with joy and pride, because in the midst of his glory he knew himself to be more humble than the lepers outside the city gate. And the people prostrated themselves before Pope Jacynth, and prayed for his blessing.

And Pope Jacynth slept on the rushes in his chamber, and drank only water from the well and eat only salad, and beneath his robe he wore a shirt of camel's hair, mighty rough to the body. And he gloried in his humbleness. And he took of the money of the jubilee year, which twenty priests raked with silver rakes where the pilgrims passed the bridge by the Emperor Adrian's tomb, and would have none of it for himself, but distributed half to the poor and the widows and orphans, and with the other he caused stonemasons to quarry for marble among the temples of the heathen, and to draw thence the columns having flutings and sculptured capitals to set up in the nave, and to saw into slabs the pillars of porphyry and serpentine and Egyptian marble, for wainscoting and flooring.

And in this fashion did he build the *basilica* by the Ostian gate. And he dedicated it to St John and St Paul, slaves and servants of Flavia, the sister of the Emperor Domitian, meaning to show thereby that in the love of God the lowest are highest; for he gloried in his humbleness. And they brought him blind men, and those with grievous sores, and lepers, to bless, that they might recover. And Pope Jacynth blessed them, and washed their sores and embraced them; and Pope Jacynth gloried in his humility.

Now when Satan saw this, he laughed; and the sound of his laughter was as a rushing wind, that burns the shoots of the wheat (for it was spring), and nipped the blossom of the almond-tree and plum-tree, causing it to fall in great profusion, as every man could testify. And Satan went before the Lord and said: 'Behold, O Lord, I have won my wager. For the man Jacynth, once Odo, has sinned against Thee, even the sin of vaingloriousness; so do Thou give him to me, body and soul.'

And the Lord answered: 'Take thou the man Jacynth, formerly Odo, his body and his soul, and do therewith whatsoever thou please, for he has sinned the sin of vaingloriousness; but for Myself I reserve that which remaineth.'

So Satan departed. And he took the body of Pope Jacynth, and touched it with invisible fingers; and lo, it did gradually turn into stone; and he took the soul of Pope Jacynth, and blew on it, and behold, it shrank slowly and hardened, and became a stone, even a diamond, which, as all know, burns forever.

Now the people and the pilgrims were so amazed at the humility of Pope Jacynth, that they clamoured to see him; and they attacked the gate of the palace over against the Church of St. Peter, the gate which has a gable, and in it our Lord clad in white, on a ground of gold, with a purple halo round his head, all done in mosaic by the Grecians. So the priests and the barons were afraid of the violence of the people and particularly of the pilgrims from the north, and they promised to bring Pope Jacynth for them to worship. And they dressed him in his vestments of beaten and riveted gold, set with precious stones and graven stones, and placed him on his throne of cedar-wood, and the eight bearers, three counts, two marquises, two dukes, and the Exarch of the Pentapolis, raised him on their shoulders and bore him through the square, with the censer-bearers before and the trumpeters and the fans of white peacock.

And the people fell on their knees. Only there stood up one, who afterwards vanished, and was the Apostle Peter, and he cried, 'Behold, Pope Jacynth has turned into an idol, even an idol of the heathen.' But when the people had dispersed, and the procession had entered the church, the throne-bearers knelt down, and the throne was lowered, and behold, Pope Jacynth was dead.

But when the embalmers and the physicians took the body

after three days that it had lain in state, surrounded by tapers, with lamps hung all round, under the mosaic of the dome, they found that it was uncorrupted, and had turned into marble, even marble of Paros, like the idols of the ancient Grecians. And they wondered greatly. And the learned men disputed, and decided that Pope Jacynth, formerly called Odo, must have been a wizard, for this certainly was devilry. So they caused his body to be taken and burned into lime, which, being turned to the finest marble, it readily did. Only, when they came to remove the lime, they found in the midst of it a burning diamond, that instantly vanished, nor was any man in time to seize it. And likewise a thing of the consistency of a dead leaf, and smelling wonderfully of violets, but it was shaped in the image of a heart And it also vanished, nor was any man quick enough to seize it.

Now when he came down from the palace, hard by the pine cone of the Emperor Adrian, Satan did meet an angel of the Lord, even Gabriel, who was entering, wrapped round in wings of golden green. And Satan said, 'Hail! brother, whither goest thou? for there remaineth of the man Jacynth, called formerly Odo, only a little lime, which was his body, and this stone that burneth eternally, which was his soul.' And Satan laughed.

But the angel answered, 'Laugh not, most foolish fellow-servant of the Lord. For I go to seek of the man Odo, sometime called Pope Jacynth, only the heart, which the Lord has reserved for Himself for all eternity, because it was full of love and hope in His mercy.' Now as Gabriel passed by, behold! a pomegranate tree along the wall, which had dried up and died in the frost ten years before, sprouted and put forth buds.

The Legend of Madame Krasinska

A story from *Vanitas*

It is a necessary part of this story to explain how I have come by it, or rather, how it has chanced to have me for its writer.

I was very much impressed one day by a certain nun of the order calling themselves Little Sisters of the Poor. I had been taken to these sisters to support the recommendation of a certain old lady, the former door-keeper of his studio, whom my friend Cecco Bandini wished to place in the asylum. It turned out, of course, that Cecchino was perfectly able to plead his case without my assistance; so I left him blandishing the Mother Superior in the big, cheerful kitchen, and begged to be shown over the rest of the establishment. The sister who was told off to accompany me was the one of whom I would speak.

This lady was tall and slight; her figure, as she preceded me up the narrow stairs and through the whitewashed wards, was uncommonly elegant and charming; and she had a girlish rapidity of movement, which caused me to experience a little shock at the first real sight which I caught of her face. It was young and remarkably pretty, with a kind of refinement peculiar to American women; but it was inexpressibly, solemnly tragic; and one felt that under her tight linen cap, the hair must be snow white. The tragedy, whatever it might have been, was now over; and the lady's expression, as she spoke to the old creatures scraping the ground in the garden, ironing the sheets in the laundry, or merely huddling over their braziers in the chill winter sunshine, was pathetic only by virtue of its strange present tenderness, and by that trace of terrible past suffering.

She answered my questions very briefly, and was as taciturn as ladies of religious communities are usually loquacious. Only, when I expressed my admiration for the institution which contrived to feed scores of old paupers on broken victuals begged from private houses and inns, she turned her eyes full upon me and said, with an earnestness which was almost passionate, "Ah, the old! The old! It is so much, much worse for them than for any others. Have you ever tried to imagine what it is to be poor and forsaken and old?"

These words and the strange ring in the sister's voice, the strange light in her eyes, remained in my memory. What was not, therefore, my surprise when, on returning to the kitchen, I saw her start and lay hold of the back of the chair as soon as she caught sight of Cecco Bandini. Cecco, on his side also, was visibly startled, but only after a moment; it was clear that she recognised him long before he identified her. What little romance could there exist in common between my eccentric painter and that serene but tragic Sister of the Poor?

A week later, it became evident that Cecco Bandini had come to explain the mystery; but to explain it (as I judged by the embarrassment of his manner) by one of those astonishingly elaborate lies occasionally attempted by perfectly frank persons. It was not the case. Cecchino had come indeed to explain that little dumb scene which had passed between him and the Little Sister of the Poor. He had come, however, not to satisfy my curiosity, or to overcome my suspicions, but to execute a commission which he had greatly at heart; to help, as he expressed it, in the accomplishment of a good work by a real saint.

Of course, he explained, smiling that good smile under his black eyebrows and white moustache, he did not expect me to believe very literally the story which he had undertaken to get me to write. He only asked, and the lady only wished, me, to write down her narrative without any comments, and leave to the heart of the reader the decision about its truth or falsehood.

For this reason, and the better to attain the object of appealing to the profane, rather than to the religious, reader, I have abandoned the order of narrative of the Little Sister of the Poor; and attempted to turn her pious legend into a worldly story, as follows:—

1

Cecco Bandini had just returned from the Maremma, to whose solitary marshes and jungles he had fled in one of his fits of fury at the stupidity and wickedness of the civilised world. A great many months spent among buffaloes and wild boars, conversing only with those wild cherry-trees, of whom he used whimsically to say, "they are such good little folk," had sent him back with an extraordinary zest for civilisation, and a comic tendency to find its products, human and otherwise, extraordinary, picturesque, and suggestive. He was in this frame of mind when there came a light rap on his door-slate; and two ladies appeared on the threshold of his studio, with the shaven face and cockaded hat of a tall footman over-topping them from behind. One of them was unknown to our painter; the other was numbered among Cecchino's very few grand acquaintances.

"Why haven't you been round to me yet, you savage?" she asked, advancing quickly with a brusque hand-shake and a brusque bright gleam of eyes and teeth, well-bred but audacious and a trifle ferocious. And dropping on to a divan she added, nodding first at her companion and then at the pictures all round, "I have brought my friend, Madame Krasinska, to see your things," and she began poking with her parasol at the contents of a gaping portfolio.

The Baroness Fosca—for such was her name—was one of the cleverest and fastest ladies of the place, with a taste for art and ferociously frank conversation. To Cecco Bandini, as she lay back among her furs on that shabby divan of his, she appeared in the light of the modern Lucretia Borgia, the tamed panther of fashionable life. "What an interesting thing civilisation is!" he thought, watching her every movement with the eyes of the imagination; "why, you might spend years among the wild folk of the Maremma without meeting such a tremendous, terrible, picturesque, powerful creature as this!"

Cecchino was so absorbed in the Baroness Fosca, who was in reality not at all a Lucretia Borgia, but merely an impatient lady bent upon amusing and being amused, that he was scarcely conscious of the presence of her companion. He knew that she was very young, very pretty, and very smart, and that he had made her his best bow, and offered her his least rickety chair; for the rest, he sat opposite to his Lucretia Borgia of modern life, who had meanwhile found a cigarette, and was puffing away and explaining that she was about to give a fancy ball, which should be the most *crâne*, the only amusing thing, of the year.

"Oh," he exclaimed, kindling at the thought, "do let me design you a dress all black and white and wicked green—you shall go as Deadly Nightshade, as Belladonna Atropa——"

"Belladonna Atropa! why my ball is in comic costume" . . . The Baroness was answering contemptuously, when Cecchino's attention was suddenly called to the other end of the studio by an exclamation on the part of his other visitor.

"Do tell me all about her;—has she a name? Is she really a lunatic?" asked the young lady who had been introduced as Madame Krasinska, keeping a portfolio open with one hand, and holding up in the other a coloured sketch she had taken from it.

"What have you got there? Oh, only the Sora Lena!" and Madame Fosca reverted to the contemplation of the smoke-rings she was making.

"Tell me about her—Sora Lena, did you say?" asked the younger lady eagerly.

She spoke French, but with a pretty little American accent, despite her Polish name. She was very charming, Cecchino said to himself, a radiant impersonation of youthful brightness and elegance as she stood there in her long, silvery furs, holding the drawing with tiny, tight-gloved hands, and shedding around her a vague, exquisite fragrance—no, not a mere literal perfume, that would be far too coarse but something personal akin to it.

"I have noticed her so often," she went on, with that silvery young voice of hers; "she's mad, isn't she? And what did you say her name was? Please tell me again."

Cecchino was delighted. "How true it is," he reflected, "that only refinement, high-breeding, luxury can give people certain kinds of sensitiveness, of rapid intuition! No woman of another class would have picked out just that drawing, or would have been interested in it without stupid laughter."

"Do you want to know the story of poor old Sora Lena?" asked Cecchino, taking the sketch from Madame Krasinska's hand, and looking over it at the charming, eager young face.

The sketch might have passed for a caricature; but anyone who had spent so little as a week in Florence those six or seven years ago would have recognised at once that it was merely a faithful portrait. For Sora Lena—more correctly Signora Maddalena—had been for years and years one of the most conspicuous sights of the town. In all weathers you might have seen that hulking old woman, with her vague, staring, reddish face, trudging through the streets or standing before shops, in her extraordinary costume of thirty years ago, her enormous crinoline, on which the silk skirt and ragged petticoat hung limply, her gigantic coal-scuttle bonnet, shawl, prunella boots, and great muff or parasol; one of several outfits, all alike, of that distant period, all alike inexpressibly dirty and tattered.

In all weathers you might have seen her stolidly going her way, indifferent to stares and jibes, of which, indeed, there were by this time comparatively few, so familiar had she grown to staring, jibing Florence. In all weathers, but most noticeably in the worst, as if the squalor of mud and rain had an affinity with that sad, draggled, soiled, battered piece of human squalor, that lamentable rag of half-witted misery.

"Do you want to know about Sora Lena?" repeated Cecco Bandini, meditatively. They formed a strange, strange contrast, these two women, the one in the sketch and the one standing before him. And there was to him a pathetic whimsicalness in the interest which the one had excited in the other.

"How long has she been wandering about here? Why, as long as I can remember the streets of Florence, and that," added Cecchino sorrowfully, "is a longer while than I care to count up. It seems to me as if she must always have been there, like the olive-trees and the paving stones; for after all, Giotto's tower was not there before Giotto, whereas poor old Sora Lena—But, by the way, there is a limit even to her. There is a legend about her; they say that she was once sane, and had two sons, who went as volunteers in '59, and were killed at Solferino, and ever since then she has sallied forth, every day, winter or summer, in her best clothes, to meet the young fellows at the station. May be. To my mind it doesn't matter much whether the story be true or false; it is fitting," and Cecco Bandini set about dusting some canvases which had attracted the Baroness Fosca's attention. When Cecchino was helping that lady into her furs, she gave one of her little brutal smiles, and nodded in the direction of her companion.

"Madame Krasinska," she said laughing, "is very desirous of possessing one of your sketches, but she is too polite to ask you the price of it. That's what comes of our not knowing how to earn a penny for ourselves, doesn't it, Signor Cecchino?"

Madame Krasinska blushed, and looked more young, and delicate, and charming.

"I did not know whether you would consent to part with one of your drawings," she said in her silvery, child-like voice,— "it is—this one—which I should so much have liked to have— to have . . . bought." Cecchino smiled at the embarrassment which the word "bought" produced in his exquisite visitor. Poor, charming young creature, he thought; the only thing she thinks people one knows can sell, is themselves, and that's called getting married. "You must explain to your friend," said Cecchino to the Baroness Fosca, as he hunted in a drawer for a piece of clean paper, "that such rubbish as this is neither bought nor sold; it is not even possible for a poor devil of a painter to offer it as a gift to a lady—but,"—and he handed the little roll to Madame

Krasinska, making his very best bow as he did so—"it is possible for a lady graciously to accept it."

"Thank you so much," answered Madame Krasinska, slipping the drawing into her muff; "it is very good of you to give me such a . . . such a very interesting sketch," and she pressed his big, brown fingers in her little grey-gloved hand.

"Poor Sora Lena!" exclaimed Cecchino, when there remained of the visit only a faint perfume of exquisiteness; and he thought of the hideous old draggle-tailed mad woman, reposing, rolled up in effigy, in the delicious daintiness of that delicate grey muff.

2

A fortnight later, the great event was Madame Fosca's fancy ball, to which the guests were bidden to come in what was described as comic costume. Some, however, craved leave to appear in their ordinary apparel, and among these was Cecchino Bandini, who was persuaded, moreover, that his old-fashioned swallow-tails, which he donned only at weddings, constituted quite comic costume enough.

This knowledge did not interfere at all with his enjoyment. There was even, to his whimsical mind, a certain charm in being in a crowd among which he knew no one; unnoticed or confused, perhaps, with the waiters, as he hung about the stairs and strolled through the big palace rooms. It was as good as wearing an invisible cloak, one saw so much just because one was not seen; indeed, one was momentarily endowed (it seemed at least to his fanciful apprehension) with a faculty akin to that of understanding the talk of birds; and, as he watched and listened he became aware of innumerable charming little romances, which were concealed from more notable but less privileged persons.

Little by little the big white and gold rooms began to fill. The ladies, who had moved in gorgeous isolation, their skirts displayed as finely as a peacock's train, became gradually visible only from the waist upwards; and only the branches of the palm-trees and tree ferns detached themselves against the shining walls. Instead of wandering among variegated brocades and iridescent silks and astonishing arrangements of feathers and flowers, Cecchino's eye was forced to a higher level by the thickening crowd; it was now the constellated sparkle of diamonds on neck and head which dazzled him, and the strange, unaccustomed splendour of white arms and shoulders.

And, as the room filled, the invisible cloak was also drawn closer round our friend Cecchino, and the extraordinary faculty of perceiving romantic and delicious secrets in other folk's bosoms became more and more developed. They seemed to him like exquisite children, these creatures rustling about in fantastic dresses, powdered shepherds and shepherdesses with diamonds spirting fire among their ribbons and top-knots; Japanese and Chinese embroidered with sprays of flowers; medieval and antique beings, and beings hidden in the plumage of birds, or the petals of flowers; children, but children somehow matured, transfigured by the touch of luxury and good-breeding, children full of courtesy and kindness. There were, of course, a few costumes which might have been better conceived or better carried out, or better—not to say best—omitted altogether.

One grew bored, after a little while, with people dressed as marionettes, champagne bottles, sticks of sealing-wax, or captive balloons; a young man arrayed as a female ballet dancer, and another got up as a wet nurse, with baby *obligato* might certainly have been dispensed with. Also, Cecchino could not help wincing a little at the daughter of the house being mummed and painted to represent her own grandmother, a respectable old lady whose picture hung in the dining-room, and whose spectacles he had frequently picked up in his boyhood. But these were mere trifling details.

And, as a whole, it was beautiful, fantastic. So Cecchino moved backward and forward, invisible in his shabby black suit, and borne hither and thither by the well-bred pressure of the many-coloured crowd; pleasantly blinded by the innumerable lights, the sparkle of chandelier pendants, and the shooting flames of jewels; gently deafened by the confused murmur of innumerable voices, of crackling stuffs and soughing fans, of distant dance music; and inhaling the vague fragrance which seemed less the decoction of cunning perfumers than the exquisite and expressive emanation of this exquisite bloom of personality.

Certainly, he said to himself, there is no pleasure so delicious as seeing people amusing themselves with refinement: there is a transfiguring magic, almost a moralising power, in wealth and elegance and good-breeding.

He was making this reflection, and watching between two dances, a tiny fluff of down sailing through the warm draught across the empty space, the sort of whirlpool of the balloom— when a little burst of voices came from the entrance saloon. The multi-coloured costumes fluttered like butterflies toward a given spot, there was a little heaping together of brilliant colours and flashing jewels. There was much craning of delicate, fluffy young necks and heads, and shuffle on tiptoe, and the crowd fell automatically aside.

A little gangway was cleared; and there walked into the middle of the white and gold drawing-room, a lumbering, hideous figure, with reddish, vacant face, sunk in an immense, tarnished satin bonnet; and draggled, faded, lilac silk skirts spread over a vast dislocated crinoline. The feet dabbed along in the broken prunella boots; the mangy rabbit-skin muff bobbed loosely with the shambling gait; and then, under the big chandelier, there came a sudden pause, and the thing looked slowly round, a gaping, mooning, blear-eyed stare.

It was the Sora Lena.

There was a perfect storm of applause.

3

Cecchino Bandini did not slacken his pace till he found himself, with his thin overcoat and opera hat all drenched, among the gas reflections and puddles before his studio door; that shout of applause and that burst of clapping pursuing him down the stairs of the palace and all through the rainy streets. There were a few embers in his stove; he threw a faggot on them, lit a cigarette, and proceeded to make reflections, the wet opera hat still on his head. He had been a fool, a savage. He had behaved like a child, rushing past his hostess with that ridiculous speech in answer to her inquiries: "I am running away because bad luck has entered your house."

Why had he not guessed it at once? What on earth else could she have wanted his sketch for?

He determined to forget the matter, and, as he imagined, he forgot it. Only, when the next day's evening paper displayed two columns describing Madame Fosca's ball, and more particularly "that mask," as the reporter had it, "which among so many which were graceful and ingenious, bore off in triumph the palm for witty novelty," he threw the paper down and gave it a kick towards the wood-box. But he felt ashamed of himself, picked it up, smoothed it out and read it all—foreign news and home news, and even the description of Madame Fosca's masked ball, conscientiously through.

Last of all he perused, with dogged resolution, the column of petty casualties: a boy bit in the calf by a dog who was not mad; the frustrated burgling of a baker's shop; even to the bunches of keys and the umbrella and two cigar-cases picked up by the police, and consigned to the appropriate municipal limbo; until he came to the following lines:

This morning the *Guardians of Public Safety*, having been called by the neighbouring inhabitants, penetrated into a room on the top floor of a house situate in the Little Street of the Gravedigger (Viccolo del Beccamorto), and discovered, hanging from a rafter, the dead body of Maddalena X.Y. Z. The deceased had long been noted throughout Florence for her eccentric habits and apparel.

The paragraph was headed, in somewhat larger type: "Suicide of a female lunatic."

Cecchino's cigarette had gone out, but he continued blowing at it all the same. He could see in his mind's eye a tall, slender figure, draped in silvery plush and silvery furs, standing by the side of an open portfolio, and holding a drawing in her tiny hand, with the slender, solitary gold bangle over the grey glove.

4

Madame Krasinska was in a very bad humour. The old *Chanoiness*, her late husband's aunt, noticed it; her guests noticed it; her maid noticed it: and she noticed it herself. For, of all human beings, Madame Krasinska—Netta, as smart folk familiarly called her—was the least subject to bad humour. She was as uniformly cheerful as birds are supposed to be, and she certainly had none of the causes for anxiety or sorrow which even the most proverbial bird must occasionally have. She had always had money, health, good looks; and people had always told her—in New York, in London, in Paris, Rome, and St. Petersburg—from her very earliest childhood, that her one business in life was to amuse herself.

The old gentleman whom she had simply and cheerfully accepted as a husband, because he had given her quantities of bonbons, and was going to give her quantities of diamonds, had been kind, and had been kindest of all in dying of sudden bronchitis when away for a month, leaving his young widow with an affectionately indifferent recollection of him, no remorse of any kind, and a great deal of money, not to speak of the excellent *Chanoiness*, who constituted an invaluable chaperon. And, since his happy demise, no cloud had disturbed the cheerful life or feelings of Madame Krasinska. Other women, she knew, had innumerable subjects of wretchedness; or if they had none, they were wretched from the want of them. Some had children who made them unhappy, others were unhappy for lack of children, and similarly as to lovers; but she had never had a child and never had a lover, and never experienced the smallest desire for either.

Other women suffered from sleeplessness, or from sleepiness, and took morphia or abstained from morphia with equal inconvenience; other women also grew weary of amusement. But Madame Krasinska always slept beautifully, and always stayed

140

awake cheerfully; and Madame Krasinska was never tired of amusing herself. Perhaps it was all this which culminated in the fact that Madame Krasinska had never in all her life envied or disliked anybody; and that no one, apparently, had ever envied or disliked her. She did not wish to outshine or supplant any one; she did not want to be richer, younger, more beautiful, or more adored than they. She only wanted to amuse herself, and she succeeded in so doing.

This particular day—the day after Madame Fosca's ball—Madame Krasinska was not amusing herself. She was not at all tired: she never was; besides, she had remained in bed till midday: neither was she unwell, for that also she never was; nor had anyone done the slightest thing to vex her. But there it was. She was not amusing herself at all. She could not tell why; and she could not tell why, also, she was vaguely miserable. When the first batch of afternoon callers had taken leave, and the following batches had been sent away from the door, she threw down her volume of Gyp, and walked to the window. It was raining: a thin, continuous spring drizzle. Only a few cabs, with wet, shining backs, an occasional lumbering omnibus or cart, passed by with wheezing, straining, downcast horses. In one or two shops a light was appearing, looking tiny, blear, and absurd in the gray afternoon. Madame Krasinska looked out for a few minutes; then, suddenly turning round, she brushed past the big palms and azaleas, and rang the bell.

"Order the brougham at once," she said.

She could by no means have explained what earthly reason had impelled her to go out. When the footman had inquired for orders she felt at a loss: certainly she did not want to go to see anyone, nor to buy anything, nor to inquire about anything.

What *did* she want? Madame Krasinska was not in the habit of driving out in the rain for her pleasure; still less to drive out without knowing whither. What did she want? She sat muffled in her furs, looking out on the wet, grey streets as the brougham rolled aimlessly along. She wanted—she wanted—she couldn't tell what. But she wanted it very much. That much she knew very well—she wanted. The rain, the wet streets, the muddy crossings—oh, how dismal they were! and still she wished to go on.

Instinctively, her polite coachman made for the politer streets, for the polite Lung' Arno. The river quay was deserted, and a warm, wet wind swept lazily along its muddy flags. Madame Krasinska let down the glass. How dreary! The foundry, on the other side, let fly a few red sparks from its tall chimney into the grey sky; the water droned over the weir; a lamp-lighter hurried along.

Madame Krasinska pulled the check-string.

"I want to walk," she said.

The polite footman followed behind along the messy flags, muddy and full of pools; the brougham followed behind him. Madame Krasinska was not at all in the habit of walking on the embankment, still less walking in the rain.

After some minutes she got in again, and bade the carriage drive home. When she got into the lit streets she again pulled the check-string and ordered the brougham to proceed at a foot's pace. At a certain spot she remembered something, and bade the coachman draw up before a shop. It was the big chemist's.

"What does the *Signora Contessa* command?" and the footman raised his hat over his ear.

Somehow she had forgotten. "Oh," she answered, "wait a minute. Now I remember, it's the next shop, the florist's. Tell them to send fresh azaleas tomorrow and fetch away the old ones."

Now the azaleas had been changed only that morning. But the polite footman obeyed. And Madame Krasinska remained for a minute, nestled in her fur rug, looking on to the wet, yellow, lit pavement, and into the big chemist's window. There were the red, heart-shaped chest protectors, the frictioning gloves, the bath towels, all hanging in their place. Then boxes of *eau-de-Cologne*, lots of bottles of all sizes, and boxes, large and small, and variosities of indescribable nature and use, and the great glass jars, yellow, blue, green, and ruby red, with a spark from the gas lamp behind in their heart. She stared at it all, very intently, and without a notion about any of these objects. Only she knew that the glass jars were uncommonly bright, and that each had a ruby, or topaz, or emerald of gigantic size, in its heart. The footman returned.

"Drive home," ordered Madame Krasinska. As her maid was taking her out of her dress, a thought—the first since so long—flashed across her mind, at the sight of certain skirts, and an uncouth cardboard mask, lying in a corner of her dressing-room. How odd that she had not seen the Sora Lena that evening.... She used always to be walking in the lit streets at that hour.

5

The next morning Madame Krasinska woke up quite cheerful and happy. But she began, nevertheless, to suffer, ever since the day after the Fosca ball, from the return of that quite unprecedented and inexplicable depression. Her days became streaked, as it were, with moments during which it was quite impossible to amuse herself; and these moments grew gradually into hours. People bored her for no accountable reason, and things which she had expected as pleasures brought with them a sense of vague or more distinct wretchedness. Thus she would find herself in the midst of a ball or dinner-party, invaded suddenly by a confused sadness or boding of evil, she did not know which. And once, when a box of new clothes had arrived from Paris, she was overcome, while putting on one of the frocks, with such a fit of tears that she had to be put to bed instead of going to the Tornabuoni's party.

Of course, people began to notice this change; indeed, Madame Krasinska had ingenuously complained of the strange alteration in herself. Some persons suggested that she might be suffering from slow blood-poisoning, and urged an inquiry into the state of the drains. Others recommended arsenic, morphia, or antipyrine. One kind friend brought her a box of peculiar cigarettes; another forwarded a parcel of still more peculiar novels; most people had some pet doctor to cry up to the skies; and one or two suggested her changing her confessor; not to mention an attempt being made to mesmerise her into cheerfulness.

When her back was turned, meanwhile, all the kind friends discussed the probability of an unhappy love affair, loss of money on the Stock Exchange, and similar other explanations. And while one devoted lady tried to worm out of her the name of her unfaithful lover and of the rival for whom he had forsaken her, another assured her that she was suffering from a lack of personal affections. It was a fine opportunity for the display of pietism, materialism, idealism, realism, psychological lore, and esoteric theosophy.

Oddly enough, all this zeal about herself did not worry Madame Krasinska, as she would certainly have expected it to worry any other woman. She took a little of each of the tonic or soporific drugs; and read a little of each of those sickly sentimental, brutal, or politely improper novels. She also let herself be accompanied to various doctors; and she got up early in the morning and stood for an hour on a chair in a crowd in order to benefit by the preaching of the famous Father Agostino. She was quite patient even with the friends who condoled about the lover or absence of such. For all these things became, more and more, completely indifferent to Madame Krasinska—unrealities which had no weight in the presence of the painful reality.

This reality was that she was rapidly losing all power of amusing herself, and that when she did occasionally amuse herself she had to pay for what she called this *good time* by an increase of listlessness and melancholy.

It was not melancholy or listlessness such as other women complained of. They seemed, in their fits of blues, to feel that the world around them had got all wrong, or at least was going out of its way to annoy them. But Madame Krasinska saw the world quite plainly, proceeding in the usual manner, and being quite as good a world as before. It was she who was all wrong. It was, in the literal sense of the words, what she supposed people might mean when they said that So-and-so was *not himself*; only that So-and-so, on examination, appeared to be very much himself—only himself in a worse temper than usual. Whereas she. . . . . Why, in her case, she really did not seem to be herself any longer.

Once, at a grand dinner, she suddenly ceased eating and talking to her neighbour, and surprised herself wondering who the people all were and what they had come for. Her mind would become, every now and then, a blank; a blank at least full of vague images, misty and muddled, which she was unable to grasp, but of which she knew that they were painful, weighing on her as a heavy load must weigh on the head or back. Something had happened, or was going to happen, she could not remember which, but she burst into tears none the less. In the midst of such a state of things, if visitors or a servant entered, she would ask sometimes who they were. Once a man came to call, during one of these fits; by an effort she was able to receive him and answer his small talk more or less at random, feeling the whole time as if someone else were speaking in her place. The visitor at length rose to depart, and they both stood for a moment in the midst of the drawing-room.

"This is a very pretty house; it must belong to some rich person. Do you know to whom it belongs?" suddenly remarked Madame Krasinska, looking slowly round her at the furniture, the pictures, statuettes, knick-knacks, the screens and plants. "Do you know to whom it belongs?" she repeated.

"It belongs to the most charming lady in Florence," stammered out the visitor politely, and fled.

"My darling Netta," exclaimed the *Chanoiness* from where she was seated crocheting benevolently futile garments by the fire; "you should not joke in that way. That poor young man was placed in a painful, in a very painful position by your nonsense."

Madame Krasinska leaned her arms on a screen, and stared her respectable relation long in the face.

"You seem a kind woman," she said at length. "You are old, but then you aren't poor, and they don't call you a mad woman. That makes all the difference."

Then she set to singing—drumming out the tune on the screen—the soldier song of '59, *Addio, mia bella, addio.*

"Netta!" cried the *Chanoiness*, dropping one ball of worsted after another. "Netta!"

But Madame Krasinska passed her hand over her brow and heaved a great sigh. Then she took a cigarette off a *cloisonné* tray, dipped a spill in the fire and remarked,

"Would you like to have the brougham to go to see your friend at the Sacré Coeur, Aunt Thérèse? I have promised to wait in for Molly Wolkonsky and Bice Forteguerra. We are going to dine at Doney's with young Pomfret."

6

Madame Krasinska had repeated her evening drives in the rain. Indeed she began also to walk about regardless of weather. Her maid asked her whether she had been ordered exercise by the doctor, and she answered yes. But why she should not walk in the Cascine or along the Lung'Arno, and why she should always choose the muddiest thoroughfares, the maid did not inquire. As it was, Madame Krasinska never showed any repugnance or seemly contrition for the state of draggle in which she used to return home; sometimes when the woman was unbuttoning her boots, she would remain in contemplation of their muddiness, murmuring things which Jefferies could not understand. The servants, indeed, declared that the Countess must have gone out of her mind.

The footman related that she used to stop the brougham, get out and look into the lit shops, and that he had to stand behind, in order to prevent lady-killing youths of a caddish description from whispering expressions of admiration in her ear. And once, he affirmed with horror, she had stopped in front of a certain cheap eating-house, and looked in at the bundles of asparagus, at the uncooked chops displayed in the window. And then, added the footman, she had turned round to him slowly and said,

"They have good food in there."

And meanwhile, Madame Krasinska went to dinners and

parties, and gave them, and organised picnics, as much as was decently possible in Lent, and indeed a great deal more.

She no longer complained of the blues; she assured everyone that she had completely got rid of them, that she had never been in such spirits in all her life. She said it so often, and in so excited a way, that judicious people declared that now that lover must really have jilted her, or gambling on the Stock Exchange have brought her to the verge of ruin.

Nay, Madame Krasinska's spirits became so obstreperous as to change her in sundry ways. Although living in the fastest set, Madame Krasinska had never been a fast woman. There was something childlike in her nature which made her modest and decorous. She had never learned to talk slang, or to take up vulgar attitudes, or to tell impossible stories; and she had never lost a silly habit of blushing at expressions and anecdotes which she did not reprove other women for using and relating. Her amusements had never been flavoured with that spice of impropriety, of curiosity of evil, which was common in her set. She liked putting on pretty frocks, arranging pretty furniture, driving in well got up carriages, eating good dinners, laughing a great deal, and dancing a great deal, and that was all.

But now Madame Krasinska suddenly altered. She became, all of a sudden, anxious for those exotic sensations which honest women may get by studying the ways, and frequenting the haunts, of women by no means honest. She made up parties to go to the low theatres and music-halls; she proposed dressing up and going, in company with sundry adventurous spirits, for evening strolls in the more dubious portions of the town. Moreover, she, who had never touched a card, began to gamble for large sums, and to surprise people by producing a folded green roulette cloth and miniature roulette rakes out of her pocket. And she became so outrageously conspicuous in her flirtations (she who had never flirted before), and so outrageously loud in her manners and remarks, that her good friends began to venture a little remonstrance. . . .

But remonstrance was all in vain; and she would toss her head and laugh cynically, and answer in a brazen, jarring voice. For Madame Krasinska felt that she must live, live noisily, live scandalously, live her own life of wealth and dissipation, because . . .

She used to wake up at night with the horror of that suspicion. And in the middle of the day, pull at her clothes, tear down her hair, and rush to the mirror and stare at herself, and look for every feature, and clutch for every end of silk, or bit of lace, or wisp of hair, which proved that she was really herself. For gradually, slowly, she had come to understand that she was herself no longer.

Herself—well, yes, of course she was herself. Was it not herself who rushed about in such a riot of amusement; herself whose flushed cheeks and over-bright eyes, and cynically flaunted neck and bosom she saw in the glass, whose mocking loud voice and shrill laugh she listened to? Besides, did not her servants, her visitors, know her as Netta Krasinska; and did she not know how to wear her clothes, dance, make jokes, and encourage men, afterwards to discourage them? This, she often said to herself, as she lay awake the long nights, as she sat out the longer nights gambling and chaffing, distinctly proved that she really was herself. And she repeated it all mentally when she returned, muddy, worn out, and as awakened from a ghastly dream, after one of her long rambles through the streets, her daily walks towards the station.

But still . . . What of those strange forebodings of evil, those muddled fears of some dreadful calamity . . . something which had happened, or was going to happen . . . poverty, starvation, death—whose death, her own? or someone else's? That knowledge that it was all, all over; that blinding, felling blow which used every now and then to crush her. . . . Yes, she had felt that first at the railway station. At the station? but what had happened at the station? Or was it going to happen still? Since to the station her feet seemed unconsciously to carry her every day. What was it all? Ah! she knew. There was a woman, an old woman, walking to the station to meet. . . . Yes, to meet a regiment on its way back. They came back, those soldiers, among a mob yelling triumph.

She remembered the illuminations, the red, green, and white lanterns, and those garlands all over the waiting-rooms. And quantities of flags. The bands played. So gaily! They played Garibaldi's hymn, and *Addio, Mia Bella*. Those pieces always made her cry now. The station was crammed, and all the boys, in tattered, soiled uniforms, rushed into the arms of parents, wives, friends. Then there was like a blinding light, a crash.... An officer led the old woman gently out of the place, mopping his eyes. And she, of all the crowd, was the only one to go home alone. Had it really all happened? and to whom? Had it really happened to her, had her boys . . . But Madame Krasinska had never had any boys.

It was dreadful how much it rained in Florence; and stuff boots do wear out so quick in mud. There was such a lot of mud on the way to the station; but of course it was necessary to go to the station in order to meet the train from Lombardy—the boys must be met.

There was a place on the other side of the river where you went in and handed your watch and your brooch over the counter, and they gave you some money and a paper. Once the paper got lost. Then there was a mattress, too. But there was a kind man—a man who sold hardware—who went and fetched it back.

It was dreadfully cold in winter, but the worst was the rain. And having no watch one was afraid of being late for that train, and had to dawdle so long in the muddy streets. Of course one could look in at the pretty shops. But the little boys were so rude. Oh, no, no, not that—anything rather than be shut up in an hospital. The poor old woman did no one any harm—why shut her up?

"*Faites votre jeu, messieurs*," cried Madame Krasinska, raking up the counters with the little rake she had had made of tortoise-shell, with a gold dragon's head for a handle—"*Rien ne va plus—vingt-trois—Rouge, impair et manque*."

How did she come to know about this woman? She had never been inside that house over the tobacconist's, up three pairs of stairs to the left; and yet she knew exactly the pattern of the wall-paper. It was green, with a pinkish trellis-work, in the grand sitting-room, the one which was opened only on Sunday evenings, when the friends used to drop in and discuss the news, and have a game of *tresette*. You passed through the dining-room to get through it. The dining-room had no window, and was lit from a skylight; there was always a little smell of dinner in it, but that was appetising. The boys' rooms were to the back. There was a plaster Joan of Arc in the hall, close to the clothes-peg. She was painted to look like silver, and one of the boys had broken her arm, so that it looked like a gas-pipe.

It was Momino who had done it, jumping on to the table when they were playing. Momino was always the scapegrace; he wore out so many pairs of trousers at the knees, but he was so warm-hearted! and after all, he had got all the prizes at school, and they all said he would be a first-rate engineer. Those dear boys! They never cost their mother a farthing, once they were sixteen; and Momino bought her a big, beautiful muff out of his own earnings as a pupil-teacher. Here it is! Such a comfort in the cold weather, you can't think, especially when gloves are too dear. Yes, it is rabbit-skin, but it is made to look like ermine, quite a handsome article.

Assunta, the maid of all work, never would clean out that kitchen of hers—servants are such sluts! and she tore the moreen sofa-cover, too, against a nail in the wall. She ought to have seen that nail! But one mustn't be too hard on a poor creature, who is an orphan into the bargain. Oh, God! oh, God! and they lie in the big trench at San Martino, without even a cross over them, or a bit of wood with their name. But the white coats of the Austrians were soaked red, I warrant you! And the new dye they call magenta is made of pipe-clay—the pipe-clay the dogs clean their white coats with—and the blood of Austrians. It's a grand dye, I tell you!

Lord, Lord, how wet the poor old woman's feet are! And no fire to warm them by. The best is to go to bed when one can't dry one's clothes; and it saves lamp-oil. That was very good oil the parish priest made her a present of . . . *Aï, aï,* how one's bones ache on the mere boards, even with a blanket over them! That good, good mattress at the pawn-shop! It's nonsense about the Italians having been beaten. The Austrians were beaten into bits, made cats'-meat of; and the volunteers are returning tomorrow. Temistocle and Momino—Momino is Girolamo, you know—will be back tomorrow; their rooms have been cleaned, and they shall have a flask of real Montepulciano . . . The big bottles in the chemist's window are very beautiful, particularly the green one.

The shop where they sell gloves and scarves is also very pretty; but the English chemist's is the prettiest, because of those bottles. But they say the contents of them is all rubbish, and no real medicine . . . Don't speak of San Bonifazio! I have seen it. It is where they keep the mad folk and the wretched, dirty, wicked, wicked old women. . . . There was a handsome book bound in red, with gold edges, on the best sitting-room table; the *Æneid,* translated by Caro. It was one of Temistocle's prizes. And that Berlin-wool cushion . . . yes, the little dog with the cherries looked quite real . . .

"I have been thinking I should like to go to Sicily, to see Etna, and Palermo, and all those places," said Madame Krasinska, leaning on the balcony by the side of Prince Mongibello, smoking her fifth or sixth cigarette.

She could see the hateful hooked nose, like a nasty hawk's beak, over the big black beard, and the creature's leering, languishing black eyes, as he looked up into the twilight. She knew quite well what sort of man Mongibello was. No woman could approach him, or allow him to approach her; and there she was on that balcony alone with him in the dark, far from the rest of the party, who were dancing and talking within. And to talk of Sicily to him, who was a Sicilian too! But that was what she wanted—a scandal, a horror, anything that might deaden those thoughts which would go on inside her . . . The thought of that strange, lofty whitewashed place, which she had never seen, but which she knew so well, with an altar in the middle, and rows and rows of beds, each with its set-out of bottles and baskets, and horrid slobbering and gibbering old women. Oh . . . she could hear them!

"I should like to go to Sicily," she said in a tone that was now common to her, adding slowly and with emphasis, "but I should like to have someone to show me all the sights . . ."

"Countess," and the black beard of the creature bent over her—close to her neck—"how strange—I also feel a great longing to see Sicily once more, but not alone—those lovely, lonely valleys . . ."

Ah!—there was one of the creatures who had sat up in her bed and was singing, singing *Casta Diva!* "No, not alone"—she went on hurriedly, a sort of fury of satisfaction, of the satisfaction of destroying something, destroying her own fame, her own life, filling her as she felt the man's hand on her arm—"not alone, prince—with someone to explain things—someone who knows all about it—and in this lovely spring weather. You see, I am a bad traveller—and I am afraid . . . of being alone . . ." The last words came out of her throat loud, hoarse, and yet cracked and shrill—and just as the prince's arm was going to clasp her, she rushed wildly into the room, exclaiming—

"Ah, I am she—I am she—I am mad!"

For in that sudden voice, so different from her own, Madame Krasinska had recognised the voice that should have issued from the cardboard mask she had once worn, the voice of Sora Lena.

8

Yes, Cecchino certainly recognised her now. Strolling about in that damp May twilight among the old, tortuous streets, he had mechanically watched the big black horses draw up at the posts which closed that labyrinth of black, narrow alleys; the servant in his white waterproof opened the door, and the tall, slender woman got out and walked quickly along. And mechanically, in his wool-gathering way, he had followed the lady, enjoying the charming note of delicate pink and grey which her little frock made against those black houses, and under that wet, grey sky, streaked pink with the sunset. She walked quickly along, quite alone, having left the footman with the carriage at the entrance of that condemned old heart of Florence; and she took no notice of the stares and words of the boys playing in the gutters, the pedlars housing their barrows under the black archways, and the women leaning out of window. Yes; there was no doubt. It had struck him suddenly as he watched her pass under a double arch and into a kind of large court, not unlike that of a castle, between the frowning tall houses of the old Jews' quarter; houses escutcheoned and stanchioned, once the abode of Ghibelline nobles, now given over to rag-pickers, scavengers and unspeakable trades.

As soon as he recognised her he stopped, and was about to turn: what business has a man following a lady, prying into her doings when she goes out at twilight, with carriage and footman left several streets back, quite alone through unlikely streets? And Cecchino, who by this time was on the point of returning to the Maremma, and had come to the conclusion that civilisation was a boring and loathsome thing, reflected upon the errands which French novels described ladies as performing, when they left their carriage and footman round the corner . . . But the thought was disgraceful to Cecchino, and unjust to this lady— no, no! And at this moment he stopped, for the lady had stopped a few paces before him, and was staring fixedly into the grey evening sky.

There was something strange in that stare; it was not that of a woman who is hiding disgraceful proceedings. And in staring round she must have seen him; yet she stood still, like one wrapped in wild thoughts. Then suddenly she passed under the next archway, and disappeared in the dark passage of a house. Somehow Cecco Bandini could not make up his mind, as he ought to have done long ago, to turn back. He slowly passed through the oozy, ill-smelling archway, and stood before that house. It was very tall, narrow, and black as ink, with a jagged roof against the wet, pinkish sky.

From the iron hook, made to hold brocades and Persian carpets on gala days of old, fluttered some rags, obscene and ill-omened in the wind. Many of the window panes were broken. It was evidently one of the houses which the municipality had condemned to destruction for sanitary reasons, and whence the inmates were gradually being evicted.

"That's a house they're going to pull down, isn't it?" he inquired in a casual tone of the man at the corner, who kept a sort of cook-shop, where chestnut pudding and boiled beans steamed on a brazier in a den. Then his eye caught a half-effaced name close to the lamp-post, "Little Street of the Grave-digger." "Ah," he added quickly, "this is the street where old Sora Lena committed suicide—and—is—is that the house?"

Then, trying to extricate some reasonable idea out of the extraordinary tangle of absurdities which had all of a sudden filled his mind, he fumbled in his pocket for a silver coin, and said hurriedly to the man with the cooking brazier,

"See here, that house, I'm sure, isn't well inhabited. That lady has gone there for a charity—but—but one doesn't know that she mayn't be annoyed in there. Here's fifty *centimes* for your trouble. If that lady doesn't come out again in three-quarters of an hour—there! it's striking seven—just you go round to the stone posts—you'll find her carriage there—black horses and grey liveries—and tell the footman to run upstairs to his mistress—understand?" And Cecchino Bandini fled, overwhelmed at the thought of the indiscretion he was committing, but seeing, as he turned round, those rags waving an ominous salute from the black, gaunt house with its irregular roof against the wet, twilight sky.

9

Madame Krasinska hurried though the long black corridor, with its slippery bricks and typhoid smell, and went slowly but resolutely up the black staircase. Its steps, constructed perhaps in the days of Dante's grandfather, when a horn buckle and leathern belt formed the only ornaments of Florentine dames, were extraordinarily high, and worn off at the edges by innumerable generations of successive nobles and paupers. And as it twisted sharply on itself, the staircase was lighted at rare intervals by barred windows, overlooking alternately the black square outside, with its jags of overhanging roof, and a black yard, where a broken well was surrounded by a heap of half-sorted chickens' feathers and unpicked rags.

On the first landing was an open door, partly screened by a line of drying tattered clothes; and whence issued shrill sounds of altercation and snatches of tipsy song. Madame Krasinska passed on heedless of it all, the front of her delicate frock brushing the unseen filth of those black steps, in whose crypt-like cold and gloom there was an ever-growing breath of charnel. Higher and higher, flight after flight, steps and steps. Nor did she look to the right or to the left, nor ever stop to take breath, but climbed upward, slowly, steadily.

At length she reached the topmost landing, on to which fell a flickering beam of the setting sun. It issued from a room, whose door was standing wide open. Madame Krasinska entered. The room was completely empty, and comparatively light. There was no furniture in it, except a chair, pushed into a dark corner, and an empty bird-cage at the window. The panes were broken, and here and there had been mended with paper. Paper also hung, in blackened rags, upon the walls.

Madame Krasinska walked to the window and looked out over the neighbouring roofs, to where the bell in an old black belfry swung tolling the *Ave Maria*. There was a *porticoed* gallery on the top of a house some way off; it had a few plants growing in pipkins, and a drying line. She knew it all so well.

On the window-sill was a cracked basin, in which stood a dead basil plant, dry, grey. She looked at it some time, moving the hardened earth with her fingers. Then she turned to the empty bird-cage. Poor solitary starling! how he had whistled to the poor old woman! Then she began to cry.

But after a few moments she roused herself. Mechanically, she went to the door and closed it carefully. Then she went straight to the dark corner, where she knew that the staved-in straw chair stood. She dragged it into the middle of the room, where the hook was in the big rafter.

She stood on the chair, and measured the height of the ceiling. It was so low that she could graze it with the palm of her hand. She took off her gloves, and then her bonnet—it was in the way of the hook. Then she unclasped her girdle, one of those narrow Russian ribbons of silver woven stuff, studded with *niello*. She buckled one end firmly to the big hook. Then she unwound the strip of muslin from under her collar. She was standing on the broken chair, just under the rafter. "*Pater noster qui es in cœlis*," she mumbled, as she still childishly did when putting her head on the pillow every night.

The door creaked and opened slowly. The big, hulking woman, with the vague, red face and blear stare, and the rabbit-skin muff, bobbing on her huge crinolined skirts, shambled slowly into the room. It was the Sora Lena.

10

When the man from the cook-shop under the archway and the footman entered the room, it was pitch dark. Madame Krasinska was lying in the middle of the floor, by the side of an overturned chair, and under a hook in the rafter whence hung her Russian girdle. When she awoke from her swoon, she looked slowly round the room; then rose, fastened her collar and murmured, crossing herself, "O God, thy mercy is infinite." The men said that she smiled.

Such is the legend of Madame Krasinska, known as Mother Antoinette Marie among the Little Sisters of the Poor.

Tuscan Midsummer Magic

1

"Then," I said, "you decline to tell me about the Three Kings, when their procession wound round and round these hillocks: all the little wooden horses with golden bridles and velvet holsters, out of the toy boxes; and the camelopard, and the monkeys and the lynx, and the little doll pages blowing toy trumpets. And still, I know it happened here, because I recognise the place from the pictures: the hillocks all washed away into breasts like those of Diana of the Ephesians, and the rows of cypresses and spruce pines—also out of the toy box. I know it happened in this very place, because Benozzo Gozzoli painted it all at the time; and you were already about the place, I presume?"

I knew that by her dress, but I did not like to allude to its being old-fashioned. It was the sort of thing, muslin all embroidered with little nosegays of myrtle and yellow broom, and tied into odd bunches at the elbow and waist, which they wore in the days of Botticelli's Spring; and on her head she had a garland of eglantine and palm-shaped hellebore leaves which was quite unmistakable.

The nymph Terzollina (for of course she was the tutelary divinity of the narrow valley behind the great Medicean Villa) merely shook her head and shifted one of her bare feet, on which she was seated under a cypress tree, and went on threading the yellow broom flowers.

"At all events, you might tell me something about the Magnificent Lorenzo," I went on, impatient at her obstinacy. "You know quite well that he used to come and court you here, and make verses most likely."

The exasperating goddess raised her thin brown face, with the sharp squirrel's teeth and the glittering goat's eyes. Very pretty I thought her, though undoubtedly a little *passee*, like all the symbolical ladies of her set. She plucked at a clump of dry peppermint, perfuming the hot air as she crushed it, and then looked up, with a sly, shy little peasant-girl's look, which was absurd in a lady so mature and so elaborately adorned. Then, in a crooning voice, she began to recite some *stanzas* in *ottava rima*, as follows:

"The house where the good old Knight Gualando hid away the little princess, was itself hidden in this hidden valley. It was small and quite white, with great iron bars to the windows. In front was a long piece of greensward, starred with white clover, and behind and in front, to where the pines and cypresses began, ran strips of corn-field. It was remote from all the pomps of life; and when the cuckoo had become silent and the nightingales had cracked their voices, the only sound was the coo of the wood-pigeons, the babble of the stream, and the twitter of the young larks.

"The old Knight Gualando had hidden his bright armour in an oaken chest; and went to the distant town every day dressed in the blue smock of a peasant, and driving a donkey before him. Thence he returned with delicates for the little princess and with news of the wicked usurper; nor did any one suspect who he was, or dream of his hiding-place.

"During his absence the little princess whose name was Fiordispina, used to string beads through the hot hours when the sun smote through the trees, and the green corn ridges began to take a faint gilding in their silveriness, as the princess remembered it in a picture in the castle chapel, where the sun was represented by a big embossed ball of gold, projecting from the picture, which she was allowed to stroke on holidays.

"In the evening, when the sky turned pearl white, and a breeze rustled through the pines and cypresses which made a little black fringe on the hill-top and a little patch of feathery velvet pile on the slopes, the little princess would come forth, and ramble about in her peasant's frock, her fair face stained browner by the sun than by any walnut juice. She would climb the hill, and sniff the scent of the sun-warmed resin, and the sweetness of the yellow broom. It spread all over the hill, and the king, her father, had not possessed so many ells of cloth of gold.

"But one evening she wandered further than usual, and saw on a bank, at the edge of a cornfield, five big white lilies blowing. She went back home and fetched the golden scissors from her work-bag, and cut off one of the lilies. On the next day she came again and cut another until she had cut them all.

"But it happened that an old witch was staying in that neighbourhood, gathering herbs among the hills. She had taken note of the five lilies, because she disliked them on account of their being white; and she remarked that one of them had been cut off; then another, then another. She hated people who like lilies. When she found the fifth lily gone, she wondered greatly, and climbed on the ridge, and looked at their stalks where they were cut. She was a wise woman, who knew many things. So she laid her finger upon the cut stalk, and said, 'This has not been cut with iron shears'; and she laid her lip against the cut stalk, and felt that it had been cut with gold shears, for gold cuts like nothing else.

"'Oho!' said the old witch—'where there are gold scissors, there must be gold work-bags; and where there are gold work-bags, there must be little princesses.'"

"Well, and then?" I asked.

"Oh then, nothing at all," answered Nymph Terzollina beloved by the Magnificent Lorenzo, who had seen the procession of the Three Kings. "Good evening to you."

And where her white muslin dress, broidered with nosegays of broom and myrtle had been spread on the dry grass and crushed mint, there was only, beneath the cypresses, a bush of white-starred myrtle a tuft of belated yellow broom.

One must have leisure to converse with goddesses; and certainly, during a summer in Tuscany, when folk are scattered in their country houses, and are disinclined to move out of hammock or off shaded bench, there are not many other persons to talk with.

On the other hand, during those weeks of cloudless summer, natural objects vie with each other in giving one amateur representations. Things look their most unexpected, masquerade as other things, get queer unintelligible allegoric meanings, leaving you to guess what it all means, a constant dumb-crambo of trees, flowers, animals, houses, and moonlight.

The moon, particularly, is continually *en scène*, as if to take the place of the fireflies, which last only so long as the corn is in the ear, gradually getting extinguished and trailing about, humble helpless moths with a pale phosphorescence in their tail, in the grass and in the curtains. The moon takes their place; the moon which, in an Italian summer, seems to be full for three weeks out of the four.

One evening the performance was given by the moon and the corn-sheaves, assisted by minor actors such as crickets, downy owls, and vine-garlands. The oats, which had been of such exquisite delicacy of green, had just been reaped in the field beyond our garden and were now stacked up. Suspecting one of the usual performances, I went after dinner to the upper garden-gate, and looked through the bars. There it was, the familiar, elemental witchery. The moon was nearly full, blurring the stars, steeping the sky and earth in pale blue mist, which seemed somehow to be the visible falling dew.

It left a certain greenness to the broad grass path, a vague yellow to the unsickled wheat; and threw upon the sheaves of oats the shallows of festooned vine garlands. Those sheaves, or stooks—who can describe their metamorphose? Palest yellow on the pale stubbly ground, they were frosted by the moonbeams in their crisp fringe of ears, and in the shining straws projecting here and there. Straws, ears? You would never have guessed that they were made of anything so mundane. They sat there, propped against the trees, between the pools of light and the shadows, while the crickets trilled their cool, shrill song; sat solemnly with an air of expectation, calling to me, frightening me. And one in particular, with a great additional bunch on his head, cut by a shadow, was oddly unaccountable and terrible. After a minute I had to slink away, back into the garden, like an intruder.

3

There are performances also in broad daylight, and then human beings are admitted as supernumaries. Such was a certain cattle fair, up the valley of the Mugnone.

The beasts were being sold on a piece of rough, freshly reaped ground, lying between the high road and the river bed, empty of waters, but full among its shingle of myrrh-scented yellow herbage. The oxen were mostly of the white Tuscan breeds (those of Romagna are smaller but more spirited, and of a delicate grey) only their thighs slightly browned; the scarlet cloth neck-fringes set off, like a garland of geranium, against the perfect milkiness of backs and necks. They looked, indeed, these gigantic creatures, as if moulded out of whipped cream or cream cheese; suggesting no strength, and even no resistance to the touch, with their smooth surface here and there packed into minute wrinkles, exactly like the little *stracchini* cheeses.

This impalpable whiteness of the beasts suited their perfect tameness, passiveness, letting themselves be led about with great noiseless strides over the stubbly ridges and up the steep banks; and hustled together, flank against flank, horns interlaced with horns, without even a sound or movement of astonishment or disobedience. Never a low or a moo; never a glance round of their big, long-lashed, blue-brown eyes. Their big jaws move like millstones, their long tufted tails switch monotonously like pendulums.

Around them circle peasants, measuring them with the eye, prodding them with the finger, pulling them by the horns. And every now and then one of the red-faced men, butchers mainly, who act as go-betweens, dramatically throws his arms round the neck of some recalcitrant dealer or buyer, leads him aside, whispering with a gesture like Judas's kiss; or he clasps together the red hands and arms of contracting parties, silencing their objections, forcing them to do business. The contrast is curious between these hot, excited yelling, jostling human beings, above whose screaming *Dio Canes!* and *Dio Ladros!* the cry of the iced-water seller recurs monotonously, and the silent, impassive bullocks, white, unreal, inaudible; so still and huge, indeed, that, seen from above, they look like an encampment, their white flanks like so much spread canvas in the sunshine. And from a little distance, against the hillside beyond the river, the already bought yokes of bullocks look, tethered in a grove of cypresses, like some old mediaeval allegory—an allegory, as usual, nobody knows of what.

4

Another performance was that of the woods of Lecceto, and the hermitage of the same name. You will find them on the map of the district of Siena; but I doubt very much whether you will find them on the surface of the real globe, for I suspect them to be a piece of midsummer magic and nothing more. They had been for years to me among the number (we all have such) of things familiar but inaccessible; or rather things whose inaccessibility—due to no conceivable cause—is an essential quality of their existence. Every now and then from one of the hills you get a glimpse of the square red tower, massive and battlemented, rising among the grey of its ilexes, beckoning one across a ridge or two and a valley; then disappearing again, engulfed in the oak woods, green in summer, copper-coloured in winter: to reappear, but on the side you least expected it, plume of ilexes, battlements of tower, as you twisted along the high-lying vineyards and the clusters of umbrella pines fringing the hill-tops; and then, another minute and they were gone.

We determined to attain them, to be mocked no longer by

Lecceto; and went forth on one endless July afternoon. After much twisting from hillside to hillside and valley to valley, we at last got into a country which was strange enough to secrete even Lecceto. In a narrow valley we were met by a scent, warm, delicious, familiar, which seemed to lead us (as perfumes we cannot identify will usually do) to ideas very hazy, but clear enough to be utterly inappropriate: English cottage-gardens, linen presses of old houses, old-fashioned sitting-rooms full of pots of *potpourri*; and then, behold, in front of us a hill covered every inch of it with flowering lavender, growing as heather does on the hills outside fairyland. And behind this lilac, sun-baked, scented hill, open the woods of ilexes. The trees were mostly young and with their summer uppergarment of green, fresh leaves over the crackling old ones; trees packed close like a hedge, their every gap filled with other verdure, arbutus and hornbeam, fern and heather; the close-set greenery crammed, as it were, with freshness and solitude.

These must be the woods of Lecceto, and in their depths the red battlemented tower of the Hermitage. For I had forgotten to say that for a thousand years that tower had been the abode of a succession of holy personages, so holy and so like each other as to have almost grown into one, an immortal hermit whom Popes and Emperors would come to consult and be blessed by. Deeper and deeper therefore we made our way into the green coolness and dampness, the ineffable deliciousness of young leaf and uncurling fern; till it seemed as if the plantation were getting impenetrable, and we began to think that, as usual, Lecceto had mocked us, and would probably appear, if we retraced our steps, in the diametrically opposite direction.

When suddenly, over the tree-tops, rose the square battlemented tower of red brick. Then, at a turn of the rough narrow lane, there was the whole place, the tower, a church and steeple, and some half fortified buildings, in a wide clearing planted with olive trees. We tied our pony to an ilex and went to explore the Hermitage. But the building was enclosed round by walls and hedges, and the only entrance was by a stout gate armed with a knocker, behind which was apparently an outer yard and a high wall pierced only by a twisted iron balcony. So we knocked.

But that knocker was made only for Popes and Emperors walking about with their tiaras and crowns and sceptres, like the genuine Popes and Emperors of Italian folk-tales and of Pinturicchio's frescoes; for no knocking of ours, accompanied by loud yells, could elicit an answer. It seemed simple enough to get in some other way; there must be peasants about at work, even supposing the holy hermit to have ceased to exist. But climbing wall and hurdles and squeezing between the close tight ilexes, brought us only to more walls, above which, as above the oakwoods from a distance, rose the inaccessible battlemented tower. And a small shepherdess, in a flapping Leghorn hat, herding black and white baby pigs in a neighbouring stubble-field under the olives, was no more able than we to break the spell of the Hermitage. And all round, for miles apparently, undulated the dense grey plumage of the ilex woods.

The low sun was turning the stubble orange, where the pigs were feeding; and the distant hills of the Maremma were growing very blue behind the olive trees. So, lest night should overtake us, we turned our pony's head towards the city, and traversed the oakwoods and skirted the lavender hill, rather disbelieving in the reality of the place we had just been at, save when we saw its tower mock us, emerging again; an inaccessible, improbable place. The air was scented by the warm lavender of the hillsides; and by the pines forming a Japanese pattern, black upon the golden lacquer of the sky.

Soon the moon rose, big and yellow, lighting very gradually the road in whose gloom you could vaguely see the yokes of white cattle returning from work. By the time we reached the city hill everything was steeped in a pale yellowish light, with queer yellowish shadows; and the tall tanneries glared out with their buttressed balconied top, exaggerated and alarming. Scrambling up the moonlit steep of Fonte Branda, and passing under a black arch, we found ourselves in the heart of the gaslit and crowded city, much as if we had been shot out of a cannon into another planet, and feeling that the Hermitage of Lecceto was absolutely apocryphal.

5

The reason of this midsummer magic—whose existence no legitimate descendant of Goths and Vandals and other early lovers of Italy can possibly deny—the reason is altogether beyond my philosophy. The only word which expresses the phenomenon, is the German word, untranslatable, *Bescheerung*, a universal giving of gifts, lighting of candles, gilding of apples, manifestation of marvels, realisation of the desirable and improbable— to wit, a Christmas Tree. And Italy, which knows no Christmas trees, makes its *Bescheerung* in midsummer gets rid of its tourist vulgarities, hides away the characteristics of its trivial nineteenth century, decks itself with magnolia blossoms and water-melons, with awnings and street booths, with *mandolins* and guitars; spangles itself with church festivals and local pageants and instead of wax-tapers and Chinese lanterns lights up the biggest golden sun by day, the biggest silver moon by night, all for the benefit of a few childish descendants of Goths and Vandals.

Nonsense apart, I am inclined to think that the specific charm of Italy exists only during the hot months; the charm which gives one a little stab now and then and makes one say—"This is Italy."

I felt that little stab, to which my heart had long become unused, at the beginning of this very summer in Tuscany, to which belong the above instances of Italian Midsummer Magic I was spending the day at a small, but very ancient, Benedictine Monastery (it was a century old when St. Peter Igneus, according to the chronicle, went through his celebrated Ordeal by Fire), now turned into a farm, and hidden, battlemented walls and great gate towers, among the cornfields near the Arno.

It came to me as the revival of an impression long forgotten, that overpowering sense that "This was Italy," it recurred and recurred in those same three words, as I sat under the rose-hedge opposite the water-wheel shed, garlanded with drying pea-straw; and as I rambled through the chill vaults, redolent of old wine-vats, into the sudden sunshine and broad shadows of the cloistered yards.

That smell was mysteriously connected with it; the smell of wine-vats mingled, I fancy (though I could not say why), with the sweet faint smell of decaying plaster and wood-work. One night, as we were driving through Bologna to wile away the hours between two trains, in the blue moon-mist and deep shadows of the black *porticoed* city, that same smell came to my nostrils as in a dream, and with it a whiff of bygone years, the years when first I had had this impression of Italian magic. Oddly enough, Rome, where I spent much of my childhood and which was the object of my childish and tragic adoration, was always something apart, never Italy for my feelings. The Apennines of Lucca and Pistoia, with their sudden revelation of Italian fields and lanes, of flowers on wall and along roadside, of bells ringing in the summer sky, of peasants working in the fields and with the loom and distaff, meant Italy.

But how much more Italy—and hence longed for how much!—was Lucca, the town in the plain, with cathedral and palaces. Nay, any of the mountain hamlets where there was nothing modern, and where against the scarred brick masonry and blackened stonework the cypresses rose black and tapering, the trellises crawled bright green uphill! One never feels, once out of childhood, such joy as on the rare occasions when I was taken to such places. A certain farmhouse, with cypresses at the terrace corner and a great oleander over the wall, was also Italy before it became my home for several years. Most of all, however, Italy was represented by certain towns: Bologna, Padua and Vicenza, and Siena, which I saw mainly in the summer.

It is curious how one's associations change: nowadays Italy means mainly certain familiar effects of light and cloud, certain exquisitenesses of sunset amber against ultramarine hills, of winter mists among misty olives, of folds and folds of pale blue mountains; it is a country which belongs to no time, which will always exist, superior to picturesqueness and romance. But that is but a vague, half-indifferent habit of enjoyment. And every now and then, when the Midsummer magic is rife, there comes to me that very different, old, childish meaning of the word; as on that day among the roses of those Benedictine cloisters, the cool shadow of the fig-trees in the yards, with the whiff of that queer smell, heavy with romance, of wine-saturated oak and crumbling plaster; and I know with a little stab of joy that this is Italy.

Limbo

Perocchè gente di molto valore
Conobbi che in quel Limbo eran sospesi.

1

It may seem curious to begin with Dante and pass on to the children's rabbits' house; but I require both to explain what it is I mean by Limbo; no such easy matter on trying. For this discourse is not about the Pious Pagans whom the poet found in honourable confinement at the Gate of Hell, nor of their neighbours the unchristened babies; but I am glad of Dante's authority for the existence of a place holding such creatures as have just missed a necessary rite, or come too soon for thorough salvation. And I am glad, moreover, that the poet has insisted on the importance—"*gente di molto valore*"—of the beings thus enclosed; because it is just with the superior quality of the things in what I mean by Limbo that we are peculiarly concerned.

And now for the other half of my preliminary illustration of the subject, to wit, the children's rabbits' house. The little gardens which the children played at cultivating have long since disappeared, taken insensibly back into that corner of the formal but slackly kept garden which looks towards the steep hill dotted with cows and sheep. But in that corner, behind the shapeless Portugal laurels and the patches of seeding grass, there still remains, beneath big trees, what the children used to call the "Rabbits' Villa." 'Tis merely a wooden toy house, with green moss-eaten roof, standing, like the lake dwellings of prehistoric times, on wooden posts, with the tall foxgloves, crimson and white, growing all round it.

There is something ludicrous in this superannuated toy, this Noah's ark on stilts among the grass and bushes; but when you look into the thing, finding the empty plates and cups "for having tea with the rabbits," and when you look into it spiritually also, it grows oddly pathetic. We walked up and down between the high hornbeam hedges, the sunlight lying low on the armies of tall daisies and seeding grasses, and falling in narrow glints among the white boles and hanging boughs of the beeches, where the wooden benches stand unused in the deep grass, and the old swing hangs crazily crooked. Yes, the rabbits' villa and the surrounding overgrown beds are quite pathetic.

Is it because they are, in a way, the graves of children long dead, as dead—despite the grown-up folk who may come and say "It was I"—as the rabbits and guinea-pigs with whom they once had tea? That is it; and that explains my meaning: the rabbits' villa is, to the eye of the initiate, one of many little branch establishments of Limbo surrounding us on all sides. Another poet, more versed in similar matters than Dante (one feels sure that Dante knew his own mind, and always had his own way, even when exiled), Rossetti, in a sonnet, has given us the terrible little speech, which would issue from the small Limbos of this kind: Look in my face: My name is Might-have-been.

2

Of all the things that Limbo might contain, there is one about which some persons, very notably Churchyard Gray, have led us into error. I do not believe there is much genius to be found in Limbo. The world, although it takes a lot of dunning, offers a fair price for this article, which it requires as much as water-power and coal, nay even as much as food and clothes (bread for its soul and raiment for its thought); so that what genius there is will surely be brought into market. But even were it wholly otherwise, genius, like murder, would out; for genius is one of the liveliest forces of nature: not to be quelled or quenched, adaptable, protean, expansive, nay explosive; of all things in the world the most able to take care of itself; which accounts for so much public expenditure to foster and encourage it: foster the sun's chemistry, the force of gravitation, encourage atomic affinity and natural selection, magnificent Maecenas and judicious parliamentary board, they are sure to do you credit!

Hence, to my mind, there are no mute inglorious Miltons, or none worth taking into account. Our sentimental surmises about them grow from the notion that human power is something like the wheels or cylinder of a watch, a neat numbered scrap of mechanism, stamped at a blow by a creative *fiat*, or hand-hammered by evolution, and fitting just exactly into one little plan, serving exactly one little purpose, indispensable for that particular machine, and otherwise fit for the dust-heap.

Happily for us it is certainly not so. The very greatest men have always been the most versatile: Lionardo, Goethe, Napoleon; the next greatest can still be imagined under different circumstances as turning their energy to very different tasks; and I am tempted to think that the hobbies by which many of them have laid much store, while the world merely laughed at the statesman's trashy verses or the musician's third-rate sketches, may have been of the nature of rudimentary organs, which, given a different environment, might have developed, become the creature's chief *raison d'être*, leaving that which has actually chanced to be his talent to become atrophied, perhaps invisible.

Be this last as it may—and I commend it to those who believe in genius as a form of monomania—it is quite certain that genius has nothing in common with machinery. It is the most organic and alive of living organisms; the most adaptable therefore, and least easily killed; and for this reason, and despite Gray's *Elegy*, there is no chance of much of it in Limbo.

This is no excuse for the optimistic extermination of distinguished men. It is indeed most difficult to kill genius, but there are a hundred ways of killing its possessors; and with them as much of their work as they have left undone. What pictures might Giorgione not have painted but for the lady, the rival, or the plague, whichever it was that killed him! Mozart could assuredly have given us a half-dozen more *Don Giovannis* if he had had fewer lessons, fewer worries, better food; nay, by his miserable death the world has lost, methinks, more even than that—a commanding influence which would have kept music, for a score of years, earnest and masterly but joyful: Rossini would not have run to seed, and Beethoven's ninth symphony might have been a genuine a "Hymn to Joy" if only Mozart, the Apollo of musicians, had, for a few years more, flooded men's souls with radiance.

A similar thing is said of Rafael; but his followers were mediocre, and he himself lacked personality, so that many a better example might be brought.

These are not useless speculations; it is as well we realise that, although genius be immortal, poor men of genius are not. Quite an extraordinarily small amount of draughts and microbes, of starvation bodily and spiritual, of pin-pricks of various kinds, will do for them; we can all have a hand in their killing; the killing also of their peace, kindliness and justice, sending these qualities to Limbo, which is full of such. And now, dear reader, I perceive that we have at last got Limbo well in sight and, in another minute, we may begin to discern some of its real contents.

3

The Paladin Astolfo, as Ariosto relates, was sent on a winged horse up to the moon; where, under the ciceroneship of John the Evangelist, he saw most of the things which had been lost on earth, among others the wits of many persons in bottles, his cousin Orlando's, which he had come on purpose to fetch, and, curiously enough, his own, which he had never missed.

The moon does well as storehouse for such brilliant, romantic things. The Limbo whose contents and branches I would speak of is far less glorious, a trifle humdrum; sometimes such as makes one smile, like that villa of the rabbits in the neglected garden. 'Twas for this reason, indeed, that I preferred to clear away at once the question of the mute inglorious Miltons, and of such solemn public loss as comes of the untimely death of illustrious men. Do you remember, by the way, reader, a certain hasty sketch by Cazin, which hangs in a corner of the Luxembourg? The bedroom of Gambetta after his death: the white bed neatly made, empty, with laurel garlands replacing him; the tricolor flag, half-furled, leaned against the chair, and on the table vague heaped-up papers; a thing quite modest and heroic, suitable to all similar occasions—Mirabeau say, and Stevenson on his far-off island—and with whose image we can fitly close our talk of genius wasted by early death.

I have alluded to happiness as filling up much space in Limbo; and I think that the amount of it lying in that kingdom of Might-have-been is probably out of all proportion with that which must do duty in this actual life. Browning's *Last Ride Together*—one has to be perpetually referring to poets on this matter, for philosophers and moralists consider happiness in its causal connection or as a fine snare to virtue—Browning's *Last Ride Together* expresses, indeed, a view of the subject commending itself to active and cheerful persons, which comes to many just after their salad days; to wit, what a mercy that we don't often get what we want most.

The objects of our recent ardent longings reveal themselves, most luridly sometimes, as dangers, deadlocks, fetters, hopeless labyrinths, from which we have barely escaped. This is the house I wanted to buy, the employment I fretted to obtain, the lady I pined to marry, the friend with whom I projected to share lodgings. With such sudden chill recognitions comes belief in a special providence, some fine Greek-sounding goddess, thwarting one's dearest wishes from tender solicitude that we shouldn't get what we want.

In such a crisis the nobler of us feel like the Riding Lover, and learn ideal philosophy and manly acquiescence; the meaner snigger ungenerously about those youthful escapes; and know not that they have gained safety at the price, very often, of the little good—ideality, faith and dash—there ever was about them: safe smug individuals, whose safety is mere loss to the *cosmos*.

But later on, when our characters have settled, when repeated changes have taught us which is our unchangeable ego, we begin to let go that optimist creed, and to suspect (suspicion turning to certainty) that, as all things which have happened to us have not been always advantageous, so likewise things longed for in vain need not necessarily have been curses.

As we grow less attached to theories, and more to our neighbours, we recognise every day that loss, refusal of the desired, has not by any means always braced or chastened the lives we look into; we admit that the Powers That Be showed considerable judgment in disregarding the teachings of asceticism, and inspiring mankind with innate repugnance to having a bad time. And, to return to the question of Limbo, as we watch the best powers, the whole usefulness and sweetness starved out of certain lives for lack of the love, the liberty or the special activities they prayed for; as regards the question of Limbo, I repeat, we grow (or try to grow) a little more cautious about sending so much more happiness—ours and other folk's—to the place of Might-have-been.

Some of it certainly does seem beyond our control, a fatal matter of constitution. I am not speaking of the results of vice or stupidity; this talk of Limbo is exclusively addressed to the very nicest people.

A deal of the world's sound happiness is lost through shyness. We have all of us seen instances. They often occur between members of the same family, the very similarity of nature, which might make mothers and daughters, brothers and sisters, into closest companions, merely doubling the dose of that terrible reserve, timidity, horror of human contact, paralysis of speech, which keeps the most loving hearts asunder. It is useless to console ourselves by saying that each has its own love of the other. And thus they walk, sometimes side by side, never looking in one another's eyes, never saying the word, till death steps in, death sometimes unable to loosen the tongue of the mourner.

Such things are common among our reserved northern races, making us so much less happy and less helpful in everyday life than our Latin and Teuton neighbours; and, I imagine, are commonest among persons of the same blood. But the same will happen between lovers, or those who should have been such; doubt of one's own feeling, fear of the other's charity, apprehension of its all being a mistake, has silently prevented many a marriage.

The two, then, could not have been much in love? Not in love, since neither ever allowed that to happen, more's the pity; but loving one another with the whole affinity of their natures, and, after all, being in love is but the crisis, or the beginning of that, if it's worth anything.

Thus shyness sends much happiness to Limbo. But actual shyness is not the worst. Some persons, sometimes of the very finest kind, endowed for loving-kindness, passion, highest devotion, nay requiring it as much as air or warmth, have received, from some baleful fairy, a sterilising gift of fear. Fear of what they could not tell; something which makes all community of soul a terror, and every friend a threat. Something terrible, in whose presence we must bow our heads and pray impunity therefrom for ourselves and ours.

But the bulk of happiness stacked up in Limbo appears, on careful looking, to be an agglomeration of other lost things; justice, charm, appreciation, and faith in one another, all recklessly packed off as so much lumber, sometimes to make room for fine new qualities instead! Justice, I am inclined to think, is usually sent to Limbo through the agency of others. A work in many folios might be written by condensing what famous men have had said against them in their days of struggle, and what they have answered about others in their days of prosperity.

The loss of charm is due to many more circumstances; the stress of life indeed seems calculated to send it to Limbo. Certain it is that few women, and fewer men, of forty, preserve a particle of it. I am not speaking of youth or beauty, though it does seem a pity that mature human beings should mostly be too fat or too thin, and lacking either sympathy or intellectual keenness. Charm must comprise all that, but much besides.

It is the undefinable quality of nearly every child, and of all nice lads and girls; the quality which (though it can reach perfection in exceptional old people) usually vanishes, no one knows when exactly, into the Limbo marked by the rabbits' villa, with its plates and teacups, mouldering on its wooden posts in the unweeded garden.

More useful qualities replace all these: hardness, readiness to snatch opportunity, mistrust of all ideals, inflexible self-righteousness; useful, nay necessary; but, let us admit it, in a life which, judged by the amount of dignity and sweetness it contains, is perhaps scarce necessary itself, and certainly not useful. The case might be summed up, for our guidance, by saying that the loss of many of our finer qualities is due to the complacent, and sometimes dutiful, cultivation of our worse ones!

For, even in the list of virtues, there are finer and less fine, nay virtues one might almost call atrocious, and virtues with a taint of ignominy. I have said that we lose some of our finer qualities this way; what's worse is, that we often fail to appreciate the finest qualities of others.

4

And here, coming to the vague rubric appreciation of others, I feel we have got to a district of Limbo about which few of us should have the audacity to speak, and few, as a fact, have the courage honestly to think. What do we make of our idea of others in our constant attempt to justify ourselves? No Japanese bogie-monger ever produced the equal of certain wooden monster-puppets which we carve, paint, rig out and christen by the names of real folk—alas, alas, dear names sometimes of friends!—and stick up to gibber in our memory; while the real image, the creature we have really known, is carted off to Limbo! But this is too bad to speak of.

Let us rather think gently of things, sad, but sad without ignominy, of friendships stillborn or untimely cut off, hurried by death into a place like that which holds the souls of the unchristened babies; often, like them, let us hope, removed to a sphere where such things grow finer and more fruitful, the sphere of the love of those we have not loved enough in life.

But that at best is but a place of ghosts; so let us never forget, dear friends, how close all round lies Limbo, the Kingdom of Might-have-been.

Ravenna and Her Ghosts
A Medieval Legend

My oldest impression of Ravenna, before it became in my eyes the abode of living friends as well as of outlandish ghosts, is of a melancholy spring sunset at Classe.

Classe, which Dante and Boccaccio call in less Latin fashion Chiassi, is the place where of old the fleet *(classis)* of the Romans and Ostrogoths rode at anchor in the Adriatic. And Boccaccio says that it is (but I think he over-calculates) at three miles distance from Ravenna. It is represented in the mosaic of Sant' Apollinare Nuovo, dating from the reign of Theodoric, by a fine city wall of gold *tesserae* (facing the representation of Theodoric's town palace with the looped-up embroidered curtains) and a strip of ultramarine sea, with two rowing-boats and one while blown-out sail upon it. Ravenna, which is now an inland town, was at that time built in a lagoon; and we must picture Classe in much the same relation to it that Malamocco or the Port of Lido is to Venice, the open sea-harbour, where big ships and flotillas were stationed, while smaller craft wound through the channels and sand-banks up to the city. But now the lagoon has dried up, the Adriatic has receded, and there remains of Classis not a stone, save, in the midst of stagnant canals, rice marsh and brown bogland, a gaunt and desolate church, with a ruinous mildewed house and a crevassed round tower by its side.

It seemed to me that first time, and has ever since seemed, no Christian church, but the temple of the great Roman goddess fever. The gates stood open, as they do all day lest inner damp consume the building, and a beam from the low sun slanted across the oozy brown nave and struck a round spot of glittering green on the mosaic of the apse. There, in the half dome stood rows and rows of lambs, each with its little tree and lilies, shining out white from the brilliant green grass of Paradise, great streams of gold and blue circling around them, and widening overhead into lakes of peacock splendour. The slanting sunbeam which burnished that spot of green and gold and brown mosaic, fell also across the altar steps, brown and green in their wet mildew like the ceiling above.

The floor of the church, sunk below the level of the road, was as a piece of boggy ground leaving the feet damp, and breathing a clammy horror on the air. Outside the sun was setting behind a bank of solid grey clouds, faintly reddening their rifts and sending a few rose-coloured streaks into the pure yellow evening sky. Against the sky stood out the long russet line, the delicate *cupolaed* silhouette of the sear pine-wood recently blasted by frost. While, on the other side, the marsh stretched out beyond sight, confused in the distance with grey clouds its lines of bare spectral poplars picked out upon its green and the greyness of the sky. All round the church lay brown grass, livid pools, green rice-fields covered with clear water reflecting the red sunset streaks; and overhead, driven by storm from the sea, the white gulls, ghosts you might think, of the white-sailed galleys of Theodoric, still haunting the harbour of Classis.

Since then, as I hinted, Ravenna has become the home of dear friends to which I periodically return, in autumn or winter or blazing summer, without taking thought for any of the ghosts. And the impressions of Ravenna are mainly those of life; the voices of children, the plans of the farmers, the squabbles of local politics. I am waked in the morning by the noises of the market; and opening my shutters look down upon green umbrellas and awnings spread over baskets of fruit and vegetables, and heaps of ironware and stalls of coloured stuffs and gaudy kerchiefs. The streets are by no means empty. A steam tramcar puffs slowly along the widest of them; and in the narrower, you have perpetually to squeeze against a house to make room for a clattering pony-cart, a jingling *carriole*, or one of those splendid bullock-waggons, shaped like an old-fashioned cannon-cart with spokeless wheels and metal studdings.

There are no medieval churches in Ravenna, and very few medieval houses. The older palaces, though practically fortified, have a vague look of Roman villas: and the whole town is painted a delicate rose and apricot colour, which, particularly if you have come from the sad-coloured cities of Tuscany, gives it a Venetian, and (if I may say so) chintz-petticoat flowered-kerchief cheerfulness. And the life of the people, when you come in contact with it, also leaves an impression of provincial, rustic bustle. The Romagnas are full of crude socialism. The change from rice to wheat-growing has produced agricultural discontent; and conspiracy has been in the blood of these people, ever since Dante answered the Romagnolo Giuido that his country would never have peace in its heart.

The ghosts of Byzantine emperors and exarchs, of Gothic kings and medieval tyrants must be laid, one would think, by socialist meetings and electioneering squabbles; and perhaps by another movement, as modern and as revolutionary, which also centres in this big historical village, the reclaiming of marshland, which may bring about changes in mode of living and thinking such as socialism can never effect; nay, for all one knows, changes in climate, in sea and wind and clouds, *Bonification,* reclaiming, that is the great word in Ravenna; and I had scarcely arrived last autumn, before I found myself whirled off, among dogcarts and *chars à bancs,* to view reclaimed land in the cloudless, pale blue, ice-cold weather.

On we trotted, with a great consulting of maps and discussing of expenses and production, through the flat green fields and meadows marked with haystacks; and jolted along a deep sandy track, all that remains of the Roméa, the pilgrims' way from Venice to Rome, where marsh and pool begin to interrupt the well-kept pastures, and the line of pine woods to come nearer and nearer. Over the fields, the frequent canals, and hidden ponds, circled gulls and wild fowl; and at every farm there was a little crowd of pony-carts and of gaitered sportsmen returning from the marshes. A sense of reality, of the present, of useful, bread-giving, fever-curing activity came by sympathy, as I listened to the chatter of my friends, and saw field after field, farm after farm, pointed out where, but a while ago, only swamp grass and bushes grew, and cranes and wild duck nested.

In ten, twenty, fifty years, they went on calculating, Ravenna will be able to diminish by so much the town-rates; the Romagnas will be able to support so many more thousands of inhabitants; and that merely by employing the rivers to deposit arable soil torn from the mountain valleys; the rivers—Po and his followers, as Dante called them—which have so long turned this country into marsh; the rivers which, in a thousand years, cut off Ravenna from her sea.

We turned towards home, greedy for tea, and mightily in conceit with progress. But before us, at a turn of the road appeared Ravenna, its towers and cupolas against a bank of clouds, a piled-up heap of sunset fire; its canal, barred with flame, leading into its black vagueness, a spectre city. And there, to the left, among the bare trees, loomed the great round tomb of Theodoric. We jingled on, silent and overcome by the deathly December chill.

That is the odd thing about Ravenna. It is, more than any of the Tuscan towns, more than most of the Lombard ones, modern, and full of rough, dull, modern life; and the past which haunts it comes from so far off, from a world with which we have no contact. Those pillared *basilicas*, which look like modern village churches from the street, affect one with their almost Moorish arches, their enamelled splendour of ultramarine, russet, sea-green and gold mosaics, their lily fields and peacock's tails in mosque-like domes, as great stranded hulks, come floating across Eastern seas and drifted ashore among the marsh and rice-field. The grapes and ivy berries, the pouting pigeons, the palm-trees and pecking peacocks, all this early symbolism with its association of Bachic, Eleusinian mysteries, seems, quite as much as the actual fragments of Grecian capitals, the discs and gratings of porphyry and alabaster, so much flotsam and jetsam cast up from the shipwreck of an older antiquity than Rome's; remnants of early Hellas, of Iona, perhaps of Tyre.

I used to feel this particularly in Sant' Apollinare Nuovo, or, as it is usually called, *Classe dentro*, the long *basilica* built by Theodoric, outrivaled later by Justinian's octagon church of Saint Vitalis. There is something extremely Hellenic in feeling (however un-Grecian in form) in the pearly fairness of the delicate silvery white column and capitals; in the gleam of white, on golden ground, and reticulated with jewels and embroideries, of the long band of mosaic virgins and martyrs running above them. The virgins, with their Byzantine names—Sancta Anastasia, Sancta Anatolia, Sancta Eulalia, Sancta Euphemia—have big *kohled* eyes and embroidered garments fantastically suggesting some Eastern hieratic dancing-girl; but they follow each other, in single file (each with her lily or rose-bush sprouting from the gauze, green mosaic), with erect, slightly balanced gait like the maidens of the Panathenaic procession, carrying, one would say, votive offerings to the altar. rather than crowns of martyrdom: all stately, sedate, as if drilled by some priestly ballet-master, all with the same wide eyes and set smile as of early Greek sculpture.

There is no attempt to distinguish one from the other. There are no gaping wounds, tragic attitudes, wheels, swords. pincers or other attributes of martyrdom. And the male saints on the wall opposite are equally unlike medieval Sebastians and Laurences, going, one behind the other, in shining, white *togas*, to present their crowns to Christ on his throne. Christ also, in this Byzantine art, is never the Saviour. He sits, an angel on each side, on His golden seat, clad in purple and sandalled with gold, serene, beardless, wide eyed like some distant descendant of the Olympic love with his mantle of purple and gold.

This church of Saint Apollinaris contains a chapel specially dedicated to the saint, which sums up that curious impression of Hellenic pre-Christian cheerfulness. It is encrusted with porphyry and *giallo antico,* framed with delicate carved ivy wreaths along the sides, and railed in with an exquisite piece of alabaster openwork of vines and grapes, as on an antique altar. And in a corner of this little temple, which seems to be waiting for some painter enamoured of Greece and marble, stands the Episcopal seat of the patron saint of the church, the saint who took his name from Apollo; an alabaster seat, wide-curved and delicate in whose back you expect to find, so striking is the resemblance, the relief of dancing *satyrs* of the chair of the Priest of Dionysus.

As I was sitting one morning, as was my wont in Sant'Apollinare Nuovo. which (like all Ravenna churches) is always empty, a woman came in, with a woollen shawl over her head, who, after hunting anxiously about, asked me where she would find the parish priest "It is," she said, "for the Madonna's milk. My husband is a labourer out of work, he has been ill, and the worry of it all has made me unable to nurse my little baby. I want the priest to ask him to get the Madonna to give me back my milk." I thought, as I listened to the poor creature, that there was but little hope of motherly sympathy from that Byzantine Madonna in purple and gold mosaic magnificence, seated ceremoniously on her throne like an antique Cybele.

Little by little one returns to one's first impression, and recognises that this thriving little provincial town, with its socialism and its *bonification* is after all a nest of ghosts, and little better than the churchyard of centuries.

Never, surely, did a town contain so many coffins, or at least thrust coffins more upon one's notice. The coffins are stone, immense oblong boxes, with massive sloping lids horned at each, corner, or trough-like things with delicate sea-wave patternings, figures of *toga'd* saints and devices of palm-trees, peacocks, and doves, the carving made clearer by a picking out of bright green damp. They stand about in all the churches, not walled in, but quite free in the aisles, the chapels, and even close to the door. Most of them are doubtless of the fifth or sixth century, others perhaps barbarous or mediaeval imitations; but they all equally belong to the ages in general, including our own, not curiosities or heirlooms, but serviceable furniture, into which generations have been put, and out of which generations have been turned to make room for later comers. It strikes one as curious at first to see, for instance, the date 1826 on a sarcophagus probably made under Theodoric or the Exarchs, but that merely means that a particular gentleman of Ravenna began that year his lease of entombment.

They have passed from hand to hand (or, more properly speaking, from corpse to corpse) not merely by being occasionally discovered in digging foundations, but by inheritance, and frequently by sale. My friends possess a stone coffin, and the receipt from its previous owner. The transaction took place some fifty years ago, a name (they are cut very lightly) changed, a slab or coat of arms placed with the sarcophagus in a different church or chapel, a deed before the notary—that was all. What became of the previous tenant? Once at least he surprised posterity very much; perhaps it was in the case of that very purchase for which my friends still keep the bill. I know not; but the stone-mason of the house used to relate that, some forty years ago, he was called in to open a stone coffin: when, the immense horned lid having been rolled off, there was seen, lying in the sarcophagus, a man in complete armour, his sword by his side and vizor up, who, as they cried out in astonishment, instantly fell to dust. Was he an Ostrogothic knight, some Gunther or Volker turned Roman senator, or perhaps a companion of Guido da Polenta, a messmate of Dante, a playfellow of Francesca?

Coffins being thus plentiful, their occupants (like this unknown warrior) have played considerable part in the gossip of Ravenna, It is well known, for instance, that Galla Placidia, daughter of Theodosius, sister of Areadius and Honorius, and wife to a Visigothic king, sat for centuries enthroned (after a few years of the strangest adventures) erect, inside the alabaster coffin, formerly plated with gold, in the wonderful little blue mosaic chapel which bears her name. You could see her through a hole, quite plainly, until, three centuries ago, some inquisitive boys thrust in a candle, and burned Theodosius's daughter to ashes. Dante also is buried under a little cupola at the corner of a certain street, and there was, for many years, a strange doubt about his bones. Had they been mislaid, stolen, mixed up with those of ordinary mortals?

The whole thing was shrouded in mystery. That street corner where Dante lies, a remote corner under the wing of a church, resembled, until it was modernised and surrounded by gratings, and filled with garlands and inscriptions to Mazzini, nothing so much as the corner of Dis where Dante himself found Farinata and Cavalcante. It is crowded with stone coffins; and, passing there in the twilight, one might expect to see flames upheaving their lids, and the elbows and shoulders of imprisoned followers of Epicurus.

Only once, so far as I know, have the inhabitants of Ravenna. Byzantine, mediaeval, or modern, wasted a coffin; but one is very glad of that once. I am speaking of a Roman sarcophagus, on which you can still trace the outlines of garlands, which stands turned into a cattle trough, behind the solitary farm in the depth of the forest of St. Vitalis. Round it the grass is covered in summer by the creeping tendrils of the white clematis; and, in winter, the great thorn bushes and barberries and oaks blaze out crimson and scarlet and golden. The big, long-horned, grey cows pass to and fro to be milked; and the shaggy ponies who haunt the pine wood come there to drink. It is better than housing no matter how many generations, jurisconsults, knights, monks, tyrants and persons of quality, among the damp and the stale incense of a church!

Enough of coffins! There are live things at Ravenna and near Ravenna; amongst others, though few people realise its presence, there is the sea.

It was on the day of the fish auction that I first went there. In the tiny port by the pier (for Ravenna has now no harbour) they were making an incredible din over the emptyings of the nets; pretty, mottled, metallic fish, and slimy octopuses and sepias and flounders, looking like pieces of sea-mud. The fishing-boats, mostly from the Venetian lagoon, were moored along the pier, wide-bowed things, with eyes in the prow like the ships of Ulysses; and bigger craft, with little castles and weathervanes and saints' images and penons on the masts like the galley of St. Ursula as painted by Carpaccio; but all with the splendid orange sail, patched with suns, lions, and coloured stripes, of the Northern Adriatic. The fishermen from Chioggia, their heads covered with the high scarlet cap of the fifteenth century, were yelling at the fishmongers from town; and all round lounged artillerymen in their white undress and yellow straps, who are encamped for practice on the sands, and whose carts and guns we had met rattling along the sandy road through the marsh.

On the pier we were met by an old man, very shabby and unshaven, who had been the priest for many years, with a salary of twelve pounds a year, of St. Maria in Porto Fuori, a little Gothic church in the marsh, where he had discovered and rubbed slowly into existence (it took him two months and heaven knows how many pennyworths of bread!) some valuable Giottesque *frescoes*. He was now chaplain of the harbour, and had turned his mind to maritime inventions, designing lighthouses, and shooting dolphins to make oil of their blubber. A kind old man, but with the odd brightness of a creature who has lived for years amid solitude and fever; a fit companion for the haggard saints whom he brought, one by one, in robes of glory and golden halos, to life again in his forlorn little church.

While we were looking out at the sea, where a little flotilla of yellow and cinnamon sails sat on the blue of the view-line like parrots on a rail, the sun had begun to set, a crimson ball, over the fringe of pine woods. We turned to go. Over the town, the place whence presently will emerge the slanting towers of Ravenna, the sky had become a brilliant, melancholy slate-blue; and apparently out of its depths, in the early twilight, flowed the wide canal between its dim banks fringed with tamarisk. No tree, no rock, or house was reflected in the jade-coloured water, only the uniform shadow of the bank made a dark, narrow band alongside its glassiness. It flows on towards the invisible sea, whose yellow sails overtop the grey marshland. In thick smooth strands of curdled water it flows lilac, pale pink, opalescent according to the sky above, reflecting nothing besides, save at long intervals the spectral spars and spider-like tissue of some triangular fishing-net; a wan and delicate Lethe. issuing. you would say, out of a far-gone past into the sands and the almost tideless sea.

Other places become solemn, sad, or merely beautiful at sunset. But Ravenna, it seems to me, grows actually ghostly; the Past takes it back at that moment, and the ghosts return to the surface.

For it is, after all. a nest of ghosts. They hang about all those silent, damp churches; invisible, or almost tantalising one with a sudden gleam which may. after all, be. only that of the mosaics, an uncertain outline which, when you near it, is after all tally a pale grey column. But one feels their breathing all round. They are legion, but I do not know who they are. I only know that they are white, luminous, with gold embroideries to their robes, and wide, painted eye's, and that they are silent. The good citizens of Ravenna, in the comfortable eighteenth century, filled the churches with wooden pews, convenient, genteel in line and colour, with their names and coats-of-arms in full on the backs. But the ghosts took no notice of this measure; and there they are, even among these pews themselves.

Bishops and exarchs, and jewelled empresses, and half Oriental autocrats, saints and bedizened court ladies, and barbarian guards and wicked chamberlains; I know not what they are. Only one of the ghosts takes a shape I can distinguish, and a name I am certain of. It is not Justinian or Theodora, who stare goggle eyed from their mosaic in San Vitale mere wretched historic realities; *they* cannot haunt. The spectre I speak of is Theodoric. His tomb is still standing, outside the town in an orchard; a great round tower, with a circular roof made (heaven knows how) of one huge slab of Istrian stone, horned at the sides like the sarcophagi, or vaguely like a Viking's cap. The ashes of the great king have long been dispersed, for he was an Arian heretic. But the tomb remains, intact, a thing which neither time nor earthquake can dismantle.

In the town they show a piece of masonry, the remains of a doorway, and a delicate, pillared window, built on to a modern house, which is identified (but wrongly I am told) as Theodoric's palace, by its resemblance to the golden palace with the looped-up curtains on the mosaic of the neighbouring church. Into the wall of this building is built a great Roman porphyry bath, with rings carved on it, to which time has adjusted a lid of brilliant green lichen.

There is no more. But Theodoric still haunts Ravenna. I have always, ever since I have known the town, been anxious to know more about Theodoric, but the accounts are jejune, prosaic, not at all answering to what that great king, who took his place with Attila and Sigurd in the great Northern epic, must have been. Historians represent him generally as a sort of superior barbarian, trying to assimilate and save the civilisation he was bound to destroy; an Ostrogothic king trying to be a Roman emperor; a military organiser and bureaucrat, exchanging his birthright of Valhalla for heaven knows what aulic red-tape miseries. But that is unsatisfactory. The real man, the Berserker trying to tame himself into the Caesar of a fallen, shrunken Rome, seems to come out in the legend of his remorse and visions, pursued by the ghosts of Boetius and Symmachus, the wise men he had slain in his madness.

He haunts Ravenna, striding along the aisles of her *basilicas*, riding under the high moon along the dykes of her marshes, surrounded by white-stoled Romans, and Roman ensigns with eagles and crosses; but clad, as the Gothic brass-worker of Innsbruck has shown him, in no Roman lappets and breastplate, but in full mail, with beaked steel shoes and steel *gorget*, his big sword drawn, his vizor down, mysterious, the Dietrich of the Nibelungenlied, Theodoric King of the Goths.

These are the ghosts that haunt Ravenna, the true ghosts haunting only for such as can know their presence. But Ravenna, almost alone among Italian cities, possesses moreover a complete ghost-story of the most perfect type and highest antiquity, which has gone round the world and become known to all people. Boccaccio wrote it in prose; Dryden rewrote it in verse; Botticelli illustrated it; and Byron summed up its quality in one of his most sympathetic passages. After this, to retell it were useless, had I not chanced to obtain, in a manner I am not at liberty to divulge, another version, arisen in Ravenna itself, and written, most evidently, in fullest knowledge of the case. Its language is the barbarous Romagnol dialect of the early fifteenth century, and it lacks all the Tuscan graces of the Decameron. But it possesses a certain air of truthfulness, suggesting that it was written by someone who had heard the facts from those who believed in them, and who believed in them himself; and I am therefore decided to give it, turned into English.

About that time (when Messer Guido da Pollenta was lord of Ravenna) men spoke not a little of what happened to Messer Nastasio de Honestis, son of Messer Brunoro, in the forest of Classis. Now the forest of Classis is exceeding vast, extending along the sea-shore between Ravenna and Cervia for the space of some fifteen miles, and has its beginning near the church of Saint Apollinaris, which is in the marsh; and you reach it directly from the gate of the same name, but also, crossing the River Ronco where it is easier to ford, by the gate called Sisa, beyond the houses of the Rasponis. And this forest aforesaid is made of many kinds of noble and useful trees, to wit, oaks, both free standing and in bushes, ilexes, elms, poplars, bays, and many plants of smaller growth but great dignity and pleasantness, as hawthorns, barberries, blackthorn, blackberry, brier-rose, and the thorn called *marrucca*, which bears pods resembling small hats or cymbals, and is excellent for hedging. But principally does this noble forest consist of pine-trees, exceeding lofty and perpetually green; whence indeed the arms of this ancient city, formerly the seat of the Emperors of Rome, are none other than a green pine-tree.

And the forest aforesaid is well stocked with animals, both such as run and creep, and many birds. The animals are fox-es, badgers, hares, rabbits, ferrets, squirrels, and wild boars, the which issue forth and eat the young crops and grub the fields with incredible damage to all concerned. Of the birds it would be too long to speak, both of those which are snared, shot with cross-bows, or hunted with the falcon; and they feed off fish in the ponds and streams of the forest, and grasses and berries, and the pods of the white vine (clematis) which covers the grass on all sides.

And the manner of Messer Nastasio being in the forest was thus, he being at the time a youth of twenty years or thereabouts, of illustrious birth, and comely person and learning and prowess, and modest and discreet bearing. For it so happened that, being enamoured of the daughter of Messer Hostasio de Traversariis, the damsel, who was lovely, but exceeding coy and shrewish, would not consent to marry him, despite the desire of her parents, who in everything, as happens with only daughters of old men (for Messer Hostasio was well stricken in years), sought only to please her. Whereupon Messer Nastasio, fearing lest the damsel might despise his fortunes, wasted his substance in presents and feastings, and joustings, but all to no avail.

When it happened that having spent nearly all he possessed and ashamed to show his poverty and his unlucky love before the eyes of his townsmen, he betook him to the forest of Classis, it being autumn, on the pretext of snaring birds, but intending to take privily the road to Rimini and thence to Rome, and there seek his fortune. And Nastasio took with him fowling-nets, and birdlime, and tame owls, and two horses (one of which was ridden by his servant), and food for some days; and they alighted in the midst of the forest, and slept in one of the fowling huts of cut branches set up by the citizens of Ravenna for their pleasure.

And it happened that on the afternoon of the second day (and it chanced to be Friday) of his stay in the forest. Messer Nastasio, being exceeding sad in his heart, went forth towards the sea to muse upon the unkindness of his beloved and the hardness of his fortune. Now you should know that near the sea, where you can clearly hear its roar even on windless days there is in that forest a clear place, made as by the hand of man, set round with tall pines even like a garden, but in the shape of a horse-course, free from bushes and pools, and covered with the finest greensward. Here, as Nastasio sat him on the trunk of a pine—the hour was sunset, the weather being uncommon clear he heard a rushing sound in the distance, as of the sea; and there blew a death-cold wind; and then came sounds of crashing branches, and neighing of horses, and yelping of hounds, and halloes and horns.

And Nastasio wondered greatly, for that was not the hour for hunting; and he hid behind a great pine trunk, fearing to be recognised. And the sounds came nearer, even of horns and hounds, and the shouts of huntsmen; and the bushes rustled and crashed, and the hunt rushed into the clearing, horsemen and foot, with many hounds. And behold, what they pursued was not a wild boar, but something white that ran erect, and it seemed to Messer Nastasio. as if it greatly resembled a naked woman; and it screamed piteously.

Now when the hunt had swept past. Messer Nastasio rubbed his eyes and wondered greatly. But even as he wondered, and stood in the middle of the clearing, behold, part of the hunt swept back, and the thing which they pursued ran in a circle on the greensward, shrieking piteously. And behold, it was a young damsel, naked, her hair loose and full of brambles, with only a tattered cloth around her middle. And as she came near to where Messer Nastasio was standing (but no one of the hunt seemed to heed him) the hounds were upon her, barking furiously, and a hunter on a black horse, black even as night. And a cold wind blew and caused Nastasio's hair to stand on end; and he tried to cry out, and to rush forward, but his voice died in his throat and his limbs were heavy, and covered with sweat, and refused to move.

Then the hounds fastening on the damsel threw her down, and he on the black horse turned swiftly, and transfixed her, shrieking dismally, with a boar-spear. And those of the hunt galloped up, and wound their horns; and he on the black horse, which was a stately youth habited in a coat of black and gold, and black boots and black feathers on his hat, threw his reins to a groom, and alighted and approached the damsel where she lay, while the huntsmen were holding back the hound and winding their horns. Then he drew a knife, such as are used by huntsmen, and driving its blade into the damsel's side, cut out her heart, and threw it, all smoking, into the midst of the hounds. And a cold wind rustled through the bushes, and all had disappeared, horses, and huntsmen, and hounds. And the grass was untrodden as if no man's foot or horse's hoof had passed there for months.

And Messer Nastasio shuddered, and his limbs loosened, and he knew that the hunter on the black horse was Messer Guido Degli Anastagi, and the damsel Monna Filomena, daughter of the Lord of Gambellara. Messer Guido had loved the damsel greatly, and been flouted by her, and leaving his home in despair, had been killed on the way by robbers, and Madonna Filomena had died shortly after. The tale was still fresh in men's memory, for it had happened in the city of Ravenna barely five years before. And those whom Nastasio had seen, both the hunter and the lady, and the huntsmen and horses and hounds, were the spirits of the dead.

When he had recovered his courage, Messer Nastasio sighed and said unto himself: "How like is my fate to that of Messer Guido! Yet would I never, even when a spectre, without weight or substance, made of wind and delusion, and arisen from hell, act with such cruelty towards her I love." And then he thought: "Would that the daughter of Messer Pavolo de Traversariis might hear of this! For surely it would cause her to relent!" But he knew that his words would be in vain, and that none of the citizens of Ravenna, and least of all the damsel of the Traversari, would believe them, but rather esteem him a madman.

Now it came about that when Friday came round once more, Nastasio, by some chance, was again walking in the forest-clearing by the great pines, and he had forgotten; when the sea began to roar, and a cold wind blew; and there came through the forest the sound of horses and hounds, causing Messer Nastasio's hair to stand up and his limbs to grow weak as water. And he on the black horse again pursued the naked damsel, and struck her with his boar-spear, and cut out her heart and threw it to the hounds: the which hunter and damsel were the ghosts of Messer Guido, and of Madonna Filomena, daughter of the Lord of Gambellara, arisen out of Hell. And in this fashion did it happen for three Fridays following, the sea beginning to moan, the cold wind to blow and the spirits to hunt the deceased damsel at twilight in the clearing among the pine-trees.

Now when Messer Nastasio noticed this, he thanked Cupid, which is the Lord of all Lovers, and devised in his mind a cunning plan. And he mounted his horse and returned to Ravenna, and gave out to his friends that he had found a treasure in Rome: and that he was minded to forget the damsel of the Traversari and seek another wife. But in reality he went to certain money-lenders, and gave himself into bondage, even to be sold as a slave to the Dalmatian pirates if he could not repay his loan. And he published that he desired to take to him a wife, and for that reason would feast all his friends and the chief citizens of Ravenna, and regale them with a pageant in the pine forest, where certain foreign slaves of his should show wonderful feats for their delight. And he sent forth invitations, and among them to Messer Pavolo de Traversariis and his wife and daughter. And he bid them for a Friday, which was also the eve of the Feast of the Dead.

Meanwhile he took to the pine forest carpenters and masons, and such as paint and gild cunningly, and waggons of timber, and cut stone for foundations, and furniture of all kinds; and the waggons were drawn by four and twenty yoke of oxen, grey oxen of the Romagnol breed. And he caused the artisans to work day and night, making great fires of dry myrtle and pine branches, which lit up the forest all around. And he caused them to make foundations, and build a pavilion of timber in the clearing which is the shape of a horse-course, surrounded by pines. The pavilion was oblong, raised by ten steps above the grass, open all round and reposing on arches and pillars; and there was a projecting *abacus* under the arches over the capitals, after the Roman fashion; and the pillars were painted red, and the capitals red also picked out with gold and blue, and a shield with the arms of the Honestis on each.

The roof was raftered, each rafter painted with white lilies on a red ground, and heads of youths and damsels; and the roof outside was made of wooden tiles, shaped like shells and gilded. And on the top of the roof was a weather-vane; and the vane was a figure of Cupid, god of love, cunningly carved of wood and painted like life, as he flies, poised in air, and shoots his darts on mortals. He was winged and blindfolded, to show that love is inconstant and no respecter of persons; and when the wind blew, he turned about, and the end of his scarf, which was beaten metal, swung in the wind.

Now when the pavilion was ready, within six days of its beginning, carpets were spread on the floor, and seals placed, and garlands of bay and myrtle slung from pillar to pillar between the arches. And tables were set, and sideboards covered with gold and silver dishes and trenchers; and a raised place, covered with arras, was made for the players of fifes and drums and lutes; and tents were set behind for the servants, and fires prepared for cooking meat. Whole oxen and sheep were brought from Ravenna in wains, and casks of wine, and fruit and white bread, and many cooks, and serving-men, and musicians, all habited gallantly in the colours of the Honestis, which are vermilion and while, parti-coloured, with black stripes; and they wore doublets laced with gold, and on their breast the arms of the house of Honestis, which are a dove holding a leaf.

Now on Friday the eve of the Feast of the Dead, all was ready, and the chief citizens of Ravenna set out for the forest of Classis, with their wives and children and servants, some on horseback, and others in wains drawn by oxen, for the tracks in that forest are deep. And when they arrived, Messer Nastasio welcomed them and thanked them all, and conducted them to their places in the pavilion. Then all wondered greatly at its beauty and magnificence, and chiefly Messer Pavolo de Traversariis; and he sighed, and thought within himself, "Would that my daughter were less shrewish, that I might have so noble a son-in-law to prop up my old age!" They were seated at the tables, each according to their dignity, and they ate and drank and praised the excellence of the cheer; and flowers were scattered on the tables, and young maidens sang songs in praise of love, most sweetly.

Now when they had eaten their fill, and the tables been removed, and the sun was selling between the pine-trees. Messer Nastasio caused them all to be seated facing the clearing, and a herald came forward, in the livery of the Honestis, sounding his trumpet and declaring in a kind voice that they should now witness a pageant, the which was called the Mystery of Love and Death. Then the musicians struck up. and began a concert of fifes and lutes, exceeding sweet and mournful. And at that moment the sea began to moan, and a cold wind to blow: a sound of horsemen and hounds and horns and crashing branches came through the wood; and the damsel, the daughter of the Lord of Gambellara, rushed naked, her hair streaming and her veil torn, across the grass, pursued by the hounds, and by the ghost of Messer Guido on the black horse, the nostrils of which were filled with fire.

Now when the ghost of Messer Guido struck that damsel with the boar-spear, and cut out her heart, and threw it, while the others wound their horns, to the hounds, and all vanished, Messer Nastasio de Honestis, seizing the herald's trumpet, blew in it. and cried in a loud voice, "The Pageant of Death and Love! The Pageant of Death and Love! Such is the fate of cruel damsels!" and the gilt Cupid on the roof swung round creaking dreadfully, and the daughter of Messer Pavolo uttered a great shriek and fell on the ground in a swoon.

Here the Romagnol manuscript comes to a sudden end, the outer sheet being torn through the middle. But we know from the Decameron that the damsel of the Traversari was so impressed by the spectre-hunt she had witnessed that she forthwith relented towards Nastagio degli Onesti, and married him, and that they lived happily ever after. But whether or not that part of the pine forest of Classis still witnesses this ghostly hunt, we have no means of knowing.

On the whole, I incline to think that, when the great frost blasted the pines (if not earlier) the ghosts shifted quarters from the forest of Classis to the church of the same name, on that forest's brink. Certainly there seems nothing to prevent them. Standing in the midst of those uninhabited rice-fields and marshes, the church of Classis is yet always open, from morning till night; the great portals gaping, no curtain interposed. Open and empty; mass not even on Sundays; empty of human beings, open to the things of without. The sunbeams enter through the open side windows, cutting a slice away from that pale, greenish twilight; making a wedge of light on the dark, damp bricks; bringing into brief prominence some of the great sarcophagi, their peacocks and palm-trees picked out in vivid green lichen.

Snakes also enter, the Sacristan tells me, and I believe it, for within the same minute, I saw a dead and a living one among the arum leaves at the gate. Is that little altar, a pagan-looking marble table, isolated in the midst of the church, the place where they meet, pagan creatures claiming those Grecian marbles? Or do they hunt one another round the aisles and into the crypt, slithering and hissing, the souls of Guido degli Anastagi perhaps, and of his cruel lady love?

Such are Ravenna and Classis, and the Ghosts that haunt them.

The Featureless Wisdom

A Story from *Pope Jacynth and Other Fantastic Tales*
(*Ex Libris Augustine Bulteau*)

The manner in which Diotima, a wise woman of Mantineia, came to possess an effigy of Athena, conspicuous by the absence of all features, was as follows:—

This Diotima was also a priestess, nobody knows exactly of what But the position gave her an opportunity of knowing a great variety of remarkable persons, as Socrates, Alcibiades, Zeno, Protagoras, Gorgias, and a number of highly-gifted youths who came to nothing. Their conversation dispelled all vain prejudices from the soul of the Priestess of Mantineia; and she felt that the only wisdom to which she could possibly bring worship and service would have to be a wisdom entirely and exclusively her own.

This being the case, she betook herself one day to the workshop of Pheidias, who, as is well known, received orders for divinities of all sorts and dimensions. And she requested him to make her an image of Athena of a size to fit into her hat-box, and with a set of features easily distinguishable from those of the idols handed down by the past and still adored by the common herd. Pheidias had heard his friend Socrates speak of Diotima, and had even suspected that, as may happen between ladies and philosophers, the wise man had attributed some of his own remarks to the Priestess of Mantineia. Pheidias undertook the commission with much pleasure. And, at the end of eight days, Diotima returned to his workshop. She was shown an image of Athena, most excellently carved out of a cocoanut, and uniting, in her finely-modelled limbs and graceful drapery, all the well-known merits of the Periklean school of sculpture. Diotima took the image in her hand and turned it round with admiration.

'There's only one thing I don't much like,' she said after a minute. 'Isn't that head you have given her a little of what archaeologists are going to call (for I have the gift of prophecy, you know) *the type of the infernal goddesses?*'

'Perhaps it is, a trifle,' answered Pheidias; 'we'll alter it by next Wednesday.' Next Wednesday Diotima ordered her chariot and returned to the workshop.

'You must try and not think me too great a bore, *cher maître*, she said, after a pause, 'but this new head is—isn't it?—just a little bit too like that of an Aphrodite. Oh, I have no sort of prejudice against Aphrodite—only .... well, you know, there are statues of her in the fishmarket and horrid places like that, I believe, and the associations. . . . . But you *would* be a dear to alter this.'

'All right,' answered Pheidias, 'shall we say Monday week?'

But when that Monday had come and the Priestess of Mantineia had alighted at the workshop, there was a new surprise awaiting her. 'Upon my word,' said Pheidias, 'this, my dear lady, is really not my fault.' For his pupil (Kalamis, I believe; unless, indeed, Kalamis was his master!) had fitted on to the image of Athena a very neat and expressive little head of Silenus.

'Would you mind telling your workman,' said Diotima with exquisite politeness, 'that when he takes to fitting heads on to my little Goddess of Wisdom it is just as well he should not be drunk?'

'My dear lady,' protested Pheidias, 'you see before you the most humiliated of all your humble servants. Kalamis shall be kept on bread-and-water for ten days, and I will myself see to the new head of the figure which is to have the honour of presiding over your private devotions; and this time I will give myself the pleasure of calling in person upon you.'

At the end of a fortnight the butler of Diotima introduced,

not without some disgust, the venerable but rather untidy sculptor of the Parthenon. 'Let me have the pleasure myself, dear, dear old Pheidias,' exclaimed the Priestess of Mantineia, and proceeded to unwrap the tissue-paper from off the figure of Athena. But when she had done so there was an awful silence. For the effigy of the goddess, which Diotima held at arms'-length to look at, had indeed a most becoming helmet with three *chimaeras* tastefully curled round the ostrich feathers; it had even a face, with finely-modelled chin and delicate, flat ear. But it had no features. No eyes, no nose, no mouth—nothing!

The silence was long, and, to any soul less serene than that of a sculptor of Antiquity, would have been exceedingly painful.

Louis Norbert

Dramatis Persons Personages of the Twentieth Century
Lady Venetia Hammond, a delightful siren of uncertain age.
Earl of Arthington (her brother), personage who does not speak.
The Old Marchese at Pisa.
The Marchese's Daughter.
The Young Archaeologist.
Scene: Pisa and Arthington Manor, 1908-9.
Personages of the Seventeenth Century
Louis Norbert de Caritan.
Sir Anthony Thesiger, ancestor of Lady Venetia.
A Young Lord, personage who does not speak.
Maria Mancini (niece of Mazarin), widow of Prince Colonna, Great Constable of Naples.
A Woman disguised as a singing man.
A Masked Lady.
"Queen Berenice."
The Abbé Manfredini, a man of learning and parts, spy and assassin in the pay of the French Court.
Artemisia, a crowned poetess, afterwards abbess.
An old Spanish Captain (father to Artemisia).
Maskers, Spies, Bravoes, and Travellers.
The Scene is in Rome and Pisa, 1683-1684.

CHAPTER 1

Good heavens—why, this is *he*," exclaimed Lady Venetia, suddenly coming to a stop before a sepulchral slab in the easternmost corner of the Campo Santo of Pisa.

The young archaeologist, thus interrupted just as his companion had seemed so enchantingly interested in all he was showing her, recognised, with a little chill, that the delightful morning was over. With the resigned disinterestedness of disappointment, his eyes followed the lady's, now fixed on a marble tablet, small, unornamented and (he added to himself with vindictive criticalness) remarkably poorly lettered for its date, which was the end of the seventeenth century. It was let into the wall, breast-high, between two of those gothic windows of the famous cloister.

"Louis Norbert de Caritan"—the archaeologist read out loud, in a voice expressive of utter blankness of mind, shadowed over by personal disconsolateness, and added, for politeness' sake—"Who was he?"

Lady Venetia at first took no notice of the question and still less of the tone. Her very beautiful eyes (which had a delightful way of filling with tears whenever she was much amused) were fixed on that slab, as if she were looking through it and its wall to some distance beyond; and despite the conventional self-control she always attempted to cultivate, it was perfectly obvious that she was moved far beyond surprise or curiosity.

"Who he was?" she answered after a silence, as if the archaeologist's uninterested question had slowly worked into her own previous thoughts.

"Who Louis Norbert de Caritan was? Well, that is exactly what we none of us in my family have ever known and probably ever will know."

Then, with an effort of politeness betokening that it was no business of her companion's, she vouchsafed some further information.

"This is the name: Louis Norbert de Caritan, and very nearly the same date—

1682 instead of 1684—on a portrait hanging in my old home in what used to be called the Ghost's room."

"How very interesting," answered the archaeologist perfunctorily. He had a notion that great ladies were all addicted to some form or other of spirit-rapping. Besides, the pleasant talk they had been having was at an end, all along of this silly mystery; and she would no longer care a button about the life of Saint Ranieri or any of the paintings he had carefully selected to expound to her.

"It isn't a bit interesting except to me," answered Lady Venetia, with icy irritation.

The tone smote him. What unpardonable solecism was he being snubbed for by this woman, whose beauty, whose manner, whose very age (quite unfathomably mysterious in his youthful eyes), were already fascinating him hopelessly with mingled delight and terror? That—namely his own unknown offence—was the only riddle he could think of as he stood silently by her side, where she stooped her majestic person (being an Archaeologist he thought of her as Demeter, also because she was reddish blonde) over that tablet, reiterating the words of the epitaph as if learning them by heart, and attempting to pronounce the old-fashioned spelling.

"To think of his having died here at Pisa, *our* young Frenchman, Louis Norbert; and none of us having known anything about it. *Louis Norbert de Caritan, sixteen hundred and eighty-four, and son of Pierre Norbert sieur de Caritan and Claude de Leyrac his wife of La Rochelle*—just as on our own picture—of course it's he. And only twenty-four years old."

Lady Venetia spoke as if to herself. She had forgotten not only the archaeologist who was so kindly giving up his time to showing her the sights of Pisa, but the rest of her party, who must by this time be at the other end of the cloister. Indeed, the archaeologist began wondering whether his scientific dignity did not require him to set off after the others and leave this contemptuous and disconcerting siren to the contemplation of her certainly foolish and probably quite unauthentic mystery—in fact, assert himself in some manner he could not decide upon. But after a minute more of such silent contemplation of the epitaph, varied by raising her eyes to a ball of cloud dazzlingly white on the blue between the window tracery and the black tip of one of the cypresses of the enclosure, Lady Venetia suddenly turned to him and asked for a pencil. "I must get this inscription correct," she explained.

"Allow me to copy it for you," cried the archaeologist, suddenly reconciled and joyful. "All right—then I'll dictate it to you." But with one of her delightful, unaccountable changes of manner (delightful at least when they were changes back to one's own poor self) she became suddenly very aware of the archaeologist, and more particularly of his having pulled out his notebook.

"Oh no, not in that," she exclaimed. "I can't have you tearing out leaves from your notes about the origin of Pisan architecture and all those wonderful things you have been so awfully good telling me about—no, not your notes. Haven't you a card, or the entrance ticket—anything to scribble upon?"

The archaeologist, who had retained certain foreign habits despite his English bringing up, bowed very ceremoniously and made a little speech.

"I will copy out the epitaph for you as soon as I get home, and it shall remain, if you will allow it, among my pedantic dates and measurements, in remembrance of a very delightful interlude in the routine of my work."

"Thank you, you really *are* very nice," Lady Venetia exclaimed, unconsciously implying that she had just been thinking that he was not. So she fell to reading out loud, with minute, she evidently thought scientific, insistence on the old-fashioned and moreover faulty spelling of that French inscription engraved by seventeenth-century Italian stone masons. It was, or rather is— for you can go and read it tomorrow—as follows:

Ci-git Louis Norbert de Caritan, escuier, fils de Pierre Norbert sieur de Caritan pres de la Rochelle et de Claude de Leyrac sa femme, décédés. Lequel Lovis, avant de passer au service de S. M.

le Roy d'Angleterre voulust fair (sic) ce voyage d'Italie et estant
tombé malade a Rome pour changer d'air se porta en cette ville
de Pise où subitement il mourust et fust enterré en ce saint lieu
le XV jour d'Aoust MDLXXXIV asgée (sic) de XXIV ans.
Priez Dieu pour le salut de son ame. Fait par le très cher ami de
la nation et maison de France, l'Abbé Manfredini, chanoine de
cette cathedrale.

"Curious all this talk about this Abbé Manfredini," remarked the archaeologist, professional instinct overcoming fear of intrusion on Lady Venetia's mystery. "I mean all this talk of his being *le Très Cher Ami de la Nation et Maison de France*, on the tombstone of another man, about whom he says so little, and who was going to enter the English king's service, not the French one's. Do you remark that he never says he was the friend of the deceased or of the deceased's family?"

"How could he?" interrupted Lady Venetia; "nobody ever knew what Louis Norbert's family was, and we have always known that Pierre, his father, and Claude, his mother, must have been faked by my great-great-great-grand—whatever you would call him—Nicholas Thesiger, who brought him up."

The archaeologist was too shy to express any surprise at this additional information, which Lady Venetia gave as if she were mentioning some well-known recent detail of her own family affairs.

"All the more," he said, glad to get over that—"all the more it seems odd that this Abbé Manfredini should have thought it necessary to assure the public that he himself was a friend of the French Crown, a circumstance which didn't concern the deceased. It almost looks as if Manfredini may have been one of the unofficial diplomatic agents that kings and ministers employed in those days, especially in Italy, wandering *abbés*, monks, barber surgeons, even opera singers, people who were paid for secret information and occasionally for something worse."

Lady Venetia's eyes had settled on the archaeologist's face as he spoke the last words. "That explains," she burst out when he had barely done. "That explains everything! I mean Louis Norbert's death here and our never having heard of it. It was this Abbé Manfredini who did it. I have always felt sure there must have been foul play. And it was by order of the French court. They had some secret reason against him. And of course they couldn't kill him while he was living with my people in England; so they waited till he happened to go to Italy. And then that *abbé* put up the tombstone with all this talk about his friendship to the French nation and crown. It was his way of sending in his bill after he had done the murdering. Do you see?"

In saying these words Lady Venetia turned upon the archaeologist a face so beautifully and wonderfully inspired as to deprive him of every reasonable reply. But instead of yielding to his sense of awe and admiration by holding his tongue, the ill-advised youth tried to show himself a perfect man of the world.

"What I see," he answered with heavy airiness, "is that your imagination not only gallops but flies." And by way of making matters worse, he even added: "Why, it is you, not I, who ought to have been an archaeologist."

"I could not possibly have disliked anything more," was her reply. Then, drawing herself together, till she loomed goddesslike, and casting an indifferent glance at the neighbouring *frescoes*—"By the way," she added, "the rest of them must be getting impatient for lunch."

Whereupon she walked silently towards the exit.

But, despite the woman of the world's dignity (mysteriously terrifying and fascinating to the archaeologist) Lady Venetia was in reality remarkably impulsive. So, by the time they had got to the gate of the cloister, she was already remorseful at having shown so much exasperation with this exasperating young pedant, just as she had previously been self-reproachful for taking him so much into her confidence.

"You will come home and have lunch with us, of course, Professor?" she said, using that title to which he had no sort of right, and avoiding looking at him.

But the archaeologist had understood. Or at all events he had smarted. So he pretended that he had an archaeological meeting which would spread over all that day. It would also, he suddenly remembered, prevent his having the honour of dining with Lady Venetia and her friends. He felt of ice and also of steel, let alone tingling (which neither of these calm substances would do) with self-defensive indignation. But when he had accompanied Lady Venetia to the steps of the Campo Santo and helped her into one of the cabs which were prowling round in the wintry sunshine, something seemed suddenly to give way inside him, the steel and the ice turned into an aching void. And, at the very moment that the lady drove off to overtake her party, he suddenly exclaimed:

"Oh, I had forgotten the inscription. I will copy it out and bring it this evening, if you will allow me to call for a few minutes after dinner to take leave of you—"

CHAPTER 2

When the archaeologist turned up at the hotel that evening, with a facsimile of the epitaph, whose artistic elaboration must have taken much of the time of the supposed archaeological meeting, he found Lady Venetia and her companions on that belated motoring tour wrapped up in furs and bent upon a walk in the moonlight. Of course they all said the Professor (for so they called him in their innocence of what professorship means) must show them their way. And of course, despite his resolutions, the "Professor "did so with alacrity.

They left the semicircle of white lights of the Arno quays, with tall white houses asleep above the wavering reflections in the river. They walked silently through the hushed emptiness of the wide Pisan streets, and naturally in the direction of the cathedral and Campo Santo. The moon was full and high; and the church and tower and baptistery stood clear as at noon, every tiny pillar and moulding drawn as in Indian ink, the pale yellow of their marble nowise bleached by that pure white radiance. Only, under the blue, luminous sky (where a single star pierced throbbing and a *cirrus* spread across like an ostrich feather) all things had a stillness, a solemnity and aloofness far beyond that of day, even in this solitary and venerable corner.

They walked—*they* were the archaeologist, Lady Venetia, her cousin the ambassador on leave of absence and his two uninteresting daughters—round and round and up and down for quite a long while, silent, and aware of the silence only the more when one of them made a remark in an undertone. The windless night was icy. But it was not merely the moon and the biting cold which made the diplomatic personage, walking ahead with his two girls, turn round comparing the wide, shining cathedral platform with the terrace in Hamlet. The long wall of the Campo Santo, with its flat buttresses, was in full moonlight, and the side of the cathedral nearest it was in its own shadow, lying deep, broad, and black upon the grass.

But as they paced this shadowy side, there met them as they came forward (seeming to steal round till it stood fully revealed) the great circular whiteness of the baptistery, with the moonlight searching all its openwork, and the buttons along its cupola-ribs black against the bright and moon-blue sky. On the other side stretched the long, low belfried wall of the old hospital, and the stone posts closing the grassy precincts glared white. And among the crenellated walls on the other hand there loomed half visible that deep, closed gate, unopened doubtless for centuries, with the archaic lion among the bushes on its battlements: that gate which always made the young archaeologist, who, after all, was secretly a poet, think most unscientifically of the East, of Saladin and Coeur de Lion, and at the same time, more unscientifically still, of primeval Greece, Mycenae or Argos.

That familiar haunting thought freed him from whatever self-conscious shyness the solemn moonlight had not blotted out already. And, with the eloquence of those shy people who can talk easily only on deep or poetic subjects, he described this impression to Lady Venetia.

"Then you are not a pedant and afraid of seeming one," she remarked with meditative frankness.

"You thought me a pedant—and I did feel afraid of seeming one," he answered quite honestly, "because I didn't know what manner to put on, and put on the wrong one, of course—this morning when you began talking about that . . . and his epitaph."

Somehow he was afraid of saying the name.

"Exactly. You did not know what to make of my romancing, as you thought it. You were wondering whether I was an amateur novelist or a *planchette* and crystal reader. And in the doubt you thought it extremely proper that I should be snubbed by a scientific mind."

It was so absurdly like the truth and at the same time so far from what he felt it to have been, that the archaeologist, having become quite natural, began to laugh.

Lady Venetia laughed also, and there was something enchanting in her laugh, first because it was often accompanied by tears, and secondly because it was nearly always more at her own expense than at others.

"There is nothing to laugh about," she protested in the midst of her laughter—" it was very, very painful. And I have never regretted anything so much in my life as having let myself talk about Louis Norbert de Caritan to a pedant I had mistaken for a sympathetic friend."

"It wasn't the poor pedant's fault though, was it, dear Lady Venetia? Heaven knows he was innocent of any attempt to be sympathetic, worse luck to him."

"People don't seem sympathetic because they try to," she answered. "You ought to know that, even at your youthful age. You had been awfully nice and kind to all of us; not minding our being dunces, and having faith in our being able to see beautiful things if somebody else was kind enough to open our eyes to them. And you had said nice things, without knowing it, about yourself. Just hinting at them in your matter-of-fact way. That Abbess, who had been a fashionable poetess and musician, that you showed us the portrait of yesterday, and whom you seemed to be rather in love with; by the way, you never told me her name? "

"She was of Spanish extraction, or rather of Moorish, de Val-

207

or y Cordoba—her name was Artemisia."

Lady Venetia looked up in the moonlight. "Really?" she remarked. "Artemisia is a name that exists in my family."

"It is a name one meets with in Italy in the seventeenth century, when she lived," he answered, little guessing that she had been on the point of adding "and it is one of my own names."

"The seventeenth century she lived in?" resumed Lady Venetia. "Louis Norbert de Caritan also lived in the seventeenth century, and died in Pisa. Perhaps they may have met?"

"Just as likely not," replied the archaeologist, with historical dryness. It was like looking the other way. And he felt obliged to look the other way. For as they loitered on far behind their companions, and she walked by his side tall and vague in her furs, he somehow knew that her fine, kind face, more beautiful and bewitching than when she had been young, was tilted upwards in that characteristic manner, gazing up as if the moonlight was full of unseen things. And, just because he knew what her face looked like at that moment, he naturally could not look at it.

"You see," suddenly resumed Lady Venetia, "you had happened to surprise, by the chance of our finding the epitaph, one of the few bits of childish romance that exist, that I cherish secretly in my remarkably prosaic, elderly heart. . . . Sixteen hundred and eighty-four—that is the date, isn't it?"

"And the fifteenth of August," chimed in the archaeologist, with an extra dose of scientific dryness.

With that easy cordiality which already made him occasionally jealous of all the other people to whom she must evidently show it, the lady had passed her long-furred sleeve through his arm, and he felt the weight of her slow, graceful, rather heavy step as she walked.

"The portrait of him hangs," she went on after a long silence, "or rather it used to hang—for heaven knows all the changes my late sister-in-law may have made!—in what was called the Ghost's room at Arthington. No one had ever seen or heard a ghost in that particular room, so far as I know; and there are ghosts enough to be seen and heard (I don't care for ghosts, do you? such prosaic twaddle it seems to me!) in other parts of the old place. But that room has always been called the Ghost's room, and has always been shut up, except when there were hunt balls and that sort of thing and people had to be crammed everywhere; Arthington is ten times too big for us nowadays! Well, about the Ghost's room.

"We children were afraid of it, at least the others were afraid and didn't like being in it. *I* was afraid and *did* like being in it perhaps all the more. It's not at all in the oldest part of the house, but in the wing added early in the Restoration by Anthony Thesiger, the one who helped to turn out James II. and who was made the first Lord Arthington (we have always been Whigs—Cromwellians first—and as to me of course I'm a socialist) . There are no mullions, or low ceilings. I suppose you'd call it imitation Italian; I often think of that part of the place in certain villas here in Italy. The room has a bed with faded sort of tulip stripes, red and yellow, on the curtains and coverlet, and a canopy with four of those cut velvet plumes or vases we saw in your friend's palace the day before yesterday.

"And there is an ebony inlaid cabinet, with mirrors inside when you open it; and the walls are hung with all manner of black blurred pictures: boar hunts, and smoky battles and flower-pieces like faded chintz; you have seen the sort of thing ten thousand times in Italy; I suppose it's all the refuse of what generations of Thesigers carted home from the Grand Tour. The portrait of Louis Norbert is the only one in the room. It's rather black too, but in a different way: he has black clothes which you can't see quite plainly, and long black hair; and his face and hands and collar stand out from all that black. I don't know whether the picture is any good as a picture. I haven't seen it since I got married, and that's more than twenty years ago. But I see it quite clearly in my mind; I mean I see *him*, for it never struck me to think of him as a portrait!

"It all began by my eldest brother one day locking me into the Ghost's room for a lark. He thought I should be frightened—I was quite a small girl—and so I was at first, because I'd never been in the Ghost's room, except when the housekeeper showed people round. Of course I wouldn't scream or howl, or bang at the door, or do any of the things my brother and the other boys expected a girl to do. I remember sitting for a long time half paralysed with terror and not daring to lift my eyes.

"The shutters were closed and a ray of light came between them, making the dark things on the wall and that dreadful bed with the hearse-plumes just barely visible; and the light ended off in a horrid white spot in a looking glass. I steeled myself to look round; then I felt ashamed and slowly crawled (feeling the whole time as if someone or some dreadful piece of furniture would claw me) to the window, and got on to a chair and contrived to unbolt the shutters. There were big trees close in front and it was getting on for evening, so that the light wasn't much use, if anything making all those black things on the wall and the bed and that dreadful mirror only more alarming. But in the light I first became aware of *him*—I mean of Louis Norbert. I ought by rights to have been only more frightened when I turned round and found his white face confronting me; and I daresay I *did* think he was the room's ghost.

"But somehow I stopped being frightened as soon as I saw him. He was so awfully kind and sad, as if he wanted to help me, and at the same time (and that was more to the point) he wanted *me* to help him. I dragged a chair up, and stood on it and looked at him and spelt out his name: Louis Norbert de Caritan. And I remained sitting there, and dozed off and dreamed all sorts of lovely things; I'm not sure he didn't want to marry me at the end, anyhow I remember I helped him in some mysterious way. When my brother, who had forgotten me, unlocked the door, late in the evening, he was horribly frightened by finding me quite numb and cold in that armchair; and I had to be put to bed, and the nurse made sure I should have brain fever, just to punish poor Arthington.

"Gracious, when I think what he's turned into now, sitting boxed up in two rooms, poor dear, thinking only of draughts! Well—after that I used to steal back to the Ghost's room and spend a good deal of my time there. Of course no one guessed I should choose it for my *secret place*, after it had given me a fright and made me half ill. And if the housekeeper ever missed the key, she certainly never suspected *me* of abstracting it; but we were a happy-go-lucky set, and most often she had the key all right, but the door wasn't locked.

"So, for years, I lived all my *secret time*—for every child who isn't an only child must have secret times and secret places unless they're mere driven cattle—in the presence of Louis Norbert. At first it may have been a matter of convenience, just as I had previously spent my secret time, carried the books I wanted to read alone and my especial doll and pet stones and general fetishes, under a bridge on a dried-up stream in the park. Then, as I grew older, it began to be distinctly for the sake of Louis Norbert. Of course I'd always been fond of him ever since that first time, and grateful, and I liked to tell him stories and invent them about him. But later I became acutely aware of his being there, and no longer felt so much at my ease, and no longer brought anything except books of poetry—which I didn't read, but thought fine—or very romantic novels—I remember Mrs. Henry Wood's—it does seem funny!

"It was the time when I discarded dolls and took to practising the piano furiously. I began to stay less at a time in the Ghost's room, but to go there in a funny, formal way, always with my hair tidy and my dress fairly straight. Once I even put on my best hat and a pair of my mother's long gloves. It was something like going to church (not of course the church one really did go to) and also like being in love. And in fact when I was in love I forgot all about the Ghost's room. But—isn't it odd? I spent one of my last hours in my old home in that room, the day before I was married. I suddenly felt awfully unhappy—women sometimes do when about to be married—and all alone in the world.

And I took a very absurd leave of Louis Norbert, standing on a chair, the same armchair my brother had found me asleep in when I was small. Since then I've not seen him, though I have been time after time at Arthington; he had dropped out of my life . . . I don't know"—suddenly concluded Lady Venetia, addressing the archaeologist and no longer, so to speak, her own self—"I don't know why I tell you all this nonsense. I suppose that when one's old enough to be a grandmother one begins to harp upon one's childhood; it's a beginning of senility. And then—have you never remarked it? (but perhaps you are still too young)—there are things one can talk about to strangers just because they *are* strangers. Why, where are the others gone?"

And Lady Venetia, disengaging her arm from the archaeologist's, looked up and down in that empty, icy moonlight, whence those great marble things shone disembodied in their pallor.

"They must have lost patience and gone back to the hotel," she added. "Which is the way? Good gracious, I fear I've kept you here till midnight with my silly stories, and that you must be half dead of cold. Let's walk a little briskly, if you don't mind."

"I was afraid—I felt sure," murmured the archaeologist half to himself, "that you would suddenly feel chilly after so long a time in the moonlight."

"Chilly and grown old, as Browning says," answered the lady.

CHAPTER 3

They talked only of indifferent things as they walked quickly towards the riverside: of the probabilities of finishing that motoring tour or whether it would not be necessary to ship the car by rail to Rome; did the "Professor" think the roads would be impassable after this early frost? Was there any likelihood of a north wind to dry them? Also about the archaeologist's work on the Byzantine origins of Pisan architecture; would it keep him there long? About the difference between foreign and English Universities. Had he liked his three—or was it six?—years at Oxford? (He had been a Rhodes scholar, hadn't he?) But of course he couldn't have seen it with a really foreign eye, since his mother was English.

"If you weren't so ceremonious," said Lady Venetia, "I shouldn't have known you from an Englishman. No accent at all."

"You mean that I don't eat with my knife," he answered grimly.

Lady Venetia's excessively sympathetic heart smote her. Was it possible that she could have sounded patronising? She was always rushing into extremes with strangers, being too familiar and then freezing up and hurting their feelings.

It was dreadful! A happy thought struck her.

"Look!" she exclaimed, ignoring the archaeologist's last remark, "isn't this exactly the square with the commander's statue? And that house, can't you imagine Donna Anna rushing out of it after Don Giovanni?"

They were crossing a small square, bluey-white in the moonlight, and Lady Venetia pointed across its smooth wide flags to a close-shuttered house, whose *escutcheon* and curved double flight of stairs were carved out in black shadows under the overhanging eaves.

"Do you not think," answered the archaeologist, "that in this house and in this square Louis Norbert de Caritan may have lived and died in August 1684?"

"I may have given you a right to laugh at me, but you are a prig, after all, to do it."

But as she turned her indignant eyes on her companion she was surprised to find that he was perfectly serious and deeply moved.

"I didn't mean it literally, you know," she murmured.

"And I did," he answered curtly; and they proceeded in silence.

But when they had warmed themselves by the fire of olive logs in the hotel sitting-room, and answered the remarks and questions of the rest of the party whom they found sitting round it, Lady Venetia opened the yellow hotel piano, and having drawn from its chattering strings the great opening chords of the overture of *Don Giovanni*, she broke suddenly into the music of the duel, the rushing and lunging little scale passages, the death wail of the commander and the lamentation of his daughter.

"I suppose I'm dreadfully old-fashioned," she said, "and of course I don't deny that Strauss would have made one's flesh creep and given one bad dreams for six weeks with such a subject; but this music is my idea of romance; you know what I mean? The sort of thing that square with the statue in the moonlight means, and then that phrase of Ottavio's immediately afterwards, trying to console Anna; one connects it—well, not with the horrid sort of thing people call tragedy—but with all sorts of things sad and mysterious and yet very consoling in a way, death and misfortune, but which didn't make people horrid. I daresay," she wound up with a radiant smile to the whole party, as she pushed in the desk and pressed down the lid, "I daresay I'm talking awful rubbish!"

But when the archaeologist rose to take his leave and wish them a good journey—

"Don't forget us," she said, stretching out her hand; "and"—holding his for an imperceptible instant in hers—"don't forget Louis Norbert de Caritan, in case you can find out anything about him here at Pisa."

"I promise to find out something about Louis Norbert de Caritan," answered the archaeologist, "since you will allow me to take an interest in him," and he kissed Lady Venetia's hand in the foreign fashion, and bade them all "goodbye."

LETTER 1

From the Archaeologist to the Lady Venetia Hammond

Pisa, December 6, 1908

Dear Lady Venetia,

In obedience to your desire, I went to the town archives the day following your departure, but learned, to my great disappointment, that the seventeenth century records (I had intended looking more particularly through the police reports as well as those of the *Misericordia* and other funeral confraternities) are at this moment in process of removal to a new wing, and consequently inaccessible for the next weeks to all students, even privileged ones like

214

your humble servant. I have therefore been unable to obtain any information about the stay in Pisa and the death there of the personage in whom you take an interest.

But curious coincidence has given me, so to speak, a glimpse of that Abbé Manfredini who put up the epitaph in the Campo Santo, and whom, through some sympathetic clairvoyance, you judged in an unfavourable light, but one which, as you will see, seems in a certain way justified. (By way of parenthesis: if there were no odd coincidences there would be no archaeology, no archaeologists, and perhaps no human beings at all.)

This information was obtained in consequence of a perfectly idle interest in a certain palace, which you may remember pointing out to me (saying it made you think of the duel in *Don Giovanni*, do you remember?) on the evening when I had, for the last time, the honour of escorting you to your hotel. It may amuse you to hear how it all came about.

Having heard, the morning of your departure, that you had decided not to continue the journey in your motor, but to take the Roman express, I hastened to the station in case I might be of any service to you and your cousins—perhaps, I thought, in sending off the car. But I was a little late, and though the Roman train had not yet left, there was, alas! (really that Pisa station is the most disgracefully mismanaged, as well as one of the most antipathetic and gloomy of stations) another interminable train blocking the platform, so that, by the time I could run round to the further line, *your* train had just begun moving away, to my infinite regret.

I was on the point of leaving that place of disappointment (for I had hoped you might have remembered some commission or some other enquiry to entrust me with)— well, I was about to leave, feeling also rather ridiculous by reason of the bunches of violets in my hands, when I was stopped by old Marchese Viscardi, whose palace I had had the honour of showing you, and whose acquaintance I shall always regret that you did not make, for he is the most exquisite and, alas! the last example of one of the most characteristic and enchanting of Italian types: the provincial nobleman who is at once a farmer, a sportsman, a scholar, and a man of great artistic taste.

And, what happened to be even more to my purpose, a passionate antiquarian who seems to have inherited from his many illustrious ancestors every minutest historical tradition of his native town. He had just come from boar-hunting in the Maremma; his clothes seemed still to carry the smell (perhaps it was only my fancy) of the thickets of myrtle and lentisk in which he had been reducing them to raggedness. He was going to see his grandchildren near Lucca and consequently to have his midday meal at the station while waiting for a train, instead of going to his house. I adore this old man, not only for his learning and kindness, but also for his look of stepping out of a Van Dyke picture.

So I asked leave to join in his very frugal repast. When he had told me all about the boars that had been shot (the mere names of those woodland hills with their views of Etruscan capes and islands are like music to me) and also the measurements of a certain church-cornice I had once admired in his company, I watched for my opportunity.

"You who know every stone in Pisa by heart, *Marchese*," I said, "will, of course, know all about a slab in the easternmost wall of the Campo Santo, to the memory of a young Frenchman who died in Pisa late in the seventeenth century."

"Louis de Caritan—let me see, there's another name too (I have entirely lost my memory with advancing years!)— yes! Louis Norbert de Caritan—of course! Not *quite* the easternmost as you say, but rather, I venture to correct, *north-eastern* by north, since it is near the figures treading the grapes and about twenty metres from the famous sarcophagus with the Amazons. Yes, Louis Norbert de Caritan, *escuier, fils de Pierre*," etc.—and the marvellous old gentleman repeated the whole inscription with scarcely any hesitation and only one mistake.

I had to make an effort not to interrupt him, I can assure you.

"Then, *Marchese*," I exclaimed, before the last words were fairly out of his mouth, "then you will be able to tell me all about this Frenchman." But with a courteous regret (and yet he couldn't have guessed my disappointment!) the *Marchese* answered that he knew nothing about the personage I alluded to.

"You see," he added, "I am not a real *savant* like you; my scanty knowledge of local history is confined, I am ashamed to say, to my own family records, and so I am ignorant (I often feel it with shame) about the many interesting foreigners (your poet Shelley, I believe, among others) who used to come to Pisa for their health and of whom several died here; you remember in the Campo Santo the monument to Count Zamoyski, and another to Prince Ratibor and—"

"Yes, yes, but that doesn't bear on my point." I had scarcely said it before I felt horribly shocked at my rudeness, particularly when the adorable old gentleman merely answered with courteous dignity:

"I regret my ignorance particularly when, as in your case, it prevents my satisfying the curiosity of my learned friends."

What a brute my disappointment had made me! So, wishing to atone a little by giving his know) an opportunity of displaying itself, I bethought me of that house which had struck your fancy during our walk in the moonlight, and I asked him what he knew about it.

He knew half an hour's worth of detail: who had built that house, who had built every preceding house on the same site, ever since Pisa had existed, the alterations from the original plan, the number of the windows, the thickness of the walls, the orders of the architecture, let alone all the people who had ever leased any part of it. He was forgetting his train.

"For an archaeologist like you," he at last said, "the house in question has moreover another interest, as having once contained (and more precisely, between 1679 and 1693) one of the most celebrated private collections of antique gems existing at that epoch, that of a certain Abbate Manfredini, sometime canon of the cathedral."

"The Abbé Manfredini!" I exclaimed, "indeed! Why, of course I have heard of him." I didn't mention where or in what connection, for fear of returning to the sore subject of his ignorance about the epitaph. "Do tell me about him."

My request was unnecessary.

"His collection," went on the *Marchese*, "contained, as you doubtless know, some of the finest antiques now existing in foreign museums, for instance, a sardonyx by Pasiteles which is one of the glories of the cabinet of gems of St. Petersburg; and a celebrated hunt of the Caledonian boar (that has remained in my poor memory because of our own boar-hunts, in which I trust you will again partake)—a Caledonian Hunt, I was saying, supposed to be after a *fresco* by Polygnotus. Besides this collection of gems Canon Manfredini possessed also a torso of a faun which was bought by the Elector of Saxony on the disposal of his property in consequence of the painful conclusion of his career."

"What painful conclusion to his career" I asked, trying not to be too much interested (that the *Marchese* had dated as 1693 and the epitaph was of 1684—no, there could be no connection!).

"The Abbate Manfredini," resumed the *Marchese*, "was a man of very great parts and most cultivated taste, thanks to both of which he had risen to a condition much above his birth, for he is said to have been the son of Prince Ludovisi's cook. He was a very fine Latinist, even in a time when Latinists were more plentiful than they are, alas! nowadays. Some of his odes (one, I remember, is on the raising to the purple of my great-great-grand-uncle Cardinal Spini) have been printed in Bachofen's *Florilegium*; and some of his epigrams have recently been re-edited to celebrate the marriage of my cousin Lanfreducci. He was also well versed in natural science and made some interesting discoveries in chemistry, as I am assured by my old friend Professor Bimboni, for I have no competence in such things, unfortunately.

"He was one of the many persons of that time (you will remember the notorious Cavalier Borri) who dabbled in the transmutation of metals; unfortunately also, so at least it was asserted, his studies extended to the preparation of poisons; those were the days, as you remember, of so-called Acqua Tofana and the *Poudre de Succession* of Brinvilliers and Exili. Be this as it may, he fell into ill repute with the Grand Ducal Government, and more particularly awakened suspicion under Pope Innocent XII. , and was confined, on a charge of atheism, in the castle of St. Leo in Romagna, where he died in the pontificate of Clement XL, to whose family my grandmother, I am proud to say, belonged. But I am forgetting my train in the pleasure of conversing with you—and my little grand-daughters had promised to meet me with the carriage."

I snatched his bag and gun-case and ran with them to the Lucca train, which he was just in time to catch. But as the guard shouted *Partenza* and tootled the horn of this operatic country, the old man leant out of the window and said quickly:

"As regards that Canon Manfredini, I have found in a letter of Cardinal Azzolino, a relation of my wife's, and also, as you know, Queen Christina of Sweden's testamentary executor, a reference to him, to the effect that this Queen

always averred that this same Manfredini was a dangerous man who possessed the secret of the so-called Iron
Mask and many others, and would someday have to be
suppressed by the court of France, on whose blackmail
he subsisted, eking out what he got by spying for various
potentates by turns."

So you see, dear Lady Venetia, that you were quite right
in guessing that the Abbé Manfredini was a villain, and
thinking of that house in connection with romance and
violence (you remember the *Don Giovanni* music?). But
I, therefore, was right in saying (though you took the remark, if I may speak and live, rather ungraciously) that *you*,
rather than I, ought to have been an archaeologist.

I am, dear Lady Venetia,

Yours, etc.

LETTER 2

From Lady Venetia to the Archaeologist

Arthington Manor, Burton Saxon,

February 16, 1909

My dear Professor,

Do not think me ungrateful for your long and delightful
letter. The very circumstances which prevented my answering only made it more welcome, for I read it (two
months late!) in the midst of very sad solitude and dreariness, when one was thankful to be reminded that such a
thing as romance had ever existed!

But I ought to explain, in case you should not have heard
it, that I had scarcely been in Rome three days after we
left Pisa (what a time ago it now seems—that wonderful
moonlight walk! and all about Louis Norbert!) before I
was sent for to look after my eldest brother (my sister-
in-law died about a year ago) who had had a stroke and
was despaired of. He is now out of danger, unless another
stroke comes, but crippled, and likes me to stay on. But for
six weeks the danger was continual. That's why your letter

has remained unanswered so long, and now I'm answering it from my old home. Don't think I wasn't grateful for your letter.

When Arthington was once out of danger it gave me a lot of pleasure (I couldn't read books, somehow, or newspapers) and something to think of—I mean all about Louis Norbert. It's odd that it was different while the danger was there. Have you remarked (no, you're too young probably) how one can live one's life in the constant face of death? I suppose one braces oneself and makes the best of all small mercies, and when the danger is over one just plops down. During those weeks—seven, I think—one either sat up all night or went to sleep ready to be called to hear that the worst had come; but it ends by becoming in a dreadful way natural, as if there could be nothing else (men have told me it was like that with soldiers in the trenches or in a besieged town).

And the odd thing, and which makes one hot with shame sometimes, is that one isn't miserable the whole time. I hated myself for it, but during that dreadful stress one seemed at times so keenly aware of some things being so good and so interesting, one's breakfast, for instance, after a bad night, or dawn with the bare trees against it as one came downstairs. For a great many days—weeks, in fact—I never dared leave the house for more than half an hour every day, and then always leaving word where I could be signalled to; and do you know, in those hurried runs, I seem to have discovered, for the first time in my life, how beautiful this old place is: the red brick (it really is like oranges and geranium) where it has got a little chipped, against the white stone-coping, and the courses of black (you know the sort of thing) gave me a sort of stitch of pleasure.

Also there seemed something inexpressibly harmonious and at the same time romantic in the round niches with Roman busts, and in the terraced balustrade, looking down the green walk between the old, old pines, which are almost like cedars. I really seemed never to have seen any of it before.

Now my brother is better, the doctor out of the house, only one nurse remaining (who will, I fear, be permanent). He is beginning to be able to speak again, in a way that wrings one's heart. And he, who used to be the most gruffly unsentimental of men, now likes to look at the trees with me holding his hand, also to listen to music, which he used to hate.

How tragic, tragic the way that illness and old age sometimes make people spiritual, susceptible of things they never felt before. It's as heartrending, don't you think, as the transfiguration of dead people's faces? but I daresay you are too young to have much experience of such matters.

Of course it's *I* who have to make the music, a very little at a time; but when he's a bit stronger I shall send for a nice little hump-backed fiddler who is starving in a slum at present. For poor Arthington likes to look over a lot of old instruments, really almost a collection and some quite good, which have accumulated in the house. They are brought in, spinets and harpsichords and all manner of fiddles, one every day; and he puts a finger on the keys or pulls a string and looks pleased in a way that makes me want to cry.

Well! I have told you all this to explain why your letter remained unopened under a constantly increasing pile, and why, since I have been able to read it, it has been a great pleasure and in a way company. I like to think of Louis Norbert, though I haven't had the energy to go and see his portrait again. I am utterly at a loose end now—I can't read, except the advertisements in the *Times* or a page of poetry now and then (funny, I read the *Penseroso*—fancy, it must have been quite "recent verse "in Louis Norbert's day, or at least like Browning to us). You see, my mind still runs on "our mysterious young Frenchman," as my father used to call him. So I do want you, as soon as those archives are open again, to go and see whether you can't find out something about him. Or, if you can't find out anything, make it up! After all, aren't you archaeologists ever-lastingly inventing?

I am, dear Professor,

Yours, etc.

PS.—You don't mind my continuing to call you Professor, although you explained you couldn't possibly be one? There's something comfortable in it, better than plain "dear Mister So-and-so." And then it's nice you should know such a lot and be so young. Why, you could be my grandchild, if I had married very early, like people in the Sandwich Islands.

LETTER 3

From Lady Venetia to the Archaeologist

Arthington: March 1 1909

My dear Professor,

I wonder whether you have got a long letter explaining my silence and all that has happened? I sent it to Pisa.

I am now writing to ask you to be very kind and order for me a collection of old Italian music (*not* Parisotti, which I have) you once mentioned at Pisa. I find that the only thing my poor brother (I told you how dreadfully ill he has been) cares for now are the old instruments which have accumulated in this house. He isn't *really* musical, you know, and it bores him hearing the same thing over again often, so we are getting rather to an end of our supply; and as the instruments are principally seventeenth-century harpsichords and violins and thereabouts, what he likes is hearing the sort of music written for them. It's no good telling him you can play Brahms on a Strad (not that we have a *real* Strad!)—*he* wants nothing later than Corelli. And one must humour him, poor dear.

223

So be very kind and tell them to send me that collection you mentioned.

Any news of Louis Norbert, I wonder?

Yours, etc.

LETTER 4

From the Archaeologist to Lady Venetia

Pisa: March 5, 1909

Dear Lady Venetia,

I found both your letters yesterday on return from a walking tour in the Abbruzzi. You will know, without my fumbling to tell you, how deeply I sympathise in your recent trouble, and how sincerely I hope that Lord Arthington's recovery may not be liable to the dangers which are still giving you anxiety. I hope you will receive even before this the collection of old Italian music you asked me about. I telegraphed to the publisher at Leipzig to send it you direct.

I am now adding a volume which I picked up last year at a bookstall. As I am not capable of coping with figured basses and all the various old clefs, I had got a friend of mine (the rather odious youth who bored you so about his book on Gluck) to transpose it all into intelligible characters, and this I send you, but also the rather jolly old printed copy of which I beg your acceptance.

The youthful music-historian in question condescended to bestow on these compositions the adjective which, I remember, made you so indignant (and really the attitude of us professional critics is insupportable), calling them, as I think he did the baptistery of Pisa, "*amusant.*"

But I want very particularly to know whether you like them, because they happen to be by a certain seventeenth-century Abbess, who in her worldly days was a "tenth Muse and fourth Grace" of Italy (she was even crowned in the Capitol, like Mme. de Staël's Corinne) and in whom I take a faint, romantic interest, as I think I mentioned (but

224

of course you wouldn't remember) when you first did me the honour of telling me about the young Frenchman of the Campo Santo epitaph.

The name of the abbess and crowned poetess-composer (her father was originally a Spaniard) was Artemisia de Valor y Cordoba, called in Italian Artemisia del Valore, which makes rather a pretty name, don't you think, for a heroine and a genius?

So far I have had the pleasure of executing your musical commission. But alas! not the one about Louis Norbert de Caritan, for the archives are still closed to students. But has it not struck you that your own family archives might possibly yield some information about a personage who, after all, seems to have spent the greater part of his life under your roof?

Or have you reasons for knowing that such researches have already been made and have led to nothing? If, as you suggested, he had been murdered in Italy, would his English protectors not have made some enquiry about his untimely end?

Please command me in anything wherein I can hope to serve you, and believe me,

Yours, etc.

PS.—I notice that you say, "if you can find out nothing, couldn't you make it up?" Ah, dear Lady Venetia, you little know with what a dreadful temptation you are besetting a hitherto innocent student of history!

LETTER 5

From Lady Venetia to the Archaeologist

Arthington: March 8, 1909

My dear Professor,

Thanks for the music, which will probably turn up to-morrow. And thank you above all for your friendly interest in my poor friend Louis Norbert. Your letter has just come, and excited me quite awfully; as soon as I can get a few hours' freedom I shall make straight for our Muniment Room.

Now doesn't it show what silly idiots we frivolous yokels are! It had *never* struck me that there might be something—must be something—about Louis Norbert among our family papers. Yet of course I knew—I always have known that there is a Muniment Room and exactly where—up three steps from the middle landing of the north staircase which creaks so awfully and where Lady Bridget is said to walk (there is a round window which frames the white deer in the park rather nicely).

The room has a square door studded with nails like a safe, as if anybody wanted to get in, bless your heart! and it has a mullioned window over the big cedar. I have only been there once in my life, when some Americans who had been civil to my sister-in-law insisted, after coffee and *chartreuse*, upon being shown letters of eye-witnesses of the execution of Mary Queen of Scots or some other horrid stuffy Yellow Starch and Star Chamber sort of tragedy, the worst about which always strikes me (but I have no historical mind!) was the want of air and the people having gone about (at least so their portraits show them) always in furs, even in midsummer landscapes.

I have always associated the contents of the Muniment Room with those Americans who said, "My! ain't it just cunning!" or words to that effect, and also with some dreadful psychical researchers whom Arthington had to show the door because they tried to spirit-rap among our family papers. (I'm sure I would have let them so long as they didn't bore us about it all.)

By the way, I have a notion *you took me for a psychical researcher* when I first told you about L. N. that evening in Pisa, and that's what riled me so dreadfully. I can tell you now you've been so kind and we're such good friends. But it never once occurred to me to associate the Muniment Room with dear Louis Norbert.

226

Of course I've always known he was brought up at Arthington; indeed, it's just all I do know about him, and that my father called him "our mysterious young Frenchman," which always struck me as a bit pompous. But it had never occurred to me to put two and two together. That's what comes of being brought up by the stud groom, as we all were! I remember you said at Pisa (I thought you so sententious, but how true it was!) that frivolous people (you didn't say "frivolous," because you're too polite, but you implied it)—well, that frivolous people like me divide the world's contents into things they like and things that bore them, and never suspect there may be any other order in the universe.

I fear I can't get a free hour until a cousin comes to relieve guard with my brother early next week, for the poor man hates being left alone.

But *then! then* I will fly up Lady Bridget's Ghost's staircase and revel in the Muniment Room—though I can't help feeling that dear Louis Norbert can't possibly have any connection with all those stuffy horrors, and belongs to a totally different world from the execution of Mary Queen of Scots and Thomas Thesiger, Knight and Privy Councillor of Queen Elizabeth, who witnessed it and wears a little fur-lined motoring bonnet and a grey beard and a ruff.

I fear that I have utterly disgraced myself in your wise young historical eyes and that you will cease to take any interest in this foolish, frivolous old woman and her seventeenth-century friends.

But the doctor has today told me that my brother is at last quite out of danger, and so I am rioting in the mirth of my second childhood.

I am, dear Professor,
Yours nevertheless very truly,
Venetia Hammond.

From Lady Venetia to the Archaeologist

Arthington: April 2, 1909

My dear Professor,

Do you know they are quite beautiful, those compositions of your seventeenth-century abbess? Odd, isn't it, that we should each of us have a friend in the seventeenth century, in the selfsame town too; and that these two friendly ghosts should probably never have met in their mortal life, but only in the idle fancy of us two modern friends!

Thank you awfully for giving me that beautiful volume, *Ricercari et Inventioni—*

della Nobil donzella Artemisia del Valore—accademica filarmonica et Alfea—I do love that old book so much, with the fine volutes wasting so much space, and the abbreviations saving so very little. You oughtn't to have given me anything so valuable!

As to the compositions themselves, all of them are interesting and some really *very* fine. Of course I am only a frivolous dunce about music, as everything else, and I have no doubt that odious youth (who was not *amusant* himself, was he?) would say they were nothing but imitation, as was natural with a *femme du monde* (do you remember how he withered all *my* musical likings with that word?). Of course, I am, as I've said, only a frivolous dunce (which is what he meant) about music, but I *do* know what I like. And I *do* like some of Artemisia's work quite tremendously.

By the way, I never told you one of my own names is Artemisia (so much nicer than the silly geographical one I am called by in honour of Venetia Stanley in Charles I.'s time), and perhaps that's one reason why I like her music! But seriously, I am rather less a dunce about music than other things, and at this moment particularly about old Italian music. You see, my poor brother wants to hear things appropriate to his old instruments, so the domestic fiddler and I have been playing a good deal of Corelli and Vivaldi and such like, and I have taken heart of grace and even sung a little to please poor Arthington, things of Carissimi and Scarlatti and Stradella, etc. And I assure you that in this company the Nobil Donzella Artemisia holds her own.

The music of that time has still something a bit awkward in modulation and phrasing (the Italians got, if anything, too glib later); and in the midst of a great deal of learning and even of pedantry (but then *I* am ashamed to say Bach sometimes bores me to tears with his science!) something pathetically helpless—do you know what I mean? Like babes in the wood who have run away from their lessons, or the look in the eyes of puppies, *dreadfully* sad without knowing why and just because they don't know why; as if, in the midst of all their inventing and *ricercare'ing* (I am speaking of seventeenth-century composers and especially Artemisia, not about pups!) and their perpetual helping themselves out with counterpoint, they were trying to catch hold of melodies which they may have heard from the reaped fields as they sat at noon behind closed villa-shutters, or in the moonlight, thrummed along the paved lanes between their garden walls in town.

Good heavens! how eloquent I have become—it comes of consorting with the ghost of a learned poetess and lady composer! But *you* know what I mean if I seem to talk nonsense, that's what's so comfortable about a learned man. Well! Artemisia has all that, perhaps more, because she was a bit of an amateur—and it goes to my heart, like certain scents of burning wood that meet one in Italy on fine cold days.

Her poetry, poor dear (for I see the words are also hers where there are any), is rather funny. So crammed with mythology, one never knows who or why or what among all those Almanachs de Gotha of Olympus and all the attributes and *chronique galante* of gods and goddesses. Now *do* explain to me, you who are a learned man, how it came about that the same people, in this case the same woman, should have endured and I suppose liked all that *Smith's classical dictionary* and all the pedantic, far-fetched conceits about the Spear of Achilles which heals the wounds it makes (why on earth did it?) and so forth, and who were able to appreciate and to compose just this sort of music, with its little *bitter* (not sour like Wagner's) modulations and melancholy dances and its scraps of recitative which are something between a lyric ode and crying passion.

Anyhow, I am tremendously pleased to have Artemisia's music. And Artemisia is reconciling me to learning to manage our Dutch harpsichord with stops and pedals and manuals, and a sound something between a crazy old clock and a divine unknown kind of violin.

And so you can imagine us—supposing you have time to imagine us at all!—with the old pines swaying outside the windows, or the pale river fogs creeping along the terraces and round the dripping leaden statues—imagine us in the music-room my poor brother has made himself (and most uncommonly bad it is for sound, with its low *stuccoed* ceiling and tapestry, but very good for *listening*, one's eye going along those twistings and starrings overhead to where they meet the faint watery green of the windows); my brother (he has become so handsome, diaphanous, and aquiline, poor dear, since his illness) propped in his chair, and the sister of charity (he wouldn't have an ordinary nurse) and the domestic fiddler, who is a pathetic hump-backed person with lovely eyes—and me, seated round the harpsichord and playing those sad, sad ditties which perhaps once sounded gay.

Have you ever thought that people may have actually *danced* to some of those *Sarabands* of Bach, which seem full of all the resigned mournfulness of man and the dignified indifference of God!

Well—well—I have written you a screed about your Abbess. Tomorrow or the day after I shall attack the Muniment Room, and who knows? perhaps write you something about Louis Norbert. How dreadfully exciting!

Yours, etc.

From Lady Venetia to the Archaeologist

Arthington: April 10, 1909

My dear Professor,

My cousin has not yet come to relieve guard with Arthington, so I have not yet been able to attack the Muniment Room. But I have not wasted my time, as you shall hear! Having told my brother about the grave of Louis Norbert, he remembered that there was something about him in the inventory of the Arthington pictures. I got it out at once. It was made in the middle of the eighteenth century by the Reverend Rupert Thesiger "at the desire of his present Lordship." It would amuse your archaeologist's mind!

Of course we really have one or two fairly good pictures at Arthington and some quite good ones in the London house. But the Rev. Rupert is content with no less than five Raphaels, ten Leonardos, a Michelangelo, and *twelve* Giorgiones ("a rare master," he nevertheless remarks), let alone "some of the greatest masterpieces of the divine *Guido Reni* and the *Carracches*." Well, of course, I didn't read all that at first, but went straight to the portraits, and, sure enough, between the Van Dyke of Sir Nicholas Thesiger, Bart., and Dame Priscilla, his wife, and the Lely of the first Lord Arthington and his two wives, *there* was Louis Norbert.

> 310.—Portrait of Louis *Norbert* de Caritan, usually called 'Sir Nicholas' young Frenchman'; half length, painter unknown.

Louis *Norbert* was of noble *Huguenot* family, of *La*

Rochelle near *Bourdeaux*; his family having been ruined, and his father and mother having perished in the siege of that place during Cardinal Mazarin's persecution of the Protestants" (my brother and the *Encyclopaedia Britannica* say it was Richelieu who besieged La Rochelle and that Mazarin *didn't* persecute them; is that true?) "the orphan was adopted by Sir Nicholas Thesiger, at one time Ambassador of Oliver Cromwell to Cardinal *Mazarino*, and by him educated along with his son Anthony, afterwards Viscount, then first Earl of Arthington.

Louis *Norbert* accompanied his noble friend to the University of *Oxford* and on his travels abroad, and died young and much regretted by the family of his Benefactor and particularly by Dame Priscilla, widow of Sir Nicholas, having distinguished himself by his studious and pious disposition and by his hatred of the *Popish* superstition.

There! I read this entry to my brother, and he remarked that the Rev. Rupert was drawing the long bow about La Rochelle and the persecutions, as the siege of that place by Richelieu took place in 1627, so that if L. N.'s parents had perished there he would have been born at least twenty years after their death, since he was twenty-four in 1684. And I am sorry to say that Arthington went so far as to take away the reputation of our austere Cromwellian ancestor by adding that "the fellow" (*i.e.*, Louis Norbert) "was probably some son of the old boy's, the effect of the Paris embassy on an English puritan, and that all this romancing about perishing protestants and La Rochelle was probably invented for Dame Priscilla's benefit, who hadn't got the *Encyclopaedia Britannica*" (not even the old edition which he had let himself be swindled into buying cheap!) "to consult about points of history."

I told Arthington that was just his horrid, modern *club* way of viewing things, and that in L. N.'s time people were far more romantic; but he only said, "Oh, gammon"—and perhaps he was right.

But tomorrow I really hope to attack the Muniment Room, and then we shall perhaps know everything. Just think how splendid!

What about those old archives at Pisa? Are they *never* going to be opened? Or perhaps you are too busy—how selfish and thoughtless I am!

Yours, etc.

LETTER 8

(Crossed preceding)
From the Archaeologist to Lady Venetia

Pisa: April 12, 1909

Dear Lady Venetia,

At last the sixteenth and seventeenth-century town records have become accessible, and I have been able to give myself the very great pleasure of hunting for traces of your mysterious young Frenchman. Alas! without any result. Never once have I come across any name in the slightest degree like his. But as the police registers were removed to Florence, I will have a look when next I go there; also there still remain some boxes of unclassified documents among which we may, eventually, find something. I trust you will have better success with your Muniment Room; my search here is rather of the needle in the haystack kind. Oddly enough, in looking for the key of one mystery, I seem (as often happens with us historians) to have laid my hand on the walled-up door of another one, or rather of *two* apparently different mysteries.

Indeed, I am inclined to think (after a week in these Pisa archives) that the whole life of the seventeenth century was honeycombed with mysteries, and that there were as many secret chambers as inhabited ones! A good third of the papers I have read over appear to be the reports of spies; and when not salaried official ones (and these of every imaginable sort, physicians, priests, entire orders of monks, astrologers, postillions, actresses, fiddlers, singers, pedlars, poets, and ladies of light conduct)—then amateur spies in the shape of quiet persons who kept diaries for their own amusement.

Well, to return to the two unexpected mysteries I have hit upon—although to do so is no consolation for the fruitlessness of my researches about your young Frenchman's death—one of them is connected with a lady, apparently a great lady, who seems to have been causing anxiety to the grand duke, to the Pope, and to a personage called in some code language "number 109" and also "the Great Sophi of Hyrcania." What this lady was expected to do I cannot for the life of me make out, except that she also seems to have been bent on unravelling mysteries, neither more nor less than you and I, dear Lady Venetia; except that she is usually described as "that madwoman," "that foolish female lunatic who has given Hyrcania and other countries so much worry for so many years"—and "who has got this new suspicion into her crazy brain."

There is no further indication of her status or whereabouts, and she is sometimes called "the mad Berenice"—for everybody in these letters has at least one code name, and often several. Well, I hope poor Berenice, whoever she was, may have been more successful with *her* mystery, whatever it may have been, than I, alas, have been about Louis Norbert!

The other mystery, which is quite separate, though playing about, so to speak, in the same year, namely, that of Louis Norbert's death, concerns a foreign royalty who haunts Italy, or at least the imagination of Italian princes and spies, about that same year 1684. He is described as a Turk, but, for that reason, is just as likely to have been something else. "The successor of Mahomet of whom you desire news has not yet arrived," writes Father Girolamo Nuti, minor observant, to some personage merely described as "his

Excellency."

Then there is a barber, nicknamed *Finocchio* or *Fennel*, who says, "the person of whom you desire news is now in Rome. Be assured we shall keep an eye on him." Another and anonymous informant writes—"the distinguished Mahometan arrived in Pisa two days ago, and is ill of Malaria, doubtless caught in Rome."

I shouldn't bother you with all this odd mysterious gossip of two centuries and a quarter ago, if it were not that your old enemy the Abbé Manfredini—"*très cher ami de la couronne et nation de France*" (rather, as you say, than of poor Louis Norbert)—is mixed up in all this, and evidently held in no higher esteem than by yourself and by old Christina of Sweden, who, perhaps you may remember, told Marchese Viscardi's great-great-grand-uncle that this Manfredini was a spy and a blackmailer, or worse.

I have found a letter addressed on the back to his Excellency Monsignor Del Nero, Bailiff of the Order of St. Stephen (a Tuscan Military Order), and in it this sentence among a lot of cryptic code phrases:

> His Highness also desires that an eye be kept on the usual *abbé* (*il solito Abbaté*), who, from all we hear, appears to be up to his usual tricks (*fa delle sue*), forgetting that Pisa is not Baalbek (query: Rome?), and that we will not suffer scoundrels of his kind to have a finger in the affairs of great kingdoms. His Highness has reason to know that this Manfredini is in Rome and muddying the water, the better to fish in it.

> He intends to steal the *Ace of Hearts* and keep it up his sleeve, hoping to make a fine profit on his cards. But this His Highness is determined not to suffer it. The said *abbé* shall be warned to return home at once from Rome, else it will cost His Highness nothing to hear the last of him (*farla finita con esso lui*).

And finally:

> What you advised me through the soprano singer
> (*il musico*) Sandro, that there might be risk in touch-
> ing that *abbé*, he being already in possession of cer-
> tain facts and perhaps already selling his wares to
> the great merchants beyond the Alps, most certainly
> points to prudence.
>
> But His Highness is more and more incensed with
> this fellow's impudence who has long since deserved
> the law's rigour for illicit alchemy and worse, let
> alone his notorious atheism; and if he meddles any
> further in the question of the mislaid crown jewel
> His Highness is greatly minded to suppress him al-
> together and with no more ado.

I keep racking my brains as to who this "ace of hearts"
and "mislaid crown jewel" and "successor of Mahomet"
can be. Isn't it odd that in seeking for details of the death
of the obscure *protégé* of your ancestors we should have
come upon the traces of some mysterious personage
about whom the various courts seem to be intriguing?
I had thought of Monmouth, Charles II.'s son, but the
dates don't fit. I wonder whether this may lead to some
brand new theory about that intolerable bore, the Man in
the Iron Mask, and reinstate the old wives' tale of a twin
brother of Louis XIV.?

But I have taken up too much of your time with matters
which do not concern Louis Norbert and perhaps don't
interest you; forgive. By the way, have you no documents
at Arthington concerning the date of birth and the parentage of your young Frenchman?

And if not, are there no family traditions as to his origin?
How I wish I might have the honour of assisting you in
your Muniment Room, which will, I hope, make up for
the failure of my own attempts. I am, dear Lady Venetia,

Yours, etc.

From Lady Venetia to the Archaeologist

Arthington: May 10, 1909

My dear Professor,

Good heavens! What marvellous, patient creatures you historians must be! I am beginning to appreciate you and your virtues after six mortal mornings spent in that detestable Muniment Room.

For it is a sickening place. I had expected dust and cobwebs, perhaps a few broken twigs brought by rooks, like one sees in church towers; or even (didn't I long for it as a child!) a huge magpie's nest with chicks sitting on the family's long-lost tea spoons. But I never bargained for a dull orderliness like a country solicitor's, and under that nothing but the most sordid accounts with an illegible writing and without a vestige of spelling (even *I* feel sick at it!). Nothing but how much farmers paid, how much corn horses got, what was spent on repair of harness (*item* for a "surcingle to her laddyship her mair," and suchlike) and making of liveries. Of course I know it's only because I am so frivolous that it all bores me to tears. I suppose you learned folk would find out all manner of interesting things. But it is a bit rough upon me, coming to a place athirst for romance and mystery. And so far not a vestige of anything of the sort have I come upon. How I *do* envy you all those dear spies and "successors of Mahomet" and villainous *abbés*, and even "Berenice with her crazy brain" in your Pisan archives!

Not a word, of course, about Louis Norbert! Nothing but a growing conviction that however poor a figure we Thesigers may be cutting nowadays (all blue Tories and dunces!) the Thesigers of the past were a set of horrible old screws, as is proved (if all they write about didn't show it) by their squalid economies of writing paper, crossing in every conceivable and inconceivable sense, abbreviating half their words and writing on backs of letters and torn-out fly-leaves of books. They have pretty well broken my spirit, and if Louis Norbert doesn't make his appearance tomorrow morning, I shall give him up as a bad job and never set foot again in that odious Muniment Room!

Thursday.

I wrote like that on Monday, and, as if he had heard me, Louis Norbert *has* turned up! At least, I mean, a reference to him has.

On Thursday I had what I thought was my last go at the Muniment Room, and behold! I found a box of letters (so nice and yellow and with such lovely f's and s's like fiddle clefs—the very look of them made my heart beat). And inside was an index (which of course wasn't an index) by the usual Rev. Rupert Thesiger, D.D., stating that in 1753 he had "put the contents in order (which wasn't a bit true) and that among it were some interesting letters of Sir Anthony Thesiger, Bart., afterwards Viscount," etc., etc., "during a journey to Paris in 1683."

1683! The year before Louis Norbert's death! And sure enough, in one of them of Sept. 16th, 1683, there was a mention of Louis Norbert! Just think how I felt! It was the *fourth* time I have seen his name (on the picture, on the epitaph, on the Rev. Rupert's inventory of portraits, and now)—that I have seen his beloved name except written by you or me. Just think of that! But then archaeologists are accustomed to such emotions, digging up Troy and the Olympia Hermes and things like that.

Well, Anthony Thesiger writes to his mother (the widow Dame Priscilla I told you of) from Paris. And after endless enumeration of all the fine folk he met at the Court of Louis XIV. (a rare young snob my ancestor was), and masses of description, which his poor old mother couldn't possibly have followed, of the palaces and gardens of Marly and Versailles, he suddenly ends off:

Your adopted son is in no danger of being seduced

to Popery (as you seem to apprehend) by the sight of all this magnificence. He looks upon these polite and delightful splendours with the eyes of a Cato and compareth this place (Versailles) to Babel in the building and the builder thereof to Ahab and Pharaoh by reason of his cruel dealings with the Huguenots and the great lavishness of his court in the midst of much misery of the poor, whereat he noticeth justly, those accustomed to our happier country can scarce believe their senses, so ragged and starved do all the husbandmen of France appear. I have tried to soften our friend's ferocious virtue, to sacrifice, as they choicely say here, to the Graces, but so far all in vain."

"Like Babel in the building." Those are the very first words that Louis Norbert has uttered in our presence, dear Professor, and of *course* they are *exactly* what we should have expected of him, just exactly what we ourselves would have thought (for I'm a socialist, aren't you?), and he's a *friend*, and it doesn't matter, does it, how long ago friends may have been born and died, they always know and love each other when they meet! I always thought that if Louis Norbert had lived in our day he would have been a sort of Cunninghame Graham (how awfully good those last stories of his are!) and held pro-Ferrer meetings in Trafalgar Square, and ridden a mustang and gone to prison for his opinions, and all the time dreadfully an aristocrat and hating publicity.

And how exactly like that mean-spirited young Thesiger (I have not bothered to copy his grotesque, illiterate misspelling) to want Louis Norbert to "sacrifice to the graces" and enjoy all these "polite and delightful splendours"—he, I mean Thesiger, the son of a Cromwellian stalwart and "Avenge Lord thy murdered Saints" sort of person. Of *course* Louis Norbert just wouldn't, and merely quoted the Bible, which, after all, is a deal finer than all their Corneilles and Bossuets and the other things in the *Cours de Dictées* we were bored with.

By the way, how did our delightful young Huguenot come to be buried in a Catholic cemetery? Surely some part of that villainous *abbé's* plot!

These words of our dear Louis Norbert (I can't get over their happening to have just been his first to us!) have brought home to me how much I have always loathed Louis XIV. and his court. It isn't really because of the *Cours de Dictées* and the six months I was made to spend at a school at Versailles. I've been back there time after time, and often in awfully good company (I like dining there after a hot day in Paris, don't you—much better than the Bois); but all the Louis XIV. part has *always* seemed to me utterly dull and pompous (just think of Villa d'Este at Tivoli or even the Boboli gardens!), except when autumn makes it untidy and—is it the right word?—*elegiac*.

And just think what it must have looked like when it was all new, tons and tons of brand new stone, and *stucco* like whipped cream, and trees the size of brussels sprouts, and lamentable, transplanted saplings wilting away in the gravel! "Like Babel in the building, and the builder like Ahab or Pharaoh"—how true, and what a real *friend* Louis Norbert proves to be! Indeed he is far too lenient in his judgment, like all nice people (Cunninghame Graham, whom he's so like, when he writes in the *Clarion* against capitalists).

I mean about Louis XIV. For I rather liked Ahab in Renan's *Peuple d'Israel* (Jezebel was *rather grande dame*, don't you think?), and as to Pharaoh, of course Louis Norbert had never been in Egypt, else he could never have been so disrespectful to those wonderful statues as to think of them in the same breath with that odious, bedizened vulgarian of a *Roi Soleil*. So like a magnified, vulgarised Sir Willoughby Patterne, with "he has a leg" (though I always think Meredith overdoes that leg!), perpetually posing and expecting the women to do all the love-making and the faithfulness! Faugh!

And all those sickening *grandees* waiting about for him to pass (and the pompous wretch used to complain if they weren't there every day and every hour, do you remember?) in hopes of getting a *tabouret* or an office or money at the end of ten or fifteen years of bowing and scraping. Don't you hate the silly way that people, particularly old ladies with intellectual pretensions, say to one, "My dear, you *must* read Mme. de Motteville—or the Cardinal de Retz"—or "*Do* let me lend you a volume of Saint Simon—he is such a psychologist, my dear, and such exquisite wit," etc., etc., etc., when they ought to be *ashamed* of reading all that abominable gossip, like the lowest society papers and much more indecent, and all the cock and bull poisoning of people with pounded diamonds in *eau de chicorée* (of course pounded glass would have been too cheap for such *grandees!*).

How I loathe it all, and how glad I am Louis Norbert loathed it also! That brute of a Louis XIV., behaving like that to poor Mile. de La Vallière! And how like him to end off with marrying a retired governess—so just what he *would* do. And then that little niece of Mazarin whom he jilted—what was her name? She *did* score off him when he sent her away and she said, "*Vous êtes Roi, Sire, et vous pleurez et me laissez partir.*" I hope it's true and that he felt properly humiliated once in a way. Wasn't her name *Berenice,* like the lady of your Pisan spies—or why do I associate her with that? Isn't it a play by Racine, dreadfully dull, but which one's French friends pretend to find *exquis*—and all exclaim (you know their tone) "oh-o-o-o-oh—" about?

Write to me at once what you think of Louis Norbert's first appearance on our scene; and whether you don't think all he says about Versailles and Louis XIV. So true.

Yours, etc.

From the Archaeologist to Lady Venetia

Pisa: May 18, 1909

Dear Lady Venetia,

I am so glad you foresaw how enchanted I should be at Louis Norbert not disappointing your search, and making his appearance upon (as you are kind enough to word it) *our* scene. And particularly with sentiments so very much in harmony with your own, in which I have the honour of quite concurring. I am moreover quite personally obliged to your interesting and mysterious seventeenth-century friend for having, however unintentionally, elicited the enchanting attack on Louis XIV. which you have done me the honour of addressing to me. I believe it to be of extraordinary historical value; and I keep reading and re-reading it with infinite enjoyment.

By a curious coincidence, I believe you have already solved, if not the riddle of your young Frenchman's end (but this will surely come out of your Muniment Room!), at all events one of the two historical mysteries I have come upon during my, unfortunately still fruitless, researches in these Pisan archives. You have discovered the identity of that enigmatic *Berenice* whose crazy fancies somehow exercised the Grand Duke of Tuscany's spies and diplomatists. Of *course* she was Marie Mancini, Mazarin's niece, and widow of the Constable Colonna.

I ought to have guessed it at once, but it required your nimbler wits to put two and two together. You associated Mazarin's niece and "*vous êtes Roi, Sire, et vous pleurez et me laissez partir*"—with Racine's *Berenice* for the excellent reason that that play (on which I find you unduly severe) was suggested by Marie Mancini's treatment at Louis XIV.'s hands. Titus, who sacrifices his love for the Jewish princess to the *Raison d'Etat* of ancient Rome is Louis XIV.; Berenice, who refuses to be jilted, is Marie Mancini, and so the grand duke and the grand ducal spies would naturally allude to her by that stage name. It is transparent; only it took you to see it! And the crazy fancy which frightened the grand duke was doubtless one of this lady's many schemes for forcing her way into the royal presence and attempting to reassert her former sway upon her quondam would-be bridegroom.

Being, alas! unable to send you any news of Louis Norbert (although I *did* send you some in my last of the *abbé* you suspected of having murdered him), I shall take the liberty of posting you a rather delightful little book by Arvède Barine, which I happen to have by me (don't return it, it is of no value), containing a most entertaining account of the *Berenice* in question.

She is really rather a fascinating creature, the most wonderful of those wonderful *Mazarines*, all with tragic or romantic adventures and splendid names: Olympe, Hortense, Laure, Soissons, Mercoeur, Mazarin, Conti, and so forth, amazons, wits, saints, astrologers or poisoneresses, driving seventeenth-century princes and ambassadors and prelates distracted with their charms, their ambitions, or their crimes.

Marie was the strangest of this handful of dangerous and amusing sirens, who were always scouring from one end of Europe to the other—Savoy to Spain, Rome to Brussels, sometimes dressed as men (Marie herself escaped from her Colonna husband in men's clothes and was very nearly taken by *Corsairs* and to the Great Turk's *harem*), sometimes dressed in the most genuine rags (do you remember Madame de Sévigné's daughter lending her shifts?), now receiving the College of Cardinals in bed, now being put under lock and key in convents and fortresses; making verses, playing the guitar, drawing horoscopes, and two of them, Olympe and Marianne, brought before the magistrates for poisoning. But I am merely spoiling Arvède Barine's little book for you with my pedantic summary.

Forgive my dullness, as well as my (I trust temporary) inability to find any traces of Louis Norbert, and believe me, dear Lady Venetia,

Yours, etc.

PS.—Should the little book I am sending have the good fortune of interesting you in the Berenice whom you have so happily identified, there are two thick (and rather dull) volumes about her by Lucien Perrey which you will certainly be able to get from the London Library.

LETTER 11

From Lady Venetia to the Archaeologist

Arthington: May 31

My dear Professor,

I have found two more mentions of Louis Norbert in Anthony Thesiger's letters to his mother. (I must say that ancestor of mine is rather nice with the old lady, though he was a snob trying to make L. N. admire Versailles.) The first is of Oct. 21, 1683. He writes:

> You need be under no apprehensions about your adopted son. These Frenchmen know not the difference between strangers. None of them guesses that *Norbert* is not an English name, and his French they find much less excellent than mine." (What a coxcomb!) "He consorteth only with persons of our own nation and a few learned men of Paris, and his heresy is accounted the fault of being English. I have moreover always believed that there was but little truth in what we were told of his parents being protestants ruined by Mazarin.
>
> I am informed that up to the rigorous measures of his present Majesty, the protestants of this kingdom have not been maltreated although they were in Savoy already in Oliver's time. Also I am informed that the only family bearing your adopted son's name is one of very small gentry, or as they say here,

hobereaux, in Gascony, and has suffered no exiles or other severities. But you well know what my dear father always thought. —

(Evidently Dame Priscilla did *not* think what Arthington thinks about L. N.'s birth, and there must be some further mystery.)

The *second* mention of L. N. is in a letter of Nov. 20, 1683. By the way, these letters were carried "by His Excellency's Gentleman" or by "a safe opportunity of His Lordship of Elgin returning home," not by the post.

Well, it appears that a lawsuit had arisen requiring the presence of Anthony Thesiger. He therefore gives up, very unwillingly, the remainder of his stay in France and his intended journey to Italy. He tells his mother that he will travel with all diligence to Arthington, hoping to arrive there in about ten days' time "if the sea be calm," but that her "adopted son" has already left Paris for Rome by way of Marseilles and Leghorn, with some personage who is called merely "his Lordship" and who is evidently some young gentleman with a numerous company of bear-leaders, for he adds:

> "Your adopted son will find himself at ease in this society, particularly by reason of his Lordship's tutor and interpreter, the learned Mr. Humphrey Standish, who is well acquainted with the antiquities and other rarities of Italy, besides being no mean physician and a philosopher in correspondence with the famous academy of the Lynxes. His Lordship is likewise followed by a good musician, Mr. Bob Lowndes, who is, in truth, in orders and serves as travelling chaplain in Popish countries."

After which reassurances to the old lady's protestantism he goes on:

> Despite what I writ to you in my last, I have since such information and suspicions as make me none

the less pleased your adopted son should stay no longer in this country, but have cleared out before I leave it.

Isn't that all very mysterious? Then—the story of the dangers run by L. N.'s family proved true after all. Or else perhaps Anthony had discovered that L. N. really belonged to some *other* family which did entail danger or disgrace. How could one find out *who* was likely to be in disgrace or danger about the time of L. N.'s birth—I suppose about 1660 wouldn't it be, since the tombstone says he died at twenty-four?

I mean, of course, in France; I mean, of course, sufficiently in disgrace for an orphan to have been spirited away to England by old Nicholas Thesiger. Would the *Fronde* be any kind of use? I have a dim idea it—whatever it was— took place about that time, but perhaps it's all nonsense—I mean my idea, not the Fronde, though I daresay that was nonsense too.

You told me you were "working up" the origins of Pisan architecture in the twelfth century. That seems rather a far cry. But I have a notion, dear professor, that knowing about any history you must know about all! So do be kind and look in your memory for some family which *mysteriously came to grief about 1660.*

Yours, etc.

LETTER 12

From the Archaeologist to Lady Venetia

Pisa: June 3, 1909

Dear Lady Venetia,

I congratulate you on your further success! You ask what family was likely to be in danger in France, or persecuted or extinguished there about 1660? I shall put the question, which is beyond my competence, to a French historian whom I expect to see in a few days in Florence, where, by the way, I will have a hunt for traces of Louis Norbert among such documents as have been removed from Pisa. My learned but rather uncommunicative friend may be willing to part with some of his carefully-secreted knowledge in return for what I can tell him about the grand ducal spies having been all agog about a mysterious "Ace of Hearts" who was abroad in Italy at the time of Louis Norbert's death, as I think I told you.

I am very glad you have given me this opportunity of showing my zeal for Louis Norbert, and removing an impression my last letter may have given, that I have transferred my interest to Berenice.

That discovery—I mean her identity with Marie Mancini—is yours, not mine; and that is my only reason for being interested in it.

You seem to think that your discoveries have come to an end with the Reverend Rupert's boxful. Do not be so impatient with your Muniment Room! Do remember what you have already discovered for yourself, namely, that our ancestors (or rather *yours*, for I don't know whether a man called Schmidt has any) were excessively avaricious of paper, and apt to turn old documents to unexpected uses. Only last week the daughter of Marchese Viscardi (that exquisite old antiquarian I met the day that you left Pisa) showed me a list of Turkish galley slaves and their rations (of food and perhaps also of lashes) which she had discovered as the stiffening of a brocade chalice-cover in their chapel. So expect to find news of Louis Norbert wherever—well, wherever you least expect it.

Besides, there are other and perhaps better ways of getting news of him. Do you remember writing to me that if I could find out nothing I was to "make it up"? Well, I venture to say the same to you—*invent!* it is but another form of the Latin word which means to *discover!* One of the evenings I had the honour of passing with you and your cousins at Pisa, I shall never forget how you entertained us all with the doings of a romantic German couple—his

247

name was *Hermann* and hers, I *think*, Isabella—yes, Hermann and Isabella Süsskind, and their sentimental adventures with a certain bassoon (or was it double bass?) player and an Italian landlady who possessed a small boy called *Italo*—Italo who was always expected to catch cold.

The bassoon player aroused fearful jealousy in this lady's husband, and somehow also in Hermann, by his unfailing alacrity in helping little Italo into his great-coat. Do you remember? And then, when you had told us exactly what each of them had felt and said, you explained suddenly that none of these people had ever existed outside your own imagination, and you seemed considerably incredulous when your ambassador cousin admitted that he had never possessed any Hermanns and Isabellas and bassoon players and Italos of his own!

Well—how shall I put it? *Invent* your Louis Norbert. Believe me, you have begun already, long, long ago, when you first saw his portrait in your childhood. Why not continue? After all, are not all the persons in whom we take the most vivid interest just, to that extent, creations of our own? And what is loving people except making them up to please one's heart's desire?

I am, dear Lady Venetia,

Yours, etc.

LETTER 13

From Lady Venetia to the Archaeologist

Arthington: June 10, 1909

Dear Professor,

I hate you, and your "inventions." Can't you tell the difference between a creature making up absurdities about Hermanns and Isabellas and bassoon players (as if everybody didn't, except my "ambassador cousin," as you call him) and a woman taking quite an inconceivable trouble—hours and days in the Muniment Room—about a real historical personage, almost a member of her own family, in whom she has been *deeply* interested all her life? It is really disappointing; I mean *you* are!

Many thanks for the little book about the Mazarin nieces. It is, I admit, amusing, and shows the French court in a more supportable light. I ought to be grateful, and I am, only I feel it was somehow intended to help me to, as you put it, *invent*, as if *inventing* were what I was bent on. And never have I felt less inclined to *make up*, to turn Louis Norbert into a Hermann and Isabella (really, how you could!) than at this moment. For this very day *I have come into his real presence,* the first time since, as a small girl, I discovered his portrait; and really, I don't think I have had such another emotion between that time and this!

I have discovered two whole long—very long—letters of Louis Norbert. Do you understand? *Letters in his own writing,* giving his own impressions of Italy to my ancestor Anthony Thesiger. They were in quite another box of papers, on a topmost shelf.

You really do not deserve to hear anything about it, you with your "invent"! But after all, you have only just taken to such odious ideas, and up to now you have really been a great dear about Louis Norbert. And I daresay you are no longer in that stupid frame of mind (I suppose it's some new-fangled *pose* of you *jeunes!*), pretending that when one is interested in people it's because they don't really exist except in one's own wonderful brain. Besides, I love copying these letters; I've already copied them once, and I'm going to learn to typewrite in order to copy them tidily.

The first is signed "your less, but more than brother L. N." And it is addressed, on the back of the first sheet:

To Sir Anthony Thesiger, Bart, of Arthington Manor, my honoured Master, these, favoured by the Duke of Winchester his Grace. Rome, Jan. 5, 1684 N.S. (New Style).

Here they both are, dear Professor, with my forgiveness. Your deeply misunderstood *old* friend,

PS.—I have not copied the misspellings. And there aren't more of them, very likely, than in my own letters.

LETTER 14

From Louis Norbert to Sir Anthony Thesiger

When we had crossed the Ciminian forest, Sir Christopher and I and other gentlemen riding on horseback alongside of his lordship's coach, each with his pistols at half-cock, and the servants with blunderbusses for fear of outlaws in those lonely places, we saw over against us a blue mountain rising out of a green and empty valley, which Mr. Humphrey Standish, my lord's interpreter, and a great antiquarian, pointed out to us as Mons. Soracte, of which Horace sayeth:

Vides ut alta stet nive Candidum
Soracte.

And Virgil, in his Æneis:

Summe deum sancti custos Soractis Apollo.

But our way lay only across big green moors, for leagues without a house or cottage, bare and covered with coarse dry grass whereon pale cattle were browsing, with here and there a gnarled oak whose trunk was raw for tearing off its bark whereof the Italians make cork, a cruel sight, methought, and fitting this forsaken country in which it became hourly more difficult to believe that we should come upon the former capital of the world, and, as papists pretend, of Christendom; or indeed, any place at all with civil inhabitants and customs.

Yet not an hour later we came in sight of an infinite number of towers and domes, among which our postillions pointed out the vastest as of the famous Church of St. Peter. And soon after, having crossed a great muddy river which was the Tiber, we rode under a gateway and into a huge enclosure adorned magnificently with fountains and an Egyptian obelisk, a curiosity I had never seen or heard described, being in shape much like a needle or thorn, but of basalt or other hard stone, and over a hundred feet in height with four basalt lions spewing water into tanks at its base.

LETTER 15

From Lady Venetia to the Archaeologist

Arthington: June n, 1909

My dear Professor,

After all, I sent you only *one* of L. N.'s letters yesterday. I wanted you to have time to enjoy it thoroughly; *what* a poet he was and how nice about Horace and Virgil—at least, it was nice in him, for I can recollect thinking them a great bore when my grandfather used to quote them over his port.

Well, today I am sending you the second one, *which is even more wonderful.* When I think of all those silly, memoire-reading old dotties with their St. Simon and so on, I should like them to see this. (No, I should *hate* them to, and no one except you shall ever see L. N.'s letters as long as I'm at Arthington.)

PS.—On recopying the letter (I am not going to bother with the queer spelling, final e's and so forth, it would look like faking, like "Ye Olde Tea-Rooms," etc.)—well, on recopying, it strikes me that L. N. must have been drawing the long bow a little about Italian wickedness; what do you think?

When people have such a gilt for writing they are apt to become just a bit abusive, as I always tell Cunninghame Graham. But, after all, perhaps they all richly deserved it, just as the capitalists do nowadays. I seem rather incoherent; it's because this is really *too* wonderful and exciting, isn't it?

Yours, etc.

251

From Louis Norbert to Sir A. Thesiger

Rome: January 15, 1684 N.S.

My Friend and excellent Master,

You ask me how I like Italy and its inhabitants. They are, indeed, of admirable learning and refinement, passing that, methinks, of the French, by reason of their sweetness and simplicity.

Thus I have been entertained with infinite kindness and wit by certain learned men, disciples of the famous *Galileo*, at *Florence*; where we sojourned some weeks on our way from the sea. The towns also are incredibly magnificent, not only for their many curious and beautiful monuments of variegated precious marbles, but also the great number of splendid private houses, rightly called *palaces*, of all the persons of consequence and even of the lesser citizens. These are never of wood, or brick, but of stone, symmetrical, lofty, the windows strangely high, and having interiorly a fine pillared yard with paved columnades for shade and rain, with often a noble fountain or antique statue in the centre.

The very streets are paved as is the habit to pave only palaces in other countries, with broad stone flags, smooth and united, whereon there is no mud and coaches roll as smooth as in a courtyard. The squares before the principal edifices are vast and regular, with abundance of water playing in marble basins among the feet of huge *colossi*.

These people live with incredible delicacy and a cleanliness so nice that they have open lofts upon their roofs, whereon to dry their linen, whereof they have strange abundance. Likewise they make incredible provision for the sick, not in paltry wooden alms-houses, but in such lofty hospitals they look like churches, where the infirm are attended by the most famous *chirurgeons* and physicians like the celebrated Monsieur Malpighi; also they have profusion of excellent music, both in their great theatres and churches, some of which I am causing to be copied for you, in especial that of *Carissimi*, who is for this country as *Mr. Purcell* or *Lully* for England and France; also a famous Sicilian, one *Scarletto*.

I am also causing drawings to be made of rare statues and collecting prints of the finest pictures and architecture, of which the excellence and abundance passeth believing.

The splendour and politeness and their loving kindness towards strangers maketh it difficult to credit what one is told of the manifold wickedness of this country. Yet it is so, as the natives themselves all too readily admit. Every man doeth justice and taketh vengeance for himself, and the life of a man is held no more sacred than a pullet's.

Duels are fought here in the Spanish fashion, the seconds engaging and often getting killed along with the principals in such manner that the streets become no better than a shambles, for some trifle of one coach taking precedence, or a dispute of saucy chair-men. And this is greatly increased by the rabble of ruffians whom all persons of quality find fit to dangle at their heels, rarely going forth without a guard of cut-throats, whose rags are barely hidden under the liveries and silver badges which place them, like their patrons, impunely out of the law's reach.

And as if such defiance of God's command, "Thou shalt not kill," sufficed not for their pride and hatred, they add to this flaunted violence wherein their person is at least exposed, all kind of secret, sudden, and dastardly murder at the hands of their servants, of whom certain, called *bravos*, or, as we should say, bullies or swashbucklers, are kept openly by these nobles, for the avowed purpose of executing their vengeance.

More than once already, since we disembarked in this country, it has happened that some person we had met at an assembly was thus dispatched by salaried spadassins or been obliged to pass into some neighbouring principality (whereof Italy affords a convenient number) to escape less the pursuit of justice, which winks and turns a deaf ear to the evil doings of people of birth, than the wrath of an injured family.

More than once hath it happened to me, and his lordship's other companions, to hear screams of murder even in broad daylight, and find a corpse weltering in blood round some blind corner or under an archway, on which occasion the street empties as if by miracle, those about vanishing like rats into drains, while doors and shutters are incontinently barred for fear of being called on to give evidence, it being the custom that those in authority should hide their impotence towards high-born offenders by racking and tormenting any poor devils they may sweep up on their way.

After which the murdered man is thrown across a barrow, or carried away by one of the congregations of mercy, cowled and masked, with torch and taper, and fitter, methinks, to strike terror than bring comfort. Indeed, I will tell you privily that it would seem as if his lordship's self had once been the intended victim of such villainous attempts, thanks doubtless to his carrying the so-called gallantries of King Charles's Court into a country as profligate indeed, but where a show of jealousy is enforced by fashion and maintained by such practices as above described. For going to a concert of music at Cardinal Chigi's, Mr. Lowndes and myself and an Italian gentleman in one of his lordship's coaches, one day that my lord had been let blood and kept the house, some ruffians, thinking he was one of us, discharged a volley from blunderbusses as we passed beneath the arch of Portugal so called, breaking a glass and grazing a footman's cheek, and what was stranger, piercing my hat with a slug without wounding me, and this by the mercy of God and the interposition of an ostrich feather. Do not, I pray you, communicate this circumstance to the lady your mother, who might be concerned for my safety, which is perfect, that murderous attack being notoriously directed to his Lordship and not to me, whose religion as well as natural moodiness preserve from giving umbrage to any man, even in this strange and dangerous land.

Vouchsafe to hold me in your affection, as I shall ever hold you and all yours in my devout and loving gratitude.

Your obedient servant,

L. N.

LETTER 17

From the Archaeologist to Lady Venetia

Villa Viscardi, Evola, Prov. di Pisa,

June 12, 1909

Dear Lady Venetia,

Your letter enclosing the first of Louis Norbert's made me feel that through some unintended and so far unintelligible *gaucherie* I had forfeited the right of taking any further interest in the personage who interests you. Indeed, I had decided not to intrude any more letters upon you, feeling as I do rather paralysed by the fear of again incurring your displeasure without even understanding why or wherein; a woman of the world like you cannot know what it is to feel oneself hopelessly awkward just where one would least wish to be so. Excuse all this talk about myself, which does not diminish my *gaffe!*

But I wish to explain my silence, and also the unpardonable rudeness (I seem perpetually committing the *unpardonable sin*, and, like religious persons, not knowing in what it consists) of delaying to return you the copies of both the letters which you have kindly communicated to me. Owing to my absence from Pisa, the second was delayed; I got it only yesterday here in the country. You are quite right in considering them as very interesting documents, nor has the very slight study I have made of the Italian seventeenth century (mainly in the archives in your service) led me to tax Louis Norbert with any exaggeration in his account of the lawlessness then existing. I have just been looking over an interesting volume, *Vita Barrocca*, by the well-known antiquarian Corrado Ricci, who repeatedly sums up the state of Italy between 1650 and 1700 in exactly the same manner.

I ought to add, perhaps, that I have been less fortunate than you, in so far as I have been unable to discover any mention of Louis Norbert's *name*. It is true that documents have lately come under my notice which *may* contain certain important references to him, but this is mere conjecture, and such as to expose me once more to the reproach of suggesting that you should *invent*, which I did, I assure you, in the most respectful intention, and, I might almost add, in a truly scientific spirit. For a hypothesis is a scientific *invention*, and after your identification of the *Berenice* of the grand ducal spies with Mazarin's niece, I wished to encourage you to make a further hypothetical identification towards which some of our facts seemed, in a way, to point.

Be this as it may, I cannot sufficiently express my regret that my advice should have been such as to deserve your displeasure.

I am, dear Lady Venetia,

Yours regretfully, etc.

LETTER 18

From Lady Venetia to the Archaeologist

Arthington: June 24, 1909

My dear young Friend,

What are you talking about? What is all this nonsense about *displeasure* and *rudeness?* Never have I suggested such a thing! If anyone has been rude it has been I. (Although I must say you did rile me with your Mazarin nieces book and your invent and your inconceivable bracketing of L. N. with Hermann and Isabella). Well, I mean if anyone has been rude or committing *gaffes*, it is always sure to be

I; and worse than *rude, ungrateful* in forgetting even for an instant how infinitely patient and sympathetic you have shown yourself in this matter, which, after all, concerns only me.

It is so long since you last wrote, and this letter of to-day has an unknown address, so I don't even understand *where* you are; that is why I don't send you the copy of some other letters of Louis Norbert's which I have recently discovered, *very* extraordinary and mysterious letters I am sure you will say. Please let me know where I can send them, and whether you will get them if I *register* them? Italian country posts are sometimes unaccountable in their methods.

Yours, etc.

PS.—What are the new references to L. N. which you think you have found? And what do you mean by saying that perhaps they involve *inventions?* Please explain by return of post.

LETTER 19

From the Archaeologist to Lady Venetia

Villa Viscardi, Evola, Prov. di Pisa,
July 1, 1909

Dear Lady Venetia,

I hasten to thank you for your gracious forgiveness of my stupidity, of which the worst was thinking I had offended you.

There is no danger in sending your copies here even if you do not register them. You have, I see, got thoroughly in touch with Louis Norbert's century as regards fear of the post. Or have *femmes du monde* always a preference for registering?—registration and telegrams, isn't that a generalisation worthy of your friend Henry James?

Well, if you will not invent, it is not my place to urge you to frame a hypothesis. Only you must allow your humble scientific friend to desist, on his part, from precipitate formulation of the one he sees looming before us.

I am, dear Lady Venetia,

Yours, etc.

20

Telegram from Lady Venetia to the Archaeologist

Arthington: July 5, 1909

Dear Professor,

Earnestly request formulate historical hypothesis.—Hammond.

Reply paid

21

Telegram from the Archaeologist to Lady Venetia

Evola, Prov. di Pisa: July 6, 1909

Infinitely regret disobey request. Premature formulation always dangerous. Respectful greetings. Letter follows.

LETTER 22

From the Archaeologist to Lady Venetia

Villa Viscardi: July 6, 1909

Dear Lady Venetia,

I cannot at present explain why (and the scientific reasons would be a mere impertinence) I was obliged to telegraph yesterday declining to formulate any hypothesis. Allow your humble servant merely to explain that for the present saying "formulate" to him is exactly the same as saying "*invent*" to you.

As regards the documents I alluded to, I cannot as yet tell you much about them, for the simple reason (among others, however) that I cannot as yet read them; I mean that they are, if they exist at all and are not mere imagination (like Hermann and Isabella), in cypher, or rather *cryptogram* (not mushrooms!). That is to say, that, if they exist, they exist in single words and phrases which must be picked out of books according to a clue which has in each case to be discovered.

This much, however, I can tell you—these documents (if documents they prove to be) form part of the library of that learned Pisan Abbess Artemisia del Valore, who was, in her young and worldly days, a crowned poetess (like Corinne!), and whose compositions you think so interesting. This library, or rather a very small selection thereof, she did not give to her convent when she took the veil in 1687, but handed to a cousin who had then recently married the head of the Viscardi family. And it is in the library of Marchese Viscardi's villa that I have discovered these books once belonging to the abbess, and in them—well, the documents which are perhaps, after all, mere coincidence and fancy.

Feeling a little (and quite unreasonably) discouraged by your *aversion* to inventing (forgive my reverting to this incident), I gave the goodbye to Louis Norbert and accepted the invitation of Marchese Viscardi to spend some weeks in a villa of his which happens to be within a walk of some curious *Proto-Pisan* churches, which I am drawing and measuring and photographing in the company of this delightful old man, while helping him with the "Guide to the Mediaeval Antiquities of the Pisan Province," upon which he has been engaged some thirty years.

It was his unmarried daughter, the same young lady who had found the list of galley-slaves in the chalice-cover, who first got wind of the cryptogram and the clue to it; and it is she (she has an amazing archaeological *flair*) who is now helping me in my attempt to decipher these (supposed) documents.

It would amuse you to see us poring over the mystery after dinner by the big round table in the great *sala* of the villa, portraits of ancestors in scarlet and armour, and immense heads of wild boars looking down on us from under the dimly-lit, far-off arches, while the rest of this hospitable family and their country guests amuse themselves with reviews and illustrateds, and the dear old *Marchese* takes his nap like an Elizabethan *grandee's* effigy of painted alabaster more than ever...The end of my sentence has got lost in my vain attempt to make you see this extraordinary characteristic and charming Italian interior.

If only I were a novelist instead of a mere plodding pedant, *what* romantic things I could write about this great old house, of noblest, simplest architecture, where you find your way to bed by the light of an oil lamp in a corner of the great sounding corridors hung with portraits and coats of arms, and there is an old spinet outside my door and a perch for combing out periwigs in the closet alongside of my bathtub!

Well, there we are, the *Marchesina* and I, poring over old yellow volumes of the *Pastor Fido,* of Virgil, and other classics, and books on natural science having belonged to the learned, the once gloriously crowned, abbess, and over piles of manuscript music, in search of faint, faint marginal marks which mean that here she is (so at least we imagine) addressing her correspondent, or being so addressed by this mysterious, anonymous, *perhaps non-existent*, (quite as non-existent as Hermann and Isabella!) creature.

Meanwhile around us the rest of the company discuss the coming vintage, the municipal elections, the shooting of the various boars on the walls, until perhaps the *Marchese* suddenly awakes, quite on the spot, and inconceivably courteous and dignified, and joins in with some amazingly exact and to the point piece of chronology, or natural history, or family tradition. Or else some of the innumerable batches of grandchildren troop in, delightful hoydens masquerading in the garments of the guests mixed with those of long-deceased ancestors, and extemporise charades or play riddles in verse which the old butler has composed and laid alongside the menu.

It sounds like nothing at all when I write it, and it is, in reality, such an incomparable mixture of the past and present, spacious, airy, friendly, simple and yet full of mysterious shadows and gleanings. . . . I often think how much it would appeal to your (I mean no offence) imagination and love of romance.

The *Marchesina* has inherited her father's antiquarian gifts. She is, besides, an excellent horsewoman (and it takes one to deal with her Maremma colts!), and knows more about plants and animals than any naturalist of my acquaintance, or any schoolboy (for she has pet toads and suchlike); she knows all about the real life of the peasantry, and can tell me their biographies like one of themselves, as well as their fairy tales and poetry. And with all this a certain shy self-irony, with a charm like the bitter of mountain herbs. Some day you must really know her and her father.

Meanwhile, and until the cypher of the abbess has been mastered, I will merely tell you that we have made out— or imagine we have made out (for *we* invent, dear Lady Venetia)—that Artemisia, before her religious time, engaged in a clandestine correspondence by means of books and music borrowed and returned; and that the subject of this correspondence was to warn some person in whom she took an interest against the machinations of his enemies. The idea arose in my mind (and was accepted by the *Marchesina's* almost intuitive knowledge of the past of her fellow countrymen) that there must be some reason for the verse

Heu! fuge crudeles terras, fuge littus avarum

being not only underlined in a fine Elzevir Virgil, but copied out on the flyleaf of the same book in a large, bold hand; and that at the end of the Virgil there was a note— "*Vide Æneid: LIB II. versus 44*"—which verse was no other than that same admonition to "fly from these cruel shores." Indeed it was this arrangement which first led us to notice that the backs of some of the abbess's books contained lists of pages corresponding to underlined verses or single words, thus constituting a sort of little code or dictionary.

Besides the verse in question the Virgil contains faint pencillings under the words "enemies"—"danger"—"death," and the word "*dapes*" and every other meaning food. In short, we have come to the (perhaps over-hasty) conclusion that the lady whose music you admired was carrying on an elaborate secret correspondence in order to warn someone against *poison*.

"Those were the days of Acqua Tofana," remarked the *Marchesina* with a slight shrug, as she might have said, "These are the days of telephones"—and turning to her father—"*È vero Babbo?*" she continued, "they were always poisoning or getting poisoned, or thinking they were getting poisoned, in the seventeenth century."

"*Eh già*," answered the *Marchese* from his newspaper; "you remember the case of our cousin Lanfreducci's Neapolitan great-grandmother."

But the wonderful tale here related would be too long to repeat, and spoilt in the repeating. Besides, I have already taken up too much of your time with things in which Louis Norbert, alas! plays no apparent part.

And—well—my hypothesis is not yet ripe enough to formulate!

I am, dear Lady Venetia,

Yours, etc.

LETTER 23

From Lady Venetia to the Archaeologist

Arthington: July 20, 1909

My dear Professor,

How awfully interesting about your delightful friends, and the villa and your discovery (I can't quite make out what you discovered) about Artemisia and the crypts—

no, I won't try for the word, you yourself said "*ne pas confondre* with mushrooms—"

The fact is I have only had time to glance at your letter—for I have just found another from Louis Norbert! And what is far more exciting even—whom do you suppose he introduces into the scene? Guess! Try and guess! But you can't, although it is so simple! Why, who could it be except the villain, the *Abbe Manfredini!*

I shall begin to believe that I have the second sight, as my silly Scotch cousins imagine themselves to have! For didn't I see, at the very first glance (I mean at the epitaph), that it was the *Abbé Manfredini who had done it?* It's *too* strange, and at the same time too utterly obvious, when you think of it. But now behold the *Abbé* in person!

Your (rather excited) friend, etc.

PS.—*Please acknowledge by return of post.* I must know what you think of it all.

PS. 2—Was *this* perhaps your hypothesis you couldn't formulate at once? But after all, haven't we known it from the very first time we clapped eyes on the epitaph?

LETTER 24

Louis Norbert to Sir Anthony Thesiger, Bart.

Rome: Jan. 16, 1684 N.S.

My good Master and beloved Brother,

I am, as you see, still in Rome, and like to remain as long at least as his lordship, returning with him after a sojourn at Naples. And this partly to make all possible and diligent profit by a teacher whom good luck hath sent me, being such that no man is better able to explain all the wonders and curiosities of this place, illustrating them with polite learning, he being indeed the deepest antiquarian *virtuoso,* besides profoundest historian and scholar, I have met. This is a certain Abbot Manfredini, a native of Pisa, whom I knew at a sitting of the famous academy of the Lynxes, at a discussion of the physical inventions of the celebrated Torricelli.

Lest your lady mother and my good benefactress, whom I devoutly reverence, should take alarm at this popish frequentation, let me set forth how *Abbas* is the title given in this country to any ecclesiastic, or indeed any layman, lawyer, or scholar, however little a clerk in orders, who hangeth about the Papal court and wears the collar and black cloak for cheapness and protection.

As regards Manfredini, although (by some popish simony) he benefiteth by the title and stipend of canon of Pisa, he is but such a half-baked priest, averring moreover only kneaded of pagan dough with the devil's own leaven. Indeed, his freedom from any superstition, even if it savoureth at times of the doctrines of Epicurus, obligeth him to a shallow pretence of conversion, whereof himself is the first to laugh, in order to consort unccnsured with heretics, with whom, as with all strangers of distinction, he mixes greatly, being well travelled, versed in all modern tongues, and a favourite of the French court in especial, whose legal adviser he purporteth to be in matters ecclesiastic, though better able to advise, I suspect, in the purchase of gems and statues, whereof himself possesses a rare collection.

From our first time of meeting he hath shown me a degree of friendship marvellous towards such a tyro in learning as I feel myself, and hath lost no occasion of obliging me even beyond all my wishes. Wherefore I am his grateful debtor and most attached friend, he being moreover of infinite sweetness and courtesy and a modesty rare in the learned, so that my attachment suffereth only from a certain irreligious ribaldry and gross levity, which, however, he showeth towards others in my presence but never towards myself, excusing himself by the need of *barking with the wolves* and also by the hatred of hypocrisy bred by Rome in a quick, free spirit. By his kindness I have had all curiosities thrown open to me, and been given an opportunity of seeing many famous persons, wherein Rome, as always, abounds.

By him, *exempli gratia*, have I been presented to the learned Court of the Queen of Sweden, who liveth here in voluntary exile, a crazy, foul-mouthed old harridan enough, but versed in every science and of curious mother-wit.

And yesterday I was carried by him to view the library of Prince Columna, on which occasion I was introduced to another personage who, albeit not a queen, might have become one. The story told me by the Abbot Manfredini is singular and little known, so I deem it deserving your attention. It seems the present king of France, in his minority, loved a niece of the famous Cardinal Mazarino, at that time minister of France; and would have wedded her after long wooing, but for the opposition of the queen, his mother.

This Mazarine lady was accordingly married by proxy to Prince Columna, Constable of Naples, and the chief, with his rival Orsini, of all the Roman barons. But whether disdaining such meaner alliance, or fearing his jealousy, since she ceased not flaunting her passion for the French King, she, having borne him sundry children, fled from Rome, and habited like a man, took ship to France where, after all manner of strange adventures, she sought an interview with the king, her former sweetheart.

Which, being refused, and herself threatened with return to her jealous husband, she wandered for many years from court to court, sometimes setting all by the ears through her favours, but oftener confined in convents and fortresses, and obliged to hairbreadth escapes and penurious voyages, wherein she was assisted by the fidelity of a Moorish slave-wench; and always flouting her enemies, by her invincible daring and the magic she exercised over men's minds, whereunto the vulgar add the knowledge of astrology and necromancy, she being now sister to two French duchesses arraigned for meddling in such unlawful knowledge at the time of the notorious Marchioness of Brinvilliers and La Voisin, poisoners and sorceresses.

The lady I am telling of, whose right name is Maria Mancini, Constabless Columna and Duchess of Tagliacotio, is now a widow and lives very retired though in great state, wearing it is said, day and night, the necklace of pearls given her by King Louis, in whom, 'tis thought, she never despairs of reviving his old flame; moreover spending much time in the vain practices of astrology and sortilege, doubtless in hopes of gaining through them such access to the king as himself hath constantly denied her.

It is this lady's story which the famous Monsieur Racine hath set forth in his play of *Berenice*, wherein that Jewish Queen, beloved of Titus, when that Emperor, respectful of the majesty of Rome, repudiates his youthful promise to wed her, is made to use the words with which this lady is said to have reproached her royal lover—"You are a king, sir, yet while you weep, allow me to go hence."

As we were examining the precious manuscripts collected by a late Cardinal Columna (whereof I enclose you an inventory hastily made by myself) who should enter the library but the Lady Constabless, attended by two maids-in-waiting, a chaplain, and an old Moorish female, marvellous ill-favoured.

Abbot Manfredini instantly made three deep reverences, and falling on one knee, offered to kiss her hand as of a queen, exclaiming, in his irreverent fashion:

"*Salve Regina!*"

Whereat she, scanning him disdainfully, turned to that old Moorish woman saying:

"See, see whom we have here! by my faith the learnedst man in Rome, most agreeable of spies and delicate of blackmailers, acceptable above every other eavesdropper to the polished Court of Versailles.

"Well, Abbot," she continues, laughing and signing him to rise up, "well, when will you be given the Collar of the Holy Spirit? or will it be the collar (as these Italians call it, *Strozzo*) of the garotting block offered you by His Holiness himself in recognition of the many enemies whom you have killed?"

Whereon she waved her hand in mock salute, and made to leave the room.

But the abbot took her words as jest, and throwing himself in her way, vowed he was ready to put his head in any noose to please so lovely a lady, but would rather it might be the two white hands of one of her handsome serving wenches.

"And, madam," he adds, pushing me before him, "vouchsafe a glance of those Jove-conquering eyes to this sweet youth, English, or as St. Augustine said, Angelical, in form and breeding, yet, 'tis said, French of birth, that he may tell it to his nephews when an aged man."

I confess these pleasantries had much embarrassed me, and more so when I found myself laughingly thrust by the abbot into the princess's presence and almost on to my knees.

"English and yet French!" cries the *Constabless*, stopping on her way to the door. "What entertaining riddle, fit for the *ruelle* of *precious* ladies, may this be, *Monsieur l'Abbé*? or has your elegant wit invented some sham mystery lacking a real one to offer your royal employers?"

But while she spoke, half jesting, half angry, she fixed her eyes on me with an odd intention, and as she did so I noticed the *abbé* watching us anxiously.

I bethought me of the lady's reputed madness, and was heartily glad when she departed and this strange comedy, yet flavoured with somewhat tragic, had come to an end.

When we were alone the *abbé*, no doubt to reassure me, jested not a little about the impression I had made on the *Constabless*, calling me Louis XIV.'s successor, till I bade him cease such pleasantry unseemly to his cloth, whereon he told me very seriously beware of this lady, she being the maddest woman in all Rome, albeit Rome holds the queen of Sweden.

And *anon* told me the story I have just related to you, to which I would add that the Constabless Columna is still well-favoured and of majestic mien, and has a certain magic of eye and voice which explaineth the fear the King of France is still said to feel of her ever returning to his presence.

I would not have you judge the Abbot Manfredini by this anecdote; he being, indeed, of those whose only fault is jesting affectation of the vices they have not, and taking ironic amusement (as being a declared misanthropos or disbeliever in men) in the foolish gossip whereby the wicked folly of the city explaineth the great fortune and influence due only to his unparalleled learning and universal helpfulness, making him beloved of all the great and hated by all the mean and envious.

LETTER 25

From the Archaeologist to Lady Venetia

Florence: July 26, 1909

Dear Lady Venetia,

Your letter containing copy of Louis Norbert's has followed me here, and I answer it at once, excited, as you can imagine, by this *entrée en scene* of the learned and villainous *Abbé*.

But, dear Lady Venetia, I am more excited even at another detail, which you seem almost to have overlooked—the simultaneous appearance of the Constabless Colonna. Do you forget that you yourself have ingeniously identified this lady with the mysterious *Berenice* of my Pisan spies?

You do indeed take your historical discoveries lightly; why, one of us would hope for a professorship for less!

The matter strikes me perhaps because, taking the opportunity of these few days in Florence to rummage in the grand ducal archives, I have found those reports from the usual grand ducal spies, and among them more allusions both to the *abbé* and the mysterious *Berenice*, who is never mentioned without the title of this *madwoman*. One of these allusions, in a letter from a Fra Barnaba, Servite, is as follows:

> The *Abbate* you know of excuses himself, saying he is busy preventing that madwoman embroiling His Highness in her crazy ambitions, which, after continuing a good twenty years with ceaseless displeasure to the court of France, and worry to those of Spain and Savoy and all persons who have come across her path, have, it seems, got a new lease of life from the rumours that the Ace of Hearts is now abroad in Italy.

I am returning to Pisa tomorrow, and soon after to the villa of Marchese Viscardi, where I hope to hatch the hypothesis I have alluded to, unless indeed, as I half expect, you and Louis Norbert himself will have forestalled me in the discovery.

I am, dear Lady Venetia,

Yours, etc.

Letter 26

From Lady Venetia to the Archaeologist

Arthington: Aug. 1, 1909

My dear Professor,

I now know who Louis Norbert de Caritan really was. And I believe you know it also, but you have wanted to leave me the joy, the *intoxication* of lighting upon the discovery, you dear, kind young friend.

That was what you meant when you made me so cross refusing to "formulate a theory" (what a pedant I did think you!) and went on in that maddening way insisting I should invent! Well! I have not invented, unless inventing may mean (by the way, you hinted something to this effect)—may mean *discovering the truth.*

And the *truth*—the truth you also know, I feel sure, my dear professor, the truth is—that L. N. was the heir to the throne of France, inasmuch as the legitimate son of Louis XIV. and Marie Mancini. It flashed across me this morning a good hour after reading your last letter, and in the strangest way. I was feeling ungrateful and annoyed at your still refusing to tell me what you and your young friend have discovered in the abbess's letters (now I know!) when my eye fell on that book about the Mancini niece which you had sent me. It had got unbound, as French books do, and Arthington had spelled slowly through it, dog's-earing as he does; so it looked untidy because *I* was cross with you. (I hate books that fall to pieces, worse than roses messing a carpet almost.) I rang for my maid to put it in a parcel which was going to the binders—really merely to get rid of it because *you* had not been kind, I thought, and meanwhile picked it up and opened it at random.

I fell upon the description of that little seaport Brouage where Marie spent an autumn in enforced or voluntary exile after that last passionate interview with the king at St. Jean D'Angely, and made up her mind, or, as the writer thinks, pretended to, to give him up forver.

I had thought it rather twaddle (the usual French *psychologie de son prochain*, as Bourget used to call common or garden gossip years ago), when suddenly now I had a sort of vision of Brouage (by the way, Arthington had sent for Perrey's big book *Le Roman du Grand Roi*, and I'd looked it over and there is all about Brouage in that); well, I had a vision, *quite* distinct: a tiny dismantled fortress, all grown with wild fig and caper, above the half-silted harbour and the dreary, dreary salt marshes; underneath the castle was the town or village, low houses, white-washed but all weather-stained, and a rampart with pollard elms separating the one from the other; and the sea far away at the end of that half-choked canal, with distant capes and towns, I think one must have been La Rochelle—gleaming fitfully like liberty and happiness.

I assure you I saw the place *as if I were in it.* A coach drawn by six grey mules—I suppose they used them in the South of France—drove slowly round and round the bastions, with the brown toasted elm leaves raining down on it. In the coach was that governess of the Mazarin nieces, that Mme. de Venel, who played the spy for Mazarin and told him whenever his niece got a packet from the young king; also two girls, one almost a child (that was the funny, pert little Marianne, the one who afterwards told the judge in the witch trial that she had seen the devil in his figure), and one very lovely and silly—that was Hortense, the one who was at Charles II.'s Court.

But Marie Mancini, the king's would-be bride, was not with them. Then I saw inside of the *chateau* or fortress, the great grim rooms with tall chairs marshalled against the walls, and card tables with wax *flambeaux* guttering in the draught, and these same two sisters and two friends they had sent for to play with. Then a room looking towards the sea, a salt wind blowing in among the curtains of the bed like a hearse—Marie was in it, insensible, like dead. There was an old Arab (do you remember she took lessons in astrology at Brouage, from an Arab physician whom Mazarin grumbled about?) with a white beard and turban sitting near the bed calculating a horoscope, and a tiny Moorish slave girl hiding behind a curtain.

And bending over the pillow was that governess or *duenna*, Mme. de Venel, all in black and yellow with a high, starched cap like the *femmes savantes* wear. The woman in the bed suddenly moaned and turned over on to her side away from these people. Then the Arab quickly got up, and lifting the counterpane took something from her side, covering it with his sleeve, and the *duenna* fetched a wrapper from a chest, and took the thing in it from him. A man in grey, with big boots, was in the door, and Mme. de Venel handed the wrapped-up thing to him; and as he took it, it screamed dreadfully, and was a new-born child. Then the woman in the bed suddenly sat up like galvanised and stared as if she didn't see, and then shrieked and shrieked and twisted her hands until she began to sob and fell back exhausted—and then I saw nothing more. For, mind you, I *did* really seem to see it much as crystal-gazers say they do.

But at the same time I knew I was *thinking* it all, not really seeing, and I heard myself say to myself, "Of course, that's how it all happened," and noticed that the book had fallen and that my maid was there waiting for orders, so I said, like an idiot, "Oh, Banks, I wanted you to send this book with the others to the binders, and after I'd rung it suddenly struck me I'd like to read it again. I'm so sorry to have troubled you—and would you bring me my garden hat and the scissors." I felt such a fool when she answered, "Quite so, my lady," as if that was the way sane people usually behaved or looked, for I'm sure *I* must have been staring into space like a lunatic. And I just longed to tell her all about Louis Norbert; and if it had been my dear little French Anna, who got married last year, I should like a shot, and she would have understood and been very sympathetic.

But English servants are a sort of *memento* not *mori*, but *memento* whatever is Latin for *not making a fool of oneself,* don't you think? I was horribly agitated and felt I must rush out into the open. I thought I'd walk to Harlow Heath, where there's air and space, but I found myself walking up and down, up and down the old bowling green in the lee of the house, stopping to stare like an idiot at the old stone bowls, or cannon-balls from the Royalist siege, and mumbling silly words to myself.

And suddenly a tune came into my head. It was one of those seventeenth century things, the lament of Jephthah's daughter by Carissimi, with a long minor *rifioritura* on the word *ululate.* And I said to myself: "Yes—of course—Jephthah's daughter and Louis XIV.'s son!' There was a high wind, and the old trees (they are pines almost like old, old cedars) creaked and moaned and seemed to repeat ululate. I suppose I was really a bit off my head.

Since then I have been absurdly calm, as if it had happened years ago, I mean the discovery of who Louis Norbert was, and as if I had always known it. And of course I always *ought to have* known it (as I suppose you did, but why not tell me?) all the time. For it is so simple and so obvious how it all happened. I know every detail. But before telling you, with your dreadful historical mind, I will have a go at those books again (I believe Arthington hasn't sent them back yet to the London library) and work it all out, dates and all.

No, on second thoughts I won't delay sending this off and telling you merely that I now know it all (as I feel more and more sure you *did* all along!)—I mean that Louis Norbert was the legitimate son of Louis XIV. and Marie Mancini.

And so goodbye for today.

Yours, etc.

LETTER 27

From the Archaeologist to Lady Venetia

Pisa: Aug. 4, 1909

Dear Lady Venetia,

I have read your letter twice over and feel positively stunned; what a poet and a novelist you are!

Know it all along? I? that Louis Norbert was what you say? The thing is so colossal my pedant's pen scarcely dares copy it! Never did such an idea enter my brain.

The evidence in the abbess's secret correspondence, even if it refer to Louis Norbert *at all* (which is my *half-fledged* hypothesis), has absolutely nothing to do with Louis Norbert's *birth; if anything* (for I am not sure) with Louis Norbert's *death.* I sent you the Arvède Barine book merely because I thought you would be pleased to have identified the *Berenice* of my Pisan spies with Mazarin's niece; I believe you have utterly forgotten that real first-rate bit of guess work on your own part!

As to your present theory, I fear that had it ever entered my mind I should have felt bound to dismiss it in the light of the documents published by Lucien Perrey and which I have consulted since getting your letter this morning. If that book (*Le Roman du Grand Roi*, also another, *Une Princesse Romaine*, which you should get) is still at Arthington, as you thought, you will doubtless have convinced yourself that your delightful notion does not, alas! hold historical water. This book contains the complete series of letters from Mme. de Venel, the *duenna*, informing the cardinal uncle, almost day by day, of the health and doings of the Mancini girls. And these reports leave absolutely no room for such a supposition as yours.

Moreover, there are letters of Cardinal Mazarin (see Perrey) to the Queen Mother, and one at least to Louis XIV. himself, expressing the utmost reprobation of any such possible marriage. Of course, as Arvède Barine, I think, points out, Marie Mancini's letter from Brouage to her uncle, saying that she gives up all hope of the royal marriage, may have been a mere feint on her part, since she continued in correspondence with the king. But that does not alter the evidence of Mazarin's spy, the *duenna* de Venel.

Besides, if the child had been born in wedlock, even if it had been spirited away as you describe, do you suppose Marie Mancini would ever for a moment have given up the king and let herself be married off to Prince Colonna? We know that even after she had been married for years to the constable, she never gave up the hope of seeing Louis XIV.; and it seems very probable that her flight from Rome was less due to her alleged fear of the constable's jealousy (he had closed an eye to very violent flirtations with Cardinal *Chigi* and the Chevalier de Lorraine) than to a hope of forcing her way into the king's presence.

Would not such a woman have moved heaven and earth if she had actually had a legitimate child as a trump card?

But of all this you are doubtless thoroughly convinced by this time. Do not let it diminish in your eyes (it could never in mine) the value of your wonderful vision of the castle by the sea, of the sick room and the spiriting away of a new-born child.

My contention is that it does not refer to a child of Marie Mancini and Louis XIV. But why should it not refer to Louis Norbert? You are, no doubt, less of a disbeliever in occultism than you boast yourself.

And what, given such belief, could be more natural or rather supernatural than that your strange sympathy with the poor youth who died in 1684 should enable you to see into his past, however hidden from ordinary investigation?

After all, it is only what would have happened to a poet or novelist; and, as I have already ventured to say, a poet and a novelist are lost (or perhaps gained!) in you, dear Lady Venetia; only I, a poor plodding historian, am bound to protest, in the name of historical documents, against the gratuitous interpretation of your vision of Louis Norbert's birth in the light of a marriage between Louis XIV. and the Berenice of our Pisan spies. Who knows whether your Muniment Room, methodically examined, may not at last prove that both of us are right! Meanwhile pray bear up with the scientific cavillings of your fervently appreciative though sceptical pedant, etc.

28

Telegram from Lady Venetia to the Archaeologist

Arthington: Aug. 7, 1909

Objections already disposed of in a letter you will receive tomorrow. Governess utterly untrustworthy. Uncle really delighted.

Venetia Hammond.

From Lady Venetia to the Archaeologist

Arthington: August 4, 1909

My dear Professor,

It has taken me longer to work out than I thought—I mean all the dates and things in Lucien Perrey's book and also Amedée René's *Les Nieces de Mazarin*, which my brother *most* luckily sent for after reading your Arvède Barine.

But I don't grudge the hours I spent over those dull, dull books, because it all works out quite *marvellously*, as you will see, leaving absolutely *no* doubt that first: Louis XIV. married Marie Mancini secretly in Dec. 1658 or Jan. 1659; second, that a child of this marriage was born at Brouage, near La Rochelle, in autumn 1659; third, that this child was spirited away instantly after its birth by Cardinal Mazarin's agents, the mother being deceived into the belief that it had never lived; and fourth, of course, that this child, whom my ancestor Nicholas Thesiger, formerly Cromwell's envoy to Mazarin, took charge of and educated, unconscious of his real parentage, was the person afterwards known as Louis Norbert de Caritan, who died at Pisa in 1684, presumably poisoned by the Abbé Manfredini.

See how businesslike I have become! Isn't that how you historians do when you (what you refused so *long et pour cause!*) *formulate a hypothesis.* Only, of course, this isn't a hypothesis. It's fact. And this is how it all came about.

You remember that the Queen Mother and Mazarin wanted the proposed marriage of Louis XIV. with a Princess of Savoy to miscarry—the queen because she hoped for a Spanish marriage which would make peace with her brother, and Mazarin—well, of course Mazarin hadn't made up his mind whether it wouldn't be quite possible for Louis XIV. to marry his niece, since he had been so long in love with her and since two other nieces had meanwhile married royalties of sorts.

Mazarin wasn't sure how the Queen Mother would take the *fait accompli* of such a marriage; you remember the old fox once asked her, pretending to joke, how she would like Marie Mancini for a daughter-in-law, and Mme. de Motteville, who was present, writes that the queen answered very hotly that if such a thing happened all France would rebel against her son and she herself would head the rebels; whereupon Mazarin drew in his horns and pretended to snuff out all that romance and work for the boring Spanish marriage.

Anyhow, at the time we're dealing with (I've looked up all the dates, it was in 1658) there was still this Savoy marriage on the *tapis*, which had to be offered to the king for one reason or another (and my belief is that Mazarin just used it to push Louis into his niece's arms, as actually happened)—had to be offered to the young king. But in order to make this match miscarry Mazarin suggested to the stupid old queen (fancy her having married that vile half-priest herself, faugh!) that Marie Mancini should be employed, she having been brought up as the King's play-fellow and already having made red-hot love to him for about a year, taking her as one of the party to meet the poor little Savoy girl with whom these old schemers had determined to disgust Louis XIV.

So they all went to Lyons. Do you remember that the Queen Mother and the other Mazarin nieces travelled in coaches (the journey was a royal progress and took weeks), but Marie Mancini insisted on riding the whole way on horseback by the king's side, through mud and frost and rain from Paris to Dijon and from Dijon to Lyons? At Lyons the king went out to meet the Savoys coming to be looked at, and, like the poor, mean-spirited creature he was, seemed quite resigned to marrying the princess. But as soon as he was home Marie Mancini made him a fearful scene, saying among other polite little things, "How can you allow them to give you in marriage *à une si laide femme?*"—whereupon that feeble, pompous young egotist ("he has a leg," like Meredith's Sir Willoughby Patterne) began to be horribly rude to the Savoys and let the duchess know, in the brutalest way, that he did not fancy her daughter. Then the poor Savoys were given emerald earrings or something and sent back across the Alps, like housemaids who don't suit. The vulgarity of those old people is too sickening!

The Queen Mother began machinating the Spanish marriage she wanted, and Mazarin pretended to aid and abet her. But how well he aided her is shown by the Court remaining two whole months at Lyons, which two months were entirely taken up in *fêtes* given by Louis XIV. to his ex-playfellows the Mazarin nieces, and particularly in walks, card-playing, endless novel-reading and so forth, *tête-à-tête* with Marie Mancini. There were even some rather charming little youthful idylls, if you remember, like that of the king drawing his sword and throwing it away because Marie had hit against it as they walked side by side; also the king (fancy the afterwards peruked Caesar on the rocking-horse in—is it Place Royale?) getting on to the box of the Mazarin nieces' coach and driving them home evening after evening with his royal hands.

These young people were always in and out of the queen's residence and the Mazarin lodgings, and one has an impression of Place Bellecour and Lyons in general having no other inhabitants and being utterly given over to their amusements and flirtations. That was in December 1658 and January 1659. Well, *during those two months at Lyons* Louis XIV. *secretly married Marie Mancini.* Whether he did it freely from sheer mad love, or to assert himself against his mother and her Spanish match, or whether Marie, who was always ready with scenes on the smallest occasion (what a mad, headstrong, violent creature she was!), bullied him into it, of course we don't know.

Nor whether the cardinal uncle closed an eye or actually abetted, intending to recognise or disavow the marriage according to what turned up in the meanwhile—all this we don't know. But this is certain, *married they were.* No one says so, but it must have happened; a young gentleman of Louis XIV's later gallantries doesn't go on philandering two whole years round a passionate young siren without making her either his mistress or his wife.

But a creature as ambitious, as bent on a royal marriage, as astonishingly able to command herself, a niece, in fact, of Mazarin, is not La Vallière, who makes an end of all her ambitions with an "all for love." And remark, not a creature has even suggested that Marie was Louis XIV's mistress. It is always of marriage, a promise of marriage that old Mazarin affects to be afraid, and instead of his and the Queen Mother's pushing the young people into an illicit connection and have done with it, these two old sinners are always interfering with meetings and correspondence on the score of possible marriage.

Well, once safely married to Marie, Louis XIV. pretends to agree to the Spanish match; Mazarin goes off to negotiate the peace of the Pyrenees. He orders his unmarried nieces away from Paris, sends them to La Rochelle—(La Rochelle, which is Louis Norbert's reputed birth-place!)—and when Louis XIV. has insisted on meeting Marie Mancini at St. Jean d'Angely, she is packed off with her *duenna* and younger sisters to Brouage (and why to Brouage, a tiny little God-forsaken fortress, *but on the sea*, except because a place was wanted where a child could be secretly born and secretly spirited away?).

At Brouage, after two months' pressure put upon her, Marie Mancini at last writes that famous letter to the cardinal promising to give up all thoughts of the king—despite which letter the king keeps on, spies or no spies, sending her immense letters and even (you remember?)

a puppy of his favourite dog, and he finds excuse for delaying the promised marriage. Then freed from Brouage Marie is reported to be flirting with the Duke of Lorraine; immediately Louis XIV.'s (Sir Willoughby Patterne) vanity is incensed; he marries his Spaniard forthwith, and Mazarin having meanwhile unexpectedly died, Marie is sent off in great state as the wife by proxy of the Constable Colonna. And it is then she says, "*Vous êtes Roi, sire; et vous pleurez, et me laissez partir.*"

That's the story. Of that secret marriage, which must have taken place (Mazarin doubtless conniving) at Lyons in December 1658 or January 1659, a child was born next autumn, in the secrecy of the exile at Brouage. *And that child was Louis Norbert.* Mazarin had him taken from his mother instantly on his birth, sent to the neighbouring La Rochelle (once the stronghold of protestantism, whence the notion that he was a southern protestant), and then conveyed to my ancestor's in England. Marie, who was dangerously ill, was told by the *duenna* and the Arab doctor that her child was either still-born or had died at birth; she was delirious for days and knew nothing of it all.

Of course Mazarin might have had the child killed; it would have been simpler, and people were so fond of murdering in those days. But you must remember that at the moment of its birth Louis XIV. had not yet married his Spaniard and was on the contrary perpetually putting off the ceremony. So of course Mazarin preferred keeping the child as a card up his sleeve to take the queen Mother's trick with, I mean oblige her to recognise the Mancini marriage when the right moment came.

And of course Mazarin, in his daily letters to the Queen Mother (horrible old woman! fancy a King of France's widow becoming the morganatic of that oily clerical adventurer, and going on writing him cypher love letters when they were both of them well over sixty!)—well, of course, in those fulsome letters to the queen, Mazarin kept assuring her that he was working his head off (always whining about his gout and his services to France, the old villain!) trying to come to an agreement with the Spanish Court.

But in reality he was doing all he could to make that Spanish match miscarry. Otherwise, I ask you, why should it have taken him all those months at St. Jean de Luz to settle it all up? The gullibility of those great political personages (let alone the people who write about them nowadays!) is really something portentous, when a duffer like me sees at a glance through all this rot. Of course it's only fair to say that the Queen Mother didn't know there was such a person as Louis Norbert, not having been brought up at Arthington or seen the epitaph at Pisa or the letters in our Muniment Room as I have. Still, allowing that much, these seventeenth-century intriguers weren't worth their salt, were they? never putting two and two together.

As to these modern historians, Barine, and Perrey and Amedée Rene, and the rest of them! Well, *you* aren't a historian, are you, only an archaeologist, which is so much more sensible, so you don't mind my letting fly at these people. I suppose these *historians* would say that none of all this can have happened, because of the letters they have discovered in the national library or the *Affaires Etrangères*, or wherever it is; letters, particularly those of the *duenna de Venel* to Mazarin, purporting to give the minutest account of Marie Mancini's health and doings while at Brouage, and leaving not the smallest chink, so to speak, by which to introduce the baby; nothing but assurances that Marie was being well *surveillée* and that everything was being done (though in vain!) to intercept any correspondence.

How is it that these historical bigwigs don't see *at a glance* that the letters they are publishing are a *sham?* Really, it's too droll to imagine Mazarin, who, after all, was a great diplomatist and had contrived to become prime minister and morganatic husband or lover to a queen although his father kept a hat-shop—it's too much of a good thing to imagine that Mazarin would have kept letters telling all about the marriage of his niece with Louis XIV. and the birth of Louis Norbert! Why, of course these printed letters are faked-up reports written by the duenna according to Mazarin's instructions, in order to be sent to the queen and make her believe that he was taking every precaution against the king and his own niece, and the real reports of the *duenna* were all in cypher (I've learned that much from you!), and such horrible compromising things (that my common sense suffices to tell!) Mazarin instantly put into the fire, so that these silly blinds have remained. Why, if the Queen Mother had found them she'd have off with his head'ed at once, surely?

Well, I am too tired to write any more today—and surely *this is enough!*

Your historically-minded friend, etc.

LETTER 30

From Lady Venetia to the Archaeologist

Arthington: August 7, 1909

My dear Professor,

I have just sent you a wire telling you that all your objections were forestalled in the letter I sent off *before* getting yours.

Well, I suppose scientific people *have* to cultivate scepticism at any price and at any cost; there is doubtless (isn't that how you reason?) some advantage to the race which compensates for the individual silliness. But I must say I expected something better from you, my dear professor. But there it just is, and all men, historians or not historians, are *exactly* alike in this—once you get a wrong notion into your head at the beginning, no power on earth will ever get it out again or prevent your seeing the most *obvious* fact distorted through it!

I mean that you having, long ago, heard me talk about

some imaginary friends and make up foolish stories and dialogues about them (as every human being except historians and my dull ambassador cousin naturally does)—well, having chanced to hear me talk about Hermann and Isabella and the double-bass player and Italo, you have written me down as a foolish woman with a hopeless tendency to romancing about everything, what you call a *born poet or novelist*. Almost the most riling part of it is this amiable attempt (so like a man towards a woman!) to turn an *unjustifiable accusation* into a compliment—

of course that all hangs together with your recommending me to *invent*. (I was perfectly right in being angry with you, although you afterwards explained it away.) And now you think I am inventing, I suppose. And all the time it is you, my poor young, learned friend, who have been inventing, *inventing a me* utterly unlike the reality. It is really pitiable.

Well, I hope my letter has put an end to that invention, *yours*, I mean, by showing that I am serious in this matter, whatever *you* may be!

As my telegram told you, I had already forestalled your objections, or rather the facts and *dates* themselves have disposed of them. As to further objections of yours, *viz.*, *that Marie Mancini would never have let herself be married to the Colonna man, in fact would never have let go of the king if there had been a child*, why, my dear man, the *whole point is that she didn't know that a child existed*, because Mine, de Venel and the astrologer and the rest of them stole it during her delirium and then made her believe either that it had been born dead or had died immediately after birth. Indeed, that was why she wrote from Brouage to her uncle giving up all further thoughts of the king.

That letter was the result of her terrible disappointment and grief at the loss of the child, and her recognising she now no longer had any hold on that selfish young brute of a king. *That letter of renunciation was perfectly genuine* on

Marie Mancini's part, and it's really rather amusing that just *it* should have been selected as a hoax by the historians (particularly that Arvède Barine, who is besides a woman, and therefore malignant towards other women!) who took the de Venel *duenna's* bogus reports as so much gospel. "*Et voila comment s'écrit l'histoire!*"—Who was it said that? Certainly not a historian!

PS.—I have been thinking more about the point whether M. M. *ever* got to know that her child by Louis XIV. had survived; and I've had another look at the facts given by those books. Of course I suppose "historians," at least *these* historians (for I know *great* historians like Michelet and Carlyle, and like you're going to be some day) aren't tied by bogus documents—I suppose they'd *point out* (that's the form, isn't it?) that there is absolutely no mention either of a marriage or a child in the memoirs which Marie M. herself published. But then these memoirs were published during her lifetime, and, *what is more important*, while she still entertained hopes of getting permission to return to France; they would therefore not contain anything that could compromise or incense the king; just as (even these "historians" point this out) she carefully refrained from saying anything in them against her husband, whom she was afraid of, although in her private letters she made no bones about explaining her flight from him by the fear of Colonna trying to kill her.

And now I come to think of it, all those fears of Colonna killing her were probably a mere excuse she gave her friends for trying to get back to France and a way of awakening Louis XIV.'s sympathy (which she didn't)—for if Colonna had been so jealous as all that he'd not have tolerated all her goings-on in Rome with the Chevalier de Lorraine (all those rowdy swimming parties in the Tiber—rather amusing they must have been, at the Acqua Acetosa, I suppose, but not decent at *her* age), and that Cardinal Chigi, with the bulgy eyes; besides, Colonna had his Mme.

Paleotti, and they all evidently lived quite shamelessly and peacefully together. All that fear of Colonna's tardy blood-thirstiness was therefore evidently mere shamming, and this leads us to a very important conclusion.

Don't you think that M. M.'s extraordinary flight from Rome (you remember how she and her sister Hortense drove to Civita Vecchia—or was it Fiumicino?—after audibly giving the order "to Frascati," and put on men's clothes in the carriage, and then wandered about, half dead from fatigue and fright, on the seashore, waiting for the faithful butler to bring a boat round; and then the meeting of the boat ruffians—I was once on the Tiber with two totally drunken boatmen and had to take an oar, so I know what it feels like—and the blackmailing and the escape from Barbary pirates)—well, don't you think it probable that M. M. decided on this extraordinary escapade because she had somehow got wind of the survival of her child by Louis XIV.?

That would also account for her change of attitude towards Colonna (you are a man of science, so one can talk freely with you like a doctor), whom after all she had rather liked by her own showing, and which she explained by an astrologer warning her that if she had a fourth child she'd die in the process. For, of course, if a woman discovers that she is the mother of the King of France's legitimate successor, she does not want any more little Colonnas, even if she did like the Colonna man.

It may have been that little Moorish slave girl who told her, the one who had been given to her in her girlhood and was always so faithful afterwards, *and who accompanied her on her flight.* You see, the little Moor may have seen the astrologer and Mme. de Venel do something queer which she understood only later when she herself was grown up. It's all very possible. But mind, I do not for an instant insist that it must have happened.

Marie Mancini may *never to the end of her days have suspected her child's survival*, just as Louis Norbert may never, to the end of his life, have suspected (let alone that this was why the *abbé* poisoned him) that he had a father and mother alive, still less who they were.

And Sir Nicholas' widow and son, that rather intolerable Anthony, may never have dreamed who their "young Frenchman" was nor troubled their heads about it. People take things so extraordinarily for granted when they're in their own family, don't you think? And we Thesigers have never been noted for the nimbleness of our wits nor exuberance of our fancy, although you *do* think that *I* am a "born novelist and poet"—or whatever your polite phrase is!

By the way, this letter, and the way in which I have summed up all the evidence to you (*and my complete open-mindedness as to whether or not either M. M. or L. N. ever suspected their relationship*) must have convinced you that I am of the genuine stock of Sir Peter Thesiger, Elizabeth's Privy Councillor, of whom it was said, "that he was a man of weighty judgment, albeit slow in the forming it."

Yours, etc.

PS.—Do write at once. What a lot of misunderstanding and waste of time merely because you're in Italy and I in England!

LETTER 31

(Never sent)

From the Archaeologist to Lady Venetia

Pisa: August 12, 1909

But, dear Lady Venetia, don't you see that what you call *consulting the facts* is merely referring the whole matter to your own fervid fancy, interpreting everything in the light of the little romance yourself has made up, and sweeping aside as "bogus" whatever evidence goes against your own wishes . . .?

There is a volume of William James's essays called *The*

Will to Believe—you are that Will in this case. Or—are you merely playing at Hermann and Isabella after all? It is a rule of that game to pretend that you aren't, and is it my silly pedantry and lack of worldly experience which makes me fail to play up to you? I feel so utterly lost, such a hopeless, owlish, priggish duffer.

If only I knew what you were about, whether in earnest or not, or both, but anything for certain, so as not to be making perpetual wrong moves if it is a game, or hurting your feelings genuinely if it isn't one. For, prig though I am, I also could "invent."

I am afraid to think how well I could invent, forge documents and all! if once I set about it, merely to please you, or rather to keep up this enchanting romance, which is worth all the Louis Norberts and Artemisias of all the seventeenth century.

But then you may be in earnest. In fact, I am sure you *are* in earnest and that it is merely my priggishness which sees your ways as a game; after all, exquisite beings like you do not walk, they *dance*, they do not speak, they *sing*, at least compared with the hideous movements and sounds that such as I have recourse to! And if you *are* in earnest, good heavens! what an ass, what a bounder would you think me if I ventured to treat the whole matter as a game and attempt to play up to it!

And the worst of it is that the only person who could ever tell me what is really the case is yourself; and you are the only person I never dare ask.

This letter begun to you has ended off merely as an expression of my own puzzled feelings, but not to you, dear, adorable, unintelligible lady of my thoughts.

One thing at least I can tell you, or rather tell myself: so far, at least, I have never been guilty of deceiving you, nor of prolonging this correspondence which is the romance of my life.

And now for the waste-paper basket!

(Sent instead of preceding)

From the Archaeologist to Lady Venetia

Same date

Dear Lady Venetia,

All that you say is very plausible, splendidly thought out. Almost too plausible, for historical fact usually presents a less tidy appearance.

What remains for you to do is that, having what we call "formulated your hypothesis"—

and a most ingenious hypothesis it is—you should patiently work through whatever further documents may still be hidden in your Muniment Room. It is quite possible you may thus acquire absolute certainty for or against. Meanwhile, I will continue my researches here, although they do not seem to bear upon your notion. Still—fancy if the abbess's secret correspondence contained even the smallest reference to Louis Norbert!

Yours, etc.

LETTER 33

From the Archaeologist to Lady Venetia

Same date

Dear Lady Venetia,

Since writing this morning I have come to the conclusion that I must go to England to settle a historical difficulty which blocks my way. I may possibly be going to Cambridge for a day or two. Is it at all possible, in Lord Arthington's present condition, that I should be allowed the honour of calling on you for half an hour? I think I may be near your part of the world. If it is possible, would it be pushing presumptuousness too far to ask you to send me a wire here to Pisa? My departure is not absolutely certain yet, so I cannot give you an English address to answer to, and I should be too sorry to miss an opportunity of presenting you my homage and talking over your discoveries.

At the same time, please believe how perfectly I should understand if Lord Arthington's illness or any other reason made you unable to grant my request.

Yours, etc.

PS.—If I come I will bring you as much of the abbess's correspondence as we have hitherto deciphered. I wish I could say I was quite sure that it refers to Louis Norbert.

34

Telegram from Lady Venetia to the Archaeologist

Arthington: August 16, 1909

Enchanted prospect meeting. Arthington hopes you will spend few days with us. Joint attack on Muniment Room. What fun.

A rivederci presto.

Venetia Hammond.

INTERLUDE

1

Despite a nervous desire for perfect correctness, nay conventionality, of behaviour, the archaeologist contrived to make his visit to Arthington quite disconcertingly unconventional.

As his train approached the station where Lady Venetia had told him he should be fetched, his fervid imagination presented him with a picture of himself arriving in the motor with his luggage, and possibly facing Lady Venetia at the top of the steps (he saw those Jacobean steps with increasingly painful distinctness) while he hesitated whether the right thing was to jump over the side of the car (it was, of course, open in some mysterious way at the back) or wait to be released by some pompous menial. And this picture, nay drama, became more intolerable with every forward jolt of the slow local train.

Moreover he discovered that this meeting, which he had longingly brought about with a duplicity whereat he blushed, had suddenly become a matter of icy indifference verging on positive repulsion. He did not want to see Lady Venetia. Not only not now, but, if possible, never again in all his life. He became aware that he had made her up during the past seven or eight months; he could have told you how and when he had added each touch to her wholly imaginary image; he could have recited (indeed did recite to himself) every item in her various letters which now brought home the wilfully disregarded certainty that the reality of this lady was utterly unlike his portrait of her.

And with this overwhelming recognition came a feeling that in thus allowing himself to paint an imaginary Lady Venetia, he had taken an unpardonable liberty with the real one, a liberty that the real one, could she guess at anything so monstrous, would resent beyond expression.

For what right had an obscure young pedant, his priggishness fresh from Balliol and a dreadful German university, to think so many times a day, let alone all day long, about a woman (he coldly admitted it) old enough to be his mother, belonging to a totally different caste and set, and whom he had seen during the space of exactly four days? That Lady Venetia Hammond should think of him only as the purveyor or recipient of information (or thereabouts) about a historical personage more or less her own invention—this knowledge, so far from arousing his resentment towards the lady, merely overwhelmed him with the sense of his own ludicrous presumptuousness.

For high-flown sentiment alters its fashions like lesser things; and nowadays Don Quixote, so far from openly performing antics in Dulcinea's honour, would, on the contrary, be horrified that his love should be suspected by any creature in the world, and worst of all by Dulcinea herself. Even the lady who never told her love would, so far from pluming herself on her monumental silence, probably have felt intolerably forward at having any love to be silent about.

Be this as it may, when the archaeologist was within such distance of the appointed station as to begin wondering which side of it Arthington Manor might be situated, he found it quite impossible to face the terrible situation himself had artfully created. So sinking back in the empty compartment, and veiling his countenance in the *Daily News*, he allowed the train to halt without getting out; and only when it had resumed its slow career, he ventured to look back to where the ticket collector and porter stood opposite a small heap of unclaimed possessions in company with an impassive though inquiring footman. And there, as the train swished round an embankment, there waited the motor from Arthington.

The archaeologist felt an ineffable, cool, trickling relief. But instantly after came the sense that he had made an utter fool of himself and brought about a situation more thorny than the one he had thus childishly evaded. What should he do next? Allow the train to carry him to the terminus, Birmingham or Northampton, whatever it were, thence return to London and telegraph some silly excuse? But his luggage would meanwhile have been taken to Arthington.

And his whole soul revolted at the thought of Lady Venetia— or through Lady Venetia the Arthington butler—being called upon to restore these articles, which suddenly took on the most ignominiously sordid appearance. Besides, when it came to giving up the whole visit, he discovered that, agonisingly as he dreaded it, to give it up, to return to London and Italy without having seen or heard Lady Venetia, felt exactly like the removal of a limb with preliminary local freezing, only that the limb was somehow his heart.

So at the next station he jumped out desperately; enacted dramatic surprise at his mistake and even horror at separation from his luggage; paid the excess on his ticket and enquired whether he could hire a fly; and, on bare sight of that ignominious vehicle, started off on foot in the direction, as sundry loafers told him, of Arthington Manor. The distance was seven miles, and he knew that the walk, particularly in the boisterous autumn wind, would steady his utterly disgraceful nerves. Thus he walked, fortunately without the further shamefulness of dust or mud, through the regulation kind of midland landscape, which little by little appeared to him as fantastically poetic and well nigh paradisaic.

He became indeed so taken up by the curves of the newly-reaped fields, accentuated by stacks, with the various green bands of market garden and grass, the red brick villages smelling of sweet peas, and the sedgy river reappearing under bridges with whirr of waterfowl, that he really began to look upon his previous nervousness as a bad dream, and to face his meeting with Lady Venetia as the most natural of events, elaborately connecting it with a hope for tea.

2

He was therefore quite steady of nerve, almost too perceptibly steady, when he walked up the soughing avenue of old twisted pines and towards the terrace, which he recognised so well, where Roman Emperors looked out from circular niches. Then the road swung round where the deer grazed, and there was the entrance to the house. He did not shrink from grasping the bell. He pronounced his own name in unfaltering accents. He manifested no shame at beholding his properties in the hall; and gave a monosyllabic explanation of the occurrence while being deprived of his hat and stick and asked whether he would like to be shown his room or go in at once. . . .

But at that moment a door was noisily opened, and there, between the Ionic columns of the hall, stood Lady Venetia. He heard her exclamations of pleasure and interrogation without understanding them; he heard himself answer something which he did not understand either, and saw himself advance towards her as he would have seen a foreign body. And then it was all over. He had never seen this lady before and had never, in all his life, heard her voice. She was Lady Venetia Hammond, the friend of a friend and about whom he knew a lot, cordial, gracious, impulsive, enchanting, as he had been informed; and towards her he, the stranger, felt calmly, politely appreciative, and absolutely nothing besides. As to himself, he was himself. It was quite simple.

She led him into a big room, whose seventeenth-century furniture and portraits and view of terrace and roe-deer he was quite lucidly admiring. She gave him some tea, which had grown cold and bitter, and she waved away the butler's attempts to bring any fresh, all in the pleasure and excitement of talking at once about *their* discovery. She called it *our* discovery and poured out volumes about it, while the archaeologist listened resignedly, eating undue quantities of bread and butter and wondering whether this gracious and ample lady, with a beauty more fascinating for being on the wane, could possibly be the woman to whom he had been writing, not merely the posted and written letters, but scores of unposted, unwritten, barely formulated ones, for many months past. Her voice, for one thing, was much more like everyone else's than like the one she had had at Pisa; if anything, rather bell-like with an imperceptible drawl and blurring of *r*'s. Instead of which he recollected it, quite distinctly, as dusky, a little veiled, decidedly *contralto* and Duse-like. And he himself, how much more massive, weighty, older he was than he had thought. If this lady was of an age past all defining, he, decidedly, was no longer a boy.

"Shall we go and see Louis Norbert's portrait?" she said, eyeing his bread and butter impatiently. "If we are quick there will just be light enough for a first look."

He bowed, in the fashion he had so stupidly acquired on the Continent, and opening the door, passively followed her. But when she had swept across two or three ground floor rooms, she suddenly stopped at the foot of a Charles I. staircase, and turning sharply, exclaimed with vehemence:

"No, not today; I *am* really becoming an intolerable bore with Louis Norbert. Fancy my calmly forgetting that you have come all the way from London and Pisa and walked for hours from that dreadful station, and in this wind! I am disgracefully inconsiderate. And it isn't quite respectful to our dear Louis Norbert to be selfish and idiotic about him. So we'll see him quietly tomorrow. And now you go and rest or have a quiet smoke in your room before dinner."

And she pressed his hand lightly, warmly, freely, in her large and beautiful one.

"I *am* glad you have been able to come," she said—"it's awfully kind of you to have thought of it."

She was adorable, no doubt of it, but she *wasn't* the lady he had written to; only a sister or cousin, with some features and gestures, some grace of character and manner in common.

The whole of that evening, which seemed extraordinarily roomy and full of well-spaced incidents, was spent by the Archaeologist in wondering what had become of *his* Lady Venetia.

This one was really much more beautiful. He had never before seen her, he reflected, in evening dress, and had thought of her as existing permanently in the motoring garments or the travelling tea-frock he had known at Pisa. And accustomed as he had become to the rustic simplicity of his Italian friends' villa-life, the unexpected appearance of the real (or unreal?) Lady Venetia, with shining shoulders and glancing diamonds, filled him with a kind of superstitious awe, the dining table (even with poor Lord Arthington's cripple's chair and the nursing sister's habit disturbing the effect)—the dining table affecting him, with its silver and flowers and wax-lights, as some manner of altar.

Patet dea, he afterwards discovered himself inwardly repeating. Moreover he discovered that Lady Venetia—*this* Lady Venetia—had (how to express the thing without going wide of the mark?) what in anyone else he would have called (but such words were evidently unsuitable to her) an *intellectual prestige* he had never before guessed. Indeed, he wondered how he could ever have written to her as he had: she was now unattainable by his criticisms, and he might be justifiably afraid of getting himself into disgrace by what he said, but he laughed bitterly though internally at his former fear of hurting or discouraging *her*.

The prestige of Lady Venetia, vague, looming, effulgent, grew even greater (and his own importance in the moral landscape accordingly smaller) when she set to making music after dinner.

What he had heard her play at Pisa, that duel and death scene music of Don Giovanni on the jangling hotel piano, had indeed haunted him ever since, but rather as part of a whole romantic situation, in which his modern self and sundry seventeenth-century ghosts were co-involved; not at all as a specimen of more or less musical proficiency on the part of the player.

Now, in the music room at Arthington, he became massively aware of her being a great, a wonderful musician. She did indeed occasionally stumble, and frequently swept whole passages aside with a toss of her head (he noticed her head's constant slight upward tilt, ready for such tossing) and a "and so on"—but she made the music step out and take its place, and, while it was there, fill the world with its ways of greatness. She was a wonderful musician.

But somehow he did not enjoy it. And during the whole evening he kept self-consciously fearing that she would leave Beethoven and Bach, and play—oh terror of embarrassment !—that Don Giovanni music, or worse even, some of the seventeenth- century music he himself had sent her; above all, he was insanely shy of the compositions of the abbess. For he was thoroughly well aware that although he did not mind how much Lady Venetia might pour out about Louis Norbert and the rest of that story, he would dislike quite extremely having to talk about any of it himself. Not, heaven help him, because of any romantic shyness, connected with those dim romantic puppets in themselves, but because they had been discussed in letters of which he was painfully aware that he had often re-read them when they were hers, and often rewritten when his own.

But, at the end of the evening, when she had decided that her invalid brother must not have any more music (Lord Arthington was about as much stage property in the archaeologist's eyes as the invalid chair in which he was propped up) and she had asked "our young friend" (so she called him) to close the piano for her, she paused with the electric switch in her hand, and suddenly remarked:

"You see, one of the things which made poor Isabella feel

so sore was that Hermann got into the habit of fussing over the lamps or the candles (he pretended they smoked or guttered) whenever Italo's mother began playing the *intermezzo* of *Cavalleria* on the pension piano (it had an embossed ebony head of Beethoven in its waistcoat). Isabella, of course, imagined she disliked it because it was so fussy of Hermann, and that *Cavalleria* thing (Italo's mother never played anything else on any occasion) was such *very* trashy music; and besides, the two hands always went one after the other, perpetual broken chords; and Hermann, being German and having been one of the Bückeburger Gesangverein, ought not to like sugary Italian rubbish. Of course that wasn't a reason for Isabella also hating the double-bass player glowering at Italo's mother from a corner of the piano; but she just did.

"And one day—about six weeks ago—poor Isabella's worst, inexplicable feelings (they're called *Ahnungen* and only Germans have them) were justified. For Hermann and the double-bass player both rushed violently to help little Italo into his overcoat, each from his end of the *salon*, and they came bang up against each other and bumped their foreheads with incredible violence. So then, of course, there *had* to be a duel, and Hermann had the choice of weapons . . .

"Upon my word," she interrupted herself, "you ought all to be ashamed of having such a fool as me for a friend or relation, perpetually talking such awful rot; and as to Arthington, I believe he feels like sinking into the earth at his sister making such an idiot of herself before a learned man, don't you, Dick? So we had better invoke the mantle of night to veil such foolishness—"

And as she extended her hand (which he had some difficulty in not kissing Italian fashion) to the archaeologist, she smiled a wide, pale blue, luminous smile of the eyes, so simply, humorously, maternally, divinely friendly, that the archaeologist, when he got to his room, felt like one delivered of a ridiculous spell and restored to unparalleled reason and happiness.

This was yet another, a quite unexpected Lady Venetia. And

it was the real one.

In the perfect happiness of those ten days (for Lord Arthington insisted on nothing less) spent by the archaeologist in Lady Venetia's society, there were, it is almost needless to remark (for human beings must always spoil their own good luck, especially when they are young human beings), moments when that happiness seemed very near to wrecking.

Not indeed openly, indeed it is extremely doubtful whether Lady Venetia ever dreamed of such dramas, but in the squally depths of the archaeologist's unspoken feelings.

One of these occasions of tragic stress was the first time, the very day after his arrival, that he stood before the portrait of Louis Norbert.

Lady Venetia had introduced him summarily to the Muniment Room, and then showed him (with a sudden self-reproachful spasm of hostess-ship) the rest of the magnificent old house, its pictures and furniture and china closets, and its stately, efficiently-haunted rooms and mirrored galleries and monumental staircases. But she had put off the visit to Louis Norbert's portrait till after their walk among the white deer of the park to where the herons rise out of a marshy stream.

"The room looks west," she explained, "and I have a fancy for your seeing Louis Norbert the first time at the hour that I first did, all those endless years ago; that's why I've been putting off taking you to him."

The archaeologist answered, of course, "What a capital idea," and then felt he had not said quite the right thing, and that this was too much *mise en scène*, too *voulu*, somehow.

After all, Louis Norbert was only so much paint and varnish on an old canvas. . . .

"Here he is," said Lady Venetia, when she had introduced the archaeologist into a room so darkened that he remained on the threshold for fear of stumbling over looming furniture.

"Here he is; or rather, here we are in his presence," and with a sudden sharp movement (he had noticed what strong hands, almost like very exquisite man's hands, she had, at the piano, last evening) she unbolted and threw open the shutters, letting in the low afternoon sun.

The archaeologist was aware (as people occasionally are) of its all having happened before, only he couldn't think when; it being this *tête-à-tête* with Lady Venetia and the words she had just uttered in the presence of Louis Norbert's portrait.

Perhaps because he recognised all the surroundings: there were the smoky battle-pieces and the varnish-blackened boar hunts she had spoken of at Pisa, and the faded Rachael Ruysch nosegays, all in ebony fretted frames closely packed on the walls; there was the canopied bed, with cut velvet vases like hearse plumes; and there the console with huge lion's feet which she had feared would claw her in the dark, when she—good heavens, what a thought!—had been a small girl. He had visualised it all so often in his mind.

And *there* was the portrait.

As Lady Venetia had intended, the low sunlight cut the room in a narrow, silvery, dusty beam; and broke, golden and mellow, on the portrait, shifting now from the face to the hand on the sword, or on to some portion of the black dress, revealing gold threads here and there or a gold tassel—according as it moved with the sway of the cedar branches outside.

The archaeologist stepped close and looked carefully. It was a fairly good picture; or rather a fairly bad one of a very good school, some belated disciple of Van Dyke's at a time already given over to Lely; and well preserved. All *that* the Archaeologist made a note of in order to remark upon to Lady Venetia. For he knew at once that he could not, somehow, remark to her on what was his instant and growing impression, namely, how astonishingly handsome and fascinating this painted young man was, with his white, eagle face between long brown hair, and eyes like deep dark pools drawing one in. Although the date must have been the end of Charles II.'s reign, the dress had a Cromwellian austerity; and, instead of having the few pert bristles giving men of the Restoration a look of supercilious satyrs, this youth's beautiful firm mouth stood clean and pure like Milton's.

It is almost impossible to put on paper the utterly foolish things which the archaeologist was aware of thinking and feeling. It was intolerable that men of past centuries should have been so romantic and good-looking; only women were allowed that nowadays. And, at the same time, this lovely, languishing youth was manly—that was the worst of it! Manly like a drawn sword or a finely-rowelled spur, not manly after the style of a starched shirt-front or severely well-rolled umbrella. It was unfair and intolerable. It was, in a way, shameless to be at once so appealing and so mysteriously dignified. And all the while those men of the past were a hundred times more prosaic than oneself. But, like tenors, they *sang*, and oneself only *spoke*; or rather, if oneself had any common sense and breeding, oneself held one's tongue.

The archaeologist did the latter. He stood for a long while before the portrait; and when at last he decided to turn round, he nodded gravely and merely said "Yes."

He was still further at a loss for words when he noticed that Lady Venetia, whom he had thought of as standing by his side during that station before the portrait, had retired to the open window; and that when she turned her face towards him he thought her lips trembled a little, and fancied (but it was doubtless only fancy!) that through the exquisite little veil of powder there stole a blush.

"Confound Louis Norbert," he said to himself quite articulately; "all this is really too much of a good thing; it is silly." But he knew, for he was analytical and also just, that far the silliest was himself.

4

[From the archaeologist's notebook, between some quotations of the Chronicle of Basil Commenius and the hours of trains between Paris and Périgueux, doubtless in view of visiting the Byzantine Church of St. Front. This note is dated "August 28th, in train, after leaving Arthington," and is headed "A decoy."]

The last evening of my stay Lady V. H. took me to see a decoy, one of the few, she tells me, still remaining in this part of England.

You pass by a keeper's cottage, with puppies about. The decoy is in a little blackish wood, very close set, in the midst of burnt-up stubble fields: a series of wattled screens or large hurdles, not unlike the straw mats Italian gardeners make for *spalliered* lemons, with glimpses between them of wired-over canals. And then, quite unexpected, a big pond, almost a lake, overhung by big, dark trees and high bushes; black water half hidden under blackish lily-leaves. A whirr overhead! and three wild ducks pass; the false wild duck, tamed, who decoys the travelling ones into the lake and up those water-traps, to have their necks wrung, after vainly beating against wire roof and wattled walls, among those closed canals.

A heron rose as we came away, and disappeared high among the trees. When we were out of the black wood with its black lake, the sun had set; there was a wonderful broken, filmy sky above the dry, pale fields. Lady Venetia shuddered; and when we had climbed, for the view, on to the terrace roof of an old gate-house nearby, she told me to warm my hands on the parapet still tepid from the sun; the old grey stone is encrusted with almost invisible mosses, and it was like touching some rough and furry creature, after the tragic chilliness of the decoy.

"I don't know why I took you to that dreadful place," she said, as we looked down from the gate-house. "An ill-omened place, don't you think, that pond and woods, with the horrid deception to the poor travelling birds? It made me feel as if long ago one of us might have been decoyed by false friends, entrapped among those wicked screens, and the black water closed overhead."

She remained silent for quite a long while, her head tilted up in that characteristic, rather lyric attitude; and looking over the stubble fields to the last red vestiges of sunset.

Then she began to talk once more about L. N., whom she has now taken to calling the *Dauphin*.

"Of course," she said, "that is exactly what happened to him. I daresay it was thinking of him made me remember the decoy."

That evening some neighbours came to dinner, so that we had no further conversation together. And I left Arthington next morning—rather by choice than by necessity—too early to take leave of Lady Venetia.

LETTER 35

[This and the following are copies made by Lady Venetia of the most important passages in letters discovered in the Muniment Room by herself and the archaeologist during his stay at Arthington.]

From Louis Norbert to Sir Anthony Thesiger

Rome: January 28, 1684 N.S.[1]

On our recent journey back from Spoleto, whither we went to view the temple of the River Clitumnus mentioned by the divine Maro, to Narni, where is the bridge of the Emperor Augustus, there happened a circumstance which foolishly gave me umbrage, and hath set me musing, more than is judicious, upon the mystery surrounding my birth.

As we sat on the top of the pass in a miserable inn among muleteers and charcoal burners, for we were surrounded by oak-woods, drying our garments after riding in heavy rain, a horseman clattered into the yard, and alighting, sate himself at the table. He ordered wine and entered into talk with us; and from his womanish voice and mien I took him for one of such singers as this unholy country delighteth in.

He surprised us by speaking the French language very

---

1. N.S. means that the writer adopted the Gregorian calendar in use abroad, and called by the English, among whom it was not officially introduced till the middle of the eighteenth century, New Style. [Note by the archaeologist.]

readily, and entertained my lord with many stories of the Court of France, whither he had, he said, been called in his youth to sing. Asked what his name was he answered one very common in Rome, Mario Mancini, "but I had not the luck," he adds with a ribald jest, "of being a favourite kinsman of Cardinal Mazarino." He had the manner and address of the parasites of princes, and spake in knowledge of many curious circumstances. He affected to ask each of us his name and business, with the forwardness of such pampered fellows, and pointing suddenly to me, and fixing his bold eyes:

"Were we in France, and this honourable company not English, I should not need ask after the family of this pretty cavalier, for from my recollection of his Gallic Majesty when last I sang before him, I should swear he must be a bastard of the blood royal."

"Bastard thyself, thou impudent semi-vir," I exclaimed, rising, much angered. But as I was about to draw, he merely tapped my shoulder and with marvellous assurance bid me put up my sword.

"My son," he saith, using that familiar Italian fashion, "no harm is meant. All who seem bastards may not be so, and I know some, wearing crowns today or preparing to wear them tomorrow, who are less honourably begotten, perchance, than yourself: *Experto crede.*"

And saying he must look after his nag, he left the room, but only after bending quickly over me in passing, and whispering something which I failed to hear, for my lord, enlivened by the fellow's sauciness, mistook whatever it was for some obscene jest, and burst out laughing and shouting to me to be of good cheer.

Presently, when all the company save me, who was indeed foolishly humbled, had forgotten that impudent and ambiguous rascal, the man—if he was a man—returned with a lute he had borrowed of the innkeeper, and offered to give his lordship a sample of the skill he had once had, before an adventurous life and many hairbreadth escapes had cracked his lovely voice.

It was in truth far from good, and indeed not that of a singer at all, but rather of a wheezy, superannuated strumpet.

He seemed, moreover, in his cups, and the song which he sang was sure not such as he or any other had sung before kings, but foolish stuff of the loves of Jove, how he deceived Semele, with a refrain tagged on from some bawdy snatch—'*Tis a wise bird knows its own father, quoth the cuckoo*—singing the which, in order to raise a laugh again, he fixed his eyes upon me, when for some reason I cannot find, methought I had seen those eyes and something like his mien before, though he was freckled and sunburnt and had a great stain across his face like a mask—but this must surely have been a fancy, bred of my secret disturbance at the adventure.

When he had done he distributed my lord's present to the ostlers and muleteers, not without a dignity that staggered his lordship, saluted all around, and, turning to me very seriously, craves my pardon for seeming to speak lightly of my lady mother, who was, he'd take his oath, as honest a matron as ever wore a wedding ring. Whereupon he thrust his hat over his eyes, and springing on his horse with more grace than we expected, kissed his finger-tips to me and rode off, followed by an old black groom whom we had not noticed.

Mr. Bob Lowndes, his lordship's secret chaplain and a profound musician, said nothing should make him believe the fellow had ever learned to sing least of all sung before a court; and Mr. Humphrey Standish, the interpreter, was convinced he was no singing man at all, but some wandering trollop in men's clothes; his lordship opining for his part that 'twas most likely a spy set on himself as a protestant nobleman. But as regards me, this adventure hath made me wonder, more than I am wont to let myself, whether my birth is such as your excellent father and my benefactor's kindness would have had me believe, and I fear some contemptuous suspicions may have arisen in the minds of my fellow-travellers.

LETTER 36

From Louis Norbert to Sir A. Thesiger

Rome: February 8, 1684 N.S.

Excellent Friend and Patron,

This will acquaint you that his lordship hath suddenly decided we shall spend Lent at Naples, at which place he would already be, if his departure before carnival, to witness which he had hired windows in the chief street, might not have savoured of timidity after an accident that happened lately.

Of this, lest you should hear and be apprehensive for my person, I will tell you, albeit my lord desireth holding it privy. So I would remind you of what I writ already, touching the habits of vengeance and secret violence of these Romans, and in especial of an attack on his lord-ship's coach, on which occasion my hat was traversed by a slug intended not for me but for him. This time the villains hurt his lordship's own person, although but light-ly, cutting him in the hand as he wrenched the sword wherewith one of the two *bravi* (for so these mercenary cut-throats are styled) was like to run me through as we promenaded one evening before the grand duke of Tus-cany his gardens.

His lordship having thus disarmed one of the ruffians, both took to their heels, and we set off in their pursuit. But as we thought to overtake them near the Triton fountain, or rouse some help with our cries of murder (forgetting that such cries meet but deaf ears in Roman streets), the *spa-dassins* disappeared over a monastery wall, taking asylum, as is here the habit, in the precincts of a church. This event decided me to telling my lord how I had noticed fellows dogging my steps of late, lurking in blind alleys and *porticoes*; and had even, passing at dusk up the Spanish steps, heard a shot whistle past and fall a few yards off, a window snapping to hard by. All of which attempts were manifestly aimed at his lordship's self, we being of the same stature and complexion, and my lord in rivalry (to Christ's further shame!) with a great personage ecclesiastic, for the favours of a notorious Bolognese *meretrix*.

In consequence I advised his lordship that, not desiring to be killed for another man's fornications, I must part company, whereon he hath decided to sacrifice that mincing Rahab to his safety, and leaving Rome awhile, abandon her to her purple- gowned paramour. All this I tell you lest you be disturbed by rumours of dangers surrounding me, which, as I have explained, is not the case, I being at strife with no one, even in this evil land.

His lordship thinks, however, that this brief absence may suffice (the prelate meanwhile wearying of his *moecha*), and we return to view the famous Easter functions in St. Peter's church.

Wherewith I would bid you kiss your good mother's hand most reverently for me and take my constant love and service for yourself.

LETTER 37

From Louis Norbert to Sir A. Thesiger, Bart.

Naples: March, 1684 N.S.
[Beginning not copied.]

Having answered your questions touching the Phlegraean Fields, the Bay of Baiae and Avernus, and enclosed an opinion of his lordship's physician on the vexed matter of the Tarantula or Dancing Madness of these regions, I would now wish to beg a favour of your friendship. This is to question your mother (and my dear benefactress) touching the circumstances of my birth and parentage, which she may have forgotten or deemed it seemlier to forget, but wherewithal, methinks, I have some right, and perhaps necessity, to be acquainted.

And since the lady is aged and infirm, ask her not as from me, neither put direct questions to her, such as may beget defiance in the mind of the old in years. But rather place before her such indifferent questions as will gently stir her recollections or move her to contradiction. As, *exampli gratia*, whether her adopted son may not in truth be a nephew, or other illegitimate and natural issue of the family; what reason your father could have had for calling an Englishman by a French name.

Also, whether there exist not, or have existed, papers declaring the place and year of my birth? And such like points, the ascertaining of which may lead perhaps to the excellent and reverend lady declaring more than we credit her with knowing. And, should she ask reasons for your sudden inquisitiveness, tell her, which is the truth, that you have reason to think his lordship holds me for a bastard of the Thesigers, even alluding thereunto, to my certain mortification.

LETTER 38
From Louis Norbert to Sir A. Thesiger, Bart.

(Favoured by His Excellency the Spanish Ambassador)
Palermo: March 15, 1684 N.S.

Honoured Master and more than Brother,
It hath occurred to me it may be unworthy of our loving kindness to hide from you aught concerning my person, even if it turn out but trifling and fantastic. Therefore I will relate to you a carnival adventure, that happened to me the eve of our leaving Rome, wherewith I have acquainted no man else. This I do the more willingly as it may explain, or at least excuse, in your rational eyes, sundry untoward questions I had requested you to put to your mother, whereof I sometimes feel ashamed, wondering whether what I shall now narrate may not be merely

a jest practised by those who deem me over thin- skinned and sensitive.

You should know that the Romans celebrate their carnival with astounding splendour and licence, compensating their everyday hypocrisy ecclesiastical, the whole population rioting in masks and disguises for eight whole days, and filling the principal street, which is magnificent with many princes' and prelates' palaces, and an obelisk at one end and the columns of M. Aurelius and Trajan at the other, with pageantry, horse-races, and races, meseems more indecent than diverting, of Jewish elders sewn up in sacks.

The day before Ash Wednesday (whereon we took our departure hither) the licence reaches its highest at dusk, when everyone carries a lit taper, and seeks to blow out his neighbour's, keeping his own alight or lighting it afresh off some other man's, wherein ariseth an indescribable hubbub and tussle between the maskers in the street and those at the windows, throwing not flowers only but anything coming to hand on their assailants' lights; all which with yells and roars more worthy of demons than men, and wherewith are not infrequently mingled the shrieks of those trampled by mischance or stabbed by enemies on such a favourable occasion.

Having witnessed enough of this foolery on the previous afternoons, I determined to spend the hours of the *Corso* (for so they call this horse-play) in hearing an *oratorio* or sacred opera, whereof one is given at the church of St. Philip Neri, with the intent of tempting men from those ribald scenes to the thought of God, though in fact rather to that of music fitter for the feasts of Cupid than of Christ, and the warblings of eunuchs whose vocal nimbleness is watched and betted on like the running of those riderless barbs in the chief street.

Be this as it may, having heard the *oratorio*, by one Alexander Scarlatto, an excellent young master, to the end, methought I would regain the Carnival street and witness that last scene (which taketh place only on Shrove Tuesday) of putting out the wax-lights, from the windows my lord had hired at an apothecary's over against Prince Pamphyly, nephew of Pope Innocent X. The streets of Rome were strangely deserted, save those nearest the Corso, whereto all the inhabitants had crowded, and I was able to make my way quite unmolested.

But just as I was turning round the back of the great church which was once Agrippa's Pantheon, I was caught all unexpecting in a rout of some twenty maskers, harlequins, pantaloons, and scaramouches, who set upon me with animal cries and obscene caperings, they having the privilege, on these days, thus to molest any citizen caught unmasked; nor do the customs of the place allow any defence against their violence. I was thus unable to get loose of these unseemly knaves—some of whom dressed as women in dresses of Columbine or Esmeralda—and perforce let them carry me along, doubting not it was towards the great street or Corso.

When behold! a Captain Matamoros among them waves his red cloak over his head and I suddenly found myself in utter darkness, vainly struggling in the thick folds, while those around crowed like cocks and shouted bawdy songs, one of them, with the treble, nosey voice these maskers make themselves, whispering in my ear that no harm was meant and I should stay quiet for the Blessed Virgin's sake. Thus I was carried off my feet and meseemed up a stair, and set down at the top in solitude and silence, doubting not that the jest would end in some strumpet's lodgings, and suspecting that his lordship himself might be privy to it, having ofttimes railed me for my puritan manners.

When I could free me from the cloak, I found myself in a large room and, as expected, in presence of a woman, completely masked and veiled. She sat quite motionless, and having waited that one whom I recognised as the

Captain Matamoros of that gang should have finally extricated me from those ignoble wrappings, she signed for himself to withdraw and, with a gesture, bid me advance to the table where she sat and whereon stood sundry globes, planispheres, and other astrologer's baubles.

The room was lighted only by a double *flambeau*. But I could see the woman's very dark eyes under her vizard. She began speaking in that masker's mincing voice, hiding her own, but was unable to keep it up, whereon I noticed her natural voice was of the kind Italians call *contralto*, a little muffled but very sweet. She asked whether I were the young Englishman of the count (for so they call him) of S.'s company. Then, whether it were true I was the son of French parents, albeit reared in England? On my answer it was the case, but in what this might concern her, she put her hand upon my arm and said, because, being versed in astrology, she wished to give me certain warnings. And continueth to interrogate me, whether I had remembrance of my parents or birth-place? What things I could remember of my infancy?

Whereto I answered that my memory went no further than your father's hospitable home. Finally she bid me tell her the day and hour of my nativity. Whereat I was constrained to confess I knew them not, being but a waif adopted by your father's beneficence, and having only been told that my age, being near your own, must be twenty-four or five.

At this she seemed to wonder and vainly sought to extract more, which I, not knowing, could not give. But I on my side bid her tell me her name, and for what reason she asked these questions.

"My name," she saith, "is not that it should be, nor is it useful you should know it. The maskers call me Queen Berenice, and that suffices. "For the rest she added there was reason to believe she had known my parents, although she was forbidden to tell their name.

On my conjuring her, if she guessed it, to tell me, she shook her head; and when I seized her hand bid me beware of violence, for the maskers tarried without; and said she had no certain knowledge of aught, and perhaps knew no more than myself. "Nor," she adds, "is it any of this I have to speak about, but to give you warning that it is written in the stars that your life is jeopardised in your twenty-fifth year, and more especially should you ever learn your parentage," as, having studied astrology all her life, and having never proved mistaken in her calculations, she could assure me.

Whereat a thought struck me.

"But, madam," I exclaimed, "if you have been able to draw my horoscope, 'tis evident you must know what myself does not, namely, the day and hour of my nativity and therefore who I truly am."

And I flung myself at her feet, embracing her hands and imploring her to speak. But she merely raised me up, kissing me on the cheek through her vizard, whereby I learned herself was shedding bitter tears. And:

"Go, go," she cries; "seek not to learn any more nor imagine myself acquainted with aught but doubts. These may well be the wild fancies of a mind half crazed by too much rumination of the past. And it may well be you are not him I seek for and tremble to find. But whosoever you are, the very doubt, and alas! perhaps my own inquisitiveness concerning you, encompass you with dangers; wherefore let me conjure you leave this town and country and return to the safety of your adoptive home."

Thus, embracing me once more, she left the room, bearing the *flambeaux* in her hand, whereon I was once more in darkness, and once more muffled in that cloak and carried away, this time however in a coach at full gallop of six horses, as I clearly felt. When I could see again I found myself on the steps of a little closed church at the foot of the Aventine, among weeds and cypress trees, and not far from the place of public execution at the "Mouth of Truth," so called.

The earliest stars were showing in a sky as fair as ours in summer, exceeding peaceful. And as I sped along, amazed and wondering, I heard the guitars and songs of bands of maskers, and the hum of the crowd returning from the Corso, some still carrying lit tapers, and prancing about the winding streets with laughter and revelry.

LETTER 39

From Louis Norbert to Sir Anthony Thesiger, Bart.

Rome: June 2, 1684 N.S.

[Description of the Temple of Minerva Medica and palace of Prince Falconieri omitted in copying.]

. . . To the strange sights it hath been given me to witness in this country—whereof a burning of relapse Jews at Palermo, an eruption of Mons Vesuvius and the Roman Carnival, one has been added quite unexpected, and compensating by its rarity for the wedding of the Sea by the Duke of Venice, that having happened already on Ascension Day. This singular spectacle is no other than the crowning of a poet at the Capitol of Rome; or rather, making it but the more unlikely, of a she-poet.

I was carried there by my good friend, the Abbot Manfredini, who never neglects an occasion of pleasing my curiosity. This ceremony hath, I believe, taken place once already since the death of Tasso, who, you will remember, untimely died beforehand, but the poet's name escapes me at this moment. The first thus to be crowned was Francis Petrarcha, for I see no evidence that, as some of these Romans pretend, the same was done by Virgil, nor seemeth it likely that the ancient Romans, whom that same divine Vates admonished they should leave arts and letters to Greeks, caring themselves only for arms and legislations, should have turned the Capitol or the Victor's Crown to such effeminate uses.

How effeminate they could become is indeed shown by the ceremony I witnessed, albeit I must confess that were it ever seasonable to bestow such honours on a female, this one deserves them, not only for her genius and learning but her maidenly decorum and manly gravity. This maiden is barely out of her teens, but hath already filled Italy with her fame, not merely as a poet, scholar, and natural philosopher, but also, whereof this country is an eminent judge, a musician.

The ceremony took place in the hall painted with the battle of the Horatii and Curatii, over against the famous equestrian statue of Marcus Antoninus Philosophus. There was a vast concourse of all the first nobility, ambassadors and many cardinals, the coaches reaching to the church of the Jesuits; and a huge crowd of the commoner sort, since in this country even the unlettered and the mendicants respect letters and arts, and even rustics and boatmen will quote whole staves of the poems of Tasso and their curious Gothick Dante.

The Capitoline bell rang, mortars were fired from the Castle of St. Angelo, and I own I could but smile that such to do, in the very places that witnessed Scipio's and Caesar's triumphs, should now be made because a young gentlewoman writeth Greek and Latin verses and singeth extempore *stanzas* in her own tongue to the lute. All of which she did do to our universal admiration, showing herself indeed a marvellous fine scholar; nor could I fancy anything more similar to how we figure the enthusiasm or *oestrus* of a Muse or Apollo, than this maiden's air and expression when inventing her verses, which she chanted to the accompaniment of an archi-lute in her own hands. But, as already mentioned, more than at her genius, I wondered at the modesty and nobleness of her demeanour, and the manner wherewith she thanked for this great honour; and, handing her crown of bays to her aged father, addressed him, on the spur of the moment, in a Latin elegy recounting how he and no other had led her infant steps towards the Muses and Apollo.

And, from all I learn of Signora Artemisia, for such is her name, this admirable lady's virtue and discretion do emulate her genius. In this modern Babylon no noble nor ecclesiastic, however high placed, hath boasted of her favours, nor is the faintest breath upon her youthful virtue. She resideth retired enough at Pisa, a town of the great Duke of Tuscany, with her venerable father, a scholar and former captain of the Spanish garrison of Orbetello; and only here in Rome has obligation to her benefactors made her admit much company into her presence.

I have had the good fortune, always through the aforesaid Abbot Manfredini's friendship, of being presented to her at a great academy (for such they call it) of poetry and music in the palace of Don Livio Odescalchi, and been graciously admitted to present my respects to her and her excellent parent in their lodgings over against the church of St. Ignatius, where every other evening they entertain much company, both learned and of high birth, the cardinals themselves disdaining not to clamber to the top of the house where this tenth Muse and fourth Grace holds her Parnassus.

We have already discoursed on many points of learning and taste, and the Signora Artemisia adviseth me to return to Tuscany, her native province, where, she says, letters and arts are cultivated to much better effect, and life is richer in humane virtues than in Rome, which is indeed, meseems, the *Cloaca Maxima* of all wickedness, as it was once the citadel of all virtue and glory.

This young gentlewoman left Rome yesterday, a great concourse of nobility accompanying her on horseback and in coaches to the gate. The Abbot Manfredini urgeth me to cultivate her learned friendship, inviting me in most obliging fashion to visit him in their native Pisa, where, it seems, they live as neighbours, although meseems he hath more partiality for her than she for him; and whether for that reason or weariness of my company, she hath dissuaded me from accepting such hospitality, saying I should find better company in Florence, for which city she offered me letters, adding we might meet there later belike, but discounselling me the sojourn of Pisa during the summer heats, the air of that city being, she says, thick and feverish, and no better for strangers than that of Rome.

Yet, were it not that I seem to guess her strongly disinclined to our continued acquaintance, I own I would readily risk an ague and yield to the *abbé's* hospitable importunities. But, matters being such, and the air of Pisa thus unfavourable to my complexion, it seemeth likely I shall continue in the company (whereof I feel well-nigh sated and weary) of his lordship, and accompany him soon to Bologna and Venice.

Moreover I am impatient of your answer to a letter dispatched to you some couple of months back, touching some questions put to your reverend mother, an answer you will doubtless send me by the new gentleman who is coming to join his lordship's company.

LETTER 40

From the Archaeologist to Lady Venetia

Villa Viscardi, Evola, near Pisa,
September 28, 1909

Dear Lady Venetia,

I am so excited following up a discovery in the Abbess Artemisia's secret correspondence, that (hoping always to give you some definite news) I have delayed thanking you for your copies of Louis Norbert's letters. Do not think me unappreciative. I have re-read them several times, both for their own extraordinary interest, and also, I confess, because they remind me of the mornings when I had the honour of assisting you to find them during that happy week under your brother's hospitable roof.

Those mornings in the Muniment Room! How long, how incredibly long ago do they seem! And how far, far off are your lawns smelling of cedar and yew, your flocks of white deer in the beechmast; and how arid and desolate has not Tuscany seemed on return, with its autumn look of being an old bone, shapely like the ram-skulls on antique altars, gnawed and bleached by the centuries and the elements!

To return to the Abbess's secret correspondence. Thanks to the Marchesina Viscardi (I am, as you see, back at the villa for the vintage), we have got beyond the mere scrappy enigmatic messages conveyed in quotations and underlined words of various books—messages, you may remember, which seemed to harp perpetually on plots and dangers, and particularly on danger from poison. And at last we have been able to decipher a whole letter.

The book containing it is, of all unlikely things, a treatise on the Kingdom of Sweden (*De Svedicis Rebus libri* XX. etc.) by Abraham Vossius, printed in Leyden 1652, an octavo of four hundred and fifty pages, fine Elzevir type. It is bound, unlike any other of the Abbess's books, not in vellum, but in greyish paper with pale blue flowers, or rather in common cardboard covered with a grey flowered wrapper, labelled in a fine, scholarly hand, which I love to believe the abbess's own! What has made the cypher easier to read is that not merely single words of the book have been used, but whole sentences.

By the way, perhaps I ought to remind you of the system of the correspondence, which I explained to you before coming to Arthington, and once, I think, there. Well, the abbess's correspondent probably writes his letter first, in this case in Latin. He then takes the book he is going to send her (a book lent or returned) and hunts in it for words and sentences suitable to his purpose, probably altering his letter whenever he does not find exactly what he needs.

Then he draws up at the end, or on the inside flyleaf, a list of pages, the pages on which the sentences composing his letter will be found, interspersing this list with a certain number of notes intended to mislead a casual reader; for instance, *vide* p. 12, 35, 80, 115 *et seq*: *Swedish militia* p. 135—*Character of Gustavus Wasa*, p. 120—*idem of Gustavus Adolphus*, p. 300, with blank numbers in between; also occasionally Latin expressions, as if the reader were collecting them for reference to a dictionary, instead of which, if put in connection with other words faintly underlined in the indicated pages, they serve as connecting links, while giving an air of *bona fide* scholarship to the whole business.

Also there are other passages, more visibly underlined, which have no reference at all to the message, and are merely intended as a blind to an indiscreet, unintended reader. All this involves an immense waste of time and ingenuity for those who are *not* in the secret (as is shown by the *Marchesina* and I having made so very little progress hitherto); but I have no doubt that previous correspondence had already settled some points for those who were in the secret—for instance, "next book I lend you read chapter so and so, or from verse so and so to so and so"— besides, the *Marchesina* and I are merely antiquarians playing with a historical riddle; whereas the abbess and the unknown correspondent were dealing with life and death, poisonings and hairbreadth escapes, and, unless I am greatly mistaken, they were lovers.

("*Eh già,*" says the *Marchesina*, all *jeune fille* proprieties disappearing before the hereditary antiquarian's instincts, "*eh già,* nuns did not renounce worldly interests in those days.")

To return to the letter in the Abraham Vossius—here it is, translated for your benefit, such as I have this very morning finally pieced it together (if only the *Marchesina* does not prove to me this evening that I have pieced it all

316

wrong!). It is headed: "To the Muse Urania, from Thyrsis, an obscure and unfortunate shepherd." But it is all in the third person, as follows:

That he is prepared to die, knowing himself, though innocent, surrounded by enemies and persecuted by the gods. That being an obscure orphan no one will miss him. And that, as he cannot induce the only one who makes his life worth having to escape with him to the Hyperboreans, he prefers to await his fate consoled at least by her presence.

Have you any idea, dear Lady Venetia, who this unlucky shepherd Thyrsis might be?

Same date—11.30 p.m.

Have you any idea, dear Lady Venetia? Yes, I am sure you have, for (although you hated me for saying it!) you are a born poet and novelist, that is to say, a superlative historian! But the Marchesina Viscardi is not a poet nor a novelist, but a hereditary antiquarian and born archaeologist, that is to say, considerably of a detective.

When, after dinner this evening, and when her father had already dropped off to his nap, I placed the Abraham Vossius and my Latin copy of the letter rather triumphantly on the big table among the illustrated papers, she merely glanced at the letter (this young lady, only less astounding than Artemisia, reads Latin as easily as she drives an unbroken Maremma mustang!) saying: "We will go through that presently. But first of all, let us have a careful look at the book itself."

"Careful look!" I cried indignantly. "Why, dear *Marchesina*, do you think I have extracted all that without careful looking?"

But the *Marchesina* laughed.

"I mean the *outside*," she said. "First of all, this is a *borrowed* book."

"Evidently," I answered rather impatiently, wondering

whether she could be trying to avoid an enquiry into the abbess's love affairs, "or rather it is a *lent* book, since the letter it contained could be conveyed only by lending or giving the book to her."

"That is not what I mean," said the *Marchesina*; "it is a borrowed book because it is a covered book; and it is covered because there is something on the binding which would have identified the sender. *Con permesso*"—and so saying, this marvellous young detective, after passing her thumb over the face of the paper wrapper, adroitly slipped a paper-knife into its corners, and lifted it off. And there, instead of the coarse cardboard I had taken for granted, was a limp calf binding, and on it, embossed, but half erased with a penknife, a coat of arms and a scroll. And what that coat of arms is the *Marchesina* does not know; but you do, dear Lady Venetia, and you know it, *not* because you are a "born poet and novelist," but because you are an Arthington.

For rubbing her finger along the defaced inscription above that obliterated shield, the *Marchesina* spelt out slowly and letter by letter, these letters:

Ex libris:
. . . XI . . . H . . . AU . . .
H . . . SI . . . R . . QU . . . S.

which, being interpreted, means that this *De Rebus Svedicis* of Abraham Vossius once belonged to the library of Nicholas Thesiger, Knight; and therefore that the correspondent of the Abbess Artemisia, the unfortunate, obscure Shepherd Thyrsis whom she warned against poison and who refused to save his life by flying from her presence, was Louis Norbert de Caritan. And *he* was . . . well, that is *your* contribution to this web of fact and fancy.

I am, dear Lady Venetia,

Yours, etc.

From Lady Venetia to the Archaeologist

Arthington: October 5, 1909

My dear Friend,

"My contribution to this web of fact and fancy"!

Oh my dear, dear young historian, what a moment you have chosen to return to that theme with variations! To begin with, I can't help laughing quite loud at the drama of solemn surprise with which you have staged the discovery of my great-great-great whatever he was's *ex libris* on the abbess's book, as if you had not known all along, *as if you had not been hinting in all your letters, that the Abbess's correspondent must be Louis Norbert*; as if either you or I would have troubled a button about the Abbess and her secrets unless Louis Norbert had been at the bottom of them!

And now you strike an attitude of amazement when your nice young Italian friend slips a paper-cutter through a paper binding and reveals what we have known for ever so long! I suppose that you do it just as very scrupulous persons deliberately persuade themselves of a lie before telling it to others: it keeps up the standard of truth! And then, when I have the straightforwardness to say that I feel sure when I do feel sure, you talk of my contribution to a mixture of fact and fancy!

Has it never struck you how a little modern comedy of errors between a *very simple* aged woman and a very *complicated* (but *very* nice) young man has spun itself, like a cobweb, round this terribly solemn tragedy of men and women who have been dead more than two hundred years?

Well, I wonder I can write all this, except that experience has shown me that one's sense of humour sometimes gets uppermost at tremendously serious moments. And this is one.

For, just as you are talking of mixtures of fact and fancy, here is L. N. coming forward *himself* to tell the secret of his birth!

I found this letter last night, absolutely unexpectedly, as I was giving a farewell look (for I may soon be leaving Arthington) at the Muniment Room. It was in a box labelled "Miscellanea, 1750-1800," among a heap of drawings by great-grand aunts and my great-grandfather's copybooks. You will notice it contains a request to destroy it; and this request probably resulted in the partial acquiescence of Anthony Thesiger not putting it with L. N.'s other letters, and its eventually getting not destroyed, but mislaid. I have at once copied it for you, and you will perhaps read it with difficulty, because my hand shook so. Meanwhile goodbye, dear professor; and what a pity Pisa is so far from Arthington!

Yours, etc.

LETTER 42

From Louis Norbert to Sir A. Thesiger, Bart.

Rome: (date not given)
Dear friend, my honoured Patron,
Mr. Thomas Wyndham arrived yesterday from London, bringing me yours informing me how your reverend mother (whose kindness hath made her more than mine) declareth ignorance of my birth and origins, and gently chideth me for giving my thoughts to such vain wonderings; whereby it is moreover plain you also blame me, howsoever the harshness is blunted by undeserved brotherly benevolence.

That I put questions touching these things was indeed perhaps, at the time of writing my letter, mere derogation from the resolve (wherein your mother and yourself had schooled me) to accept unquestioning the mystery of my origin and even perhaps its shame, as not affecting my own will or duty, but put such strength as God may lend me into cultivating virtue and knowledge that may compensate the involuntary shortcomings due to the fault of others or malice of fortune. But there hath happened since wherewithal to give me reason, and justify my strangeness. Whereof I now will communicate to you as much as prudent, albeit I was decided, until your letter came, that my lips should remain forever utterly sealed for sheer amazement.

The thing I tell you of happened to me weeks ago, when we returned to Rome, not, as intended, for Easter, but, owing to his lordship's changeable passions, only for Whitsuntide.

The second night of our journey back from Naples we lay at San Quirico, but not at the inn. For on his lordship's coach and our saddle-horses entering the village, they were surrounded by men with torches, who invited my lord to lie that night at the castle of the Duke of Columna, which is on a cliff above the river and very ancient. It is indeed what we call a donjon, but with a fine house built into its defences with ceilings painted with mythologies and brave silk hangings and gilded leather of Cordova on the walls.

But it appeared to have been disused for many years, and the serving men who had met us with the torches, and who indeed were mostly peasants and clad in little better than rags, though with silver badges and laced hats of the duke's colours, had no food but such husks as themselves eat to set before us, nor sheets to the beds, which were very fine of cut velvet and cloth of silver, but wherein we lay in our clothes, in part also because my lord misdoubted that this hospitality might not hide some villainy such as these mountains abound in, where bands of outlaws sometimes possess themselves of a nobleman's house, or a nobleman himself disdaineth not to become no better than a robber chief.

We were glad however of drying ourselves at the bonfires they lighted in the largest chimney-places I have ever seen, for such of us as came on horseback were wet to the bone. We were treated also to the choicest wines, out of the bailiff's cellar, whereof my companions partook overmuch, but I refused to touch, partly for fear of drugs, and also hatred of the swinishness whereby, as Shakespeare sayeth of the Danes, we English make ourselves the fable of these soberer Italians. And this abstinence I mention lest you should interpret amiss the strange recital I shall now make you.

I had been put to lie by myself, separated by some vast saloons from my lordship's suite. I sat up till the castle clock struck midnight, reading in the pocket *De Amicitia* which was your parting gift. And when I had laid me down I could long find no sleep, but lay with wide-open eyes in that great room, listening to the rats and the rain and wind, and scanning the ceiling very nobly but lewdly painted with the loves of Jove, as I could distinguish by the glare of my dying fire.

The fire had died down all but a few embers, and I was still broad awake, but with closed eyes seeking sleep, when meseemed a door creaked and a rustling crossed the floor. I was like to have called out, yet merely felt for my sword and pistols under my pillow. But having placed them in readiness, and neither seeing nor hearing aught else, I closed my eyes and was about to sleep, when a light smote my lids and a hand fumbled very gently at my collar. It was a woman's hand, and a woman was bending over me, screening the light of a lanthorn from my eyes. She instantly moved that hand to my mouth, enjoining rather than enforcing silence, and let the light shine full on me, leaving herself in the darkness.

My first thought had been of some robbery, then of such adventures as young men meet but the more for the jealous Spanish prudery of this country. And knowing his lordship much inclined to such, made sure I was mistaken

322

for him. The more so that the woman remained attentively scanning my features, nor interrupted her scrutiny when I did ask what she sought.

There was in her manner that which removed all thought of such light tales as had occurred to me, moreover persuaded me she was not young. Perchance, I thought, she is such as walk in their sleep, and whom to wake is to set a-raving. In which belief I lay still, decided not to thwart her.

After a while of fixed gazing on my face, she took my sleeve, I lying on that bed dressed all but my coat, and rolling it up to the shoulder, carefully scanned my right arm in the light of her lanthorn, a process she repeated for the left one. Having done which she sighed deeply, and unfastened my shirt at the throat, I having removed my *steenkirque* the better to sleep. You are to understand that all this time, which seemed eternal, I could not see her face at all, but merely her person's outline cloaked and hooded; whereas I lay, blinking, in the full glare. When, as she stooped closer and closer over my neck, a sudden recollection of tales of vampyres, being evil spirits that suck men's blood, laid hold of me, and I began saying my prayers.

Which noticing by the movement of my lips, she pointed to a birth-mark on my throat and asks me whether I had always had it? employing to my surprise the *French* language, and not with the pronunciation of these Italians, but, meseemed, rather as I had heard it spoke in Paris.

I answered, with as much of the language as I possess, I believed it to be so. But almost without awaiting my words she flings herself upon me, embracing my head and kissing me; withal sobbing so bitterly she seemed like to die, with a sound that wrung my heart yet filled it with terror, crying, "My son! my son! they have stolen my son!"

Whereat I made sure she must be some poor crazed woman, perhaps imprisoned in this lonely castle, as the wives of even great princes may sometimes happen to be in this lawless country where the great live but for their lusts and vengeances. And indeed, revolving what she then told me, I often think that either she or I, or both, must have been mad.

But of these matters I dare not write, not merely from the fear that others may read, but because the very words would seem, as perhaps they would be, madness.

This only would I have you believe. Ever since that night my life, albeit unchanged in other men's eyes, seems turned into a bedlam haunted by evil spirits of worldly ambition and suspicious amazement. Wherefrom I vainly seek to distract myself by study, converse, and I may now add, love; and that I spend many hours on my knees imploring the Lord to enlighten my spirit and save it from the abyss yawning around me, were it only by giving me, if such His pleasure, safety and peace in immediate and premature death.

For I awake of nights dreaming of that woman's wailing embrace, and start up sobbing myself; but, worst of all, my waking hours are haunted by her words, and by the ceaseless strife of belief and doubt, hope and fear concerning their import. For which reason, I would implore you also for your prayers, standing so bitterly in need, not of human, but of Divine aid to my distracted spirit.

Having meditated this my letter, keep its contents secret from all men, and speedily destroy it.

Thine,

L.N.

PS.—Despite the little encouragement received from the learned young gentlewoman whereof I writ in my last, I am inclining to accept the Abbot Manfredini's invitation to go with him to Pisa, and this in hopes of growing perchance absorbed in other thoughts and even in other despairs and sorrows.

LETTER 43

From the Archaeologist to Lady Venetia

Florence: October 25, 1909

Dear Lady Venetia,

Your letter containing Louis Norbert's astonishing account of what happened to him in that castle has followed me here after some delay. And although, in my despised capacity of self-deceiving sceptic, I might point out that it by no means contains absolute proof of his identity or even absolute proof of the identity of his mysterious visitor, I am a great deal too upset to do so, owing to a discovery I have myself just made, and which shatters a great deal of our historical construction.

This discovery, which I have made, thanks to a friend's researches in the Florentine archives, is nothing less than this:

> *Louis Norbert was not poisoned; he was not murdered by the Abbot Manfredini. He died, as any normal young gentleman might have died at that time, in a duel.*

You remember how vainly I have searched for any notice of his death in the police registers of Pisa, and in those of the burying confraternities, who ought to have mentioned him, since, although he was a heretic, the Abbé Manfredini had contrived (probably by some story of having converted him) to get him buried in the consecrated (nay, arch-holy!) ground of the Campo Santo. Well, this morning my good friend Professor Aronson, to whom I had told of my researches, handed me a copy of a letter he has meanwhile discovered among a miscellany of seventeenth-century grand ducal documents. It is from a "Grand Prior" (I suppose of the order of St. Stephen) writing on behalf of the grand duke.

After a variety of other allusions there is as following:

> With reference to the death of the young Englishman recently killed in a duel, about which His

325

Highness has been extremely agitated in his mind for the reasons you are aware of, that renegade Moor (Marrano) of an Abbate has begged me to point out to His Highness's consideration, that from certain information which he obtained from the young man himself concerning things which passed in Rome and wherein the mad woman (*quella matta*) His Highness knows of played a part, this accident at the hands of that foolish captain has happily delivered His Highness and many others (*altri non pochi*) of a responsibility which might have been troublesome"—(and in a postscript adds):

Perhaps it has not yet come to His Highness's knowledge that there were no seconds involved in the duel, and that the captain having shortly afterwards died of a wound from the Englishman's sword, we have been happily saved all the tiresome judicial enquiries; nor could the whole business have possibly received a more satisfactory and truly providential solution at the hands of fate.

Satisfactory and truly providential solution! That is poor Louis Norbert's sole funeral oration—pronounced to reassure a little timorous Medicean Grand Duke.

Is this, I wonder, the last we shall ever find out about your dear friend's—and perhaps you will allow me to add—*our* dear friend's end? Shall we never discover who was the "foolish captain"? Evidently not a *bravo*, for that kind of gentry was *not* foolish, and never risked getting killed like this unknown duellist who had killed Louis Norbert. I fear all this will remain forever hidden in the gulf of two centuries and a quarter, which, odd as it seems, separates us, unpassably, from those men.

I am, dear Lady Venetia,

Yours, etc.

From Lady Venetia to the Archaeologist

Arthington: November 2, 1909

My dear Professor,

What is all this? Louis Norbert not murdered by the *Abbé*? Killed in a duel like any other young gentleman of his day?

But it isn't possible, my dear young friend. It . . . well, *it can't be the case*, whatever nonsense those Medicean spies (of course spies are *all* liars) may choose to write.

As to the curtain having dropped and our never discovering anything more, why, my dear professor, you surely don't mean to sit down calmly under such a dispensation, at the very moment too that the plot has most thickened! Seriously, do you intend our joint work to *come to an end?* Do you mean that L. N. and Berenice and Artemisia and the Abbé Manfredini are now going to be wrapped up in tissue paper like so many puppets and the box containing them to be put away on a shelf of our lives which neither of us will ever touch again?

Well, you are young and an archaeologist, and I suppose you have dozens of other mysteries awaiting you in the future—archaeologists are a kind of Don Juan passing from mystery to mystery, instead of from mistress to mistress. So it's all very well for *you*.

But think of me! *I* can't begin taking interest in Saxon churches or who wrote the letters of Junius, or Kaspar Hauser, or the Etruscan language, can I, *at my age?* And just, as it happens, at the moment that—well, I don't mind telling, you are such a friend and will feel indignant—just at the moment that my poor silly old brother thinks fit to solemnise his comparative recovery by marrying a woman (and you guess *who*) who has been entangling him for the last two months, so that, having fought my fight against her, I shall have to depart from Arthington and become once more a wanderer on the earth's surface. Think what a moment to say to a woman, after stirring her up all you were worth to historical researches: "*Finis*; no more of *that*, my dear lady."

And to say it merely because someone has discovered that a grand ducal spy says L. N. was killed in a commonplace duel!

Really, your letter is enough to push one to strange resolutions!

But there *must* be more documents. What became of the *abbé*, what became of Artemisia? And who was the "foolish captain "who killed L. N. in that duel and died of his wounds?

Captain! Now I come to think of it, hasn't there been a captain somewhere before in this story? Let me think. Now *where* could a captain have come in? I have it! Artemisia's father had been a captain in the service of Spain (something about a Spanish garrison—is there such a place as Orbetello?). L. N. says so in a letter. *And I believe* it was Artemisia's father who killed Louis Norbert. So, instead of the story being at an end, we are now in the very thick of it!

Your very disappointed and dispirited old friend, etc.

PS.—This is a silly letter, but it expresses my firm conviction that, *with good will* and being so kind a friend, let alone so wise an archaeologist, you may find the means of not letting this story drop at this particular minute.

LETTER 45

From the Archaeologist to Lady Venetia

Pisa: November 6, 1909

My dear Lady Venetia,

First let me say—so far as I can without intrusiveness—how deeply I grieve at any annoyance which may be threatening you. Also, how much I would give to be able at least to divert you from the thought of it.

You are quite right. I was a mean-spirited wretch. This wonderful story must not finish off miserably in mere doubt and darkness. We will know how things went with L. N. and Artemisia, and whether, as you suggest, her father was the "foolish captain "who killed him.

I will stickle at nothing; and you shall not be sent away with a *no* to your curiosity, even if I have to sell my soul to satisfy it, as the alchemists and master-builders do in mediaeval legends!

I am proud and happy to be allowed to remain, dear Lady Venetia,

> Your devoted fellow investigator, etc.

Letter 46

From Lady Venetia to the Archaeologist

Arthington: November 10, 1909

My dear Professor,

A very strange thing has just happened, enough to make one superstitious. As if he had heard the words with which your letter ends, Louis Norbert has appeared once more! This is how it happened. There is a mirror in the room I have been occupying here, which — I mean the mirror— has always had an odd fascination for me, although quite the most eerily unbecoming one I have ever looked into. I ought to tell you that, for the convenience of my brother's illness, I was, on my arrival last winter, put into what is called the Queen's Room—the usual room of the usual Queen Elizabeth, which is habitually kept only for show. It is rather grue, as such low-ceilinged, mullioned rooms always are to my mind, particularly when hung with life-sized tapestry, whence huge arms and legs and the flagons of the Marriage of Cana or Anthony and Cleopatra are always striking out.

But when I came I was far too anxious and miserable to mind, and then I got accustomed and rather liked it. Anyhow, in the dressing-room adjacent, called the King's

Closet (no scandal about Queen Elizabeth, I trust) there is this mirror. It isn't very old—Queen Anne or thereabouts; it is round, on a swing frame, and stands on a kind of parrot-perch by the window, so that you can tilt it to see all kinds of unexpected views of the park in it, rather like a camera *obscura*, for it's awfully tarnished. It amused me to turn it about and see my face, which was turned into a ghost's by the blackened, spotty glass, with a change-able background of leafless trees (they are leafless again) of brown beechmast with the deer in and out, or of terrace and grass walks.

But when I turned the mirror so as to get the room itself for background (bluish-green hunting tapestry this King's Closet has, looking very dusty in that tarnished glass) I always felt rather eery, as if some other face were going to appear in it alongside my own. I never once thought of L. N. in connection with it, so don't imagine I am going in for the natural supernatural and such rot!

Well, this morning as I tilted the glass to see a particular cedar in the sunlight, what must needs happen but the thing comes down with a crash on to the floor—I mean the oval mirror itself—the hoop in which it pivoted re-maining on the stand, like an empty parrot's hoop. I hate breaking mirrors—don't you? and was very much relieved to see the glass quite intact, merely separated from the wooden frame. My maid, who had joyfully hastened in at the crash, consoled me for the accident by remarking that the glass had come loose before, "and," she added, "they must have mended it—people were very untidy, I think, my lady, in those days—by sticking in an old piece of letter."

And she handed me the paper which lay under the circle of glass on the floor. It was a piece of thick yellow paper, folded wedge fashion to keep the glass in place. My heart beat a little, for I thought I recognised the hand. I thrust it in my pocket and went down on to the terrace (the stags were roaring in the woods all round) and read it in the twilight. It was Louis Norbert's last letter.

Here it is, copied for you.

LETTER 47

From Louis Norbert to Sir A. Thesiger

My honoured Master and dearer than a Brother,

Opportunity having offered of getting these to your hands through the politeness of Mr. Nathaniel Ingram, an English merchant, about to sail from Leghorn, who hath ridden over to Pisa for sundry business, I take it to let you know of myself and present you and your mother with my affection and gratitude, which will end only with my life. Albeit, this may, indeed, be nearer unto its end than my youth warrants.

Howsoever it be, I resign myself into God's merciful hands, well satisfied that if my end is near it should be through no intended fault of mine, but only the malice of enemies whose motives I do not even know.

Let me explain to you, my benefactor and more than brother (as indeed your father and mother have been more than such to me), that after the things whereof I writ you from Rome I was near dying of a wound from a dagger four inches long, given me one afternoon as I was returning from the sacred opera of Jephthah at the church *in Miranda*, and precisely as I was turning a blind corner near the famous fountain of the Tortoises, where I felt myself caught by the cloak and stabbed, but was, by the mercy of God, able to pursue the two villains who had thought to end me, but being hirelings, flew for their lives to the nearest church, outside of which I fainted and was presently carried to an apothecary's and thence to the hospital of the *Consolation*.

This was the fourth attempt from which Heaven allowed me to escape. But as his lordship had long since and very publicly departed from Rome to Venice, it became evi-

331

dent that this attempt must be intended not for him (as, owing to his many gallantries we had hitherto thought) but for myself, which tallies likewise with sundry warnings I had myself received, and some of which I writ you of in due course. In which fears I was confirmed by a learned gentleman whose friendship, as I writ you, I had made, and by whose urgent advice I removed to Pisa as soon as my wound allowed, taking leave of all my English friends and even of my servant, who elected to follow his lordship to Venice.

Of the wisdom whereof I now have sundry misgivings, and from many things misdoubt me whether I have not been betrayed into the hands of worse enemies and am not a hostage imprisoned in that false friend's house; whether it is indeed thus only time and God's will can reveal. But I have been warned that nothing good is intended, and that sicknesses whereof I am fortunately recovered were by no means accidental, nay, rather meant to have finished me. Indeed for this reason I am taking what may prove my last opportunity to present my love and duty to you and the lady your mother, and explain how it has gone with me in the event of your learning my end.

Not that I am without a friend in this place. Heaven in its goodness hath sent me such an one that even yourself could not be more beloved. But this person, while urging me to fly and putting all means at my disposal, for instance the ship of Mr. Nathaniel which will bring you these, this same incomparable friend is the very reason why I cannot think of my safety, but only of hers, which is jeopardised daily for my poor person.

And for the love of this unparalleled friend I will ask what may be a last favour of you, dear patron and brother, to wit, that when as I pray it may please Heaven that you take a wife and get children, you shall call your daughter Artemisia, in memory of the friend of your friend L. N.

At Pisa in the house of the Abbé Manfredini,
canon of the Cathedral.

August 13, 1684 N.S.

Postscript to the copy of this letter:

My own second name, and that, I am told, of *every* eldest
daughter of an Earl of Arthington, conforms to L. N.'s last
request.

Venetia Artemisia Hammond.

LETTER 48

From the Archaeologist to Lady Venetia

Pisa: December 21, 1909

My dear Lady Venetia,

I told you that, rather than leave your curiosity unsatisfied,
I was ready, like Faust and others among my fellow ped-
ants, to sell my soul.

I have now done so, and I venture to send you herewith
registered, and as a humble Christmas greeting, its price.

These Memoirs of the Abbess of St. Veridiana, previously known in the world as Artemisia del Valore, were
composed in a language you are not quite familiar with,
though (for reasons which I will later explain) I am unable to inform you whether that language is Latin, Greek
(which that learned muse possessed fluently) or mere Italian; so what I send you is a translation made to the best of
my slight powers.

It will, I trust, satisfy you, if of nothing else, at least of the
utter devotion of

Your humble servant, etc.

PS.—I must not forget to warn you that, like other persons who have entered into similar agreements with the
Evil One, I am bound over to complete discretion concerning the details thereof. I must therefore entreat you
to desist from all questions concerning the original of this
document and its whereabouts, let alone the manner in
which it has come into my hands.

Done into English, for the Lady Venetia Artemisia Hammond, by her humble servant, "The Professor."

Albeit while I lived in the century the voice of slander had never found wherewithal to impugn my fair fame and maidenly honour, and I was held up to the admiration of mankind not merely for my learning, but my virtue; yet none the less my life, until it pleased Heaven to touch my heart with grace, was in truth given over to naught but vaingloriousness and worldly emulation; and that to my twentieth year, when I received, or desecrated by receiving, the crown of Petrarch.

Even from my tenderest infancy, for it happened that my dear father, being already white-haired and disabled by wounds got in the service of his Catholic Majesty, was left a widower with me an only daughter but a year old, and as soon as I was returned from nurse and able to speak, instead of confiding me, like other young damsels, to the sluttish sordidness of serving wenches, or handing me over to the ignorance and apathy of nuns, my father, I say, lacking a son, and I a mother, determined he should be the latter to me and I the former to him, accordingly applying his every thought and care to my upbringing.

Thus did it come about that I early learned such things as only few women are taught, and more precisely those for which I was destined to become famous in this foolish world; particularly humane letters, poetry, the Castilian and French languages as well as my own Tuscan, philosophy both natural and metaphysical, mathematics and music, in all of which, by his kindly indulgence in teaching and a certain natural readiness of my own, I made huge progress without suffering in health or taking too much the habits of a pedant.

But although my body did not suffer, since I was able to dance and ride as well as any other gentlewoman, and men praised the good looks wherewith Fate had endowed me—

although therefore suffering not in my bodily vigour or my maidenly decorum, yet my soul, as already hinted, grew up entirely devoid of spiritual grace.

Almost the earliest of my recollections is being stood by my father on a table and made to recite, with puerile voice, the death of Dido and the lament of Hecuba to an audience of learned men. At five years old I was carried to Florence, there to extemporise verses before the Grand Duke Cosimo dei Medici, on which occasion, bursting into sobs, the good Grand Duchess Victoria took me in her arms and soothed me with sweetmeats and kisses, sowing the seed of direst worldly vanity in my childish soul.

Soon after, being but seven years old, I was elected a member of the Philharmonic Academy of Bologna and of the Alphean of Pisa, and subsequently of others more than it is profitable to enumerate; on the first occasion the cardinal legate, afterwards His Holiness Innocent XII., stuffing me with morsels taken from his own plate, not without my infant disgust. And by the age when other maids still play with dolls, I had been carried from one end of Italy to the other, receiving on all hands universal flattery and such homage as ill beseems any of God's creatures, all of which I swallowed with greediness, vanity growing with that it is fed upon; until, in the twenty-first year of my age, it pleased the Senate and people of Rome, in the reign of Pope Innocent XL, that I should receive publicly at the Capitol the crown of poetry.

It was at this moment of my life, and indeed on this very occasion, that my eyes were opened to the vanity of the world and of my ways in it. As I knelt in the midst of that vast assembly, bowing my head to receive the laurel from the hands of the Senator of Rome, something seemed suddenly to give way within me. My heart, which had been beating violently, stood still, freezing my limbs and checking my breath; my mouth filled, as it seemed, with bitter ashes, and I was aware that I had, in some manner, died, and was looking on, I knew not whence, at a *simulacrum* or *eidolon* of myself moving and speaking with a semblance of life. This *simulacrum* it was which rose and gave thanks, and then, using my limbs and voice but not my will, swept the lute with unreal fingers and improvised a poem which my real self heard as through an incalculable distance.

While this was proceeding, and I knew that in some inexplicable manner I had died and left but this ghost behind me, the eyes of my spirit (in whatsoever way those of the body may have been busied) were led into the crowd before me, and without seeing a single one of the hundreds of spectators I had seen hitherto all too vividly applauding me, they, *id est*, my spiritual eyes, rested on the face of an unknown youth (such at least he might be described) which met them with a look that transpierced my soul and restored it to life, though to a changed one.

Such a face our painters have given to the youthful saints and martyrs, Stephen and Sebastian, or indeed that Angel who carried the lily to the living Lily of Carmel and spake the words—"Hail Mary." So that I doubted not I had beheld a vision, and so soon as I was restored to my lodging hastened to my closet and there wept bitterly and thankfully for many hours, which proceeding my good, foolish father and the worldly-wise men surrounding him explained very learnedly and with abundant Greek and Latin *vocables*, as the prostration of bodily spirits following too long and high-pitched a tension of those curious parts anatomists cut out and examine with their glasses, especially as Renatus Cartesius has taught, of the gland called *Pinealis* where the soul resides.

When, after some few days of solitude and meditation, cloaked as sickness, I was enabled to resume my ordinary existence, I did so without difficulty, but feeling that it concerned me no longer save in so far as it pleased my father, and that, save for him only, it was the same to me if God had sent me instant death or bid me live on to fourscore and ten, all happenings having grown indifferent and dropped from me like the cloud which the sun first lowers from the mountain-tops and then sucks away into nothingness.

Such was my happy, nay blessed, state; too blessed, alas! for me, unworthy, to remain in, since it pleased the Origin and Fount of All Things and Love which moveth the Sun and the Stars, to withdraw me from the sight of Its ineffable ways and plunge me once again into the fires of worldly passions, albeit such, this time, as may be accounted rather purifying than destructive to the Soul. For it happened that, but a few days after the events I have described, and while my father and I tarried in Rome after that foolish pomp at the Capitol, that, being present (though only in the body) at a festivity in the house of a Roman noble-man, there was brought to my father and me a young English cavalier in whom, to my amazement, I seemed to recognise the face which had met my gaze during that first strange fading away of my baser self.

Though whether, as the sceptical followers of Aristippus might say, it was this youth's countenance that had taken on prophetic and supernatural meaning because of the disturbance of my spirits; or whether, as I incline to think, there was but an accidental resemblance (as a real man might bear to the effigy of an angel) between that messenger of the Eternal and the youth in question, no man's wits are sufficient to decide. Howsoever, so soon as I beheld him and that resemblance which seemed well-nigh identity, I felt as the poet Dante sayeth, that love had appeared for the first time in my life, taking the guise of this youth and making me exclaim, "*Ecce Deus, fortior me qui veniens dominabitur mihi.*"

And this was really my first, as it had been my last, experi-ence of love, the habit of applause having hardened my heart, and the many attempts of wicked men upon a damsel exposed to the public gaze, and protected only by an aged father, having up to that time inspired me with such disdain of the other sex as is fabled of the virgin amazons. But, for this reason, and likewise the indifference or timidity of the young Englishman, who was an orphan of no estate and dependent on the benevolence of a nobleman of that country, this passion of mine found no out-let or expression; and albeit we met frequently and discoursed lengthily of many things, there appeared not in the demeanour of either aught revealing the love I felt and afterwards learned was not unrequited.

But worldly though was my passion, it was ever mingled both with a wish to be worthier for the beloved one's sake, and also with an ardent desire to serve him if possible at my own expense and even to the sacrifice of my very love. Of which latter an opportunity offered all too soon, whereof, alas! I fear my sinful weakness took but a half-hearted grip. For learning that my father and I resided at Pisa, this cavalier showed himself greatly inclined to go to that city for the pursuit of his studies, and thereby awakened the evil designs of a wicked man who makes it his trade (since Hell has still to claim him) to serve kings and courts by extracting unsuspecting men's secrets, and dispatching these victims, if desired by his patrons, with silent, decent means *ad inferos*.

Since it would seem that the uncertainty of this youth's origin had attracted the suspicion of sundry among the great of this earth, and perhaps raised the hopes of certain others, in such a way that, all unsuspected by himself, he walked for ever among the traps and pitfalls of some and the snares and larks' mirrors of others, an innocent and helpless victim. The aforesaid evil man and atheist priest, perhaps egged on to further wickedness by jealousy, he having more than once proffered me filthy love and been contumeliously repulsed, although I had kept this secret for fear of damaging my poor old father, this mercenary eavesdropper and murderer, I say, took the occasion of possessing himself of my beloved (since such he will ever remain in my heart), as he might have done of secret letters which he could sell one by one, threaten to make public or destroy to extort payment from powerful and guilty persons; inviting the poor youth to accompany him to Pisa (where none of his English friends should be near him) and there board with him and make free use of his library and collections.

These things, which later events proved, alas! but too true, I did not at this time know, being ignorant of the circumstances of that cavalier's life; yet was I filled with deep suspicions of his would-be friend and host, and such evil forebodings as must, methinks, have been sent by Heaven. In consequence of which, my passion transcending its own wishes, I used such arguments as I could find wherewithal to dissuade that youth from going to Pisa, withholding from him only my suspicions of that villain priest, thinking them belike uncharitable. Yet, though I argued my best, and even willingly incurred the doubt of being shrewishly averse to him I loved so dearly, it must be that I merely deluded my own conscience, using means such as I secretly knew would prove insufficient, and refraining from the one means ready to my hand to end that dangerous project but with it all my hopes, to wit, accept an invitation of the emperor to settle at Vienna in the capacity of Caesar's court poet and composer.

With these sharp scissors I ventured not to cut my love's poor hope, pretending merely to myself that I was breaking its thread with weak and fumbling fingers. By which selfish delusion of myself I brought about horrors surpassing those of any fabled Hypsipyle, destroying both my father and lover, and, but for the mercy of God, my own soul. Whereof the reader shall now judge.

Having bidden, as I lyingly told myself, a last farewell to that English cavalier, I travelled with my father to the court of the Duke of Savoy, there to exhibit myself in such poetic contests as already seemed to me not glorious but shameful. And having refused to enter into correspondence with that youth, returned to Pisa with an easy conscience, albeit hidden therein was the hope, growing to certainty with every day, that, disobeying my warnings, he would have proceeded to that city. And the joy I felt was coloured with expectation, not surprise, when the next day that cavalier came to salute us and I recognised my fraud, but recognised also the overwhelming love I bore him, whose violence I had not hitherto suspected, and whose joy laughed all my fears and scruples to scorn.

But alas! the very next meeting these proved but too justified. The English cavalier, seen in the light of day, was strangely pale and thin, and on my pressing him, admitted that he had indeed contracted some slow, insidious malady since his arrival. These words he spoke in the presence of my father and others, and also of that wicked poisoner in whose house he lodged, and who, feigning extravagant friendship, never let him out of sight, but, for one excuse or other, ever dogged him like a shadow. Neither the days following was I able to see him alone, or warn him of my suspicions, that malignant hypocrite pretending deep concern in his ailment, and a motherly fear lest any imprudence should increase it.

Thus, meeting followed meeting, without our ever being alone, that youth's virtuous diffidence forbidding his seeking opportunities of declaring his love, and my dear father's jealousy having been artfully raised by that priest, not of Christ but of Satan, well knowing that the old man dreaded nothing so much as love or marriage which would separate me from him and cut short those foolish triumphs wherein his paternal fondness overmuch delighted.

Imagine my despair, seeing my lover perishing day by day and unable to warn him of his danger! At last, seized with desperation, I bethought me of a means of communicating with him, for he had neither friend nor servant of his own, but lived in that foul assassin's house all unsuspicious, waited upon, nay jealously watched, by the villain's accomplices in the guise of serving folk; the villain's plan being perhaps not yet to kill, but so to weaken his health and spirits as to make him a prisoner, and then, if events required it, dispatch him easily and noiselessly in such a way as to avoid scandal.

And, the youth once confined to his house and couch, it was clear to that traitor that the habits of my sex and age and my father's jealousy would put that poor victim beyond reach of my warnings. Accordingly, I devised the plan of sending that sick cavalier a book wherewithal to beguile his idleness, wherein I placed a slip, stating he would find information of interest to his studies on certain pages, and on these pages I faintly wrote in the margin numbers of other pages, in which I had underlined separate words, which, added together, made this phrase:

"Beware false friends. You are being poisoned."

Having dispatched the book by my father's hand, he being

well disposed to the youth as long as sickness kept him away from me, I spent the next hours praying to God and making vows to God's Mother and the Saints that this message might not miscarry; neither is it possible to express the length and agony of the hours until there came an answer.

This was brought, all unwittingly, by the villain priest himself, who was ever seeking opportunities to see me and do me displeasure. Let those who read this confession imagine my consternation when this villain arrived, and after many fulsome compliments just as he was leaving, drew forth the book I had sent to the Englishman two days before, and fixing impudent eyes on me said that our poor friend, the English cavalier, had found this book too pedantic for his taste, and returned it to me. In order to hide the agitation of my spirit, for I felt myself grow pale and red, with fear and impatience to examine that volume, I affected anger and, snatching the book from him, threw it rudely in a corner, exclaiming that I did not hold much by his Englishman's taste in books or by his manner towards ladies.

Whereat that other one was mightily pleased and, taking snuff, merely asked what could be expected from barbarians and heretics, and went his way. Hardly was he gone when I picked up the book and tore it open. The numerals I had written had been effaced, and my first thought was it might have been by the hand of the traitor. Judge then of my joy when I discovered at the back another set of numbers which led, by the mode I had invented, to other underlinings, making the words "Greetings and gratitude. Love makes life worth keeping."

Thus was it possible to check for a while the monster's attempts, since the cavalier, feigning a sick man's whims, refused all cooked food, subsisting only on fruit and eggs, which on the pretext of my father's farm, I was able to send him; adding, on the score of its special age, wine of our vintage in closed phials. By which means the cavalier was able to keep in life and even grow strong enough to eat once more at his host's table, who, suspecting his suspicion, suspended for the time his evil plans and ostentatiously ate first of all whereto he helped his guest.

We had meanwhile become accustomed to a secret correspondence by such means as I have already described, finding great sweetness in discoursing freely of our love, which we had meanwhile confessed to each other in this fashion; while preserving in our meetings the manners of strangers to one another. Nor can I possibly tell the marvellous joy of this strange courtship, wherein never came a kiss nor barely a handclasp, nor even such language of the eyes as would have been noticed by strangers, but only riddles and symbols concerted together in those letters made up of a few words underlined in books that passed from hand to hand; and also such messages as could be conveyed by music, for the English cavalier frequenting the assemblies held in various noble houses, I composed a number of songs and instrumental inventions, which my poor guileless father hastened to get printed, wherein to express freely all that I felt for that excellent youth.

And these, on such public occasions, I would sing, turning away from where he sat for fear our eyes might meet; but putting into my voice, as I had done into the words and notes when I invented them, all the raptures and hopes and fears which love brings in its train. Indeed such was the blissfulness of our strange intercourse that we wished only for its continuance, neither hoping for aught else nor allowing ourselves to fear the future.

But an opportunity occurring of an English merchant-ship sailing from Leghorn, that cavalier, in a message conveyed in Xenophon's *Cyropaedia*, put an end to that foolish happiness by asking me to fly with him to England and become his wife, adding that it could be cloaked as a journey to show my learning before the English universities and court. To which I replied, by the same device of secret correspondence, that both my religion and my duty to my father forbade me, since he would never consent, being old, to leave his country for ever.

But even while I was answering thus, I became aware, from the altered looks of my lover and his returning ailments, and from I know not what in the manner of that devilish priest his jailer, that danger was closing around him once more. Whereupon, terrified by his obstinacy, and feeling as if the loss of my love would be as nothing compared with the loss of my poor lover, I resolved that he must seize the occasion of that ship and save his life even if it meant our parting forever. And this, not having time to convey through our usual correspondence (which might be discovered by an all too great exchange of books), I brought to his knowledge the selfsame evening of that my resolution, which will live forever enshrined in this poor heart, since it was the last time of my looking upon my lover's countenance until I saw it, O horror! rigid in death.

There was a great assembly at the house of one of the chief citizens of Pisa, whereat I was to sing, together with other musicians; and knowing this the Englishman, albeit sick of the insidious poison which was being administered to him in some mysterious manner, hastened to be present, but dogged as always by his jailer-murderer.

During the earlier part of that evening, whereon I seemed to feel my hair turn white, I tried, even recklessly, to enter into private conversation with that cavalier, but every time found myself face to face with his would-be assassin, who persecuted me with flattery and signs of partiality more fulsome than ever. At last, bidding the violins follow my lead, I wont to the harpsichord and pretended to show the assembled company various new compositions of mine; and then, suddenly calling the Englishman, asked him to second me in a duet which I was writing, wherein he obeyed me much surprised, for there were other musicians present more able to do it, although he was, like many of his nation, well versed in music and gifted with a voice which, to my enamoured ears, was sweeter in its manliness than the tones of our most famous singing men.

So, sitting at the harpsichord, I petulantly cried: "Now, English cavalier, you shall show what your nation you so boast of is truly worth in music. So read your part and follow my lead, as these worthy *virtuosos* (meaning the fiddlers) will also. And mark you, do your best, for it is not the business of a cavalier to raise a laugh against a gentlewoman's inventions."

And, looking up at the audience with a brazen boldness very unlike myself, I winked, as if inviting them to the discomfiture of that poor stranger; and began, in mock heroic guise, the entreaties of Hypsipyle, which I made ludicrous enough, imitating in buffoonish ways the graces and affectations of several famous singers there present; until the audience began to laugh. But the Englishman, pretending to enter into the sport, sang lustily, reading his part which I had scrawled a few moments previous; while I fixed my eyes on him, commanding him now loud, now soft, but in reality asking for an answer to the words, which were those of the daughter of Danaus praying her bridegroom to flee. "Say yes," I said, "say yes, that thou wilt go, beloved," and with my eyes made him understand that this buffoonery was in sooth serious.

But he, the more I sang, "Say yes," the more, insisting on his part, he sang, "No, no, I will not ever go," with such expression of resolution on his countenance as left me no doubt of his meaning, and froze my blood in my veins. Whereon I purposely tripped him with a wrong modulation and broke off, he singing, "No, no, I will not go," amidst the laughter of the assembly, upon a dissonance, which too well expressed the tearing of my heart. But I rose from the harpsichord, and turning to the assembly said this buffoonade was called *Don Quixote turned opera singer;* and thanked the Englishman for valiantly seconding me, saying I hoped he would do himself equal honour with this my musical comedy when, as I heard to my regret; he would be back in his native land; but he, affecting to laugh, hummed his part, "No, no, no, I will not go."

And thus, in the midst of peals of laughter, this dreadful evening closed. But as we descended, many of us guests, down the staircase of that palace, the Englishman, seizing my hand cried, "*Ancora,*" and with a most melodious voice sang again his phrase, wherein I joined, and the arches rang with the united declaration of our love, voice clinging unto voice. Then kissing my hand and shouting, "No, no, I will not go," he bowed and disappeared out of that festive place, among the senseless applause of those misunderstanding guests still bent upon buffoonery.

The next day, which was also the last, and the Feast of the Assumption of the Virgin, brought me a book; it was Abraham Vossius's *De Rebus Svedicis*, belonging to the Englishman, bound with the arms of the family which had fostered him, but, lest they should catch my father's eye, covered with a flowered grey paper. How many months has not that volume been the companion of my days and nights, stained with my tears as, for the thousandth time since, I spelt out the well-known riddle of numerals and words. It is, of all my worldly possessions, the only one it cost me to part from, it and its companions of our secret correspondence, on my giving myself to Christ.

And for this reason, considering it as the sign of all my offending towards God, I refused to give it, as I did all my other books and music save what had passed between the cavalier and me, to the convent which I was entering; giving these confidants of my love and misfortune to a dear friend and cousin, who little guesses how great a part of my life, and how much of my bleeding heart, is closed in that small volume which she has thrust, with one or two other seemingly insignificant companions, on to the shelves of her husband's library.

In this volume my lover repeated what he had sung. He refused to go, preferring to face death in my presence to seeking life in death far from me. "By the time you read these words," so I spelt out, "the ship will be setting sail from Leghorn to England, leaving me behind to live or die near you."

It was, as I have said, the day of the Assumption of the Blessed Virgin, and I knew he was mistaken, as no ship could leave a Tuscan port on so great a feast. In three hours, at most, of a fleet horse, the harbour of Leghorn could be reached from Pisa, and the English ship boarded under cover of the night. My resolution was instant. Calling a groom whom I had once nursed through dangerous sickness, I told him that, after the heat of the day, my spirits longed for a ride in the pinewood by the sea; but, owing to my father's fear of rheums and fevers, charged him to silence, and bade him bring two of our horses, saddled, round to our garden gate at the moment when the whole town would be preparing for the procession, and my father, with the other notables, walking in it; myself pretexting a headache against going.

My plan was to show myself to that groom habited, as is the custom of Italian gentlewomen when riding on horseback, in clothes of masculine shape and material, and then make my lover mount instead of me. Or else, taking him in place of the groom, pretend myself ready to fly, and leave him at Leghorn. The more I revolved these plans, the more aware I became that I should be obliged to choose the latter; but I decided to take counsel from the moment, fixing only in my mind that, either with or without my company, one of these horses should carry my lover to the seaport.

But how convey this to him? A message might reveal all, after the strange scenes of the previous night. So I determined to have once more recourse to song. The house which was his prison was over against ours, only a narrow square, where stands the equestrian statue of Grand Duke Ferdinand, intervening. But, owing to the heat of the season, I knew that all the inhabitants were within-doors reposing, and moreover, all shutters and windows closed to exclude the fiery air; so I must wait till evening released them.

At last the endless afternoon drew to a close. I rose and threw open my window and stepped on to the balcony. The air was still burning, and the garlands slung for the procession, and the carpet of flowers which it was to walk over, emitted a scent as of some sacrificial rite. Presently the windows opposite opened; and after a few minutes the villain priest, dressed in the robes he profaned, came forth from his house, followed by all his servants, and my father did alike, dressed as I can now see him, in the ancient Spanish fashion, in black with a gold chain, and a ruff on which his beard looked cut of alabaster. He and the priest greeted as neighbours, and, with their household, walked slowly towards the cathedral, there to receive the banners and tapers they should carry.

My lover, being a heretic (although that priest his host led people to believe him secretly converted to our faith), could not take part in this sacred show, but would, as I knew, probably await within doors until the procession should pass through our square on its homeward way, when, being already dusk, he could enjoy the spectacle thereof unnoticed. I knew that until the procession started from the cathedral there was half an hour, and after that nearly an hour till it could pass under our houses on its return journey; and during this brief time my lover's safety must be compassed.

I pushed my spinet to the window, as if in search of air, and playing loud harmonies, began to sing, feeling sure that he would hear my voice and come forth.

How long I sang without an answer I cannot tell. It seemed to me an eternity; yet no answer came. Desperate, I sang louder and louder, waking the echoes of those empty houses, all of whose inmates were gone to the cathedral. Once at the window, I could sign him to come across in the safety of that desolate place. After a few minutes a window opened, hitherto shut, and in the gathering twilight my lover's voice arose, very still and sweet, in a song of his native country, which he had once told me was called, "Come live with me and be my love."

He sang indeed in answer to me, but as if to no attention and without coming forward to the light; whereas, fearless and desperate, I stood upon the balcony facing the rising moon and singing loud to give myself courage.

"Come down," at last I shouted, pretending to be declaiming some recitative, "come quick and fly with me, your faithful bride is ready."

There was no answer and I stood petrified, awaiting him, sure he must be coming down and fearing he might lose time in seeking his money and arms. After a minute or two one half of the great house door opposite did indeed fly open with a crash, and out of it rushed my lover down the steep steps, but pursued, enveloped, by a dozen men, one or two bearing lanterns. For an instant there was a scuffle of feet and a murmur of voices,

347

then suddenly one voice arose. It was that of my father crying, "Die, thou vile heretic seducer." Then came a clash of swords and a muffled shriek, as if of one whose mouth was covered by a cloak.

I know not how I reached the street. But when I did so those men had disappeared, and there lay my lover, his dead face turned up to the moon, pierced with a number of wounds, while my father leaned against a wall, still grasping his sword, but with a great wound in his side, and presently fainted for loss of blood. I do not know what happened, save that I fell on the Englishman's body; and the last I was aware of was the voice of the traitor priest crying for help from the windows of his house, wherein he had lurked and hidden my poor father; and in the distance the tapers and torches of the procession advancing towards us with the sacred chants between the houses.

My father, when I assured him of my innocence, swore to avenge me and my dead lover on that traitorous villain who had pushed him to this hideous deed, and by whose servant's hand, and not, as was pretended, the Englishman's, he had received his own fatal wound. But he died a few hours later; and I remained alone between the dead bodies of my father and lover, men who should have been united in love for me, but whom love for me and the villainy of that monster had united in hatred and death.

My father had indeed confessed that it was the wicked priest who, fanning his foolish parental jealousy from the first, had at length made him believe myself dishonoured by that cavalier; and, having got wind of the plan of flight, hidden the old man in his house, pretending meanwhile to join the procession. But since my poor father died within very few hours, and was long speechless, the villain was able to throw the whole blame of what he chose to call a duel on him, pretending that, so far from having pushed the poor old man to this violence, he had returned home missing my father from the procession and therefore suspecting evil, and then attempted to defend my lover, asserting most impudently that the latter had, thinking himself attacked, turned upon the servants who were trying to defend him, and thereby been finally cut down by them in the confusion following on the duel.

And such was the hypocrisy of that atrocious murderer, or such the power of his employers, that my efforts to bring him to trial all miscarried, the whole occurrence being treated as an accident brought about by the light conduct of a woman in whom public applause had quenched all the scruples natural to her sex.

Thus, while I barely ventured to accompany my dead father to his resting-place, such were the taunts and gibes flung at me by young and old wherever I showed myself, that assassin was allowed, out of the money paid him for his murder, to raise a slab to his victim, having curried favour with the ecclesiastical authorities by perjuriously pretending to have converted him to the true faith; himself composing an epitaph whereon he boasted of his friendship for the deceased's alleged original nation, and called upon the passer-by to give a prayer to that poor victim of his villainy.

It was not till some years later that, rather from some caprice of his various secret employers than any recognition of his many infamies, this man was disgraced and sentenced, and then only to imprisonment in a papal fortress, whence he is doubtless at this moment machinating fresh evil.

But as for me, it behoves not to speak of my sorrow and the shame and despair that nearly brought me to lay sacrilegious hands on the life which God has lent me. Suffice it that a year or so later I took the vows in the convent of Saint Veridiana, of which I am now, however unworthy, the Superior.

May the blood of Christ and my many tears wash out the sins I have, even unwittingly, committed; and those which for my miserable sake have been committed by other poor sinning mortals!

Written at Pisa, in the year of Salvation ,1697.

From Lady Venetia to the Archaeologist

Button Street, W.

New Year's Day, 1910

My dear Professor,

I don't mind telling you that, in the secret of my chamber, I have been crying like a baby over the abbess's story. And perhaps over something else besides, which is, I rather imagine, the suspicion that my dear learned young friend is a genius. But you have told me not to ask you about the compact which has put this manuscript in your hands, so I will cheat my curiosity by telling myself that you have, on the contrary, got the Evil One to steal it for you out of the Marchese Viscardi's library; only I wish the Evil One might turn out to be in reality an angel in disguise, namely, the *Marchese's* delightful young learned daughter.

Upon my word, I really do not know (and the more I think it over the less I can decide!) whether I believe you to be a dealer in stolen goods or a poet!

Be this as it may, now, dear professor, that, thanks to you, the puppets into whom we put perhaps a little of our own life have come to tragic and beautiful and appropriate an end—now I must tell you something about myself.

I am going to marry my cousin R—— whom you met at Pisa. He has a son almost as old as I, and now his daughters (whom you perhaps remember) are both married, he wants someone to keep his embassy for him; and I, as you already know, have been entirely superseded at Arthington. Sir Edward R—— is an honourable and a useful man (as men go!), liberal-minded enough, and not boring, though a diplomat. And the situation will suit me all right. For how can I expect, at my age, to find another Louis Norbert to fall in love with?

And you, my dear professor, having replaced Artemisia del Valore reverently in her monastic grave, and hung some wreaths of bay around the lyre carved upon her tombstone—you, someday soon, won't you? will let me know that her place is taken in your heart by some dear living countrywoman of hers, learned and lovely as she, with whom you can, in years long hence, when the *cicala* is sawing in the noontide or the olive faggot crackling in winter, discuss the strange story which happened at Pisa in 1684. Or was it rather (the thought suddenly strikes me) in 1908?

Meanwhile believe in the constant gratitude of your affectionate old friend,

Venetia Artemisia Hammond.

PS.—Can you read the notes I have scribbled above? It is the duel music of *Don Giovanni* and Donna Anna's lament over her father. It has been running in my head ever since finishing the abbess's story. Do you remember I played it to you after that walk at Pisa in the winter moonlight? Some day or other when my cousin and I shall have been shelved from our embassy, and you will be a famous historian, we must all make a pilgrimage to Louis Norbert's grave, and then, with fingers as decrepit as that old hotel piano (do you remember it?), I will play that music for you once more.

·

ALSO FROM LEONAUR

AVAILABLE IN SOFTCOVER OR HARDCOVER WITH DUST JACKET

THE LONG PATROL by *George Berrie*—A Novel of Light Horsemen from Gallipoli to the Palestine campaign of the First World War.

NAPOLEONIC WAR STORIES by *Arthur Quiller-Couch*—Tales of soldiers, spies, battles & sieges from the Peninsular & Waterloo campaingns.

THE FIRST DETECTIVE by *Edgar Allan Poe*—The Complete Auguste Dupin Stories—The Murders in the Rue Morgue, The Mystery of Marie Rogêt & The Purloined Letter.

THE COMPLETE DR NIKOLA—MAN OF MYSTERY: 1 by *Guy Boothby*—*A Bid for Fortune* & *Dr Nikola Returns*—Guy Boothby's Dr.Nikola adventures continue to fascinate readers and enthusiasts of crime and mystery fiction because—in the manner of Raffles, the gentleman cracksman—here is character far removed from the uncompromising goodness of Holmes and Watson or the uncompromising evil of Professor Moriarty.

THE COMPLETE DR NIKOLA—MAN OF MYSTERY: 2 by *Guy Boothby*—*The Lust of Hate, Dr Nikola's Experiment* & *Farewell, Nikola*—Guy Boothby's Dr.Nikola adventures continue to fascinate readers and enthusiasts of crime and mystery fiction because—in the manner of Raffles, the gentleman cracksman—here is character far removed from the uncompromising goodness of Holmes and Watson or the uncompromising evil of Professor Moriarty.

THE CASEBOOKS OF MR J. G. REEDER: BOOK 1 by *Edgar Wallace*—*Room 13, The Mind of Mr J. G. Reeder* and *Terror Keep*—Edgar Wallace's sleuth—whose territory is the London of the 1920s—is an unlikely figure, more bank clerk than detective in appearance, ever wearing his square topped bowler, frock coat, cravat and muffler, Mr Reeder is usually inseparable from his umbrella.

THE CASEBOOKS OF MR J. G. REEDER: BOOK 2 by *Edgar Wallace*—*Red Aces, Mr J. G. Reeder Returns, The Guv'nor* and *The Man Who Passed*—Edgar Wallace's sleuth—whose territory is the London of the 1920s—is an unlikely figure, more bank clerk than detective in appearance, ever wearing his square topped bowler, frock coat, cravat and muffler, Mr Reeder is usually inseparable from his umbrella.

THE COMPLETE FOUR JUST MEN: VOLUME 1 by *Edgar Wallace*—*The Four Just Men, The Council of Justice* & *The Just Men of Cordova*—disillusioned with a world where the wicked and the abusers of power perpetually go unpunished, the Just Men set about to rectify matters according to their own standards, and retribution is dispensed on swift and deadly wings.

LEONAUR

ALSO FROM LEONAUR
AVAILABLE IN SOFTCOVER OR HARDCOVER WITH DUST JACKET

THE COMPLETE FOUR JUST MEN: VOLUME 2 *by Edgar Wallace*—*The Law of the Four Just Men & The Three Just Men*—disillusioned with a world where the wicked and the abusers of power perpetually go unpunished, the Just Men set about to rectify matters according to their own standards, and retribution is dispensed on swift and deadly wings.

THE COMPLETE RAFFLES: 1 *by E. W. Hornung*—*The Amateur Cracksman & The Black Mask*—By turns urbane gentleman about town and accomplished cricketer, life is just too ordinary for Raffles and that sets him on a series of adventures that have long been treasured as a real antidote to the 'white knights' who are the usual heroes of the crime fiction of this period.

THE COMPLETE RAFFLES: 2 *by E. W. Hornung*—*A Thief in the Night & Mr Justice Raffles*—By turns urbane gentleman about town and accomplished cricketer, life is just too ordinary for Raffles and that sets him on a series of adventures that have long been treasured as a real antidote to the 'white knights' who are the usual heroes of the crime fiction of this period.

THE COLLECTED SUPERNATURAL AND WEIRD FICTION OF WILKIE COLLINS: VOLUME 1 *by Wilkie Collins*—Contains one novel 'The Haunted Hotel', one novella 'Mad Monkton', three novelettes 'Mr Percy and the Prophet', 'The Biter Bit' and 'The Dead Alive' and eight short stories to chill the blood.

THE COLLECTED SUPERNATURAL AND WEIRD FICTION OF WILKIE COLLINS: VOLUME 2 *by Wilkie Collins*—Contains one novel 'The Two Destinies', three novellas 'The Frozen deep', 'Sister Rose' and 'The Yellow Mask' and two short stories to chill the blood.

THE COLLECTED SUPERNATURAL AND WEIRD FICTION OF WILKIE COLLINS: VOLUME 3 *by Wilkie Collins*—Contains one novel 'Dead Secret,' two novelettes 'Mrs Zant and the Ghost' and 'The Nun's Story of Gabriel's Marriage' and five short stories to chill the blood.

FUNNY BONES *selected by Dorothy Scarborough*—An Anthology of Humorous Ghost Stories.

MONTEZUMA'S CASTLE AND OTHER WEIRD TALES *by Charles B. Cory*—Cory has written a superb collection of eighteen ghostly and weird stories to chill and thrill the avid enthusiast of supernatural fiction.

SUPERNATURAL BUCHAN *by John Buchan*—Stories of Ancient Spirits, Uncanny Places & Strange Creatures.

* 9 7 8 0 8 5 7 0 6 6 8 6 2 *